Ruchir Joshi

Is a filmmaker and writer. Born and raised in Calcutta, he now lives in Delhi. This is his first book.

From the British and Indian reviews for *The Last Jet-Engine Laugh*:

'Several scenes are gripping – Paresh's father alighting from a train at Calcutta onto a platform thigh-deep in monsoon water, Para planning her escape from an orbiting aircraft ... There are fine observations, and many felicities of language [too]: a woman's snore "begins its soft argument with the night air", and New York highway signs above a passing taxi are likened to "guillotine blades waiting to fall".'

- *Guardian*

'A meditation on ideas of inheritance and the workings of memory ... Objects are brought vividly to life by means of a painstaking visual scrutiny.'

- *TLS*

'Ruchir Joshi's greatest strength as a writer is the gracefulness with which he treads the line between satirical exaggeration and convincing detail which all science fiction has to negotiate. His idea of the future of Indian military, headed by a crack troop of female fighter pilots, fighting a Pak-Saudi alliance over a water dispute, is possibly prescient ...'

- *Independent on Sunday*

'Compelling ... While Joshi is clearly making a statement about the trajectory of modern Indian history, his characters are by no means ciphers. We share in their lives through delicately drawn and moving vignettes and Joshi proves adept at bringing the grand historical sweep of his novel down to a human level without losing any of its power.'

- *Birmingham Post*

'Ruchir is a time traveller between generations and continents, between history and memory, between the laughter of yesterday and the sorrow of tomorrow. A novelist who has the words and means to defy and define the world he has inherited ... *The Last Jet-Engine Laugh* makes Joshi the legitimate midnight grandchild of India imagined in English. A few set pieces, which have no equal in the pages of Joshi's contemporaries, alone make that world a superpower in the post-Rushdie Indian novel.

- *India Today*

'Joshi has an exquisite eye for detail ... *The Last Jet-Engine Laugh* is a summation of three generations of trials and tribulations, loves and losses, victories and voices. Tracking times well before independence to the year 2030, memory and history, future and fantasy are in complete synergy in this entrancing web of words.'

- *The Telegraph*

'*The Last Jet-Engine Laugh* is a new fashion statement in Indian writing. To print parts of this book, instead of ink, the publishers have used adrenaline. Only this could explain the book's wildness and its speed ... some might read the novel as a homage to the past, or even a sci-fi exploration of the distant future. But what the book is really nostalgic about is the present. The thought of the banished present produces a rasp in the narrator's voice. It is this love of the moment and its loss that gives Joshi's writing its emotional undertow. At once confident and experimental, there is no denying that this voice is unstoppable and engaging.'

- *Outlook*

'Interweaves the consciousness of defeat with the joy of having lived ... What really makes *The Last Jet-Engine Laugh* stand out is Ruchir Joshi's tremendous facility with creative language, embellished by his photographer's eye for nuances and irony.'

- *The Pioneer*

'It is an amazing novel, because of the large time span it covers from 1930 to 2030 and reminds one a lot of Salman Rushdie's *Midnight's Children*. It is an unusual novel oscillating in time and mood, gripping the reader, shocking him, fascinating him, but maintaining a grip all along.'

- *The Financial Express*

'This is a book that makes you sit up and take notice. This is the rarest of phenomena – a genuinely original voice. A voice that one looks forward to hearing again.'

- *The Statesman*

'Here is proof positive that it's possible for Indian writers to be wickedly cynical, funny and bitter without the scathing edge blunting the Indianness or vice versa.'

- *Biblio*

'Joshi's forte is the evocative use of language; reminiscent of Rushdie but never self-indulgent or bombastic.'

- *Gentleman*

The Last
JET-ENGINE LAUGH

RUCHIR JOSHI

HarperCollins *Publishers* India

First published in India in 2002 by HarpeCollins *Publishers* India
First paperback edition published in India in 2003 by
HarperCollins *Publishers* India
First Published in Great Britain in 2001 by Flamingo
An imprint of HarperCollins *Publishers*
A-75, Sector 57, Noida, Uttar Pradesh 201301, India
www.harpercollins.co.in

1 2 3 4 5 6 7 8 9 10

This novel is a work of fiction. The names, characters and incidents portrayed in it are the work of the author's imagination. Any resemblance to actual persons, living or dead, events or localities, is entirely coincidental.

The author and publishers of this work would like to express their gratitude to the following: Music Sales Ltd for permission to quote lyrics from 'Shake Your Hips' (James H Moore); IMP Ltd for permission to quote lyrics from 'The Book I Read' (David Byrne, Copyright © Blue Disque Music Co. and Index Music Inc, USA); Tristran Music Ltd for kind permission to quote lyrics from 'Boom Boom' (composed by Johnny Lee Hooker, copyright © Conrad Music); EMI Music Publishing Ltd/EMI Virgin Music Ltd for permission to quote lyrics from 'Passenger' (Iggy Pop and Ricky Gardiner, copyright © James Osterberg Music / Safari Records USA); PFD on behalf of The Estate of Hilaire Belloc for permission to reproduce lines from 'I shoot the Hippopotamus'. Although we have tried to trace and contact all copyright holders before publication, this has not been possible in every case. If notified, the publisher will be pleased to make any necessary arrangements at the earliest opportunity.

AFGHANISTAN
Rawalpindi
(Pindi)
Lahore
Amritsar
PAKISTAN
TIBET
(CHINA)
NEW DELHI
(Dilli)
NEPAL
BHUTAN
Karachi
INDIA
ASSAM
BANGLADESH
DHAKA
Ahmedabad
(Amdavad, Karnavati)
Jessore
Calcutta
(Cal, Kolkata)
Bombay
(Mumbai)
Bay of
Bengal
BURMA
GOA
Arabian
Sea
Andaman
Islands
Car Nicobar
Island
Nicobar
Islands
SRI
LANKA
0 100 200 300 400 miles
0 100 200 300 400 500 600 km

This book is dedicated to the memory of my mother Satyavati Joshi, professor of literature and struggle, to her ability to remember, to her great gift of language, to her agile and fearsome wit, and in final acceptance of her repeated advice to me that I should put aside all frivolities and try and become a writer.

To the memory of my father, Shivkumar Joshi, freedom-fighter, writer, painter and photographer, who turned living into such a joyous art, who taught me how to watch and participate in the theatre of light, line and colour, who taught me how to laugh at life, and who gave me the courage to discover my own flight paths.

And to the memory of my parents' friends who became my friends as well: to Mahendra Bhagat, Praveen Pratap, Kanubhai Bhalaria, Umashankar Joshi and Harindra Dave, as a small gesture of thanks for what they have given me.

BOOK ONE

The Nation of Your Love

'No reason to get excited,' the thief, he kindly spoke,
'There are many here among us who feel that life is but a joke.
But you and I, we've been through that, and this is not our fate,
So let us not talk falsely now, the hour is getting late.'
All along the watchtower, princes kept the view,
While all the women came and went, barefoot servants, too.
Outside in the distance a wildcat did growl,
Two riders were approaching, the wind began to howl.

'All Along The Watchtower'

– BOB DYLAN

O Boatman, raise the sail!
O Boatman, don't delay!
Launch the boat, Boatman,
Take me to Medina!

– Bengali Folk Song

17 June, 2030
Calcutta

I need new prayers, the old ones don't work anymore.

I mean, I'll try the old ones again, keep turning the key in the ignition, but I know the sound that will come – I could try my father's old favourite, try like the good Brahman I've never been, *Tamaso ma jyotirgamaya, mrityor ma amrutam gama* – nope, no way, no way I can say that straight. That one just brings back a bad memory of school. I find myself doing Gyanendranath Ganguly, translating from the Sanskrit, somewhereabouts 1970 or so, 'Aut oph dhurkness o lhord, lead aas into laaight, phrom dathe lead aas o lhord, intu IMMOR-TALITHEE . . .' Nope. No way.

Try the Gayatri Mantra next. *Aum bhur bhuva swaha, tatsavitur* – you see the problem is that I need the sun for that, and this is Calcutta in the middle of a June that's come carrying an early monsoon. I haven't seen the sun for days. And '*varenyum*' always slides around in my head and becomes 'uranium' . . .

Or I could try loading the Etretat game. Etretat 3/C is the best one, and when it works it kind of works like a prayer. Something to make you happy. But it won't work. Of late the memory's been haemorrhaging, so sometimes she actually slides over the cliff, or sometimes the cops open fire. Last time I tried playing it, the waiter wouldn't bring me the bloody breakfast coff –

Wait a minute. Coffee. The water's decent today. The filter hasn't jammed. The laser is old but it's still working and today the light is a bright green. Most days it's a pheeka brown somewhere between the red – it never actually shows red – and the clear green, which basically means 'take your chances', but today it's a full green. Which means it's managed to handle all the junk in the supply. I think I will do something simple, almost a prayer, almost perfect. I will make coffee today, not almost, but actually a prayer to my Italians.

Take down the espresso machine from the shelf. Where is it? Yes there, right between the old yellow tin of Dalda and the picture of Nehru upside down in his shorts doing yoga. Take it down. Wash the water compartment, no really, the water is nice today, then fill it up to the valve – no higher – the water must reach till just under the valve. Make sure the holder is dry, make sure the holes are clean before you put it in. Now open the fridge, take the coffee out. Take a small spoon and spoon coffee into the holder. Oh shit, shuttle.

This one's the 9.30 from Haldia to Salt Lake/Jyotinagar. This bastard always flies too close, I mean sometimes right fifteen feet from my terrace, and slows down as he comes past. Must be one of their daily entertainments – come down from their standard flying height to peek into the second floor and see what the old man is up to today. This started the day they saw Sonali here. I mean we were just sitting, but obviously they thought they could tell, I don't know. Screams of 'Eijey budo ki korchhish!', Hey old man what you up to?, and 'Tor ekhono othey? Korey dekhaa baanda!', like, 'Can you still get it up? Show us!', actually, 'Show us, you big prick', 'baanda' being Bong for dick or dickhead, and then a favourite from old times, even we used to shout it at young couples walking hand in hand while we drove past at night – 'Tor baba ke boley debo!', Watch out, we'll tell your daddy!

Yeah, right, go tell him you sons of bitches. Show you, I'll show you . . . absurd they looked, hanging out of the open doors, four or five of them strapped outside, waving and shouting.

We laughed, Sonali and me, but I kept staring at the thing till it jumped over the row of palms lining the south side of the shuttle port at Rashbehari Park, kept hoping one of the bastards would fall. Apparently one of the Saab-Daihatsu engineers, a big Swede, came to Calcutta for a visit and had a heart attack and died when he saw people hanging out of his choppers at sixty, seventy feet above the ground.

At least I don't have a heart problem and yes, as Sonali pointed out in answer to the young monkeys' taunts, some other parts of my body function more or less okay still.

The shuttle shakes everything in the house as it passes. This time I've managed to spill some of the coffee grounds, which are precious in this wasteland of tea. Don't get upset, I tell myself, it's not wasted, it's part of the process. Anyway, coffee I have plenty. Deep-frozen, rare, precious, dark. If I drink the Alessi's six-demi-tasse output once every three days, I calculate I have enough for the next five years. This is, of course, if I mostly drink it alone, which I probably will. What happens after five years is not going to be my problem, I don't think. If the coffee doesn't take the heart, it will take the kidneys, and the booze is already working on the liver, so between the two that will be that. Para, my daughter, can have what's left, if she wants it. If she's still . . . well, say it . . . if she's still around.

Take the top half of the machine and screw it on, tight now, but not too tight, it won't take too many rethreadings from the idiot Tunku Mandal's lathe, though the machine has survived well for something that's thirty-two years old. It's the rubber washers that always go but I have a good stock of those too, if I don't burn too many that is.

Gas on, yes, flame low, yes, put the special mat on the fire, balance the machine on the mat. It was a design marvel in its time – a child's castle made of shining serious steel, with a copper bottom that sticks out a little and a golden ball on top of the conical lid. When it was new, the copper bottom had a tiny eagle engraved in its centre with the words 'Officina Alessi' and below that in even tinier letters 'inox 18/10', below which 'ITALY', which used to give me a lot of pleasure. There, it's going. I can now bow my head and wait. I fold my hands and I bow my head to you Italo Calvino, to you Michelangelo Antonioni, to you Carlo Levi, to you Cesare Pavese, to you Giuseppe Morandi, to you Pier Paolo P., Giuseppe? No, I think it's Giorgio, Giorgio Morandi the fascist-lover, to you Monica Vitti, and yes, yes, to you Paola Venezia, you who sent me this coffee . . . but wait, it's not the Italians' day today, it's my mother's.

I made my mother taste espresso once. 1982. I had just come back from New York and brought back a tin of Café Bustelo, not Italian, Puerto Rican, black as my hair.

'Anho kevo taste hoy?' she said, wrinkling her nose at the smell. I gave her a cup, lots of milk, lots of sugar. She took a sip and spat it out. Then she went and brushed her teeth and lay down. 'I've got a headache,' she said. And, after a moment, with panic in her eyes, 'Are you sure it's vegetarian?'

Yes, a prayer for Mummy.

You would think a seventy-year-old man would know better than to need prayers, but no. Today is the 17th of June, my mother's forty-second death anniversary, and I suddenly need to pray. I've never been able to pray like she could, just like I've never been able to make the daal she used to make. I've never regretted not being able to pray like her but the daal I do miss – nothing I've made has ever spoken to my tongue the way her daal did.

I used to think making her daal was a kind of prayer to her memory, just as, sometimes, taking a photograph, and developing and printing it, was one to my father. What could be a prayer to my daughter, who is up there, up in the sky, still alive?

What could be a prayer to friends? Lovers? To Anna Lang, mother of my daughter? To Sandhya? To Ila?

What could be a prayer to my father, teller of stories, and to the tongue he left me?

Ah, the Alessi is beginning to stutter.

'The tongue I left you is rotting in the fridge,' I can hear my father say.

'You didn't eat the daal. I had to keep it in the fridge,' I can hear my mother mumble in her sleep.

I pour out the coffee. The mug is old, Italian import bought from Macy's in New York in 1989, a year after Mummy died, a chipped old survivor, and I think the coffee tastes better in it. There it is, wide white mug with flecks of black texture, the coffee black and full, the aroma dangerous with memories from different corners of an overlong life. I add milk and sugar. I'm not a purist, not an Italian, I'm a Gujju and yes, balls, I like my milk and sugar even more than Italians do.

I go into the photo room, which is the only other room besides the kitchen and the balcony, and sit down on the sofa before taking a sip. My mother would always have her tea scalding hot but I like my coffee with the edge of heat knocked off. I wait for it to cool a tiny bit, then I blow away the wrinkly layer of fat from the top, 'tar' we call it in Gujarati, the 't' soft and the 'a' not an 'aa' but an 'a', and the tilting circle of coffee looks like a brown sea, as if seen from an airplane, and the tar the bit where the sun catches the water differently.

I take a sip. Kadvi, the dark burns even through the milk, like a zen blow to the tongue – 'Wake up!' – and then the sugar as a second pleasure and for a moment I'm back in New York, in Paris, in a hotel room in Holland, anywhere but here, anywhere but now. Back, safe, as if in a photograph with nothing before or after it, safe with the taste of coffee forever suspended in my mouth.

There's a photo of me that my parents had turned into a Diwali card. On one side of a rectangle of photographic paper a boy of about six, wearing a conical straw hat, a farmer's hat, ice-cream cone in hand, a clown-mask of vanilla around his mouth, grinning thinly at the camera. Behind the boy, out of focus, boats on the Hooghly, the ghat at Hastings. To the right of the boy, though you can't see it in the picture, a restaurant from where the ice-cream comes. Calcutta 1966.

Next to it is a photo of a little girl, also eating ice-cream next to a river. The flavour? Either raspberry or pistachio – I can't remember now and you can't tell from the black and white. They could be twins, the boy and the girl, except this second photo is taken in August 1998 in Paris and the girl has light eyes.

Whenever I think of my daughter, this is the picture I try to think of. It's the nearest thing to a prayer to her, or for her. It's very close to any prayer I may make for the boy in the photo next to it.

A prayer to my mother is complicated. A prayer to my father would be a straighter story. Not that straight, but straighter.

My Father's Tongue

My father was not the soul of tact. In fact, he had a tongue, given to him by god, with which he could slice people up into little pieces. There was the time when we went to the restaurant by the river, Gay Restaurant it was called then, though it isn't now, with my cousin Minakshiben and her father, my mother's brother Prabodhmama, and my friend Viral.

Prabodhmama and Miniben were visiting from Amdavad, and Viral's dad worked for Union Carbide. Prabodhmama, not a very smart man, asked Viral what his father did.

Viral took his mouth away from the chocolate milk-shake to reply, but my father got there first. He said, 'The boy's father is Personnel Manager of an American company here. He makes good money exploiting people. But that is more than can be said of certain others.'

If there was one thing my father couldn't stand, even more than people who worked for foreign companies, it was people who could work but didn't. Prabodhmama had left his job with Balmer Lawrie in a sulk in 1952. All he had done since then was write occasional songs that he set to music and sang on Amdavad All India Radio.

Prabodhmama and Miniben cut short their trip to Calcutta by a week and left soon after that evening. And from then on, for two years, Viral and I had to meet in secret, because Viral went and told his mother what my father had said.

Then there was the time before that, when I was in Class 2, all of seven years old. I had gone around singing, 'Haay mai hun kitna akela! Mrs Mehra ka kela! Around the world in eight dollars, Around the world in eight dollars.' Mrs Mehra broke a wooden ruler on my head, then began work with a steel one, then she thought the better of it and reported me to the Principal. Old Dwivedi then informed me that he was going to invite my father to come to the school and explain why I shouldn't be expelled forthwith. 'In order to assuage Mrs Mehra's feelings and maintain general discipline in the school,' he said.

Later, as my mother slapped me across the face every time she could breathe between her sobs, my father explained to me the nature and meaning of my crime.

'Do you know what "kela" means?' he asked.

'Yes. A banana,' I said.

'Do you know what a banana stands for?'

'A banana.'

'Suman, the child is an idiot. I told you to teach him facts. You said he was too young and now you see the result of your prudishness,' then, after waiting for another slap to land, he addressed me:

'Paresh, a kela means a banana, both of which also mean the male part which is between your legs. Now Mrs Mehra probably does not have this part, but what you were singing implied that she does. Do you understand?'

'Yes. But what's wrong with saying, "Around the world in eight dollars"? It's from the Raj Kapoor film,' I parried – to my regret – as my mother slapped me again, this time in mid-sob.

'He never stops being smart!' she wailed.

'You mean there is no end to his stupidity. And with your help there will never be,' my father said, before turning to me, 'By singing those words you implied that Mrs Mehra was using her banana to get around the world, which, given your brains, you actually will have to do.'

My mother fled the room at this point because she could not slap my father as well. He turned back to his newspaper with not the slightest sympathy for either of us.

The conversation with Dwivedi, the Principal, was, however, different. Despite our bravado all of us students were quite scared of old D. Unlike other members of staff, D. would never raise his hand against a student. But so ingenious was he in his cruelty that those who had been obliged to visit his office would, more often than not, come back wishing they had been beaten by the Class-Teacher instead.

Though we would see him at assembly every morning, and occasionally walking through the corridors, it was in his office that Dwivedi stored his terror. It was a spartan office. It smelled of Pheneol and there were three photographs on the wall behind the desk.

On the left was a smiling Jawaharlal, alias Nehru-chacha, his expression and posture conveying dignity, humility and elegance. He had what I would later identify as a certain feminine quality of grace. All that legendary, country-running, Kashmiri steel and cunning remained totally invisible to the eye of a seven-year-old.

At the centre, naturally, was Gandhiji. Short dhotyu, stick, eyes hidden behind benign spectacles, striding, it always seemed to me, on his way out past me and Dwivedi towards the sunlight and freedom outside. Being a Gujarati myself it was from this picture that I always took heart. Whenever I was called to The Office I would never look at Dwivedi. I'd keep staring at Bapu, thinking, 'Take me out of here with you,' and, alternatively, 'It took a Gujarati to win against the British and it will take another one to win against Dwivedi.'

Dwivediji took his dress sense from Nehru – long black sherwani and white chust payjamas; he took his rhetoric from Gandhi – he always wrapped the most ruthless psychological violence with some quote or the other on truth and ahimsa from the Mahatma; but his soul belonged to the third photograph in the Trinity: for some reason, the picture of Netaji Subhash was slightly bigger than the ones of Nehru and Gandhi.

But again, this is all hindsight. At the time all I knew about Subhash Chandra Bose were the two stories that Bagchi, our Maths teacher, told us. He would repeat them each year, like a shopkeeper unfurling saris he has already shown you once. By the time I left school my hatred for mathematics was inextricable from my dislike of Bose.

One of the stories was about the great man's ICS examinations. Having passed the 'written' with flying colours, the young Subhash was called for the interview by his British examiners. This was the final and most dreaded of tests.

'How would you pass yourself through this?' one examiner demanded, holding up a small gold ring. Subhash paused only a moment. Then he wrote out his name on a slip of paper, folded it and passed it through the ring – thus stunning the panel into passing him without any further questions.

Years later, when Viral became a star at the Wharton Business School, he would similarly stun his classes of freshmen by using this story as an example of lateral thinking. Aged seven, I found the story highly idiotic. I still consider it the finest illustration of the matching stupidity and vacuousness of the British and the Anglophile Bengalis who ruled so enthusiastically under them.

However, on the day my father was called to meet Dwivedi my thoughts mosquitoed around Subhash Chandra Bose and his trick with the ring. As he drove us to school I kept trying to think of ways by which my father could get me out of being expelled.

'Do you know about Netaji's ICS examination?' I ventured to break the silence. 'Hm,' he said. He seemed to be thinking about something else.

I persisted. 'Can you do something like that with the Principal?' Taking his eye away from the traffic my father gave me a pitying glance. 'No,' he said, and went back to his driving.

There was a second story about Netaji and the mystery surrounding his death. This one fascinated me when I was a little older.

I can never remember the exact details, but this much was clear: that after initial victories against Allied troops in Burma, the Indian National Army led by Bose suffered reverses; that Bose demanded more logistical support from his Japanese mentors; that when these supplies were not forthcoming he took off in a transport aircraft for Singapore to plead with the Japanese High Command there; and that the plane never reached Singapore.

Most people believe the plane crashed. Some believe that it crash-landed on an island and that Subhash is still alive, a hundred and twenty-three years old, in perfect health, waiting patiently for the right moment to return and rule India.

Another idea is that the aircraft was shot down by Allied fighters. The problem with this theory is that there were no Allied squadrons operating within several hundred miles of the route that Netaji's plane took – the sky was ruled by the Japanese Air Force. Which then leads one, as these theories do, to a cousin theory:

The transport is a twin-engine aircraft, the Japanese equivalent of the American Dakota. The weather that morning is good, a few storm clouds far to the west as the plane crosses the Burmese coastline, but nothing particularly worrying. The pilot sets course south for Singapore and relaxes. The Leader sits in the back – going through his papers with two of his generals – he wants to be ready for the Japanese when they land – time is precious.

Squares of sunlight slide across their laps and race onto the vibrating floor as the plane gently bumps across the Andaman Sea. The seats give off a smell of warm leather as the fuselage heats up a bit under the mid-day sun.

About an hour away from Singapore the co-pilot notices two dots approaching from ten o'clock. He stiffens, jabs his captain awake, points. The captain is a veteran. He takes one look at the approaching aircraft, snarls at the co-pilot and goes back to sleep. He knows a Zero when he sees one – he flew one as part of the fighter escort at Pearl Harbor.

Two minutes later Netaji himself spots the fighter planes, now much closer. He makes no mistake in identifying them – they are obviously his escort to Singapore. Suddenly he feels optimistic again – he understands the Japanese, their moods, their penchant for symbolic gestures. He taps his Sikh Lieutenant General to wake him up.

'Look, Sekhon! Our friend Takanaga has sent us his red carpet!'

The Zeros come around to take up formation a little behind and above the transport. The Flight Leader raises the co-pilot on the radio and confirms that the Commander-in-Chief of the INA is indeed on board.

After brief formalities I was sent out of Dwivedi's office to wait with the dahlia plants under the Principal's noticeboard. Frightened and miserable though I was, I was also curious. I positioned myself so that I could look through the gap in the door curtain at a glass-fronted book-case inside.

It was a standard trick for students waiting outside to position themselves here because you could see Dwivedi's face reflected in the glass panes if he stood up. He did this quite often, pacing up and down, with the Trinity's pictures behind him like a posse behind a sheriff.

Dwivedi first laid out my heinous crime. Then he started to outline the effect it would have upon the morals of the school if such a thing went unpunished. My father chimed in, 'Yes Dwivediji, I can quite understand your predicament.'

Not expecting such an early capitulation, Dwivedi stopped in front of the posse. 'So, you see!' he said, his face trying to decide between triumph and relief, visions of seeing the back of me lighting up his stupid eyes.

'Yes, indiscipline is a problem. And it is not made easy by the fact that a middle-aged lady teacher makes obscene interpretations of a seven-year-old's innocent tomfoolery.'

'Uh . . . er . . . ji . . . what?!'

I will always remember Dwivedi's face at that moment, the light catching it from a window somehow like a spotlight. It was reflected on glass against dark books with what, for a moment, seemed like Netaji's INA cap on his head.

Later, while imagining the death of Subhash, I would often put Dwivedi's face onto the great man's shoulders – the expression of shock identical as the Zeros open fire from point blank range, the jaw open in helpless anger as the realisation hits a second or two before the cannon shells hit the right engine and set it on fire.

'I mean, you know that the boy is unfortunately a bit slow. He is my child, you don't need to tell me. Definitely punish him for rudeness, we can't condone rudeness. But please, I request you, don't take too harsh a step against the poor lady, I would suggest that you don't suspend her, let her continue, but perhaps some psychiatric help . . .'

Dwivedi, who held himself to be a gentleman, had not mentioned the word 'expel' to my father. He had hoped that laying out the details of my misbehaviour would be enough to make my father, a Gandhian and a well-known writer, offer to take me out of the school in shame.

The day after Dwivedi died, a few years later, I went to the cremation with the rest of the school and watched interestedly as the flames licked through the wood into the different parts of his body. His face had been buried under a pile of sticks but I'd got a glimpse of it before they covered it up.

He had the same flabbergasted expression that I remembered from that time my father had dealt with him. When I told my father he said, 'Idiot Bahmano. They spend all their lives avoiding god and when they meet him they are shocked that he actually exists.'

The fact that my father had been a Brahman himself along with the last fifty generations of my forefathers, the fact that he had had a chotli and a janoi till he joined the Congress behind Gandhi and got a haircut and threw away his thread – causing my grandfather to stop speaking to him for four years – seemed to have escaped him. But he was under a great strain at that time and I knew that so I didn't say anything.

Also in those days of '75 – '76, when talking about me to his friends, my father would say, 'The boy's gone into himself. Doesn't talk any more. Just goes to this karate business four times a week and prays to a poster of Zeenat Aman. In fact if it wasn't for Miss Zeenat I would recommend that he join an RSS shakha. Then he could be banned and put into jail and we could stop wasting the school fees.'

By now I had learned to translate what my father said. What he meant was that, along with the Republic of India, he too was close to death, and he had hoped to see me begin to develop some dedication to the higher things of life – to writing and literature, say – before he breathed his last. What he meant was that I was wasting my time in the quiet pursuit of sex and violence while the country festered under Indira Gandhi's Emergency – that this, if ever, was a time of great sacrifice for those who believed neither in the fascism of the right nor in the fascism of Indira's 'socialism'.

I didn't give a damn. It was my father, I thought, who had gone into himself.

Late at night he would sit there at his desk, writing, his anglepoise lamp the only island of light in our dark bedroom. The desk was next to the big bed my mother and he slept in. In my own bed, which was at a right angle to theirs, I would pull the blankets up to my chin and pretend to sleep. After a while, I would hear my mother's snoring begin its soft argument with the night air, and the rhythmic scratching of my father's Pelikan fountain pen, as he filled notebook after notebook with his big round Gujarati hand. I would let some time pass, lying there and listening to these two sounds. Then I would push myself up quietly. For a few minutes I would watch my father, the grey shawl wrapped around him, his tall back bent left, supporting himself on his elbow as he wrote, trying all the while to shield my mother and me from the glare of the lamp.

My father had done this for as long as I could remember, but there was a strange unease in his body now, a fever that was new. Watching him, I would wonder who he was writing for with all that energy, now that he had had most of his readers taken away from him.

The fact was, my father's publisher had stopped distributing his old novels and stalled the printing of his new one. Many of his friends had abandoned him and most of those who hadn't, like Kalikaku, were in jail or in hiding across the country in Bombay and Amdavad. There was only one crazy editor of a daily newspaper in Bombay who still carried on publishing my father's weekly column. This terrified my mother and all our relatives. They were convinced that the only reason we hadn't all been arrested was because the government was saving us up for some special punishment.

The only exception to this was Prabodhmama, who began writing satirical songs about Sanjay Gandhi's bald patch and his tree-planting programme. He would sit in ice-cream parlours in Amdavad, singing them to other customers. Everyone also expected him to be arrested at any moment.

I didn't want to be arrested. I was happy. My plan to represent India in karate by the year 1979 was proceeding well. And, unknown to my parents, Zeenat's secretary had sent me two photographs of her boss signed by the lady herself. So that project was coming along nicely too. Had he been less tense, I would have shared this last bit of good news with my father. The letters I had written to Zeenie showed a certain flair for language, I thought, and I would have enjoyed my father's scathing comments on them because I was as addicted to the lashings of his sharp tongue as a baby is to his mother's milk.

But he was too tense. This tension showed itself to me and my mother in strange ways. He would be nice to us. He would let go opportunities for nasty comments. Instead of dismissing my mother's worries about our imminent arrest and incarceration, he would sit and explain to her why he was writing what he was in his columns. It seemed he had no acid, no bile, to spare for us. It seemed all of it was being reserved for the two he had named Ma Thug and Baby Thug (unusually, he was repeating himself here, because, earlier, he had once replaced the first part of a famous Bombay 'union' leader's last name with 'Thug' in a piece titled 'Arre! Thug! Arre!').

Despite, or perhaps because of, all this niceness my mother remained unhappy and unconvinced. The day the piece titled 'Why the Trains Are Running on Time' came out my mother called a friend's husband, a lawyer, and asked him to help make out her will.

Nothing happened of course. The year moved from a pleasant winter to a sultry spring. In the March of '76 I won my way through the quarter-finals of the Subhash Chandra Bose Karate Club's internal tournament and then lost in the semi-final because I had one eye shut tight with conjunctivitis. Viral, precocious as ever, got himself a girlfriend, an older girl whom he'd met at a Union Carbide party. My father started getting hate mail in bad English telling him that he was a traitor to the country. My mother was kept in the dark about this. Instead she discovered a half-finished letter to Zeenat that I had hidden in my Trig notebook.

My father had a small business in Badabazar, as an agent for two Bombay textile mills. This is what he did to support us, the earnings of a vernacular novelist not being enough.

One hot day in May he left for work sounding very cheerful. 'I'll be late today,' he said in a tone that made my mother turn around from what she was doing and look at him.

'Why will you be late?' she asked suspiciously.

'Writers' Union meeting,' he said merrily.

'But you always say you have no time for that lot,' she said.

'Well today I do. When a vulture comes to visit a flock of sheep, the mule may stay to watch . . .' What? I thought. But with this enigmatic comment he left. I turned my mind to my plans for the rest of that day.

My vacations had progressed to the point where they were not quite half over but they had been going on long enough for Viral and me to have washed the bad taste of school out of our mouths. We had had just enough time to get into the difficult practice of enjoying ourselves, having finished off the worst of the holiday homework, and just enough time left to make our practice perfect. That day Viral's girl was going to take the two of us to the movies.

In fact she was going to try and get us both into our first 'A' film. All I had to do was figure out what excuse to make to my mother. This was easy, since she was preoccupied with thoughts of impending doom and therefore behind in correcting exam papers for the college where she taught.

'So . . . Viral and I were thinking of going to a movie this evening.'

'Is one of the woman's films running now?'

'Which woman?'

'The love of your life. Zeenie baby.' My mother had taken to reading *Stardust*.

'It's an Englishfilm. And don't call her Zeenie baby. Her name is Zeenat.'

'Why can't you go for a matinee? Why must you go to a six to nine?'

'We didn't get tickets.'

'Oh, so the plan is an old one, is it? You're not asking my permission, you are informing me. Just like your father informs me of meetings.'

'Mummy, three to six, I get back at eight with the traffic. Six to nine, I get back at nine thirty. So the difference is one and a half hours!' Not strictly true, there was the small matter of kabab rolls and Coca-Cola afterwards, three to six I could get back by seven, and six to nine I could be back by nine twenty, but . . .

'I suppose you'll have to see Priya home, seeing as you're grown men now.'

How did she know about Priya?

'Who's Priya?'

'Why, Viral's girlfriend.'

'Who . . . ?'

'Viral's mother said she was taking you to the movies. Grown men, hah. Don't even need to ask their mothers for money anymore. Rich girlfriends to buy them ice-cream. Who needs parents anymore?'

A bad mistake not asking for money. But Viral's mother was dead and Viral was double-dead. How dare he tell his mother? And how dare she crow to my mother? What about the secret adventure? What about a man's simple privacy? But my mother was relentless.

'Besides you know your father will be late tonight. If you're such a real man, why not come home and protect your mother?'

'Protect you from what?'

'Who knows? Times are bad.'

Viral's mother had stipulated a matinee, so that is the show we went to see. We got in okay too. The guy at the gate looked at us funny, Priya gave him the tickets, he tore them in half but pocketed the five-rupee note she had put under them. So that was it for adventure, derring-do, etc.

We came out of the cinema a couple of hours later. It had rained while we were inside and the roads were dotted with little ponds of water. The sky was clearing. The sun sliced through clouds, still dark as they moved away towards Cherapunji or Chittagong or wherever our Geography teacher Sharma had decreed they go to. Cars splashed us as they drove by, the water flashing in the slanting light.

Viral was walking a little ahead of me, talking to Priya in a sly and quiet manner that I knew very well – it was the way he talked to me whenever he was trying to get me to do something I didn't want to. Walking towards Park Street, we reached the Museum before it struck me we were going in the wrong direction.

'Ei, you guys. Nizam's is that way.'

They pretended not to hear me. Their talking got more urgent.

'Ei, Viral, Priya! Nizam's is that way ya!'

They slowed down to let me catch up. Viral had a sheepish look on his face and he didn't meet my eye. Priya looked at him and then turned to me.

'Uh Paresh, we were thinking we wouldn't go to Nizam's.'

'But their kababs are the best ya,' I said, still not getting it.

'Actually, we were thinking of, like you know, taking off on our own,' said Priya firmly, a spokesman for the party.

'Oh. Achha. I see.'

Viral saw the hurt look on my face and quickly said, 'That's if you don't mind ya.'

'We just thought we'd have a coffee somewhere, and then Viri could drop me home and you needn't worry,' said Priya, adding the salt of kindness.

'Oh. Uh, fine.' I remembered my battle with my mother to get the extra time for kababs and Coke.

'Like, you know Priya and me aren't going to get to see each other for like five days now so . . . like . . . you know . . . like.'

'Yeah yeah, okay. No problem ya. And thanks for the film ya, Priya.'

'Ei Paresh, don't be like that man! You know how it is!'

'Like what, man? It's fine. Bye.' I turned on my heels.

'Viri! Come on!' I heard Priya's command. Viri indeed. Too chicken to tell me himself. To heel boy, Viri!

Suddenly, for the first time in my life, I found myself alone in the centre of town, on Chowringhee, with an hour and a half to go before I had to report home. I began to walk toward Nizam's. You don't need friends to eat an egg-chicken roll. You just need a mouth and two rupees, fifty paise – which I possessed in my pocket.

I walked to Minerva and looked at the posters of Coming Attractions. I looked across the road to Nizam's, crowded, friends sitting together on tables. Guys in parked cars with their girlfriends, mouths open, hands squeezing parathas loaded with meat, bottles loaded with Coke and Gold Spot. I began to cross and realised that I had no desire to eat one of those grotesque oil missiles. I wanted to get home and eat my mother's rotli, daal, bhaat, shaak.

I shouldered my way back out to Chowringhee. The sun had gone by now but the streets were still jampacked. I went over to the S.N. Bannerjee Road crossing, where all the buses stop, and waited for a No. 49. One came and was so crowded that it went right past. Another one appeared five minutes later. It had even more people hanging from it, fanning out of the doors like kabab rolls spilling out from a Nizam waiter's hands. It struck me that Viral-bastard and his girl, his *chick*, would probably take a taxi home after their coffee in some cosy restaurant in Park Street.

I decided I had had enough of the night-life. I began walking home, which was a good hour's walk. Just enough time to get back before my mother began telephoning Viral's stupid mother.

I turned left on Park Street and walked past Peiping, past Maple, past Trincas and The Other Room. 'Flury's is closed, so either the swines are in the Park Hotel coffee-shop, or they are in Kwality,' I thought. The ghost of the egg-chicken roll sat up in my stomach, saying, 'You should have eaten me.' I realised I was shaking with rage. I found myself turning into the Park Hotel drive-way, heading for the coffee-shop.

I walked past the sign in the lobby without really registering it. Later I would remember it very clearly:

CALCUTTA POETS AND WRITERS UNION
RECEPTION FOR SHRI YASHPAL KHANNA
(HON'BLE SECRETARY INFORMATION & BROADCASTING MINISTRY)
BANQUET ROOM, 1ST FLOOR, 6.00 PM

They weren't in the coffee-shop. I walked back out to the lobby doors to find my way blocked by a group of agitated men. I tried to push past them but it was not possible. I recognised a man in the middle of the group who was shouting at the top of his voice.

'Who the HELL he is?!? Who he IS the hell?!! Sir, Khanna sahab sir, I ASSURE you we will be expelling him from Aawaour Iunion. AND! And fartharmore! Please convhey to Madam aawaour Aandying Saappurt for Twenty-Points programme. And! Please understand on awaour behulf that this man and others like him are in no way representing AAS! I am ESHAMED!'

The man twisted the end of his dhoti in his hands as he shouted, around and around, as if trying to wipe off his shame. His name was Pramathesh Ghosh and my father had once been reluctantly obliged to invite him over to our place for a tea-party. I knew he was the Secretary of the Writers' Union, and that the only reason my father hadn't skewered him that day was because the man had been our guest. Suddenly I knew that the overdue tongue-lashing had finally been delivered. I knew it was my father he was talking about. My father who was nowhere to be seen.

The man he was addressing wasn't looking back at him. He was trying to wipe off the light spray of saliva hitting his beige safari suit and looking around for his driver to bring the car.

Another writer straightened his bush-shirt and approached him.

'Shri Khanna, namashkar. I am Dr Druba Prasad Dastidar, Editor of *Padma Little Magazine*, Democracy Press. I would also like to forward my hearty apology for this Mr Bhatt's bad behaviour and outbarst. This in the city of Tagore! I mast say if The Great Poet was Alive today he would be in full support of Ponditji's daughter. There is no kwoshchon in my –'

Khanna folded his handkerchief and turned to look at Druba Prasad Dastidar. Dastidar stepped back in mid-sentence but the hiss still caught him at point-blank range.

'Why is he your member at all? WHO invited him? Whose plan is it to sabotage this meeting? Press is here, two Forrners were there, someone of you must have planned it! You promised me a meeting of support for the PM! Why else we went to the expense of this five-star Park Hotel?'

Ghosh tried to interrupt Khanna but got swept aside.

'I don't care your little magazine, big magazine! You are 'ware I brief the PM herself every day? And this fellow has guts to talk in this way with ME? Let me tell you, Ghoshbabu, if you fellows don't care 'bout the country you will soon find out Country doesn't care 'bout YOU!'

The driver jumped out and ran around to open the door of the off-white Amby. Khanna pushed past the two men and got into the car, snatching the door from the driver's hand and slamming it shut. Ghosh's elbows went up in a saluting namashkar but Dastidar was undaunted. He reached out for Khanna, whose fingers were clutching the window rim. The handkerchief was still in his hand.

'Khanna sahab! As John F. Kennedy, a great friend of Pondit Neheru, said! "Ask not what your country can do for you but ask what you are doing for your country!!"'

'Remember that, my dear!' Khanna snarled, pulling his hand away from Dastidar as the driver let out the clutch.

'Dr Druba Dastidar! *Padma Magazine!*' Dastidar called after the car, waving, Khanna's handkerchief now held triumphantly hostage in his hand.

I worked my way around the crowd and walked quickly out onto Park Street looking for my father. On the street I passed two other writers I recognised. One was doubled up in laughter, while his friend was looking around to see if anyone had seen them. They were in front of a bar called Olympia.

'Oh I need a drink!'

'Laugh inside, laugh inside you fool, they will all be coming out any moment.'

'I don't care! Bhatt made alu poshto of that Delhi pimp.'

'Well I care, I have a job. Get inside!'

I walked on looking for where my father might have parked our car.

There was No Parking past Flury's, so I turned into Middleton Row. The street lights were off. I saw my father in the light of a paan shop, walking slowly, his old Gladstone bag looking heavy in his hand. I was too far to call out, so I didn't.

I was about a cricket pitch away when I noticed them. Two men had crossed the road in front of me and were moving towards my father purposefully. One of them tapped him on the shoulder. I thought they were writers from the meeting and I quickened my pace to try and catch up. I wanted to hear what they had to say. Something set me sprinting the moment my father turned around.

By this time I was past my obsession with stories of air warfare in the Second World War. But, every time I remembered it later, the image of two Zero fighters diving on Subhash Bose's plane would be impossible to separate from this moment. I remember my father's glasses flying up in an arc as the slap hit him, the thud of the briefcase on the pavement as he doubled up from a punch. I remember trying to shout.

I was close enough by the time one of the men swung his leg back. I saw my father on his hands and knees, naked without his spectacles, a look of fascination on his face as the kick came at him. I remember very little after that.

I only got to know the details from my father many years later. We were sitting in his hospital room waiting for the anaesthetist to come in. We both knew he would probably not survive the operation. My father decided to try and cheer me up.

What I did remember of the fight was a thought flashing through my head that it was unfair, unfair that the first man, the one trying to kick my father, had no idea of what was coming. The other memory is of the second one's knife missing me but slicing my new shirt. It was the first one I ever had without the large collars that were still going out of fashion then.

'I first thought Dharmendra had arrived, mistaking me for Hema Malini,' my father said, 'but it was only you mistaking me for Saira Banu.'

'Zeenat Aman, not Saira Banu,' I said.

'Or Parveen Babi. I remember you used to write to Parveen Babi.'

'No, it was Zeenat Aman.'

My father had begun to watch Hindi movies only recently, after he had fallen ill. He would stare balefully at the video till someone, my aunt perhaps, would ask him why he watched if he hated it so much. 'I'll have to have something to talk to Suman Begum about,' he would say.

My father mourned my mother in two ways – first by watching what had become her favourite Hindi films, and secondly by being almost as nasty about her after her death as he had been when she was alive.

'Anyway, the first chap fell down very quickly after you jumped on him. Unconscious. It was the second one who scared me because he took out a knife. But you handled him. He tried to stab you but he missed and fell down. Then he got up and came again. But you snatched up my bag and held it like a shield at the last moment – and somehow his knife got stuck in it. You twisted the bag around and suddenly this fellow was without a knife! Then you broke his arm. You would have killed him if I hadn't stopped you. You were trying to stab him in the eyes with my spectacles you know!' There was an odd tone of pride in my father's voice that surprised me.

After the fight, my father showed no pride, no gratitude, no emotion that I could discern. He had never been a coward, but with a strictness that came from both his upbringing and his total commitment to Gandhi since 1930, he had always spurned physical violence. Like an electrician disconnecting a superfluous and dangerous wire, my father had disconnected that part of his brain that threw punches, launched kicks, held guns.

But I thought my father often used his tongue like my karate teacher used the side of his hand for a chop. I sometimes used to resent my father's wit, his ability to destroy anyone who annoyed him with one knife-like sentence. Try as I might, I never could get the better of him in a verbal exchange.

We left the two men lying there and got into the car. My father said little.

'What were you doing here?'

'Walking back from a film. Buses were too crowded.'

'Which film?

'*Get Carter*. Michael Caine.'

'Did you learn all that in your karate class? Or did you see it in the cinema?'

I remembered the sound of the second man's arm snapping in my hands and wanted to throw up.

My father may have remained non-violent but that night he broke one of Gandhi's other main tenets – he lied. By agreement, we never told my mother what happened. We had met on Park Street by accident. My shirt had been torn on a rusty edge of the car door. My father's glasses miraculously survived and didn't need explaining. The next morning we discovered that his briefcase was slashed – obviously a pickpocket had tried to cut into it.

From what I could then recount of the fight, little, almost none, of my karate training had come of any use. When I reported what I had done to the men, my teacher confirmed that.

Being old-fashioned, he prided himself on teaching his pupils control. While I took little pleasure from the fact that both men probably went to hospital, I was happy that I had saved my father from being beaten up badly. But my teacher was disappointed that I had not been able to repel the attack with minimum effort and without losing my temper.

Later, in class he took this up as an example. 'In your head you were talking to them,' he said, 'arguing with them.'

I stood head down looking at the knot in my belt. The evening sun threw rectangles of light onto the mats. Other students from the advanced class stood in a row, arms clasped behind their backs, quiet. My teacher stood facing me as if about to demonstrate something, both of us in profile to the others. I could hear the baying of a small crowd watching a football match in the stadium nearby. I could hear the evening traffic on Mayo Road.

'By shouting at them you lost the argument with your sadhana, with your karate. You turned your body into a babbling tongue – and a tongue is never strong in a fight. These boys were obviously street thugs, new to the job. Had they been more experienced, you would be dead.' With which he reached across and untied my orange belt and gave me a green one, the next one lower.

'You still have a lot to learn,' he said.

1 July, 2030

Sometimes, when I wake up in the morning, before I sit up, I find myself reaching to unclick my seat-belt. Maybe it's the sofa, because that's where I sleep, but sometimes I wake up thinking I'm in an aeroplane and I need to piss before it's too late. There are only two rooms and if it's raining hard outside and the shuttles are already running, then it really feels like a bumpy landing pattern. I'm too old to believe in ghosts, meaning I don't have any ghosts that can't be put back in a drawer or pinned to a wall, but sometimes I'm sure this rooftop roomery floats. Some nights I could swear this sofa has turbulence.

Other mornings I don't have a seat-belt and I fall through the empty branches of my dreams, clacking through them, down to the ground like a dead leaf in autumn.

A long time ago – I hate saying that, but this English is a bhenchod limited language, as brittle as their dead leaves in their autumn and there is no other phrase, so – a long time ago, when I was brave about aeroplanes, in jumbos or other wide-body jets on a long flight, I would wait for the seat-belt sign to be switched off and grab any middle row that was empty. You know the ones, where they had four or five seats together in the middle, and on some flights you would find one or two rows free? Well, what I loved doing was to push up all the arm-rests and lie down.

I would make my bed as carefully as a trader in a caravanserai. After getting the arm-rests out of the way I would take one of the little pillows they used to give you and position it exactly – as far up on one of the aisle seats as possible, but not so close to the last arm-rest that it would bump my head. Most times those aisle arm-rests were fixed and they didn't move. Then, next – you're beginning to get what I mean, na? – this is when there were none of these unhealthy little force-fields you apparently have now, where they take away even more of your own control, this is when you had proper seat-belts and now I miss them, just the thought of those things, loose, uneven, dull silver buckles all higgledy-piggledy, trying to figure out which entrail belonged to which seat. What I would do is tuck all the other seat-belts in, making sure they were buried as far as possible between the seats, and just keep the middle pair out, the ones for the middle seat. The trick was to pull the adjustable end out as far as possible, that way you could trick it into thinking it was going around someone really fat. Then lie down and click it in, Laila-Majnu it, Romeo into Juliet, and there I would be, stretching out. I'm not sure why, but the plane always smelled different when I was lying down.

I would lie down, ignoring the looks of other passengers. Basically two types, either 'Is he a lunatic?' or the other category 'I wish I had thought of that', well too bad, both you kinds of jokers, I need my beauty sleep. You can nurse the stiffness of the last airport all the way to the next one, add to it on the way even – but not me! Pawan ke saharey mai tˆo chali!

I would stretch out and adjust myself. Sometimes I would need to bend my knees a bit, depending on which airline, which airplane, and then I would have to decide whether to have the blanket under or over the seat-belt. Most times it would be over the belt once I had clicked it in. It gave you more freedom that way. Sometimes I would find a pesky belt buckle poking me in the back, always just after I'd done all the work and always just as I was ready to switch off, the thing refusing to go in between the seats, and that I just hated. I always thought of the princess and the pea when this happened and I sympathised. There were tricks to fix this. You could put another blanket rolled up once or twice, not too thick, over the poking bit, or you could just pull it out and lay it over you and hope you wouldn't roll over it once you were asleep.

And asleep is what I would be. Thirty-five, thirty-seven thousand feet above the conveyor-belt of continents, sun, cloud or dark, calm, throb or rollercoaster, I would do the lunatic thing of closing my eyes, trusting my belt and trusting the pilots, without even noticing that that's what I was doing, and sleep. I can't bear to think of it now, but then, at that time, thought was not a problem and there were times, seven, eight hours, from just after take-off to just before the landing stuff began, when I would sleep and wake up feeling like I'd never slept better.

Mummy's Belt

There is a photograph of my mother that I no longer have: my mother, flanked by two of her friends – three girls standing on open ground, sunlight, white saris fluttering around their pencil-thin bodies, hands on each other's waist. Around each girl's midriff is a striped sash. Light grey on top, white in the middle and dark grey, almost black, at the bottom.

The photo is printed on good paper, thick, the matt finish only slightly yellow with age. On Sunday mornings my mother would pick it out of a pile of others and move it back and forth as if looking for something to fall out of it. When she turned it to a certain angle in the light you couldn't see the picture, just the rich, shining skin of the rectangle. Sometimes I thought a different picture would emerge from the grains when she turned the photo back towards me. But no new magic ever transformed it, every time the same three girls, all smiling. Three wide grins linking their faces, the teeth even whiter than the saris. There are other photographs too, from that time, all black and white of course, but that was never a problem – my mother used to like filling in the colours.

The sash was tirangi, a tricolour – orange on top, white in the middle and green below – Congress colours. 'Jail' colours they were called, because, in the years before the Second World War, that's where you could find yourself for wearing them.

'My friend Kanaklata, the one on the left, used to dye them at home. She would use haldar – after a few days in the sun it would turn orange – and a mixture of phudino and kothmir for the green.'

'That was in the early days,' my father would intercept, 'by '42 the Vahlabhai mills were manufacturing them by the tens of thousands – pure khadi of course, for the white base, but no kitchen spices for the colours, cheap dyes from Manchester for the orange and green . . . they made millions from the sashes, the flags, the badges. They would also charge two paisa per cup of tea at every organisation meeting held in their mansion – and believe me there were many, many meetings. Life, in fact, was one long meeting.'

'On Diwali we would even wear tirangi ribbons in our hair, and at certain marriages, where the Boy and the Girl were both Congress workers –'

My father pushing back his glasses, never taking his eyes off *The Statesman*, his bile spilling over the ramparts of newspaper. 'Cheap watery tea. Just think! Just think, that one of the great industrial empires of post-Independence India was built on selling bad tea to people about to go to jail, people wearing sashes, waving flags made from cheap English dyes!'

Colour. My daughter sends me an image in colour. It flashes on my left screen first, interrupting work as it's supposed to, then it knocks on the right monitor and transfers to the printer. The old Nambudiripad wakes up and complains out the message, the anti-curl completely dysfunctional in the humid Calcutta afternoon.

The Nambu-6CX was a glorious thing in its time – the first totally Indian-made turbo-laser colour-printer/fax/scanner. But now the cartridges are expensive and hard to find – which is why I hate receiving colour mail, which uses up more ink. The paper is terrestrial, overpriced, from Kumarbabu Stationery Co. on Rashbehari Avenue, but the message is from twenty miles up in space.

I know that somebody from the National Institute of Design has dreamed up a little logo for 'Varun-Machaan – the first Indian space station', and that they are duty-bound to use it on every single communication they send down. The tricoloured slash on top of the paper is wobbly, jiggled about by a bad space-to-earth connection. It tightens my shoulders with the same unease that the grey white and black sash in my mother's photograph did after I grew up.

The message says:

> *Dear Pups: Love: Happy Anniversary: I've sent a separate message to Ma: they call it a FGM: (Foreign Graded Message): Had to send it in black and white unfortunately: They won't let me send a private colour message outside India-Subcon Region: (Para)*
>
> *Here is a picture of the part of the Milky Way we are studying now: Ma may not get it so good in black and white so please send her a colour copy as soon as you can: Better still, get over fear of flying and go give it to her: The picture reminds me of a dried-up river bed: What looks like a sand bank is actually many stars!: I am really well!: (Para)*
>
> *Hugs and kisses: Miss you: Love: Para: (Para)*

On the last page is the image: a formation of ox-bow rivulets, blue-black space coiling through densely packed yellow dots.

And under the image:

> *Endmessage: to: Shri P. Bhatt: from:*
> *Grp. Cpt. (Rec). Paramita Bhatt*

I look around my room for a place to put the picture. My memory is going and I don't want to forget where I put it and who it's from. No matter what she does, my daughter is important to me.

The walls of my room are covered with images gathered over a lifetime and there isn't much space left, but I find a gap. It is a useful gap and Para's picture goes next to a time-lapse series capturing Howrah

Bridge after the bomb hit, as it collapsed over two days into the Hooghly in '07. The images were shot by a digital camera fixed on top of the bridge. The camera went into the water with the girders but they fished it out later.

When I first got hold of the series you could flick the pictures like one of those kinetic books and see the bridge slowly lose its pomp and settle into the river, like a tired camel sitting down. The pictures were in colour but when you riffled the pack they would become almost black and white. The last picture is deep in the water just before the camera stopped functioning and it is amazing – a close-up of a slightly blurred fish tail with the geometric patterns of girders out of focus in the background. It looks as if the fish has just knocked down the bridge. After the flurry of grey your eye becomes still on this image. The colours are lurid, digital, as unreal as the event, and Para's sand bank of stars goes well beside it.

• • •

My parents first met on a river bed, and I keep thinking of the colours that day was made of.

The Sabarmati at Ahmedabad is a strange river. I remember taking a flight from Delhi to Ahmedabad one stormy evening in '91, a good few years before I finally stopped getting into aeroplanes. Despite a schoolboy obsession with air warfare that I have yet to outgrow, I was always terrified of flying and that was one of the worst flights I ever took.

The memory of lightning gnawing at the wingtips still had me shaking with fear when I got to my hotel. The rain had stopped. From my room I could see something strange was happening on Nehru Bridge. I went down to take a closer look.

People were getting off from scooters, rickshas, buses, cycles. They were arriving in waves. They were getting off, running to the side and fighting for space to lean over the fat concrete parapet. They were looking down. A suicide? No, people were lined all the way down both sides of the bridge. I went into the crowd.

A mother held her daughter up by the waist, helping her look over the edge. 'Look! Water!' she said proudly, her fingers tightening on the girl's frock. 'So much water!' the ten-year-old exclaimed. 'But what's it doing in the river?'

The Sabarmati was in spate, overflowing.

It was something people hadn't seen for twenty years. It's not something that happened very often even in the days when my parents were children.

For most part of the year the river remained dry, though the British, as was their habit, kept building bridges over it. In 1991 the bed still curved through as it used to, dividing the old city from the new. It stretched, sandy, wide and implacable under each new structure that was put up – a ghost of what it was supposed to be – ignoring engineers' conceits like an elephant ignores street dogs.

I used to remember the names in sequence, but now I'm not so sure. From north to south: Subhash Bridge first, then Gandhi Bridge, Nehru Bridge, Ellis Bridge, and then Sardar Bridge. I am sure they had different names in the 1930s, and not all of them were even built. At least three, I think, were built after Independence.

But Ellis Bridge, the oldest and narrowest, and my favourite, must have been there. It wouldn't have been called Ellis Bridge in those days, Ellis I imagine still alive and busy designing more bridges, but it would have been there, its baleful black iron pontooning over the sand.

Political parties continued to use the river bed for political rallies till the dam project flooded the river permanently in '05. But it was the Congress that first began having their early ladhat meetings on the sand.

'What's ladhat, Mummy? Is it a fight, like a ladhai?' I would ask when I was four years old.

'No, no. We weren't allowed to fight,' my mother would snap, and then in her college lecturer's voice, 'Ladhat means struggle, the non-violent freedom struggle which brought us Independence.'

'Yes,' my father would add, mimicking my mother's textbook tone. 'The Independence to fight amongst ourselves.' And I would nod at them both, even though I was too young to understand.

'Anyway,' my mother would continue, ignoring my father's sarcasm, 'on a big day everyone in the poel would get up early, even children your age.'

Old Ahmedabad is made up of a series of interlocking casbahs called poels. On the day of a big meeting people in the poel would wake up at about four thirty or five. It would still be dark when the first prayer processions began winding their way through the lanes of the old town.

'If you looked down from a high window, and you hadn't rubbed sleep from your eyes, you would think it was a huge white snake coming down the street through the dawn mist. People would move quietly at first, shuffling from street to street. In our poel, Hajira ni Poel, a small group would start from Jheenabhai Vakil's house and pick up people as it went . . .' my mother would say.

'Then someone,' and even at sixty-eight, when she told me the story for the last time, her back still straightened at this point, 'then someone would start the singing.'

Somebody would start and slowly others would join in. One after the other – aartis, prabhatiyas, bhajans, and patriotic songs to Bharat Mata, this imaginary Mother Country still waiting to be born.

Suddenly all of them would be singing: old women, voices made strong and shrill from a lifetime of shouting at children, portly middle-aged men with thin voices, children mouthing words they didn't quite know, curiosity battling sleep in their eyes, young men with throats fervoured by the great battle that lay ahead, young women, parallel melodies of desire and patriotism lilting out of them as they examined the young men for fervour, mothers watchful of the fervour of their daughters, the boys warily eyeing the mothers, one or two of them losing the tune under a glare far more terrifying than any Englishman's.

When I was a kid we used to visit Amdavad every year and I have a distinct memory of the smell attached to early winter mornings. As you came out of the house a complex layering would form in your nose, woven out of the fragrance of open gutters, scooter engines, cows, milk and masala tea. But that was from the 1960s. I have no idea what it smelled like then, around 1930, but for some reason I imagine those dawn prayer processions smelling of incense and of the light sweat that comes with the beginning of fear.

The prabhat-feri was a daily thing, a prayer procession that would normally stay within the bounds of the neighbourhood. But on the day of a big rally, each feri would change its normal route and come out of the warren of the poel onto the main roads. There it would join up with the processions from other poels, like a tributary joining a big river, and turn towards Ellis Bridge.

Most people would be wearing white khadi. As the procession began spilling over the banks of the Sabarmati, someone standing on the bridge could see the amazing sight of a wide, dry river bed change colour from sand to white. He would be transfixed by the sight of something even more frightening than a river in full spate – the spectacle of thousands of people moving together, each dreaming of a country, and each imagining that every other person around them was dreaming exactly the same dream.

The bridge was usually an observation post for the Police Superintendent of Sabarmati Thana. Whatever fear, or awe or disgust, the Superintendent may have felt, his orders in those early days were simple: wait for the crowds to gather, wait for the speeches to begin, wait for the first two or three remarks against the King Emperor, the Government in London and the rule of Law. Then send in the mounted police. Hit as many of them as hard as you can, arrest the leaders on the makeshift platform, grab any known faces in the crowd if you couldn't cripple them first. Disperse the meeting. Make sure the little buggers remember you for the rest of their lives.

Neither of my parents ever met the Superintendent, but both of them remembered the Sergeant.

'He was a huge man,' my mother would say.

'He was a small man on a very big horse,' my father would contradict her.

'Big moustaches.'

'Big red moustaches,' my father would agree.

'Green.'

Between them my parents had only a part of the story to tell me and the part they told me I believed. The rest I made up across my childhood years. Then I forgot some of it and made it up again later. By the time I told it to my daughter it went like this:

Sergeant Green was his name and he was the terror of all Ahmedabad. Crowds had been known to scatter just from the sound of his name – 'Ei jojo hawn! Green avyo, Green!' A short bull-like man with a face perhaps a bit like Graham Gooch, Green carried a long baton that was as infamous as he was. If policemen made notches on their batons for each person hospitalised, Green's would have looked like a thick millipede.

Yes, that was Sergeant Green, the most feared policeman in the whole country. At least till the day he became responsible for introducing my mother to my father.

Not that anyone about to come under his horse's hooves would have noticed, but that day Green was not in his usual control. His horse – and I named him Pathankot for Para – was restless that day. A big horse, with something very small bothering him. Perhaps a winter mosquito in his ear, perhaps piles.

Green patted Pathankot's neck and waited for the order. The Superintendent looked again to make sure the crowd had reached full strength, he waited for the last stragglers to reach the meeting. Then he raised his right arm and brought it down in a wave. The troop came down off the bridge onto the river bed and stopped at the edge of the meeting. Many turned around and noticed. A ripple passed over the gathering, tensing the bodies, stiffening the mass. The Superintendent took a hailing tube from the man on his right and put it to his mouth. He called out to the crowd.

'Disperse!'

Everyone knew this was actually the command to charge. The speaker did not pause and nobody moved. The horses came in.

My mother had a way of telling this. 'They would really hit hard,' she would say, bringing down on my shoulders whatever stick-like object she happened to have picked up, 'hit hard or poke with their batons,' she would poke me, 'and this Green would hit hardest of all. He was really vicious. Old, young, he didn't care who he was hitting. That day I first saw him smash Kamuba in the ribs – Chandralekha's grandmother.'

I never got the full details, and years later Para played it differently, but again, this is how I imagine it: pandemonium, dust, people running in all directions. A fifteen-year-old girl sees Green knock down a frail old woman. The girl gathers up her sari and begins to run towards the woman. A boy, seventeen, also sees the old lady crumple, a huge horse rearing over her. He also starts running towards her.

From the bridge, a wider view of the one-sided battle. Three colours – swathes of white emptying out of the river like froth, the yellow sand swirling up into dust, the police in khakhi chasing after the froth. Two dots break out of the white and run in the opposite direction, into the horses instead of away from them.

Green sees the boy first. He pulls his horse around and waits for him to run into reach. He has to bend really low from his saddle, but he is good at this. The baton lands hard – just above the solar plexus. It lifts the boy off his feet and knocks him back about two yards.

Then things go wrong for Green. Normally he would straighten up, look to check whether he had caused enough damage and knee Pathankot on to the next quarry. This time though, things happen differently.

Like a sportsman replaying the crucial moment that lost him his final game, Green would spend the rest of his life trying to right himself back to balance on his saddle. On the ship home via Aden, in the hut of the radar station in Kent, till the very moment the great surprise that ended his life happened to him, in fact, Green would replay his first great surprise – the one that ended his career as a police sergeant in Ahmedabad.

A radar station in Kent? Well actually, when I was twelve I'd put it in Northumberland. But Para, who loved this part, never could pronounce Northumberland, so yes, Kent.

They say you never hear the shell that kills you, but Sergeant Green hears his death coming in from quite a few miles away.

'Morning cuppa coming in. Single Willie, low,' says his assistant to Green.

'I reckon it's a Cigar, there's two engines on that job. I'll go and look,' grunts Green and rolls his wheelchair out of the hut and onto the tongue of grassy ground on top of the cliff.

The silhouette sways on the horizon like a drunken man trying to win his feet back from the ground. Even from that distance Green can make out that the plane is neither, as he had guessed, a Heinkel bomber nor his assistant's morning reconnaissance Messerschmidt. As it comes wobbling in over the dawn sea, Green sees the plane is on fire. He recognises it as an RAF Lancaster returning from a night raid. He notes with the satisfaction of a professional that two of its four engines are dead.

He follows it as it comes low overhead. The damaged bomber has no control over its bowels and Green only hears the sound a little after he sees the bomb-doors flap open, he hears it only for a few seconds. While the bomb that kills him is a surprise, the sound isn't. He has heard the same sound on the river bed in Ahmedabad, ten years earlier.

Because my mother had wailed. Not screamed, wailed in anger.

'Something frightening escaped from inside me. I wasn't scared then but now I am. It still scares me when I think of it, when I think that this thing is still hiding inside me.'

The wail pierced Pathankot's ears and the horse reared up high, impossibly high, like a man trying to reach back over his head with both arms stretched full.

'The Sergeant hung from the horse like a sack and then . . . dropped.'

My mother would invariably pause while describing the moment when Green dangled from his horse. And I would involuntarily contract my anus, because for some reason, at that moment, I could feel Green, and he felt like a huge turd clinging on just before it finally parts from the body and slaps onto the curve of white ceramic. Every time Green fell in my mother's telling, the satisfaction I would feel was not dissimilar to one that follows a good shit.

My uncle Prabodhmama had only one thing to say to me when I was a child and he would repeat it in my ear every morning like a guru challenging a pupil with a secret mantra.

'Khawu ke na khawu?' he would ask.

'Na khawu,' I would reply obediently.

'Jawu ke na jawu?' he would then ask.

'Jawu!' I would answer loudly, and Prabodhmama would lean back with the satisfaction of a Shakespeare who has just finished rehearsing his actor for the first performance of Hamlet.

For Gujarati Brahmans the toilet is a theatre of war and Prabodhmama was no exception. He was teaching me the main tenet he claimed to live by: 'If the question is to eat or not to eat then don't eat. If the question is to go for a shit or not to go for a shit then always, and without fail, GO.'

Eased of his rider, Pathankot trotted off.

'I kept looking at the horse. I kept imagining he would come back to pick up his master. Or to avenge him. We used to read these stories you know, Rana Pratap's horse, Rani of Jhansi's horse, loyal and fierce they were, almost human, but not this horse. He just went off and stood under Ellis Bridge.'

'Obviously your brother Prabodh had told him the secret of life – he just wanted to clear his bowels.' My father would shoo in the old punch line and testily flip a page.

But my mother was not to be denied. Her wonder was fresh each time she told the story. 'Kamuba was groaning on the ground next to me. Everybody had disappeared. And there was this horse, his tail back, doing, well you know, sandaas. Precisely next to a pillar of the bridge.'

Girls normally finish toilet training earlier than boys but Para was a troubled child because of problems between me and her mother, and she took till she was five. The way it finally worked was by my telling her the story of Green and Pathankot every morning while she sat on the commode. It took a month, after which the story got put away till it found another echo much later in Para's life.

On the day Para's mother Anna and I decided we didn't need the story anymore we were in Ahmedabad staying with a cousin. Right after Para had successfully finished the Gujarati's 'daily duty', my cousin's husband, a magistrate in the sessions court, called out to his son, who was a little younger than Para.

'Beta, look! Parababy has finished! Now it's your turn to go to Pakistan!'

'But Pappa I've already been to Pakistan!'

'Pak-Istan?' repeated Para, the triumph of discovering a new word lighting up her eyes.

It took us another month before we could persuade Para to call it 'the toilet' again.

On the river bed, several years before Independence carved out three very oddly shaped turds, my mother somehow managed to tear her eyes away from Green's horse and turn her attention to the old lady. Other people had come back to help. They were lifting Kamuba onto a makeshift stretcher. The boy was doubled up in a foetal position, not moving at all. The girl went over and shook his shoulder. There was no response. For two days there wouldn't be. Despite her age, Kamuba would recover in a matter of hours. Green had saved his best shot for my father.

As she climbed up the steps from the river bed, my mother glanced over her shoulder. Green lay in a fat little pile a little distance away, also completely still. The other mounted police were busy chasing people back into the poels and nobody else had the courage to go near him. All that my parents could say of him was that he was never seen in Ahmedabad again. A few days later, city rumour had it that the fall had paralysed him.

My father was not one of those men who boasted of their scars, but my mother was quite happy to do it for him. In a sense, this bruise belonged to her, and from time to time, when my father happened to have his kurta off, she would point to it proudly. It was a near perfect circle of reddish skin about two inches in diameter, a little above the solar plexus, forming a triangle with the nipples.

From the time I was about five, I remember the bruise and it stayed constant even though the body around it changed and aged. The last time I saw it was in the Calcutta General Hospital when they were washing my father's body just before we took him for the cremation. I suddenly realised how old and wrinkled my father's skin had become, all of it except the red circle above his solar plexus which still looked strangely fresh.

My mother was too prudish to tell me this, but once I overheard her tell my aunt about the first time she laid eyes on my father's bruise. 'It was all red and swollen and someone was applying ointment to it. I had gone over to see how he was and no one had noticed. He was knocked out but I remember thinking what a beautiful body, wide chest, narrow waist, "lion-waisted" as they say in Sanskrit. He had a thick head of hair then, of course, but most of all I think I fell in love with the chest with its red bruise. I thought he would die, but he woke up one morning as if he'd just finished a good night's sleep.'

My father woke up from his sleep into a new life. Bright winter light bounced off a neighbouring wall and in through the window. Once inside the room, it played a trick with the mirror on the old dresser and ricocheted back the way it had come, stopping only to bracket itself around the face of the most beautiful girl in the world.

The most beautiful girl in the world had always played at the edges of the boy's vision. On the street he had seen her by the vegetable cart, half obscured by a pyramid of tomatoes. At marriages she had flashed past, dancing garba, spinning by too quickly for his eyes to hold but slow enough for his heart to catch on her yellow sari. On his way to school he had paused, pulled back by her black plait swinging as she went to school in the opposite direction. On the river bed, just before Pathankot's hooves shuttered the light, he had caught sight of her thin legs leaving a slipstream of sand. Far to his left, on the periphery of his life, but sprinting straight for its centre.

At seventeen, Mahadevkumar Bhatt woke up into his new life and saw Suman Pathak standing there, caught in a crossfire of light. He didn't see the other people in the room. He looked past his aunt, his third sister, and his cousin brother, looked through them as if they were shadows and locked his gaze on his future.

'Yes, my chest hurt terribly but I was young and almost as stupid as you – I thought it was my heart feeling the pain of love.'

• • •

The pain of love turned my father into a very good amateur photographer. Soon after he and my mother fell in love he borrowed a camera for the first time because he wanted to take pictures of her. During the long years they were forced to be apart he continued his photography. My parents had me late, and by the time I was born my father had been taking photographs for twenty-five years.

Our flat in Calcutta seemed to grow books and photographs. There were photographs in albums, tamped down by four sticky 'corners' on thick black paper, there were loose photographs in those big red Agfa envelopes that you still get, there were photographs pressed between the pages of books, there were photographs behind the sliding glass doors of book-cases and there were framed photographs on the wall. I sometimes feel I exchanged my mother's womb for my parents' house, where the amniotic fluid was made up in equal parts of words and images.

Now, approaching the end-game of an unsuccessful life, I have come back to Calcutta. Many of the images that fed me as a child are no longer with me but some I've managed to hold on to. They are on the walls of my room. They punctuate other pictures that I've picked up along the way – postcards from places like Poughkeepsie and Erevan, drawings from forgotten lovers, stills from films to remind me of the time when there was cinema, snapshots of my own family, newspaper photographs, still-lifes by Matisse and Morandi, digital reconstructions of lost neighbourhoods.

The pictures that my father took stand out, somehow, from this morass. It's not just that the photographs themselves were taken with an acute sense of aesthetics, a fine balance of frame and light. They were also taken with love, a lot of love. My father managed to catch many things – laughter, pensive corners, bodies telling whole stories by the way in which they were ranged against the background, faces that revealed more than their owners perhaps intended to, landscapes which talked – but it's not that either. What makes them barge into my attention is something else.

Though it was my father who took the pictures it was my mother who told me about them. She used to play a game with me on Sunday mornings. While my father read the newspaper and the maid swept the floor around our feet, my mother would pull out photographs and tell me stories connected to each picture. Then, and this was when I was smaller, she would actually shuffle around photos she had told me about and quiz me:

'What's this one?'

'That is the body of Saraswati, Motakaka's daughter. She died in Pappa's lap when she was eight months old, on 15 August, 1947, the day we got our Independence. Everybody was out celebrating except Pappa and Saraswati's mother.'

'And this one?'

'This is me crying the day Chacha Nehru died in 1964. I was crying because you slapped me. You slapped me because I threw Ba's prayer beads into the gutter . . .'

'Yes, yes, all right, and this one?'

'. . . and Pappa said you shouldn't slap me if you really believed in non-violence.'

I was one of the most photographed babies in history. And before my father's attention shifted to me, it was my mother who was the most comprehensively photographed woman in all of India. The pictures follow the trajectory of my parents' relationship – my father began to take pictures because he wanted to photograph my mother, and as the love between them died its slow death, his desire to photograph ebbed away as well. He took fewer and fewer pictures till one day when he handed me his precious Nikon F and gave me the job of official family photographer.

'You've more or less learned to focus now, so you might as well have this. Because if I wait for you to understand exposure we will be in the next century,' with which he never touched a camera again.

By the time he stopped, Mahadev Bhatt had taken thousands of photographs of Suman Bhatt, but somehow, for my mother, fate, chance and memory left the biggest residue of significance in three photographs of her not taken by my father.

'Chandrika took this snap the day before I began attending Gujarat College,' she said of the picture we knew as 'The Three Musketeers'. 'We'd all got these new sashes and she had to steal her brother's camera to take it. He was very angry when he found out because film was that precious. We had to wait five years before he gave each of us a copy of the picture.'

The next one she liked to show was a colour print. Suman Bhatt on a horse in Simla, her husband Mahadev Bhatt standing next to the horse, holding the reins. A young couple on a holiday, June 1959. It is, for India, an early colour print, strange shiny brittle paper, a thin white border around colours that had already faded by the time I saw it – sickly magentas, light pinks, the trees in the background an odd purple-ish blue, the horse an odd brown, my parents' faces almost sepia.

My mother wears a Kulu cap and underneath it her face has a proud look, as if she has just pulled Pathankot back from the pillar and mastered him. She is proud, but she is not smiling and neither is my father.

'Pain has colours,' said my mother, sixty-eight years old, waving the photograph at me as if it was Sergeant Green's baton, the day before she went into her last coma, 'and these are the colours that pain has.'

The third picture was taken in Bombay in 1952, inside a plane taking off from Santa Cruz Aerodrome. 'The day Suman made her big mistake,' my father would say, dispassionately, every time the photograph fell out of the jungle of images that overgrew our house.

Black and white, but taken with a flash, which my father never used. A woman sits erect in an aircraft seat. She is sharp, smiling for the camera, but the smile doesn't quite reach her eyes. Her body is pulling against the tight little silver seat belt that crumples her sari into a funny hourglass shape. Behind her is an oval window and through it the ground is blurred, three palm trees barely recognisable, also blurred as if in a desert storm and slightly tilted.

'This was the first time I flew in a plane. No one except for your father and his cousin Nalin knew about our marriage. Everybody in Ahmedabad was against us and your father was in Calcutta by then, so I said I was going to Bombay and took the plane secretly to Calcutta with Nalin, who bought a flash gun for the marriage.'

'When your father looks at this photo he always says I was worrying about my running away, but I was actually worried because I didn't believe any plane with me in it would ever get off the ground. I think we were in the air just after Nalin took this snap, and once we took off I was fine. The seat-belt was a bit tight, especially during the lightning storm when the plane went up and down, but I didn't care – I was in the sky. I was flying to get married to the man I loved.'

I no longer have this picture but I more or less know where it is.

There is a pair of more recent photographs on my wall and at first glance they look like the same picture. When you look more closely you can see that one copy is actually black and white, a print-out of a Web news item, and the other is a proper colour print.

'And this one?' I can hear my mother asking, though she never saw it.

The photograph is taken with a flash, but out of focus, far in the background, you can see the first streaks of dawn colouring the horizon. The photographer is looking down into the open cockpit of a jet fighter. The pilot has turned to smile at the camera just before putting on the helmet, which has three elongated stripes in the colours of the Indian flag just above the computerised visor. The stripes are even more lurid if you look at the colour print.

There is a harness which straps the pilot's body, the seat with the ejector jets and the twin parachutes into one compact unit. The straps of the harness form a cross with the centre point just under the pilot's solar plexus and the flash has turned the material bright white so it looks like someone has taken a fluorescent marker and crossed the pilot out. Sometimes I have to remind myself that I didn't put the cross there myself, that it is part of the photograph.

Underneath the newspaper version the caption reads: *Dec. 6, 2017, the Return Match for 2007 begins: Squadron Leader Para Bhatt led the first sortie of the new Ishir fighter-bombers in the pre-emptive attack against forces of the Pak–Saudi alliance early yesterday. All targets were successfully destroyed.*

Behind the colour print is a note in my daughter Para's handwriting:

Dear Pups. We hit Kharan three days ago. Don't let the smile fool you, I didn't want to go to Pakistan, I wanted to go to *Pakistan*! Please don't worry about me. As I tell the girls in my Flight – it's just a job like any other. Yeah, right.

I know you don't approve but I think Ba would have, so I took her along for the ride. You can't see it but the snap of her in the plane is in my pocket just over my heart.

Love,
Para

22 July, 2030

Open the door, I can get there, door open, go through now, go through, hold it in and keep going, you can get there.

Lift the seat, nearly there, nearly –

There.

These ghosts that I cannot get out. The mornings are the worst. Mornings in monsoon are worse than worst. Some days the suction bowl and I just look at each other in a Cold War stalemate, Yanks and Russkies eyeball to eyeball. Both jammed, neither having any truck with water, as dry as the Sahara, 'dry as a Pommie shower-curtain' as Australians used to say while describing wine. The commode-circuitry on strike and inside me a liquid tailback going all the way up behind my navel, a roadblock in front. Wanting to let go very badly but nothing coming out and the rain outside turning the screw. A fresh school of raindrops on the one frond of the date palm I can see from my bathroom window. Each drop a quivering taunt. Streets flooding below. Water, water, everywhere, but not a drop to – on really bad days, I have to manage by imagining different things.

Like the coffee spurting out of the column in the Alessi. And jumping on the sidelines, those cheerleaders from the Bantolla American Football team. As on TV the other day. 'Gimme a Peee! Pee for Paresh! Gimme an aaaaI! I for India! Gimme an essS! S for struggle! Gimme another ess! S for suicide! What do we got?! What *do we* got!?!!' Nothing worse than seeing good Bengali girls wearing American high school cheerleader uniforms, waving little coloured cotton balls. *Opor-nichey*, morons, *up* and down, up and down, *yaaay*! Enough to make you wet yourself in disgust . . . yes . . . chalo, come on old man, that's it, come on, this will pass.

And it somehow does.

I know a day will come, I know that a morning will dawn-load when it will explode inside me while I am crawling to the phone, trying to call Doctor Sanyal, Doctor, Doctor, that new German bio-catheter you were suggesting – but too late! The thing will burst like Tehri Dam, *Geeb mi a C! C for Catheter!?!!! Noooo! C for Cremayshaan!!!!*

Morning used to be my favourite time, except for those six months when I was breaking up with Ila-Teesta. As I didn't know then, the first break-up is always the worst, but when I broke up with The River I was lucky to have friends. Anirban, for one, turned all my hell into art and produced some very good songs. One in English, the 'Baby Gone Bombay' one and one in Bangla that both became cult hits. *Shokaal aashe haangorer moton*, which he then translated into English as well, bluesed it, but it didn't work so well.

Morning comes like a shark
Morning comes like a shark
Sinks its teeth lightly
Into the skin of my dark.

The tune they did for the English was still nice, but it was much better in Bangla, where he didn't try to rhyme it:

Shokaal aashe haangorer moton
Shokaal ghorey haangorer moton
Eshe halka korey daant-guli naamaay
Aamar nidra-shoron-ondhokaarer opor.

There is a sense of the dawn circling that gets lost in English; the second line should have been 'morning *circles* like a shark' but Kajol, the keyboards guy, was an idiot-purist and kept insisting that in a proper blues the repeat line could not change. And there was no way they were going to get nidra-shoron-ondhokaar right. I mean how? Sleep/sanctuary/darkness? As we know, meaning, actually, darkness-sanctuaried sleep? Chhaah. Smarter, much smarter, and this is what English does to you if you let it – like a shark, give it a toe and it will take a leg – is to make things simple. Makes you take out all the grey tones sometimes, English, leaving crude black raping naked white.

Anyway, I tell you, the moment I pull the flush, I can tell today is going to be another coffee day. The very thing that causes this pain will be needed to deal with its after-effects. It's like one of those relationships, you know, like my mother and father, or a bit differently, like me and Anna, where there is some essential poison in the other that keeps you alive, the grey tones of love-hate without which you don't have the full picture of life.

There, it's going now, the coffee, and it sounds good. Some days this Alessi also has a prostate problem. It sort of solidarnoscs with my urinary tract and silts up, a trade union of jammed pipes, and I can hear the steam pushing and nothing coming out, a trickle, an escapee drop or two, a smudge of espresso drying at the bottom of the top compartment and the smell of coffee and rubber burning. I have to act fast when that happens and it usually happens without warning. One day, the castle-prison is working perfectly and then, suddenly, the next day the inmates are rioting. Today it's fine, I can tell just from the sound. I keep an ear open for the shuttle and wait. As I wait, I contemplate the fact of mornings.

The other time morning, or, rather, the idea of morning, became a problem was when Para – I try not to remember that too often, give that memory a morning and it will take the noon as well – what was that old poem she sent me then? I shot the hippo . . . oh yeah:

I shoot the hippopotamus
With bullets made of platinum
Because if I use leaden ones
His hide is sure to flatten 'em.

To which I had a nasty reply, also Hilaire Belloc, but lines reversed, one word added, emphasis added, not really meant to be nasty but, maybe, well, yeah, if it made her cry, then too bad.

While I cannot say the same about the Kurd,
The camel is a friendly bird.

I've always been a quiet guy, but when I hit, I hit.

23 July, 2030

I normally just let it ring. When friends call they know what to do. I've worked it out. They let it ring thrice, hang up, ring thrice again, hang up again, and then at the next ring I pick it up.

Today was a mistake and I could blame it on the noise of the rain, or I could blame it on the shuttles and their racket. Or the Bhairavi on the sound system, not vocal, old man Bahauddin on the rudra veena. Okay, so there were three sounds going on, true, but I know the one thing I'm not going is deaf. The truth is I made a mistake.

What happened was that I was stuck in the bathroom, angry about the toilet suction acting up again, trying to get a packet of hand-wipes open, when someone linked and I couldn't get to it in time for the seventh ring. So, when the thing rang again a few minutes later, I clicked it on thinking it must be the same person ringing. Someone who I wanted to talk to – stupid. How idiot can an old man be? Really idiot, because I can tell you there aren't too many people left who I want to talk to. No faith in my own protection systems, no recognition that I'm really getting old, my own need to hear from someone, to talk. So – a kick in the stomach, full well hundred per cent deserved – as soon as the voice came on I knew I'd made a mistake.

Suddenly I was tripping on the snake of an unknown voice. And me still being fast, I was on to my disengagement tactics before the asshole even finished his first few words – cut him off at the gulch! – except the finished sentence was like a fish-hook. It caught inside me and after that I was struggling, flipping, and the harder I tried to get out the more the hook dug into me.

'Nomoshkar, I am linking from *The Telegraph* to get an obituary update for Shri Poresh Bhatt.'

The *fuck*! What? 'Ki? Get a what – *Ki*?'

'Obituary update, sir. Rikuwesting for our database. We need the lettest achibments and awuaards. I am linking because I hab noticed jey we have naathing new since two jiro phiphtin. And, of course you understand jey – I mean – let us prey-tu-god jey nothing happens to Poresh babu, but for all eminent people we have to be prepyared.'

Later, I messaged Para about this and she found it very funny.

Dear Eminent Pappoos,

Let us pray to god indeed! But where's the damage? Get it out of the way, I say! Nothing like 66-ing out a satisfactory obituary to help you with the seriouser business of getting on with life! I don't know if I can help, me sitting up here, but if you want I could write you an Orbituary. That's a triple pun by the way, fatzer. OR as in Alternative. Orbit as in where I am and, oh sorry, correction – quadruple. Or-Bitch-you-ary. Let's see. What should I say?

And then she went on, but that was later. The guy on the telelink was more polite.

'Excuse me sir, but I am not getting your picture on my screen, are you getting an image of myself?'

'This house is not cam-linked.' Not true, but I was damned if I was going to let some stranger gawk at me on his screen. Or vice versa. I didn't want to see his face either. But the man didn't seem bothered.

'I see sir, I see.' No, you don't you fucking chyoot. 'I tekk it sir that you are Poresh babu's secretary?'

Tekk it indeed. Everyone knew I never answered the link myself, so the idiot assumed that I had something as intrusive as a secretary. Fool. I nearly disconnected there and then. I don't know what made me hang on. Maybe ego. Curiosity. Wanting to hear what they would say after.

'Han, yes,' I said, 'Shibu Dey here,' grabbing a mix of the first two names that came into my mind.

'Sir . . . kindly . . .' his voice went delicate, 'can I tell you what we have first, for the photographs for usage after demise?'

Ah. Of course. It wouldn't just be words, would it? They would need the photographs.

'Yes, please tell me.' Me trying my best to sound like my own secretary.

'Well sir, for a photograph of Poresh babu we have one file picture from 1998, photographing some anti-nuclear demonstration in New Delhi, taken by Borun Talukdar, but sir, Poresh babu . . . he is vhery djyong in this . . .'

Not that young, thirty-eight that year, in '98, when they exploded the devices. I can still taste that Delhi May in my mouth sometimes.

'Hottest summer since they started to keep the records,' Borun said to me proudly. Then he saw me loading my camera and said, 'Ilford? You got that from There, no? Never buy Ilford here in the summer. Kodak-shodak is all right if you know who you are getting it from.' It was so hot I was surprised any film stock was safe in the shops.

Apparently April had already been brutal, and early May worse, but local people were convinced that temperatures went up even more after the first blast on the 11th. And then again after the second one on the 13th.

This was the Sansad Marg PO roundabout at five o'clock in the evening, with people standing with placards trying to catch the attention of the evening rush-hour.

Barun and I split up and began walking around. As he moved away from me, I watched him for a while. He had just bought himself a mint-condition second-hand Nikon F4 which he was very proud of. Big, massive, spaceship of a camera, titanium body, everything automatic, heavier than a Colt .45. And as I watched, Barun went up close to a demonstrator and squeezed off a few pictures. The in-built motor-drive emitted small squeals like some baby machine crying for mechanic milk. Like all modern cameras the F4 forwarded the film automatically, and Barun, never having used a motor-drive, was having a problem about what to do with his right thumb. 'It's very nice,' he'd said, 'but after each picture, my thumb moves for the lever. It's hard to lose a habit of twenty years. It feels like I'm not working.'

As I watched him, Barun crouched below a tall man with a long beard and took a couple of low-angle ones, classic city-page stuff, before sliding off towards a young woman in a crew-cut.

What a strange creature this thing, this semi-human with machinery attached to its face. This twentieth-century spawn, this one-eyed monster, this close-elbowed, crouching-bending-stalking spine-curved thing. This animal with its life centred on the nerves of one finger. This optic-driven Two-Leg. I saw something that made me bring my camera up and almost without noticing I removed myself from pretending to be a person and rejoined my species.

It's one of my favourite photographs even though it's really a nothing kind of picture.

Something made her stand out from the other demonstrators and I'm not sure what it was. Maybe just the class difference. Something, an odd pentaprisming knocking one look into another, I think I noticed how she was trying to catch people's eyes. The others stood there, silent, happy to let their placards do the talking, but not this one. As the cars passed around the traffic circle she followed them with her eyes, moving the poster she was holding up, looking for a response, for contact. It was hot and every now and then she would lower her head to her blouse sleeve and wipe the sweat from around her eyes. Then she would look up and pan the poster back towards the oncoming traffic. A dark face, thick eyebrows, from somewhere in MP or Rajasthan I guessed, her sari half over her head, a big red bindi on her forehead, smudged slightly by the sweat.

I took several pictures of her at three-quarters profile, yanking forward the film in my old F3, my thumb still quite happy without the luxury of a motor-drive. A brief look passed between us after I took the first couple of pictures. I nodded slightly as I used to do, a kind of asking for permission after the fact. She looked back at me, acknowledged my presence and then forgot all about me. No self-consciousness now that she had a camera pointed at her, and no aggression or discomfort either, just an acceptance that I was doing my job and she was doing hers. An acceptance of the overlap between my work and hers.

The picture that I like came only after I jumped over the railings into the grass lawn of the circle. In that frame you can't even see her face properly, she is in silhouette, back almost fully to camera, looking left. There is a hint of an eye as she holds up her placard and you can't read what it says, but there is an energy in her shoulders. Beyond her is a DTC bus passing with a row of people poking their heads out of the windows, staring at the woman as if she is from outer space. What happens, because of the angle, is that the row of heads seems to be coming out of both sides of the woman's own head, like some strange black and white reverse-Ravan.

I normally hate pictures like these, trick jobs, cheap jokes, like a palm tree coming out of a person's hair, that kind of thing, but this one I like and the one of Viral on the beach in Goa that kind of works the same way.

Writers can afford to shoot themselves in the head if it doesn't come. With us photographers it's slightly different. I know some have offed themselves but many of us have to go into situations to get others to do it for us. As for me, god knows someone looking at me from the outside could imagine I have enough reasons to commit suicide, but every time the thought transits through my head the woman with the placard is one of the six–seven things that stops me from taking it any further.

Mr Tekkit, the Obituary in-charge, is still meandering in my ear. He has been going through various images and he mentions all the usual suspects, all the well-known ones, the Pepsi-Cola bleeding out of the bullet holes, the clock-tower poking out of the water at Tehri Dam, the women dancing ras-garba in front of the oil refinery in Kutch . . .

'Ser, can I inkwire why there are no avhelable photos of human subject after two jiro phiptin? There are only some objects photographed. There is even that one photograph of old camera with teapot . . . and quite frankly ser, people are not understanding.'

Of course people are not understanding. People who do not want to understand will not be understanding. Just as other people who do not want to understand will refuse to understand other things. The image he's talking about is from the still-life series that I began in 2017. This one he's talking about has my first camera, an Agfa Click III and not a teapot but the first stove espresso machine I ever bought, the old classic aluminium Bialetti with the ridges all around and the half-melted black plastic handle.

I suppose I made this one and the others in the series for myself and not for some idiot non-understander. Just objects that meant something to me, put next to each other bald, like a visual list. Like an identification line-up in the police station of my memory. I don't think I even remembered Morandi and his etchings when I took those photographs but he must have been there, somewhere at the back of my head, this mad Italian who spent most of his adult life drawing nothing but bottles and pitchers and other household objects . . .

Every day this Morandi would rearrange things on a table and draw them, paint them, make etchings. Each minute change of light he would catch like a tiger catching a deer, each slight shift of visual weight between cubes, cylinders, globes. These he would take and turn into something else. The thing with the guy was that he managed to pull out stories from things. Standing alone or grouped, his objects almost become like characters in a book and you start to follow them. A jug or a wine bottle or a funny-shaped candle, whatever, you feel for it, even laugh at it and look for its shadow when it disappears and miss it when you can't find it. Sometimes you see a deliberate arrangement and sometimes you see the ultimate abstraction of chance, objects thrown on the canvas like visual dice, but what happens in the best of the guy's work is a spare poetry that I have never been capable of. Or at least I thought not, till Paola Venezia contacted me about ten years ago.

That picture Borun took of me was one I always found strange. It's almost like a still-life. I mean, here is a man, a tallish man, bending forward, short-sleeved light-coloured shirt, nondescript pants which you can't really see, frame being cut off around thigh level, camera held before face but not to the eye, looking. You would expect some sense of movement from a picture like this but what you get instead is a sense of stillness. The man bent like the handle of an art deco teapot, the sun slicing his body into two, his eyes, my mother's eyes, wide, staring at something, you can't see what. Study of Looker. Looker being looked at. A feeling I always got whenever I saw this photo, that there's always someone observing you, even while you observe someone else with all of what you have, always someone there looking at you as well, always.

I hate that photograph because it's like a hunter hung on a wall like a trophy and I was never that, never a hunter, not in the classic sense. A strange woman's voice on the international line, I had expected Anna and another screaming match, but the accent was different, the voice more high-pitched. 'I llaaik a the way your objects a look at each other,' she'd said. 'There is a ka-ranzi of look that I really llaaik.' It took me a while to understand she meant 'currency of look'. Paola Venezia of the Fondazione Morandi in Bologna wanting to buy my still-lifes for the museum's collection. Paola whom I've never met and will probably never meet, even though I think of her with gratitude every time I make a cup of coffee.

The first pictures they bought were from the Dalda tin series. The faded yellow of the tin mimicked all kinds of whites and light greys on the black and white film, with the black outline of the date-palm sharp sometimes, and sometimes out of focus, but always there like a stamp on the memory. Other objects, the tin of Bustelo, a sandsi, empty glasses all nodding obeisance to this fat round tin with the tree. The Dalda would not have had the same resonance for them as it would for Indians of my age as, and here is what people don't understand about photography, it is ultimately *not* a 'universal language' like they still keep saying. As a photographer, it doesn't matter if you don't speak English or French or German – the question is, can you take photographs in American or Dutch or English or French? Because if you can't, then there is no communication. They, over there, are not interested in making the effort to find out. So, did the Dalda tin pictures speak Italian? Well, some of them obviously did.

Paola Venezia, for example, loved the one where the tin made just a fat border on one side of the frame, The tree big and soft, just showing, with the old map of Bombay torn from an atlas stuck on the wall at the centre, the legend saying 'Mumbai' in bold Gujarati curls, and a teacup sleeping upside down on a saucer right in front of it. Hardly any shadows, everything lit by a soft straight light. Bas, that's it, nothing else in the picture, but Maria wrote to me that it moved her to tears. The photo moved me to tears too, but for completely different reasons.

How do I explain to this Tekkit joker about images creating weird bridges between two people who've never met? 'The brevitational pull of art,' as Maria said on the link once. I first thought she'd said 'gravitational pull' but she corrected me. So, yes, the brevitational pull of art cutting out the world outside the frame, creating a currency of looks between two people who've never met. On some days I barely understand it myself, so how do I explain it to this idiot who's probably never seen a real painting or a proper photographic print made from a negative in his entire short and stupid life?

How do I explain that first moment of magic, when I was six, when I pressed down on the shutter lever of my Click Three, the *kad-dank* sound it made, and then the excitement of getting the photos back from Bombay Photo Stores under the Grand Hotel arcade? And from much later in life, how do I convey the idea of a darkroom and the sea shift that happens when you first watch the paper give birth to a photograph in the developer tray? That chemical smell on your fingers as you bring a picture out to dry?

I'm obviously already a stiff for this bastard Obituary Asker, a finished book, a some kind of a file to be closed. So how do I, this fucking FTBC, convey to him that there are some strange things still alive in me? For example things my father taught me about stuff that used to matter – paintings, words, music, things that gave people pleasure, that brought some fucking sense of grace to you and sometimes, for a few moments, helped you climb out of the ordinary traps of life.

The man's voice has now developed a slithering intimacy. Like he probably thinks he's made friends or something with Poresh babu's secretary.

'Mr Dey saar, can you – off the record saar, strictly off, bujhlen tˆo saar? Can you please tell me why Poresh babu is living in this way, here now in Calcutta, alone? Why he is not in Paris, as he was?'

You slimeball little fuckshit. What business is it of yours?

But I keep a calm head and answer anyway because I'd like the record to be straight. I put on a dictation voice, hoping he will write down what I say and actually use it when the time comes.

'Well, yes, you see Paresh babu came back to India for good in 2017. He came back in protest against the new European immigration policies. He was very much a resident of France, for more than fifteen years in fact, but after what are called the "Fortress Europa" regulations, after they came into force, he could not, in good conscience, continue to live in Paris despite all the honours etc. the French and others had accorded him.'

'Oh, achha, I see.'

No you don't, because that's not the only reason. But it will do for your Web-rag. Paresh Bhatt came back to 'India' because his stupid daughter came back first to become an air force head-firster. He also came back because the pain of living in Paris, as opposed to the cost of living, was too much. He came back because he was done with women – the last of the women; mind you, there were not that many, total only five serious ones in all – because the last of all the women he'd ever had anything emotional to do with left him. He came back hoping the isolation would be less and he was wrong.

There was a time when people all over the world were worried about things like AIDS and such shit, other diseases, but they missed the real business – isolation is a disease that is far more virulent than any of these. And I've got it. That woman with the placard didn't know it, she would never have suffered from it, no matter what else she suffered from, but me, it's my new and only job, fighting this thing that's stayed climbed onto me for years. And fight I will. And lose, I know, every day till the day I die.

The West worried about diseases coming from the East, the North from the South, but the real disease is what's come the other way, what *they* transmitted – Aloneness. My mother got it late in life and eventually Mahadev Bhatt too, my father, he got it too, but not like this. A door closing, a clicking down of a phone, a cheery goodnight on the road at night. These kill you quicker than encephalitis and slower than old age. Isolated frames, cut off from each other like prisoners in separate cells, each human being trapped inside the sealed aircraft of his own life, watching the others go down, one after the other, but being able to do nothing to help.

Obituary-shobituary, what bloody obituary? How can I bring a tongue to all the unsayable things in my life? Things that look at each other and drop their eyes in shame and pain and sidle away this way and that, scurry off like rats over the edges of my conscience into the not-looking, into non-acknowledgement, into the cement of amnesia.

Para's Orbitchuary has no such hesitations, but then she's djyong. Now about as old as me in Barun's photograph, thirty-eight, but she's always been harder because she gets it from both sides of her family, (a) directly from her mother, and (b), jumping a generation as these things sometimes do, from her grandmother, Suman.

Paresh Mahadevkumar Ramashankar Bhatt. Eminence Grease, she started. *Photographer of some note many years ago, who spent most of his life suspended in an aeroplane between Europe and India. Problem for people around him because he was afraid of flying.*

No wonder he crashed his marriage along with co-pilot Frau Annalise Lang. Black box showed each pilot was trying to pull plane in opposite directions. Survived by one daughter.

Nasty on Anna who hates being called Frau just as much as my mother hated my father calling her begum, but at least now Para blames me and Anna equally. Earlier it was me and only me and then it was Anna and only Anna. But it's true, what that Larkin guy said. We fuck you up, we mums and dads. We don't mean to but we do, generation after generation, like emotional lemmings leading their young into the same vicious –

'One last kwoshchon, Shibubabu, this previous work is also a bit strange.' Who the fuck is Shibubabu? My name is – I almost correct him but catch myself in time.

'Yes?' I say tersely, I've got the picture and I'm getting tired of this conversation.

'One of the previous works also, one is not –'

'Understanding,' I finish for him. 'Which works?'

'Ser, this Landing Pattern series. Of plane wings only.'

Moron. Not of plane wings only. Plane wings with landscape, city-scape, clouds, other planes, light. Starting from the idea that.

'I'm afraid I will have to ask Pareshbabu about that. I will get back to you.'

'But ser –' But nothing. Go Obit yourself. I delink, chomping his sentence off. Suddenly Tekkit is gone and there is only the sound of the rain and the shuttles and my own slow breath bulldozering out of me.

Starting from the idea that airports are the only roots that we really have, us, the upper-middle nomads. And coming into one airport or the other has a special meaning like train stations used to do in the past or ports before that. I started taking the pictures as a way to ward off fear, especially when the planes did crazy things as they started to land. A simple realisation that my fear went away once I had my face stuck to a viewfinder and so, on one flight, landing in Johannesburg, with the jumbo's wingtip fin almost vertical over a township, I managed to pull out my camera and shoot off nearly a whole roll. The pictures weren't supposed to work but a couple were nice, more than nice, and so there it was, the Landing Pattern series. Every flight I took since then I shot photos of the landing, black and white usually. Why not take-offs as well? Why, because those were too scary to even contemplate opening my eyes during.

Once I developed the fear, I couldn't open my eyes till the pilot levelled off, till I could hear the air hostesses start to fiddle with the catering bins, not that I didn't know that a lot of flights had gone down well after reaching cruising height. Not that the airport that is your destination can't suddenly disappear in the time of your flight. There, waiting for you on the other side of the world when you take off, and gone by the time you are a few hundred miles from it. That happened to me one time I flew.

You see, people don't understand. They think I'm scared of flying because I've always been scared of flying. Where they're wrong is, first, now I'm not scared of flying – I'm scared of landing. Two, I was not always scared of flying, for many years I even enjoyed it. For instance, I remember landing one morning in Bombay, Mumbai by then, and every movement of the plane feeling like a happy slow dance with the rising sun. I didn't reach for the camera that time, probably because I had just one picture in front of my eyes, Sandy Madam grinning as she saw me coming out of customs.

I push the stop button on that and go to the system and put on another raag. Vidur Mallick this time. Dhrupad again, but vocal. Raag Bhairav as opposed to Bhairavi, Bairagi Bhairav to be precise, same family but different. I need a voice in my ear, need something to do with mornings, something sunlight to push away the rain.

Ride

'The first time? The first time what? Like, just a little lick, like, or –'

'The full thing yaar, swallow and all.'

'Ah, that.'

'Unh-huh, Mr Bhatt – ah that. Tell me.'

Viral smiles his haraami smile. He still has his haraami smile from school, the same one that he'd have after he'd sold me down the river and come back a couple of days later to try and slime back into my life. The same one that said, 'Come on ya, let's just . . . forget about it,' same one on his stupid Patel face that he would keep just out of punch range, ready to run if I wasn't mollified.

'Viral-bastard' I think as I look at the tide coming in behind him. 'Viral-fever' we used to call him, even though it's 'Veerull' and not 'Vairal'. Maybe it's the face, maybe it's the Feni, maybe it's just all these years that we haven't met, maybe it's just my insides responding to the white ropes of froth snaking out of the dark and onto the beach towards us, little white ropes that open out around Viral's neck, ropes that I watch carefully, waiting to see if one turns into a noose, but I suddenly feel some huge return wave of – of what? – affection, I guess, or some that kind of warm feeling for this asshole. I mean, who would have imagined it? Which bloody Sidney Sheldon/Jackie Collins/Shobha De type would ever dare come up with this one: two childhood friends go their own separate ways in life, they lose touch in their late twenties, do the classic gm-hk-gd, (oh sorry, Get Married, Have Kids, Get Divorced), and then bloody both of them, one from America and one from England, both decide to come across the world to the same place at the same time to lick their wounds. Actually, sach puchho tˆo, to get brainlessly laid – which neither manages – but they bump into each other instead.

We've spent two days together but I am still reeling from this Instead. Viral, being Viral, is unfazed. He looks around for the barman, finds him close-dancing a case of beer out from the insides of the beach-hut, waves at him like an emperor to a slave and turns back to me –

'So tell me, Bhatt.'

Single-minded as ever, eye on the main chance, never-let-go, that's Viral.

The first time. It was in a movie theatre somewhere on Lafayette, in post-Christmas DC, around the time of the Iran hostage crisis, which would make it late '79, early 1980. Pretty classic when you think of it really, what was interesting was what happened afterwards, but first –

• • •

They are the only ones sitting in the last row of a half-empty cinema. Cigarette smoke rises to intercept the beam from the projector window just above their heads. Paresh wonders briefly what Bethan is searching for on the floor. He likes this girl but doesn't know how to tell her, maybe he will, after the movie.

The Dolby throbs and the Wagner lifts up the helicopters and flings them low over the sea, trumpeting them into attack formation. The screen holds him and he pays no attention when he feels Bethan leaning over to reach for the popcorn tub on his lap. The sun rises, the rays stretching wide in 70 mm, the helicopters silhouetted, flying black scorpions scurrying across a tropical dawn, and he doesn't even notice his green corduroy jeans being unzipped.

The first thing he feels is Bethan's hair brushing against his hand and he looks down at the exact moment she takes him into her mouth. A question begun already – 'Has she dropped something?' – pauses in his mind as he hardens, very quickly, rising without the help of rotor blades. He feels Bethan's tongue talking to him, reading out the braille of his veins, resonating up through everything, saying things he has never heard before – crystal clear – all the way from down there. With a shock he realises that she has knelt down on the floor in front of her seat and given herself space – he realises she is quite tall. She has taken off her anorak and he can see her raised spine moving in the smudged light, snaking up and down through the faded blue t-shirt she's wearing. His eyes move up her back, up to the working of her shoulder blades, to the dolphining of her neck, to his fingers, which have found their way into her hair, and there he is stopped, forced to slap his eyes back onto the screen.

A man in a cowboy hat leans out of the open door of a chopper and yells, 'Yeeh-hah!' Paresh is suddenly scared of falling, and though he is desperate to see what is happening to him, he doesn't dare look down again.

The helicopters cross the coast and reach a Vietnamese village, their predatory shadows leap-frogging over thatched roofs. Women holding babies run screaming, straw hats falling from their heads. Houses explode in some unholy celebration. Machine-guns stitch new lines up from the mud and into the running bodies. Blood popcorns out as the bullets hit. Paresh can feel Bethan's breath quickening, her nostrils playing a tattoo around the base of his cock. He remembers her saying she's seen the movie once already. Soldiers spill out of amphibious attack boats onto a beach. Suddenly Paresh can smell the theatre, smell Bethan's shampoo, smell himself for a split second before he topples over the edge.

Bethan's mouth is still rocking on him, not stopped yet, when Robert Duvall says, 'Day-yamn! I just love the smell of Napalm in the morning!'

• • •

Viral has his fingers steepled like a professor listening to a student's paper. His eyes are closed and his fat lips are pursed together, tight as a Patel's wallet, allowing themselves to be the ball in a small game of catch-catch between his two plump cheeks.

He nods when I finish, his eyes still closed. Then he opens them and looks at me, then down to locate his drink, search and destroy, then back up at me again.

'So, the babe bombed you, huh? You think the metaphor would be the other way around but it's actually always them bombing you, no?'

'Simile,' I say.

'What?'

'Bombing in this case is a simile, not a metaphor.'

'Well, it could be both,' he shoves a Camel Light between his teeth and flips open a silver Ronson under it, 'bud eider uay, dey do de bomming.'

He tilts his head back and spews up a spray of smoke into the clear Goa night like a sperm whale in cardiopulmonary distress.

'And you?' I ask, it being my serve.

'Mhmee?' grunts Viral Patel through his Camel, pretending he's just walked into somebody else's play.

'Yah, you, you fucker.'

There is a flicker in his eyes as the memory hits and then Viral starts laughing. His long-suffering cigarette bobs up and down, trying to keep its hold between his lips. He finally takes pity on it and slam-dunks it into the ashtray as he disappears down under the table. I'm suddenly worried about his heart condition. I can hear him emitting these sounds. Emperor whale under water, having good time despite breathing difficulties. The barman looks over towards us and sees we're okay, more than okay, and he goes back to his serial on Zee.

• • •

It was damn funny ya. Unlike yours it wasn't . . . urrr . . . imported, it was . . . what do these BJP buggers call it? . . . yeah, it was fuckin' swadeshi . . . home-made . . . indigenous technology.

I didn't tell you then, but you know after I broke up with Priya?

Remember Sherman apartments and Zeenie? Well, the hell with Zeenie aunty, but do you remember me telling you about Sandhya? Sandy Agarkar the deadly Ghaatan? Remember I told you she really liked you but you were useless because you went back to Cal so, like, she and me did it? Well, what I didn't tell you was that she also went down on me the night before I left for Penn State.

Unh-huh.

Arre don't get like that ya Paresh, it was just a blow-job, okay?

Like what ya?

I know I got what should have been yours, but wait, listen to this and you won't feel so bad.

I don't feel bad yaar, Patel, this was almost twenty years ago, right?

Right, but I can also see your face now, bugger. Anyway, so we did everything, and we went all the way and all that . . . BUT. She wouldn't give me head. I'd ask, she'd come close, but no cigar. You know, just at the last moment, HORNY Ghaatan as only Ghaatans can be, but no mouth, she'd pull out.

So? How did you do it?

Patience, man. So, like, I thought. Now you have to understand that Sandy was a sporting type and she believed in honour on the field. And also, if she bet you something and she lost, she would deliver, come hell or high water. Honourable that way too. Once we bet on a Davis Cup match and she lost and the bet was she would get me the keys to Hiranandani's Porsche for a night. And she did. She made her maid servant sleep with Hiranandani's darwaan and one weekend, when Hiru was in Singapore, yeah?, she got the fucking keys one night, middle of my exams, but a deal is a deal, yeah?, so we wailed on that sucker 911 all over town before parking it back. So that way she was solid.

So I made a plan. Anyway she was getting a bit senti about my leaving, otherwise she'd never have bet head, but I sort of worked her into it.

How many days' work went into this?

Well if you put a proper time-motion analysis on it . . . I guess . . . well, you would have to say from beginning to end about twenty working days, total.

Ei, Viral? When was the last time you spent twenty whole days on a project?

Last year, setting up the finance for a machine-tools plant in Canton, but do you want to hear this story or not? So then, maybe shut up? This is what I did. Willingdon squash ladder, okay? This guy Abhay Mathur, who for three years had been killing everyone that came near him – inside Willingdon Club or out – later he once stretched Jehangir Khan, really, nearly beat him in a tournament in Leeds, he was that good. So this Mathur was at the top of the ladder. And there was this mad chap, mad Assamese bugger called Bora, Bidyut Bora, we used to call him Bidiot Bore-a, who thought he was better than Mathur even though Mathur had, like, pulverised him three times. I mean Bora was on 4 or something on the ladder but after Mathur he was probably the best in the club. He had this kind of mad energy, yeah?, like he would as soon kill you as smash an unreturnable cross-court backhand. And he could nick that ball from absolutely anywhere, which Mathur could also.

Now Bidiot was in good form that time and seething to take on Mathur yet again. And Mathur being this quiet imperious type, would play it by the book. You had to be within two numbers to challenge, like if you were 5 you could challenge 4 or 3, but not 2?, unless 2 sportingly agreed to give you a match. And Mathur, though he wasn't chicken, was in no hurry to give Bora his chance, so like every time Bora would ask, he would refuse politely. So, fingers crossed, I waited for Bora to take out Shambhu, who was on 3, which Bora obligingly did.

First thing I did was to take the jubilating dumbfuck aside and convince him that he should wait before challenging Mathur. Make him nervous, I said, let him wait, like, like I'll tell you when to challenge Mathur? At first Bore-a kept asking, 'But vhy yaa Vidal? I can beat him now,' but finally he scratched his head and said, 'Okay yaa Vidal, I'll do dat.' Dumbfuck, brand manager in ITC now, bloody fags sell themselves and he takes the credit, fucking complete moron.

So soon after that, one day when Sandy and I were knocking about on the courts, I casually said I thought Bora was getting better than Mathur. Sandy screamed with laughter. I stayed serious and then pretended to get angry. Then I blurted out the bet, not like I had planned it but like I had just thought of it? In my fury? You know, like – Fine baby, why don't you put your money where your mouth is – what I should have said was mouth where your mouth is – if Bora beats Mathur what will you give me? Oh, anything you want Viri, anything at all. Anything ya? Ya. Okay, so fine, you will suck my cock till I come, is that okay with you? That'll be the day asshole, but yeah. Sure. Okay. Bet. And boy she was deep in it.

You bastard.

Yup, that's me . . . uh . . . let me correct that Paresh – point of order – I'm a byaastrurrd, not a bawstud? But anyway, so next I started working on Mr Abhay tight-ass Mathur. Playing with him everyday, giving him psych-advice, telling him how great he was but not overdoing it, you know?, just halka. Then, one day I just let drop that he should make his point with this idiot Bidiot. It was getting annoying, some fucking chink-eyed semi-tribal thinking he could beat Abhay Mathur and going about saying it to all the chicks. 'I'll kill him ya,' says Mathur. 'What's the big deal in that, Abhay? You've done it thrice already. So this time you whip him 9–0, 9–0, 9–0 and you know what? He'll come back next week and challenge you again – bloody dhiint that he is.' 'So what should I do?' 'Make your point,' I say. 'How?' says tight-ass. I scratch my head, I pretend to think about it, I make a few sounds like I'm rejecting stupid ideas – nothing but the best for my dost Abhay – and then I come up with it.

'Why don't you . . . no . . . no . . . too risky . . .' 'What? What? What's too risky?' 'Nahi yaar, you can't take the chance.' 'What? Tell me! Tell me!' So I tell him. 'What if you say to Bora, look Bora I'm getting a bit bored with all your big talk, I'll play you left-handed, and if

I beat you, you will shut up and never challenge me again? Gentleman's Word?' Both these clowns were big into Gentleman's Word you see, Bora because his haw-haw dad owned some tea estates and Mathur 'cause his dad was some corrupt ex-ICS-IAS on the boards of some fading Brit companies.

So what did Mathur say?

Oh, Mathur loved it. 'Now *that*, you clever Gujju bastard – bashtudd – is a brilliant idea.' Then I tried to dissuade him, not too hard, halka, like. And the more I tried, the more convinced he became that thrashing Bora left-handed was the thing to do.

And did he? No, obviously not.

Well. He came close, the son-of-a-bitch. Best of five, he lost the first two games, worked it out and won back the third, all left-handed, almost won the fourth but finally Bora just overpowered him, blood-rushed him on deuce, for the crucial two points. I mean, watching that match, I sweated more than the two of them put together.

Then what happened?

Oh. Bora like, gave up squash after that? He was now on top of the ladder and there was nothing in the gentleman's agreement to stop Mathur challenging him back – right-handed this time – and so Bora resigned from the ladder and took a trip back to Dibrugarh. Business Called.

Viral. Fuck the squash. Sandy, what happened with Sandy?

• • •

The lines are an odd bright green against the dawn sky. Flat green against the warm rounded red, yellow and gold of the cirrus catching the first light of a sun still rising behind them. There is a faint smell of the plastic warming up in the cockpit, but she can't smell it because of the sealed oxygen environment in her helmet. Top right of the green head-up display, a red light flashing. Squadron Leader's screen. Top right is cluster for planes under command. Each green dot = one plane + pilot. Green turns yellow = aircraft hit, pilot ejected. Red dot = one Angel gone.

Same time, Blue Flight Leader's voice, Raksha's voice, minus flight leader's training, screaming digitally in her ear.

'Para, what happened to Cindy? What happened to Cindy? Para, Cindy's gone. This is Blue2 Leader. Blue2 Leader to SQ1. Sugar Queen One, do you read me?' Radio silence compromised. Attack sequence falling apart. Stealth profile gone. The rising sun a big red dot just behind small red dot signalling deletion of plane No. 6 from Blue Flight, dot signifying death of Flight Lieutenant Sindhu Mundkur.

Para Bhatt's brain works at speed. No rocket trace, no enemy aircraft on radar, but one of her planes has just dropped out of the sky. No signal from Sindhu, no time to register, death must have been instantaneous.

Her hands and feet have been moving by themselves, running on a parallel track, choreographed by her other brain. Her Ishir fighter is already flicking down and sideways, turning over, a pencil suddenly rolling off the edge of a desk, the desk being her altitude, now fraught with danger.

'SQ1 to Chandalika, SQ1 to Chandalika,' Para finds her voice speaking, a bit high but calm, finding the right code for an emergency message to the whole squadron, 'move to sequence 3 Charlie 3, repeat 3 Charlie 3. That was a sonar swat, possibly random, keep away from 1–5-K feet, repeat 1–5-K feet, sing your engines, keep calm, keep going.'

By the time she has finished speaking Para Bhatt's fighter is already clawing its way back up, now a vertical pencil climbing back towards the edge of the desk. Just under fifteen thousand feet Para slows her engines to almost stopping and lets herself drop out of the sky for about eight seconds.

Vertical pencil dropping. As she goes down Para Bhatt turns into three people. All three of her spines come into play. There is one connected to the eyes that watch the sky and the cascade of numbers and lights flickering on her screen, there is the second, which works the controls, pushes buttons, all centred around her left thumb, which lightly touches the switch that will kick her booster rockets back to life. And there is the third animal, the prescient one that watches these two almost from the outside, looking for a sign, for something. As she drops, Para Bhatt watches her head. She has only heard about the new sonar defences but her instincts tell her she has just come up against them.

A sonar swat was basically a carpet of deadly sound that a pair of modified AWACS aircraft flying at the same height put out for two hundred feet above and below whatever altitude they were at. The overlapping electromagnetic beams created a pincer of sound that was designed to entangle with any other sound that came in its way and create a knot of energy that no human head could tolerate. Cockpit, helmet, fireproof cap, nothing got in the way of this sound imploding the human head. The only problem with the sonar carpet was that it had to have some time to take effect, about thirty seconds, and the sound profile had to stay the same for those thirty seconds, as did the altitude of the target.

As Para falls, she feels a slight buzz around her helmet. Very slight but scary. It's something from outside her training, outside her universe. Like a bantamweight boxer punching you very fast, but very lightly, in the head. All she knows is that some pilots are more susceptible to electromagnetic buzz-fields than others, and she wonders if she will be able to take it. The punching suddenly gets harder, for about ten seconds, and then it's gone, at twelve thousand feet it's gone. AWACS nightwatchmen sleeping with their sticks out, hoping someone would trip over them. And one of her girls had. And that was it. Para hits the D-code for Plane No. 6 and tries to puts Sindhu out of her mind.

She hits her boosters at eight thousand feet, levels out, and begins to correct her mistake. Her mistake is that she has sent her squadron into a series of yo-yo manoeuvres across the Pakistani airspace. Instead of holding formation her fighter-bombers are ricocheting off an imagined ceiling, scattering like drunk birds, drawing attention from electronic eyes.

'SQ1 to Chandal –' she bites her tongue, wrong emergency code, never the same name twice, 'SQ1 to Siddheshwari, SQ1 to Siddheshwari, sequence change, repeat sequence change, Blue Flight go 2 Delta 2. Go now. Red Flight go Delta Delta 1, go now, Green Flight stay with me, go 1 Xerox 4 Zebra, go now. Siddheshwari back to radio silence.' Closing the stable door after horse had bolted – maybe. The funny code names were Cindy's idea, she always picked them in the pre-ops briefing, Cindy the intellectual, the one with the memory, the only one who sang the old songs, knew them. Cindy who was now gone, zapped.

• • •

Ah that. Well, that chick was zapped. Couldn't believe it. When I told her she just got into her Fiat and drove from Nepean Sea to Haji Ali at ten thirty at night to see the ladder for herself. Came back with tears in her eyes. Mouth tightly shut, wouldn't let me even kiss her that night.

We kept fucking and all, but finally, she gave like . . . when? This was almost a month before I left but there was no agreement on the delivery schedule, so she kept pushing it back, kept pushing it back, till my last night. That morning when her parents are out, she takes me into her room and we do it there for the first time, screw, that is. Damn strange. Till now it was always in some friend's flat or at my place or even in the Fiat, but this time we are in her room? You know those 'Love is . . .' posters? Well they looked damn funny when you are on your back and Sandy is rollercoasting on you, 'Love is . . . giving her the coffee mug the right way 'round,' yeah right, she also had one Neil Diamond poster and this litt-tul picture of Vinod Khanna on her bedside table, right next to some heavy American novel she was pretending to read, what was it? Oh yeah, Portnoy's something? Philip Roth? . . . And this was the eighth floor and Ai and Daddy were out but could come back anytime and the maid, same Porsche-wali maid, was guarding the fort, making a lot of noise cleaning up outside, and the sea was making a lot of noise and Sandy, Sandy always made a lot of noise?, and my Jethro Tull tape –

My Jethro Tull tape, thank you.

Yeah, oh yeah, your tape, what was it?

Minstrel in the Gallery, which I left for her.

Yeah well, that tape was dragging, but it was great. At the end of it she says like a goodbye, you know? 'I'll miss you Viri but . . . just go and have fun!' You know, that sort of thing? I start to point out that something's owing. She says, 'Don't worry baby, I'll see you before you go . . .' and gets me out of the house just as Mrs Agarkar comes up the lift. 'Hello beta, all packed?' 'Yes aunty, almost done.' 'We will miss you dear, don't forget to leave a little part of you behind for all of us.' 'Yes aunty, I will try.' 'Especially for your mother.' 'Yes aunty.'

So that night, right?

Right, so that night she comes over. The flat's in chaos, packing, checking tickets, passport, visa, shoes, trying on warm clothes on a hot monsoon night, my mom's organised like this huge meal, puris, undhyu, khandvis, patras, shrikhand, you name it. Mom-Dad's friends all there, half the Union Carbide Bombay top brass, all the fucking relatives, friends, people from the building – it's a riot – Viral beta is going to America, right? Jesus God. In the middle of this Sandy walks in, wearing a sari.

Sari? Sandy?

Yeah man, Sandy. In a sari. Pure traditional Ghaati, green and gold silk, probably her mother's, looking total pride of Maharashtra. No tight jeans, no bloody skimpy halter-top, no little t-shirt, no tennis shorts, bloody sari and long-sleeved matching gold-ish blouse. No ponytail, hair open, bindi even. Green eyes wide and innocent, come to see off friend. All the relatives cream, sort of 'Vahu, vahu' in their eyes? I've like forgotten about the bet, I'm trying to get ready for a continent to come and sit on me. But not Sandhya. A bet is a bet. So she waits for her chance and it comes during the aarti. Parents do this like big puja with a long, long aarti. Sandy knows because she's been to a couple before. And everyone knows I can't stand the smell of incense and even though the puja is for the departing scion of Patel family I ain't going anywhere near that stuff till it's over.

So like the puja starts in the drawing room? And Sandy and me are in the kitchen – my mom's kitchen. Food all laid out for, like, a buffet, 'cause there are too many people. Sandy goes around picking up different bits of food and tasting them. My mother hated this.

Mine too. Einthoo.

Yeah, makes it einthoo, you know how it is, so I get nervous, and like tell her to, like, stop? Sandy stops and looks at me. Then she takes a spoon and scoops off a good chunk of the lime and chilli pickle. She puts it in her mouth and then she comes and gets down on her knees in front of me.

No.

Yes. Now, Bhatt, no one's ever, you know?, like done this to me before? . . . So, so . . .

No, Viral, oh no.

Oh yes. Aarti going on full force, just a door between us and the crowd, and Sandy pulls it out and takes it . . . like into her mouth? I get hard – man, I am hard already, I don't feel anything at first, and she is quick, business-like, job to be done – do it. And cool, Jesus she was cool. Like, like once a strand of her hair gets in the way? So she stops, peels the hair off my dick and just carries on . . . phooph . . . and by now my knees have gone but I'm still standing up somehow. I'm, like, holding on to her shoulders, her gold blouse? And then I come and Sandy does this quick little thing with her lips and takes it all in. And then my mom's voice like right next to the kitchen door, 'Viru-beta! Kyaan chhu beta, aihya-aaaw!' and this girl is up and away. And me, I just shove my dick back into my pants, zip, and turn to grab the door.

Luckily my mom goes away, looking for me in my room. And Sandy's cheeks are all puffed up?, like when you're gargling? So . . . she begins to circle around the kitchen and I don't get it. She stops near the table and takes a quick look at the door, and then she bends over the Shrikand bowl and lets go . . . I say Sandy . . . what the hell –

I'm like gagging, the words don't come out almost, and Sandy coolly says, 'The deal was come in my mouth, no one said anything about swallowing,' and then you know what she does, the bitch? She then takes a serving spoon and *mixes* it all in. She was always good in the kitchen, Sandy, and Ghaatis you know they also have Shrikand, so by the time she's finished the fucking bowl is nicely decorated again, exactly like it was, you know, like fat white sworls, and the white mixing in the white and the goddam bits of pickle mixing with the little bits of pista and badaam on top . . .

• • •

My father had three brothers and four sisters. Of the four sisters Vasundhara, the one just after him, my Vasufoi, was the most beautiful. When Vasufoi was fourteen she was taken to be photographed. This was standard practice in the Bhatt family – all the daughters had their portrait taken just before they got married. 'Beta, we will lose you, but this daughter will always stay with us,' my grandmother used to say when the framed picture arrived from the photographer.

'Those photos would hang there like photos of dead people,' my father told me one time when we were in the darkroom. 'I mean, we knew that Tara was around the corner in Jethabhai Poel, Chandra and Vasu were half a mile away near Dilli Darwaja, much later Mrudula went to Mumbai . . . and they would all come home quite often, but the girls in those photographs were dead.'

'Why isn't there a photo of Vasufoi?' I asked once, when I was ten, and received no reply. Then I saw the glint of his teeth in the light of the enlarger and realised that my normally stern-faced father was grinning.

• • •

The photographer's studio was in Chakli-naka. That day they made Vasu up as if for her wedding, which was still two weeks away. Mahadev was interested in photography and went along with Vasu and Vrajendra-mama to the studio. The photographer, a portly man with a thin moustache and thick glasses, was called Hirabhai Dave. His speciality was making ordinary Amdavad girls look prettier than they actually were.

When they reached the studio, Hirabhai ignored Vasu completely.

He first greeted Vrajendramama effusively as you would an old and valued customer, then next he greeted Mahadev and for a brief moment Mahadev felt like a man. 'Yes yes, photography, interest in photography, very good, it's a very new thing but soon it will rule the world. Good boy. You can watch.'

This was 1932 and photography was already more than a hundred years old but Mahadev was fascinated.

The studio consisted of a front room on the ground floor of an old haveli, the place where business was done. Up a short flight of stairs, two back rooms, one where the photographs were actually taken and then an adjacent little, black, cupboard-like space where they were developed and printed. The framing was done by Khalid Mian at Dilli Darwaja but Khalid Mian didn't exist in Hirabhai's explanations to his clients because most of them would have been horrified at the thought of their daughters being touched, even in a photograph, by a Muslim man, old and skilled though he was.

Hirabhai's front room: a desk, a chair, a new fan suspended from the ceiling, moving slowly, circling in wonder as if it had just discovered electricity, as if it was not sure yet of this mysterious thing that set it spinning. The room was lit by a fifty-watt Sylvania bulb poking out of a flower-shaped shade made of smoked white glass. The shade held to the wall by a holder attached to a curving pipe of brass, perky, and, unlike the fan, brightly confident in the knowledge that 'electric' existed and would power it forever.

Under the fan and light was a row of bhagwans and bhagwanesses: Vishnu, Shiv, Brahma, Parvati, Amba, Saraswati, Lakshmi, Ganesh and, punctuating all these, various images, big and small, of Krishna. None of them photographs, all lithographs because they were in colour. Under the gods the photographs, black and white, sample brides, sample bridegrooms, sample patriarchs sitting, surrounded by well-organised peaks of families, flanked by wives standing next to chairs, sons and daughters sitting at feet, older ones standing next to wives. All lit brightly, but also lit by the light of an uneasy self-regard. Flies landing, for some reason, on the photographs, never on the lithographs, glued to the photographs but never on the patriarchs.

Finally, Hirabhai turned to Vasundhara, pushed his spectacles back and looked her up and down. When Hirabhai's head tilted up Mahadev could see two fans turning, one in each eye. When Hirabhai looked down you could see another kind of glint behind the chashmas. Hirabhai held Vasu lightly by the chin and moved her head around as if he was shifting the gears of a small and delicate car. Mahadev began to dislike this man. Hirabhai had a thin and scabrous voice and, though he would never live to hear it, there would be an exact replication of that sound decades later. His voice sounded like the Nambudiripad-6CX colour fax/printer/scanner when its power supply was fluctuating.

'Aah. Dikri, it's your marriage is it?'

Mahadev felt like saying, 'No, looking at you, one would think it is yours,' but he kept quiet. Vasu looked down, also saying nothing. The ghumta of the sari hid her face but from the pull of her shoulders Mahadev could see his sister was furious.

'She is a bit thin,' said Hirabhai, turning to Vrajendramama with his diagnosis. 'But I have ways to remedy that, don't worry.' Vasu kept looking at the ground.

Hirabhai led them up the narrow wooden stairs that led to the studio. An assistant was dusting a big painted curtain that stretched across the back wall. It was what Hirabhai called the Mahal Curtain – the painting was of a series of grand arches stretching away in perspective with the light coming in from the left, an odd mix between a Mughal mahal and a Baroque palace.

'Not the Mahal,' said Hirabhai curtly, printer jamming, 'she will drown in that. Pull out the Mona Lisa Akash.'

The assistant stopped his dusting and brought out a little stool from somewhere. He got up on it and with the flourish of a magician yanked away the Mahal. The decorated pillars crumpled sideways as if a soft earthquake had hit. The arches became wavy, revealing briefly the lines of paint of which they were made, and then disappeared.

'Ah,' said Hirabhai.

'Oh,' said Vrajendramama, 'this is new.'

'Yes, only the second time I am using it. I have just ordered it from Poona. It will be a novelty.'

The palace had left behind a voluptuous sky, dawn or evening light, clouds impossibly rounded, gold, pink, yellow, red, with a small, dark brown landscape – some odd relation to a scene near some river in Italy – taking up the bottom third of the painting.

Hirabhai led Vasu to a high stool-like chair in front of the backdrop and sat her down, his hands staying on her shoulders a fraction longer than necessary. Vasu gave an involuntary shiver.

'She must look like she has had fresh air,' Hirabhai rasped as he took the covering off his camera.

The camera was a Thornton Packard, with an 80 mm Zeiss lens. Mahadev's growing dislike for Hirabhai mingled oddly with an emotion that he had never felt before. Looking at the view camera, Mahadev found himself caught between desire for the object and revulsion for its owner.

The box of the camera was crafted from some dark brown wood. The corners were precise. The sides had a straightness that only vilayati things seemed to achieve. The wood had a muted sheen that contrasted beautifully with the gleaming silver of the lens body. The lens itself pulled Mahadev's eyes in, pulled them through the sparkle of the front element into a dark and deeply pleasurable cave. It was a cave from which Mahadev would take many years to emerge.

As if to spite Mahadev's gaze, Hirabhai quickly put a burkha of black cloth over the camera body and then flipped half of the cloth over his own head, joining the hated and the loved under one covering. This caused Mahadev almost physical pain. The half human, half wood, steel and glass thing looked like a mismatch from an English picture puzzle book. Vrajendramama smiled at his niece and nephew, proudly, as if he had just husbanded this strange creature into existence. After a while the creature made a muffled scratching sound.

'Light,' is what Hirabhai had said and the assistant pulled down two huge switches one after the other. Her new bangles jangling, Vasu instinctively put her arm over her eyes because the lights were so bright they hurt. After a pause Hirabhai made the same sound again and the assistant put the lights off. Mahadev and Vasu looked at each other and suddenly found themselves trying to suppress a common, insurgent grin.

Hirabhai emerged from under the cloth and shook his head as if to clear it, then he turned back to his camera and looked it over carefully, almost like a mother checking her child for mosquito bites. He flicked away an imaginary speck of dust from the aperture ring and turned to the assistant, who handed him a sealed plate. Hirabhai took the beige squarish package and immediately brought it to his mouth, his forehead puckering into a frown which pushed down behind his glasses to screw shut his eyes. Getting his teeth into the right position, Hirabhai began to gnaw at the package.

Later, when he began drowning himself in photography books, Mahadev would come across the travel journal of a sales representative of the Forbes Photographic Co. of Manchester:

> Apropos our new half-size plates, we have been instructed to take the greatest care against revealing, even inadvertently, the substance from which the package seal is made.
>
> Photographers in this country have the habit of using their teeth, scissors probably being beyond the grasp of most, to tear open the seal before placing the plate in the camera. While it may not be a problem for a Mohammedan photographer, knowledge of the fact that we find gelatine derived from beef to be the most effective sealant for our plates may cause more than a mild disturbance amongst photographers who are of the Hindoo conviction.
>
> My superior, Mr Downey, was at some pain to remind those of us being sent to India that the mutiny of 1857 had erupted from just such a 'provocation' – the rumour that cartridges supplied to

> the sepoys, cartridges which they were supposed to rip open with their teeth, had been sealed with extracts of beef and pork, each respectively anathema to the Hindoo and the Muslim.
>
> While the thought of rebellious photographers did not keep me from sleeping soundly on the ship (photographers the world over being generally less martially inclined than soldiers), I do confess to a slight trepidation on my first sales visit, which was to the Daruwalla Portrait Studio near the Taj Mahal Hotel in the Kolaba area of Bombay.
>
> This trepidation proved unfounded when Mr Daruwalla invited me to share a meal that had freshly arrived from his wife's kitchen. When I politely enquired what we would be eating, the man cheerfully informed me that we were about to be served the best beef stew in the city! For Mr D., as it turned out, was neither a Hindoo nor a Mohammedan but a Parsee . . .

Thinking back on all the gods and goddesses in Hirabhai's front room, Mahadev would feel a gleeful satisfaction because he remembered clearly that the beige packet that Hirabhai dismembered had the legend *Forbes Photographic Co.* printed on it in big bold black letters.

The assistant took the empty packet away while Hirabhai slipped the plate and covering into the camera with the skill of a pickpocket.

Hirabhai turned from the camera and said yet another isolated word: 'Mamra.'

The assistant scurried down the stairs and disappeared. Hirabhai went into a huddle with Vrajendramama and Mahadev could not hear what was being said. Vasu stared into nothing, her imminent capture on film now putting an invisible barrier between her and Mahadev. Mahadev moved closer to the magical camera.

There were words engraved around the ring that went around the lens, magical foreign words, black and neat against the shining steel: *Carl Zeiss, Jena* and then 80 mm, f4.5. On the body of the lens itself were two rings with other numbers, equally neat, equally mysterious, the two rings looking as if they had paused, caught by an outsider in the middle of an arcane, secret, dance. Mahadev's hand moved involuntarily towards the rings.

'Eeaank!' shrieked Hirabhai. 'DON'T touch!'

Mahadev snatched his hand back and moved away.

The assistant thumped up the stairs and came in holding a paper packet. Hirabhai took it and went to Vasu.

'Now beta, listen carefully. These are not to eat, do you understand? Put them in your mouth and keep them there, do you understand? After I finish, you can eat them. Now open your mouth.' Vasu looked at Hirabhai as if he had gone mad, but then she opened her mouth. Hirabhai took the packet and began pouring the puffed rice into Vasu's mouth.

Vasu took in as much as she could and then shook her head but Hirabhai continued.

'A little more dikri, just a little more, those cheeks need to be filled out so you look healthy.'

Vasu's eyes opened wide with the effort not to choke but Hirabhai showed no sign of sympathy. After an impossible amount had gone in, he stopped.

'Now close your mouth,' he said and watched as Vasu complied. He stared at her for a long time, took her by the chin and turned her head a tiny bit. 'Stay exactly like this,' he said, and skipped back to his camera.

The assistant switched on the lights and Vasu shut her eyes.

'Open your eyes, open your eyes,' said Hirabhai.

'Beta, eyes open,' parroted Vrajendramama.

'Okay dikri, now look at the camera as if you are looking at your husband. With love and devotion,' instructed Hirabhai, now standing next to the camera, his body tense as if he was about to pull the trigger of a starting gun for a race.

'Love, beta, devotion,' said Vrajendramama.

'One,' said Hirabhai. 'Two.'

Vasu glanced over at Mahadev, who had his hand clapped on his mouth. Mahadev met Vasu's eyes at the exact moment Hirabhai said, 'THREE!' and yanked the sliding cover off the plate.

• • •

I see the picture the moment the barman switches on a light behind the bar. Then he helps me a bit more by switching on a sign advertising the place. 'Braganza's Beach Hut' it says in red letters, and underneath it, in smaller writing, 'Authentik Goan Seafood'. The dim wash of light on Viral's face increases by about half a stop but it is all I need, because in my F3 I have the new Kodak 3200 ASA that I'm testing. I pick up the camera and look through the viewfinder. Viral has now begun ordering beer chasers to the feni and he knocks back a little glass and then reaches his nose into the beer mug. I wait till he is in mid-swig before asking him a question I already know the answer to.

'So Viral, did you eat the shrikhand?'

A photographer can only do so much to make a great picture. The rest is up to the universe. What I wanted was Viral spewing beer with an unspecified beach behind him. When I finally printed what I got, it was one of the most amazing images of my life. What I got was Viral bending forward, eyes wide and looking at me over the rim of the mug, Patel pupils catching the glint of the lights behind me, the spew from his mouth somehow forming two blurs that bracket his face while leaving the features clear and – and here is where the universe, or god-cheez, comes in – behind him, at the exact moment the shutter opened, a wave hitting a rock on the beach and forming a halo of spray. The spray is slightly darker than the beer, but on the black and white film it's a grey that belongs to the same joint-family of white. In the photograph it looks as if Viral Patel has swallowed the sea and is spewing it out.

Viral shakes his head and flecks of beer fly out of his hair. He chokes and coughs as the laughter fights to find its way back out of his gullet.

'Fuh – fuhk – ffuck no. Fuck no man. Fuck no – you know I don't eat shrikhand.'

I know. I know Viral hasn't touched shrikhand since my seventh birthday party when he was six and a half.

'Noh . . . no . . . but Sandy had to eat it.'

'Hunh? Kem?'

'Kem? Kem, because Mamma Patel offered it to her first. She says, my mom, says to Sandy – Beta, Viral doesn't eat shrikhand so you have to eat it for him. Sandy says no aunty, please, I am not feeling well. Mom says – what, notfeelingwell-notfeelingwell, we are all upset Viru is leaving but still you have to have shrikhand. In our house either the son has it, or a kanyaa has to have it. Sandy says please, no aunty please. Mom says – it will make you feel well, it is shrikhand after all, and none of us will have it until you have it. It's like Sandy's already the daughter-in-law, right? Ghar ni Vahu, right? Mamma Patel vs. young kanyaa Agarkar – it's a no contest and Sandy knows it's like, checkmate. So my mom takes the spoon, scoops up a bit and shoves it into Sandy's mouth. Then one more, because you never have just one spoon of anything in my house. Sandy swallows, oh boy, she swallows fast. I can still remember her face as she tries to keep it down.'

'Kanyaa, huh?' I say, grinning.

'Yeah, and she did look pretty virginal in that sari.'

We both start to laugh. In fact, we both start to do the jet-engine laugh that we'd invented in class 6, when we were eleven. The Bhatt–Patel jet-engine laugh was famous in Calcutta. One of us would start a whine and the other would pick it up and then we'd be flying, making a sort of high-pitched scream punctuated by real guffaws until we lost control and rolled on the ground, finally electrocuted by full laughter. Our enemies used to hate that sound and so did our friends. And teachers and parents it drove completely crazy.

We start well – two grown men trying to reproduce the falsetto taste of childhood. Viral goes high. I go high. We climb, but suddenly the laugh loses power halfway through take-off. The guffawing, which I was king in, is now impossible for me, and Viral chokes every time he tries the whine. Our throats are too brittle, we have swallowed too much life, too much feni, talked many hundred thousand more words since the last jet-engine laugh. Both engines go down for different reasons and both of us peter out into silence.

Viral starts coughing. He spins around out of the chair, swaying away from the table, heading towards the water. The barman's been watching us and he comes out after Viral.

'Mistermister, water's dange'rous now, sir, please don't go in. Sit back in chair, sir and I'll bring the bill.'

Viral turns around and looks at the man. He hoicks his Tommy Hilfiger bermudas up over his paunch.

'Chill man, just my feet okay? Not going in, okay?'

'Not very chilly sir, but dang'rous.'

'Okay, okay, I'll sit down, but no bill yet, okay? Evening's just starting, okay?'

'Okay, but you sit down, okay?'

'Okay, and you chill out, y'hear?' Viral suddenly has a Virginia drawl and I sense trouble. Suddenly he is a US Citizen talking to a Native.

'Ei Viral! Siddown!'

'Yenh,' says Viral as he hits the chair with his butt.

I can see the barman wondering whether he can relax yet, wondering about his bill, wondering about how much trouble Viral was going to be. I cut into his wondering.

'Two coconut fenis and a London Pilsener please.'

'Okay sir, but, please, careful.'

'Sure.'

The barman goes off. I look away, other things knocking on my brain, suddenly a memory of Gulal spraying in the air like blood, a woman's voice finishing a song.

Viral finds his cigarettes. 'Idz aboud handwriting,' he says, after a moment of communion with his Zippo.

'What?' I realise after I ask that he is still talking about the same thing.

'It's like every . . . every lover has . . . has like a handwriting? That they write on you? And the problem's always with the one you like more, ain't it? Like, when the one you *really* like goes, it's always a problem.'

'Mhm huh.'

'Fuckin' Sandy fuckin' Agarkar.' Viral's eyes suddenly get ambushed by tears. 'I've got a lot of head in my life, Bhatt, but I never forgot that one. There's a shrine in my head for that one. I didn't love her or anything . . . it was just her handwriting, like, even under duress?'

I look to the left and then to the right. The left is better because I can sense the barman coming with the drinks on my right. I lean·over as far as there is time to lean over. My puke hits the sand just a few feet short of the tide. As I let it rip out of my stomach I find myself hoping that the waves will wash away the traces by morning.

• • •

Para throws the pencil down and says, 'No-o-a!'

I pick up the pencil and give it back to her. 'Come on, Para.'

'Don't wantoo.' She makes her fighting face.

I think to myself that all this business about girls being faster learners than boys is crap.

Para sends the pencil rolling to the edge of the desk. As it drops, her hand snakes out – fast – and catches it. It's a game I'd started playing with her when she was three and she's got better and better at it. She gets to the pencil well before it nears the ground. Then she makes this hmmmmrrrhhh sound and brings it back up to the table like an aeroplane.

'Parubaby stop that! C'mon! Small "a", five times, now.'

Para scrunches up her face, slides sideways so that she is completely in the wrong position for writing and begins to strangle the pencil with four of her five fingers. She brings it down on the paper and scratches out an ugly little misshapen circle. Then she adds a little curvy worm somewhere near the bottom of it.

'There,' she says and I nearly smack her.

I'm taking it much worse than Anna. Very badly, in fact. I don't understand why it causes me almost physical pain when I see my child trying to write. No, I do understand. I take great pleasure in writing with a pen. Anna and I got together because of handwritten letters. Both my parents had beautiful handwriting. Seventeen generations of Bhatts and Pathaks had beautiful handwriting. And this, my one and only child, apple of my eye, turbine of my soul, bright, impossibly beautiful, agile in all other ways, insists on writing only when forced to and then insists on torturing the roman script beyond all recognition, leaving it all mauled and maimed, the page shuddering under her marks when she's done. I hate her 'a's the most, followed closely by her 'n's.

I try and calm down. 'Six-year-old child,' I say to myself. 'Long way to go.' 'She will get better, be patient.' Patient. 'DON'T FFORZIT!' I can hear Anna screaming at me, the German in her voice rising to the top as it does when, vfenn, she iss ankry.

'Puppi?' says Para.

'Hm?'

'Video game?'

At this point I would normally shout and squeeze more letters out of her, but today I don't.

'All right, c'mon, get your shoes on.'

'Yesssss,' Para hisses and goes off to find her sneakers.

We take the old cage down and Para rattles the gates as usual. The thing shakes and, as usual, I feel a poke of fear that the cables will go, plummeting us down to our deaths deep below the streets of Paris. The child will die with terrible handwriting, I think, and I get angry. 'DON'T!' I snap. Para does her ducking head and grinning act and steps back.

We come out of the Impasse Guiemenée onto Rue St Antoine and turn right, heading away from the Bastille. Para sprints ahead, well out of my reach, heading straight for the next side street. At the last moment, just as my mouth opens to shout, 'Stop!' she screeches to a perfect standstill and looks back at me as if to say, 'Who me? But I've been standing here for ages.' It's a game of chicken and eight times out of ten I lose and shout and get passers-by looking at me with alarm. This brown man walking along, suddenly shouts, 'STOP!' Est-ce qu'il est fou, lui? After a few moments some make the connection with the child with blue-green eyes and light brown hair. Child half a mile down the road. The looks turn to disapproval. Parisians think parents who need to shout are bad, ineffective and inappropriate parents. Perhaps they are right.

It's late August and the streets have a slightly empty feel to them, like a picture half drawn, because Paris has emptied for the holidays. In fact, everybody looks at you suspiciously because you can't be a real Parisian if you are here in August. The weather too makes for suspicion because it is as hot as Calcutta on a June day, if not as humid. Para is wearing shorts, sneakers with Thomas the Tank Engine socks and a t-shirt with a picture of Ronaldo, the Brazilian footballer. With her short hair she gets mistaken for a boy everywhere. 'Il est mignon,' the lady in the supermarket says. 'Il est vif, eh?' says the tabac-walla. And on pain of death from Para am I to tell anyone she's a girl.

'But Mamma says you always wanted a boy, Pappa, so what's the problem?'

'I never wanted a boy and I was very happy when you were born. And there's nothing wrong with being a girl, okay?'

'Yeh there is. You worry like a girl.' I object to this and we argue, but she's right on one count – like my mother, I worry. That's the difference between me and Para's mother, between me and lots of other people, that is, that if there's something to worry about, or even if there isn't, I will worry. That's also the difference between me and Para – I remember I used to worry when I was six, Para doesn't.

Take the video game for instance. Para takes the turn out of the Rue Cambon at about eighty kilometres an hour, which is normal for Parisian taxi drivers, but me, I can never go beyond fifty, try as I do. Then, when the bikes start buzzing close and weaving in front, I always brake, earlier than the guy apparently did, but my foot always jabs at the brake early. Para at this point changes to third gear and hits the gas con brio and that drives the closest ones away. Coming into the underpass I'm either too slow, so I lose according to the rules of the game because that means the photographers get clear pictures, or I'm too fast and I skid and – like Paul did – I die. Para, on the other hand, has managed to lose all of the chasing vehicles by now, so she zips clear, straight and steady, picking up speed as she rises magisterially out from under the Pont d'Alma. The last bike disappears from the rear-view mirror. The speaker makes a 'Padaang!' sound and the screen goes crazy. 'Vous avez GAGNÉ contre les paparazzi. Vous avez sauvé Lady Di. Cinq mille points! Essayez encore?!'

'Yay!' says Para. 'Pappa, can I essayer again?'

'Okay, last time now. Got to get home and make dinner.'

'No-a. Two more times.'

Despite the win of cinq mille chiffres the next essai is not free, this is France. I put the two ten-franc pieces into the slot and the game starts again. A heart made of roses comes up on the middle screen. At the centre of the heart is a photograph of her ladyship smiling seductively. This is replaced by letters that form the name. Di. Then an 'e' and a question mark are added. Then, in French, the question – 'Can you save Diana?'

The chair is a replica of the driver's seat in the Mercedes, seat-belt and all. It moves hydraulically to simulate what the driver would feel. There is one main screen and two side screens that go well behind your peripheral vision so you can turn your head to see what's coming up on the side. You can also, of course, look in the side-view mirrors, which reflect things exactly according to what you do.

Para normally likes to win, but sometimes she gets really aggressive, specially when she's missing Anna. This time I can tell by the grimace on Para's face that she's going to lose in her favourite way: coming away from the Ritz she picks up speed and then brakes hard. Her chair slams forward and then back and there is the sound of a crash. One of the chasing bikes is down, having run into the boot. 'Attention! Dodi a le whiplash! Attention!' – the words flicker on the bottom of the screen but Para doesn't pause. She is now having fun. Pumping away through the red light at the Place de la Concorde she lets one of the cars get slightly ahead and then deliberately swerves hard into it, sending it crashing. The sound of distant police sirens starts on the speakers. 'Attention! Un photographe est mort. L'agent de sécurité est blessé,' says the screen. Para grins and presses down a bit more on the accelerator, her small body sliding around on the seat, which is too big for her.

In the Alma tunnel she hits two pillars, glancing blows, rendering Dodi unconscious and Diana with a broken arm. As she comes out next to the river the sirens become louder and a police car blocks her way. Para tears at one side of the steering wheel as if pulling a rope, swinging the Merc around, trying to do a hundred-and-eighty-degree turn at a hundred and eighty kilometres an hour and the speaker gives off a squeal of tyres and a huge thud. The screen goes blank to the sound of shattering glass and then there is the noise of something big hitting the water.

'Vous avez perdu. Vous êtes dans la Seine. Dodi est mort. Lady Di est paralysée. L'agent de sécurité est mort. Vous êtes vous-même gravement blessé et vous avez tué quatre paparazzi et deux gendarmes. Le jeu est fini. Voulez-vous essayer encore?'

'Whooo,' says Para, pleased with herself.

'Formidable.' The voice sounds like cement being shovelled. I can smell the French tobacco before I turn my head. The old man is completely impassive, maybe slightly sad. Looking at Para unbuckling her seat-belt he says, 'Il conduit comme Pappa, peut-être?'

I rummage through my broken French for a reply.

'Mais pas du tout, m'sieur. Ce sont les taxis de Paris qui –'

'What's he saying, Pappa?'

'He's asking if you've learned to drive like that from me.'

'Haven't. You're boring.'

The man looks even sadder.

'Alors, mon garçon, le boring c'est mieux, unh. Wiz bohreeng you are aatlist alive-unh.'

'What?' says Para trying to claw on to the man's accent.

'Bonsoir, m'sieur,' I say putting on my best embarrassed-father look.

'De même,' he says gravely and checks Le Di(e?) game for damage before turning back to policing the teenagers hanging about the Super Virtuel.

I hustle Para out of the place into the clean late afternoon sunlight.

'Why can't I play one more game?'

'Because I don't have the money, baby.'

'That's because you're not a very good Pappa-razzi, are you? I made-a-pu-un!'

Para's into making puns nowadays and here she's made a triple pun. One, of course, I am not a good pappa. Two, I would make a lousy paparazzi, who she's been told make good money chasing after famous people. Three, I'm in Paris at the wrong time of the year waiting for Magnum to decide if they will take me on as one of their photographers. They are supposedly looking at my work and they're interested enough to want to meet me. But they are not interested enough to meet me immediately.

'Puppi?' Para slips her hand into mine as we walk.

'Yes?'

'When's Mamma coming back from Germany?'

'Told you. In two weeks' time.'

'How many days is two weeks?'

'You tell me.'

'Ummm, it's several thousand days.'

'No, try again.'

'Two weeks is fourteen days but it feels like a long time.'

'Well baby, she's been away for four weeks already, and that's a much longer time and we've had fun.'

'Yes, but now it feels like a long time, Puppi.'

'What, you're tired of Pappa already?'

'No but I want Mamma and you at the same time.'

I look at the traffic and pretend I am concentrating on crossing the road. A Twingo nearly runs us over because actually I'm not paying attention.

'Come on.' I jog across pulling Para behind me. I can tell she's a little tired now by the way she drags at my hand.

'Glace,' she pronounces and it sounds like a change of subject but it isn't. The leverage of guilt usually yields her an untimely ice-cream and she knows it.

'Okay, but only one scoop. I want you to eat your dinner.'

We like the vendor who stands near the Pont Louis-Philippe and without thinking that's where I've been heading.

The sun is right behind the cart and I have to squint to see his face.

'Bonsoir m'sieur, bonsoir mon petit.'

'Bonsoir. Un . . . Para, what do you want?'

'Raspberry, of course, you idiot!'

I flinch. I could not imagine calling my father names, or my mother. I consider a fine of no ice-cream and then think the better of it. The guilt is mingled with battle fatigue.

'Hey. Cut out the bad words, okay? Now. Again. What do you want and what's the magic word?'

Para stands to attention, puts on a solemn face and rattles off the mantra.

'Please Pappa, dearest-darling, best-thing-that-happened-to-me-after-Mamma, may I please . . . havsumeicecream?'

'Une framboise s'il vous plaît.'

'Une framboise!' the man says, washing his scoop while meditating on the word as if he's heard it for the first time. 'Une framboise . . . très bien.'

He reaches in over the other trays and decisively lops off a big ball from a pink cliff.

'Une framboise. Voilà.' He hands it to Para as if he were de Gaulle conferring the Legion d'Honneur on a hero of the Resistance.

'Mercy,' says Para, and the woman's voice, which is lower, almost gets lost under hers.

'Une pistache s'il vous plaît.'

My body reacts as if to a punch it's been expecting. My head starts to pull around but I resist. I concentrate on paying the right amount, on pulling out the paper napkins from the glass on top of the counter. Para glances at me and then past me and then goes back to her ice-cream. Then she pauses from her eating, deliberately, waiting for point-blank range before asking, 'What is pistash, Pappa?' Though it is me she is asking, the voice is designed for someone else and the flash of anger I feel is completely out of proportion to the crime.

I control my voice but I forget to ease my shoulders.

'Pistache is pistachio, baba, the green stuff. You know, the nuts?'

I turn and look at the woman, trying to smile in a casual and friendly way. After all, this is the third or fourth time we've met. And each time Para has asked the same question. But I've made a mistake this time and the woman knows it. Her smile presents its passport at the border of laughter. Shit. The last two times I'd handled it better. A brief smile at her, an indulgent irritation towards Para, 'Told you last time, baby, pistache is pistachios.' Bounced the whole thing off my armour and moved on. This is a step back and I hate my clumsiness.

'Let's go,' I say firmly, too firmly, overcompensating as I come out of the skid.

Para kills that one dead.

'No. I want to go and stand next to the river,' she says and walks away towards the embankment, which is only a few feet away. My daughter can be very sly sometimes and at moments like this I hate her. Well, not hate exactly, but whatever equivalent you can feel towards your own child. In my panic I jettison my anger and go after her. Away from the ice-cream cart and the woman.

Para turns and looks at me and I see two people in her. One is her mother and the other is mine. Anna Lang laughs and says, 'Oh yeah?' while Suman Bhatt looks disdainful, disgusted. 'Lecher,' she spits out.

The voice again, just behind me, close. I manage to think, 'God, this thing is not over yet,' before I realise what the woman is saying.

'Yu wantu try pistache?'

'Yeh,' says Para, 'I mean, oui,' and reaches out for the cone the woman is holding out.

She's about twenty-four, no older, her hair is pulled back into a little bun but I've seen it open, it's a rich brown, the colour probably comes from L'Oréal, and today she is wearing a kind of long green slip with little t-shirt sleeves and impossibly clumpy black rubber boots that add about four inches to her height. This makes her about two inches taller than me. Her face I can't bear to look at, I can't bear to describe her brown eyes, her mouth. Part of me doesn't understand why I feel in physical shock and part of me understands it all too well.

'What do you say, Para?'

'Oh yes. Thank you. Mercy.'

'Il est gentil,' says the woman, looking straight at me.

'Oui, quelquefois,' I reply, trying to smile and failing.

The woman flicks her tongue over the top of her ice-cream, not looking at me anymore. I try to find somewhere to hide my eyes.

'Is good?' she asks Para.

'Oui,' says Para.

'Wotizz your name?' asks the woman.

'Para Lang. What's yours?' says my daughter.

'Mainemizz Magali.'

They lob each other's names back and forth a couple of times, like tennis players practise rallying before a match. Then they stand next to each other and look at me, the river behind them.

'Hey Pappa-razzi! Take a photo of Magali and me eating our ice-creams,' Para orders, an ice-cream cone in each hand.

The woman leans back and lets go, the licence to laugh now hers forever. Para smiles wide. Then they both stand straight and bring a cone each to their mouths, both left-handed, like a pair of well-practised clowns. I focus and check the exposure. I press the shutter. The light reflects off the river and elbows past their faces into my camera.

BOOK TWO

Gulag Archipelago

I'm living in the future,
I feel wonderful,
I'm flipping over backwards,
I'm so ambitious,
I'm looking back,
I'm running a race,
And you're the book I read.
Feel my fingers as they touch your arms,
I'm spinning around and I feel all right,
The book I read was in your eyes.

'The Book I Read'
– TALKING HEADS

That Radha
Completely roiled,
That her being stay drenched,
In Krishna's sweat,
In that wanting,
Will wash not
That sari.

– SURDAS

24 September, 2030

Puja weather again. The monsoon gone like it came – early. Thoda for a few days, amazing that it still does that some years, for a few days there is this clean, polished, light. This light that's been taken away and washed in secret by some department of the non-stop rain, jhaadoed and ghissoed and spruced up for over four months before it's let out again. This impossible light spreading all over Cal.

The light enters the flat quietly. Confidently. How to say it? Like a wanted friend, a person with a right to be there. It comes and sits on the chairs, raising dust as it does. It drapes itself on the sofa and spreads its edges down, crosses its bloody legs – in Gujju we'd say palaanthi wali ne besey, not crossing legs but folding its legs – and settles softly but firmly on the floor, half on the old kilim and half off. Kyhaarek, at a certain time in the afternoon, around four o'clock, it touches the wall in the photo room, blanking out three soft-cornered squares from the wallpaper of images. Now, if your head's still full of the dull hammer of bastard April days and the dark, wet, poisonous stretch of monsoon that comes after, e bhinaa ni yaad ma it is difficult to believe this light, difficult to remember you are still in Calcutta. On the other hand, the only place I've ever seen this light is in Cal and I can't imagine it living anywhere else.

It makes me forget my daughter. It makes the coffee taste different. It even drives the Gujarati out of my head.

You know . . . I love this light, but I hate what it does to me. I have an old man's problem with this light. Because it's in this goddam stupid light that I always remember Ila. Bhaalo naam Teesta, as in the deadly river of north Bengal. Surname Ray, Ray pronounced 'Rai' or 'Rye'. Ila, Teesta Ray. Teesta Ray whose birthday it is today, and no, remember, that doesn't actually rhyme unless you're speaking cockney, in which case it *would* rhyme:

Teestur Ray
'oose birff-dai
I' is to-dai.

Yes, yes I know I'm losing it. A sure sign of senile dementia, Sonali says, when you start mooning over someone you've broken up with forty-three years ago. Mooning over someone who *left* you forty-odd years ago, if you want to split hairs, and sometimes han-yes, I do.

Puja light. Even the shuttles fly by more quietly, even their ghad-ghad seems more respectful of the light. The Jadavpur–Behala route copters, public here calls them 'Koptaar', have a new look. This year Boroline's gone on this massive Puja nostalgia trip and pulled out all their old ads, 1950s onwards, '80 Years of Relieving Bengal's Wounds!' – *bhoonds* as they say here, or *whoonds* if you're slightly higher class, and wrapped them around the helicopters, so when I wake up and look out from my terrace, this thing, this ekta *jinish* passes in front of my eyes, this tube of ointment, Boro-Calendula, with mini-jets attached, crowned by spinning rotor blades – 'The One Mother Trusts!'

My mom never had any truck with Boroline, she was always Dettol, but here's a nice one, I remember it from school: boy in clean & crisp white uniform, shirt/shorts, sitting, and one mother in classic '60s Sadhana haircut, high-pile bun, not a hair out of place, administering ointment to boy's knee, boy grinning away like a fool, idiot!, those things used to hurt like hell, the mother also smiling, her face painted right next to the pilot's grim mug looking the other way, stewing in the cockpit . . .

How long did Ila and me last? Aar abaar koto hobey, about three years, four? April '84 to somewhere in the middle of the dark swamp of '87, bracketed loosely on both sides by the presence of Anna Lang, or, if you like, couched by the absent presence of Anna Lang, later to be also known, reluctantly, as motherofmydaughter. So, Ila was, bas, four, three and a half years only, but sometimes a little goes a long way – as they say. Another copter lumbers by, this time with Durga's eyes stretched across the side, timeless this one, could be any year of re-living Bengal-wounds, staring at me, 'Tell the truth – did you really love her?'

Yes, the answer is yes, Bogart, fag in mouth, chewing it out of his nose, 'Yes, I wneally loved her and I b'lnieve she wneally loved me.' Then a bad variation on classic Chandler wisecrack, call me old-fyashioned, but you can't get better than Chandler, 'What *hyappened*? Well, my love twied to sit down on the lap of her love, but her love hyappened to be styandin' up.' Yeah, well. Standing up, ready to go.

Why don't I just say it straight: When she loved me and I looked at her face, I thought, this is the face that I want to die looking at, this is my death, but before that this is my life, this is the one I was made for, thought of and conceived for, designed for in some cosmic studio, a device with one function and one function only, made specifically to match with her, her only, only Ila, my Ila, the Ila who – the bell going, which I didn't hear the first time because of the copter. Get the door.

'Ke?'

'Aamra sir, pujo'r chaanda.'

Puja tax. Ila would get really angry with the neighbourhood boys. Most of the time she had a high, thin voice, very quiet, almost not there – crumbling dried petal hanging on to the page of a book – tiny bell about to crack, a fill-in-the-blanks sentence of a voice, but only a fool would get fooled by that. Like I did before the first time we made love.

'So *rude*. It's just a money-making thing and they're so brazen about it.'

The first time. When the seeing came together, when either of us could look for both, when both of us would see the same thing and need no words, no voice, thin or thick, just this brevitational pull framing out the rest of the world.

That day, we hardly knew each other then, that day wasn't Puja weather, it was April, cruellestmaanth, and we'd just finished at the electric crematorium at Kalighat. Her interviewing, me photographing. Sweat like small snakes slithering in every corner of your body, proof that you were alive, sweat infiltrating between eyelids and eyeballs, joining eyelash and viewfinder, rivering the groove between your ear and head, gluing forearm and shirt sleeve, melting down your spine –

'Iago-ing,' she'd said in the taxi going to Anirban's flat.

'What?'

'Like Iago. Slimy lying whispers. Iagoing all over the body.'

'Foi-mashi-ing,' I replied. Her turn to laugh out a what.

'Foi is Pishi in Gujju. Mashi is mashi same as in Bangla.'

'But why?'

'My father had evil aunts. I also have one or two, pishis, not mashis – my mom doesn't have any sisters – one foi, Vasufoi particularly, who'd make Iago look like a marriage counsellor.'

'Marriage counsellor?'

'They have them in America,' I explained, since I was USA returned. 'You go to them when you don't really want to get divorced. Apparently they slime you back together.'

'So that you and spouse can mix sweat with sweat again,' she says, nodding to herself as she lights up.

'Where's that from?' I ask, liking the image.

'I read it somewhere when I was thirteen, some bestseller, Leon Uris or something, ki *nongra*, I thought – I was horrified.'

Sweat Iagoing all over both of us, foi-mashi-ing, taxi caught in a jam at the Hazra–Lansdowne crossing. Us dripping, taxi seats dripping, old surdy's hands dripping on steering wheel. The hair on his arms matted, flattened like white grass after a tractor has rolled over it.

I found myself following a drop of sweat as it slid down the side of Ila's neck, watching as it pinballed slowly around the inside of her collarbone before disappearing into the wet glow in the dip below her throat. I found myself, Anna gone from life or not, found myself waiting for the next drop to appear from under her hair, like, caught myself wanting to pick it off her skin and taste it.

'Do you think different people's sweat tastes different?' Ila put a finger to the exact point of her neck I was staring at and wiped off some sweat. Then she brought the finger to her tongue and licked it pensively.

Found myself caught looking. What was she, this mouse-voice, a fucking mind-reader? Dangerous.

'Mm.' Looking at her finger as she contemplated the taste. No smile, matter of fact.

'This is just me, normal.'

Then she looked at me quite seriously, asking the expert, 'Do you think there are different sweat types? Could you tell different people with eyes closed, just by the smell of their sweat? You know, like different kinds of alcohol, could you, sort of, have a sweat cocktail and tell what all, *who* all, had gone into it? . . .Yuk!' She grimaced, disgusted by her own thought.

Don't know about the cocktail, but by the time Ila and me were done I could tell her smell all right, the taste of her sweat, her touch, you name it, I didn't need eyes, as I didn't for Anna Lang either. Or Sandy.

The first time Anna was around for Puja, October 1987 that was, after Ila and me were well finished and Anna finally came to India. She was all wide-eyed. What is this? What is that? I remember my mother explaining the concept to her and then my father and Kalikaku dismantling my mother's explanation, which led to a small ekta, chotto ekta war in the house.

Chandi Paath coming out of the pandal loudspeakers down the road. *Ya Devi Sarvabhuteshu, Matru Rupena Sansthitaa . . . Namastasye, Namstasye, Namastasye . . .*

O Goddess, You Who Are in Every Form, You Who We See in the Form of the Mother . . .

My mother in her Gujju-English, doing a cultural primer for the gora girl:

'In Gujarat we have Navratri but here in Bengal the festival is called "Durga Puja" or "Pujas" for short. This is when Goddess Durga is worshipped for ten days. She is like a daughter coming home from her husband's house and all Bengali daughters are traditionally returning from their in-laws' place to parents' place. It is also celebration of slaying of Mahishasur, who was an evil demon in buffalo shape, and Durga's vehicle, all Gods are having vehicles, is a lion.'

Nowadays, I don't dwell too much on the idea of daughters coming home. And talking about vehicles, Para's done the whole bit, trainers, ancient Jaguar two-seaters, actual combat in her Ishir, which did have a Durga sitting on a Lion painted on it and now something that's about as different from a Lion as you can get – something that looks like a bhakhri ('Gujaratis are having many different kinds of unleavened bread, like rotis and theplas, and bhakhri is Paresh's favourite. Have some more,' as my mother would say), this space station Varun-Machaan that pretends to be innocent but is deadly for all that. I guess I shouldn't be too bemused. After all, from what I remember, there is a whole passage in the Chandi Paath where the warrior Devi takes on different avatars and each avatar has a different animal that she rides.

My father taking up the guide-book in his English, which was a little better than my mother's because he read more and saw more films:

'Puja is when this whole city becomes lunatic. It is unbearable. You saw those bamboo structures? They are called pandals and there are big ones and also every little lane has one. Tomorrow they will all be covered with cloth and two days later the clay statues of Durga and her side-gods will come on trucks. Then Durga-mata will have to sit there and listen to Hindi film music, day and night, for ten days.'

Dekho! Dekho! Dekho wo aa gayaa! . . . piya tuuuuuu ab t`o aaaa jaaa! Ssolaa saawan bhadke, aaa ke bujjhaaaaaaaaja!

Hindi music interlaced with the droning of the Chandi Paath . . . *Ommmai Darliing! Uh huh huhuh huh*, Bong pandas mispronouncing the hell out of the Sanskrit.

Rupawm Dehi, Joyawm Dehi, Josho Dehi, Hrosho Johi instead of *Rupam Dehi, Jayam Dehi, Yasho Dehi, Hrasho Jahi*.

Give Me Form, Give Me Victory, Give Me Glory, Destroy My Enemies.

For her side-gods Para has two egg-heads, two men, one Ghaati called Ashok something Nalvekar? Navlekar?, and a Punj, some Gulati who is the one who photographs the universe, the one who looks up while Para looks down. And one girl, Reba Bannerjee, who is some technical whizz who keeps the whole plant running while Para hides behind all this civilian action and does what she has to do. Stuff that is 'classified' but I have a pretty good idea what it is. Stuff that's going to make some demon buffalo try and gore her sooner or later, the stuff that she does, stuff that still drives me to stupid prayers.

My mother: 'It is an auspicious occasion and it is a time to pray.'

Rupam Dehi, Jayam Dehi, Yasho Dehi, Hrasho Jahi, indeed.

Kalikaku laying down the final matrix for Anna, who is by now quite dazed: 'Though comparable to Christmas, Puja, or Pujo, as we call it, is very different in structure. There can be no easy leaning on Levi-Straussian anthropology here. Because, while Christmas is a *centrifugal* ritual, Durga Puja is a *centripetal*. Despite daughters coming home and all that, it is a time to go out. You can contrast the Christmas/Home paradigm to the Puja/Street dynamic. Also Christmas is a celebration of conservation whereas Pujos is a celebration of, of –'

My father: '– of waste. It is a time for the citizens of Calcutta to spend money that they don't have.'

O Devi! You Who We See in the Form of Worry, You Who We See in the Form of Anxiety, You Who We See in the Form of Anger . . .

Kalikaku: 'Ah-ha Modhuda, you cannot ignore the deep root of Durga Puja in the Indo-Burmese Agrarian Mother-Earth consciousness. What is Mahishasur but famine and drought? And what is Durga except the female wisdom and fecundity which overcomes that to bring plenty?'

My father: 'Plenty of noise. And crowds. And dirt. And waste.'

Ila's father would have agreed with my father had they ever met, which they never did. He was a military man, big man, who came up to almost my height, must have been five eleven, almost six, Brigadier Ray, shorter than me by an inch or so, but something in his bearing always made him seem taller and me shorter by a good few inches. One day, I wasn't there, the local boys, young men, but called boys, landed up to collect chanda for the pada's Puja and he gave them the usual fifteen rupees. One of the boys decided to be a smartass.

'Uncle, this is 1985. Nobody gives fifteen rupees anymore.'

Brig. Ray turned to the boy who'd spoken. He stared at him past the pipe clutched between his teeth.

'If you don't want it, you can give it back,' he gritted out.

The boys were taken aback, but then the smartass made another mistake. He put on his pada thug's demeanour and came slightly closer to the Brig.

'Uncle, you and your family have to live in this pada, do you understand?'

Now, the Brig. had a walking stick because of his limp, which came not from any war injury but a car accident well after he'd retired. The stick flew up and came down hard on the boy's arm. The receipt book fell to the ground. One of the other boys tried to throw a punch and missed. The Brig. didn't miss and suddenly there were these four young men running across the drive-way, one of them leaving a trail of blood on the gravel, with the Brig. crunching behind them with surprising speed.

'Young swine! Threaten me will you?'

The whole incident was resolved later, quietly, by Ila's mother, who made a conciliatory donation of a hundred and fifty rupees without telling her husband. The donation was made not in any apology for splitting open one of the boys' temples, but because Brigadier Shaheb had actually kicked the receipt book, which had a picture of Durga printed on it – a crime that no one could defend.

Today when I open the door, the boys who stand in front of me are very different.

'Hai! Good afternoon, ser! Kemon achhen?'

'Hm.'

They come out of the Japanese bow with their hands folded in a standard issue Nomoshkar, all four of them in some kind of uniform – white trousers and bright red t-shirts – and across the front of the t-shirts, just behind their perfunctorily folded palms, flashes the Koji Refrigerator logo. Koji, now bigger worldwide than even Samsung-Whirlpool, are obviously the main sponsors of this year's Deshapriya Park Puja.

Under the logo moves a slogan – *Have a cool Puja, have a Koji Puja.* And behind the English a vertical line running the same thing in Japanese. They like to remind everyone of basic allegiances, our friends from Little Nippon. No need to conjecture what would have happened if Bose had won and the Japs taken over, it's right here, right in front of my eyes. As Viral used to say, 'Not via Burma but via the Bourse.'

Yes, it's changed a lot, Puja, and it's not just all the Japs, there's one change I even like. Real incense being in short supply, very few of the pandals have real agarbattis anymore, most of them rent virtual agarbattis and the smoke is a laser projection, which suits me fine because I've hated that fucking smell since I was a child, hated it even more than Viral used to. I look at the boys and wish they were virtual as well. Actually, they almost are. Each of them has a name-tag on his shirt and I suddenly think if I tap one on the tag he will disappear. I resist the temptation to try. One of the boys, Kushal, has a little palmtop computer which he starts feeding information into. The one labelled Shuddhabrata begins his patter. He is obviously the English-speaker.

'Mr Bhatt, sir, nomoshkar and Puja greetings from your pada's Puja committee and Koji Bengal who are proud to sponsor our Puja this year. Sir, can I interest you in participating in our Puja Lucky Draw competition. The first prize is a triple-decker Koji LooseLogic refrigerator with a video-scan assist. It is the top-of-the-line Koji product and without opening the fridge door you can tell what food you have inside, when it was bought, and by when it should be consumed. You don't need to even type in the information if the can or packet are K-coded, which allows the fridge to automatically scan the foodstuffs you have purchased. And there is even a special tray to keep your water-tablets cool and a dispenser to release them into the glass without the need for you to touch them with your hands.' The Koji logo on his paunch undulates as he pauses for a breath before continuing.

'Aaro sir, there are four second prizes of the new Koji mini-fridge, which has a capacity of a handred litres and can run without power for eight days, ideal for load-shedding. And we also have eight thaard prizes of a choice of either Kont-Roll motorised skateboards or the full Barbie IndiaBabe collection, ideal gifts for children.'

My daughter already has her motorised skateboard, I want to say, and it's bigger and nastier than anything you parochial fucking south Cal louts can imagine. But I keep my mouth shut because what I want to say has nothing to do with what I *can* say and it's been that way for years.

There's a link buzz. One of the boys flicks up the mike from the rig around his neck.

'Hai! Han, Team 6, Runu here.'

Kushal immediately shows the palmtop screen to Runu, who reads off some figures into his mike. Then he listens to the other side and his face darkens. He moves away from us and goes down the stairs a bit but I can still hear his voice hissing in anger. He says something first in Japanese, which I imagine is Bangla-accented Japanese, and then breaks into pure Bonglish.

'Ota kintu Deshapriya territory. You tell those Hazra Road baanchods to jhast FACKUFF naholey gaand merey debo – Motilal Nehru Road is *awaour* area, ota neither Hazra Road na Maddox Square, bujheychho? And I'll get the boss to take it to the Puja Marketing Board *ekkhuni*, jhast now. Aami good mood ey nei, get it?'

Shuddhabrata continues his spiel, his voice slightly louder, trying to cover over Runu's phone conversation.

'And sir, Mr Bhatt, we would also like to inform that full fifteen per cent of our takings from the lottery and the advertising sales *will* go to charities such as the Mumbai Children's Rehabilitation Trust, which works with children who survived the Device and also various health and flood organisations in Banga (East) and organisations working on the epidemic in Burma.'

I look at the guy's fat and sincere face and think fuck the epidemic in Burma. I am having a hard enough time dealing with the epidemic of memory here in my own head.

In the immediate aftermath you can end up wishing whatever unhappiness on someone. Kintu jai bolo, maybe I'm a weak man, maybe it's to do with the supposed great healing qualities of time perhaps, at least that's what Sandy always mantained, but after the first couple of years I've always wished Ila well. And proper well, from the deepest inside of me, though admittedly a different deep inside from the one that was in love with her. Also a different inside from the one that wishes Anna Lang well, but that's understandable because, after all, we are and will be, forever, Mamma and Pappa.

When Ila and me broke up, *when she left me*, I kept feeling as if I had been exiled. Foolish. As if she and I were a country, as if together we formed a land, a land with borders and a currency and an Independence

Struggle and a landscape and a special, own, copyrighted, post-monsoon light. I remember feeling that Ila, when she left, had taken my land with her, or, even though I composed half of it, she had somehow made it uninhabitable for me. All those rivers that were us suddenly singed up from the earth that was us.

I look at the Koji boys and I want to get rid of them quickly. I put my thumb on the scanner of their little computer and punch in my credit code to buy the bloody lottery ticket they want me to – 'Only three thousand, two hundred rupees sir, special senior citizens' discount.'

Senior citizen up yours. 'Hai!' I snap my head at them like a warlord dismissing his Samurai and shut the door. Shut it even before they manage to turn away and shuffle back into my prison of September light.

Where was I? Ah ja, Ila-Teesta, when she left me. All that earth redistributed, all that sky shredded and scattered over different hemispheres. As if – like I'd been exiled from the atmosphere, a living view turned into a photograph floating in outer space, circling around the earth of my love but unable to re-enter its gravitational pull. Yes, the word 'exile', the not understanding of the fact of fish, just 'exile'. Only thing was that, then, in the glittering of my despair, I didn't even know the beginning of the meaning of the word.

Exiles

Two things combined to finally kill the old man. One, of course, was the temperature. The day he died, for instance, it was minus sixty degrees without taking the wind into account. Adding the wind-chill factor the temperature would have been around minus seventy-eight degrees or so. The entire gulag – prisoners, guards, dogs, work administrators – had gone silent with the shock of the cold. It was unbelievable, but the temperature actually dropped as morning broke and the sun came out. Dawn brought a wind that pushed away the night and the cloud cover that had rested with it across the peninsula. Other prisoners, far less privileged, died that day too – six of them – from various causes ranging from severe frostbite to the collapse of one man's circulation system. All of them were much younger than the old man, who was, on that January day, only twelve days away from his sixty-sixth birthday.

Sixty-six was not very old for someone like him, and his little hut in the special compound was probably the warmest place in the entire camp, including the commandant's quarters. Special deliveries of coal arrived every week from Vladivostok in sealed crates marked for intern N16/1945/CB, and it would have meant the firing squad for anyone caught tampering with the supply. Kalid-as Dutta reckoned that the second thing that got through the toughened shell was when they told the old man he could never go home. They would not have said 'never', they would have said 'not just yet', but it was the last 'not just yet' that he could take.

Also someone had made a mistake, a bad one as it turned out, in vetting the news reports that were sent to him in special packages from Moscow. Two small items attached to other news pieces from *Izsvestia*, items referring to the Chinese invasion, had slipped through, and the old man had put two and two together. Kalidas remembered seeing the photostats on one of the desks, remembered them forming a small island of paper separated from a surrounding ocean of other paper that was somehow different. The items were in Russian, naturally, but the old man was fluent in Russian by then.

India at war with China meant that the people in Moscow would now do nothing to jeopardise Khaditupi's position. The Plan would be thrown onto the garbage heap of history and He, after waiting all these years, these long eighteen years, he too would be dumped along with it. The realisation that the little hut had become his final and only destination, that Delhi was not only far, but now forever beyond the reach of his destiny, probably dealt a deadly blow to his legendary will-power.

Kalidas Dutta later calculated that the final 'not just yet' had come via coded telex, followed two days later by the package containing the lethal news items. It must have been the next day that the old man stopped speaking Russian and English, stopped communicating with his guards. He began walking up and down the compound, speaking mostly in Bengali and sometimes, as if addressing a large crowd, in Hindustani. His blood pressure shot up and he began to have difficulties urinating, indicating a problem with the kidneys or the prostate. He also stopped eating and had to be force-fed a liquid diet via a tube.

Kalidas Dutta was then a twenty-five-year-old seaman. On 10 January, 1963 he was in a prison in Vladivostok awaiting trial. He had been arrested with two other shipmates for trying to smuggle in American cigarettes. At 2 a.m. that morning, he was woken in his prison cell by an official speaking fluent English. The man shook him awake and asked him what Indian languages he spoke. Groggy from sleep and exhaustion and suddenly afraid for his life, Kalidas replied in his broken English that he spoke Bengali and Hindi.

Kalidas was whisked out of his cell, given a change of clothes and taken to one of the military airports just outside the city. On the way he was given some food and some hot tea from a thermos. The man also gave him two packets of cigarettes – Russian – and a matchbox. Kalidas didn't dare ask where he was being taken, but they seemed to be treating him kindly enough, so he relaxed a little bit. The transport was a fat little Ilyushin, code-named 'Elsa' by the Americans, and the turbo-props were already moving as the car drew up.

The official accompanying Kalidas got out and went over to another grey man in a greatcoat. The two men turned from their conversation and first greatcoat pointed a finger at Kalidas and pulled his arm back, as if he was pulling at a kite string. Kalidas understood that he was being summoned. He got out of the car and went over. The second man stared at Kalidas for a long moment. The airport lights reflected off the carpet of snow on the tarmac, reaching from below into the man's eyes. Kalidas's relaxation went out of him like air from a pricked balloon. He stood there, shivering, afraid of death once again, and crossed his hands in front of him as if waiting for the handcuffs to be put back on. The second man looked Kalidas up and down and then, suddenly, he grinned. He turned to the other official and said something in Russian: 'I don't know if this fucker can do it – his dick's on fire.' Then he doubled up with laughter. His companion looked puzzled at first. Then he looked at Kalidas, and, after a second's hesitation, pointed at Kalidas's crotch and doubled up himself.

At this point Kalidas nearly made a mistake. Actually he did make one, but no one noticed. What Kalidas hadn't told anyone was that he also spoke Russian. In fact, his Russian was better than his English. He had been a sailor for about five years on the MS *Godavari*, which was a freighter that mainly sailed back and forth between Indian and Russian ports, and over time he'd picked up more than a smattering of the language. When the second greatcoat spoke to the first one, Kalidas had understood and had already begun to look down. Luckily the first man had pointed, giving Kalidas enough reason.

As he looked, Kalidas saw that his dick indeed seemed to be on fire. There was smoke coming out from between his crossed hands. It took Kalidas a few seconds to realise what was happening. He threw down the butt of the cigarette that had almost disappeared between his fingers and carefully stubbed it out with his boot. Then he looked up and smiled sheepishly.

This was the moment that saved Kalidas's life. They seemed to trust him from then on. Greatcoat number one turned to number two and did a sort of salute before getting back into the car. 'I'd better go now.' Number two, who was obviously his superior, leaned into the window and said, 'Listen, remember, just tell Moscow that we are doing what we can, but it may be too late. It's their funeral, you understand? Not ours. And if there is a funeral here then there should be one there too, but I'll deal with that when I get back.'

The man turned away from the car and came quickly towards Kalidas. He took him by the elbow, quite gently, and guided him up the ladder. The ladder was slippery, the ribs of iron rounded over with frozen slush. If he'd had his way, Kalidas would have gone up it much more slowly. But the gentle hand at his elbow did not allow any thought of negotiation – it was that kind of gentle hand.

As the plane took off, the man handed Kalidas a hip-flask.

'Vodkiy,' he said.

Kalidas hesitated and then nodded and took the flask. The plane was a military transport and not very warm. Kalidas had one swig and, when the man made no move to take the flask back, he had another. He knew the Russians respected people who could drink.

'I am Mr Alexandrovich. But no Mister. You villcoll me Alexandrovich.'

'Yes sir.'

'Not sir, Alexandrovich.'

'Yes si— Alexander-which.' Kalidas forced himself to say 'Alexander' and not 'Alexandrovich', which he could pronounce perfectly.

During the two-and-a-half-hour flight Mr Alexandrovich told Kalidas Dutta the following things:

One, that there was an old man in a prison camp who was dying. Two, that the old man was an Indian, a criminal, who had committed unspecified crimes and was now going mad, speaking only in Bengali and Hindi. Three, that it was Kalidas's task to help the police by relaying exactly what the old man was saying. If Kalidas did this and did this faithfully, the charges against Kalidas would be dropped and he would be flown back to India within a week. If he didn't, he could spend the rest of his life in the prison camp they were going to.

Kalidas slept for a little while. He woke up when the pilot began to nudge the plane off its cruising altitude, down towards landing. The Ilyushin was happy where it was, and reacted badly when told to struggle with the air currents below it, rowdy stuff, which it quite understandably considered no longer its business. Kalidas woke up and for a moment he didn't know where he was. On a ship in a bad storm? His mother's lap? In the jail in an earthquake? Then he noticed the windows and looked outside. A blizzard slapped about the plane, getting more and more dense as the plane hiccuped lower. At one point the windows went completely white. Not the white of opaque cloud that Kalidas would see later when he flew in jet planes, but a crowd of white balls, alive and trying, for all he could tell, trying to get in through the windows.

The Ilyushin hit the strip at high speed and bounced up like a basketball. Kalidas found himself holding the arm-rests tightly, as tightly as you would an opponent's arms in a wrestling match. As the plane came down again Mr Alexandrovich woke up and briskly vomited between his own legs. He vomited forcefully but carefully, leaning right forward and managing not to spoil his trousers or his shoes.

While the plane was taxiing, a man came up from the back and handed each of them a parcel and a pair of boots. Kalidas did as he was told, and put on four layers of warm clothing, three pairs of woollen socks and solid winter boots. When the door was opened he could hardly walk because of all the clothes, but the air still cut him into half.

The walk from the aircraft to the army jeep numbed him completely. In the back of the jeep there was a brazier, and Mr Alexandrovich leaned over it and warmed his hands. His face was very close to Kalidas, the smell of vodka and puke overpowering.

'You will remembr what I said? Yes?'

'Yes, Alexanderwich,' said Kalidas.

Then Mr Alexandrovich lost interest in Kalidas. He reached into a little bag and pulled out a toothbrush that looked like it had been used for ten years. He put some toothpaste on it and began to brush his teeth as the jeep bumped its way across the frozen tundra. He didn't once spit, and though Kalidas knew there was no question of gargling, he found the sight abhorrent.

After an hour's drive they reached the gulag.

• • •

'You know,' says Kalikaku, 'you know, Paresh, I went to Gangotri last year, and it was full of Bengalis.' A pause to pour the tea. 'You know what shamed me the most? They were the most overdressed for the cold. I mean, there was a bit of cold but, ki aar bolbo, sweaters, jackets, monkey caps, shawls, gloves, gloves abar! And this is the middle of June!'

'Mummy used to bury me in sweaters when we went to hill stations. So it's not just Bengalis,' I argue.

'Nonsense! That was just your mother. I saw this Gujarati group there and they were quite normal. How did I know they were Gujarati? Well first because the women were wearing their sari pallus the wrong way around, like your mother, and second, like Sumandi they were eating theplas and that pickle, ki boley, chhundo! But the Bengalis . . . Laughing stock of all India! If they had seen their great hero in that camp. Paresh, whatever you may say about him, that man was ERECT till the last!' When he says the word 'erect' Kalikaku jerks his thin frame upwards, almost off the chair. He holds the pose for couple of seconds, exactly like a swimmer at the end of his breast stroke, before slumping back into the story.

• • •

The jeep came to a stop outside the special compound. It was snowing so hard that Kalidas could barely make out the grey mass of the hut, which was less than thirty yards away. A man ran out from the gates and opened the back door of the jeep, saluting Mr Alexandrovich in the same motion. Mr A.'s return salute flicked away an imaginary fly from near his forehead. He was out before the gesture was completed.

'He's going down, sir, rapidly. Still insists on his two walks, morning and evening. Then he collapses, sir.'

'Saying anything?'

'Nothing in Russian or English. Sometimes, something, a word, a phrase, in what sounds like German.'

'Okay, let's go.'

Mr Alexandrovich strode quickly towards the hut. Kalidas followed, stumbling, trying to keep his fur hat on as the blizzard tugged at it. As they reached the door, Mr Alexandrovich paused and turned to look at Kalidas.

'Remembr. Say nothing unless he talks to you. And. I want to know every word, no matter how stupid, how small. Yes?' He had already said this to Kalidas several times.

'Yes.'

The first thing that struck Kalidas as he entered the hut was the smell. Stepping out of the jeep, something sharp had climbed up his nose and he had placed that quickly – the diesel-blood the blizzard had drawn from the struggling engine. Here in the hut there was something else, something that Kalidas had known all his life but couldn't quite put his finger on. Something like hearing a voice you knew well, in a place very different from where you were used to hearing it.

The hut consisted of three rooms and a small kitchen. One room was for the guards and Kalidas never saw the inside of it. One was a small bedroom for the old man – a simple bed, a cupboard, a full-length mirror that he had demanded when he first came here, and a large brazier that was on twenty-four hours a day except for two months in the year.

The room they came into was the 'living room', or the 'study'.

There was a fireplace with a fire blazing in it, an armchair next to it. On the other side of the room, next to a window, were two desks that sat next to each other, covered with papers. The walls were lined with rough planks loaded with books. On a wall to one side of the desks was a large map of the Indian subcontinent, including Afghanistan and Burma.

There were two table lamps, one for each desk, and a high-wattage bulb that hung from the ceiling with an Oriental shade. Despite all the light, Kalidas had to search the room to find the old man. He saw him when the armchair developed a piece of padding that seemed to move by itself. Kalidas was, at this point, twenty-five years old, which meant that he had been seven when the war ended in 1945. It didn't matter that the face in the photographs and paintings that had pervaded Calcutta since then was frozen from a likeness from before or around 1944. It didn't matter that the death had been a famous and well-documented one, as ingrained in the public consciousness as the life itself. None of this came in the way of recognition.

It took Kalidas no more than a minute to get over the impossibility of it. It took him a terrifying further five minutes to control the shock on his face. Luckily for him, they were all looking at the old man and no one noticed.

The old man had risen from the chair, turned towards them and stared. He was wearing a fur coat and a grey fur hat that Khrushchev had sent him last year. The hat seemed too big for the crumpled face under it, in fact it seemed to be supported only by the thick spectacles and the glint in the eyes behind the lenses. The voice was reedy, not well, but it still seemed to rise out of from some deep place, somewhere well below the old army boots that stuck out from under the coat.

'Notun system banatTEI hobey. Gentlemen, this city WILL HAVE a new sewage sytem. And as Mayor it is my DUTY to ensure that no political or commercial interests come in the way of the sanitation that the People of Calcutta require. Aami kono Ingrej, ba kono babu, bania, ba businessman ke eita aatkatey debo NA.'

Having finished, Subhash Chandra Bose then looked each man in the eye as if daring someone to contradict him. Then he turned away from them and sat down in his chair. After a while his head drooped and a low sibilance filled the silent room. The Mayor of Calcutta Corporation was asleep.

• • •

When the sewage system of the city of Calcutta was built it was one of the best in the world. In 1864 Calcutta was a small town which someone had big plans for. The network of pipes and drainages that was designed and built was for the white residents of a very small part of the city – those who happened to live in, or near, Fort William and contiguous areas. The system stretched southwards from Fort William to Park Street and then made its convoluted way through the soft delta soil to Ballygunge. This was the extent of European habitation in the colonial capital, and for a decade nobody imagined that anything more was needed – the natives shat where they wanted, and the only people who required municipal sanitation were the whites dying in droves from malaria and cholera.

In 1874, the same year the first pontoon bridge at Howrah was built, the same year that the New Market was completed, the system was expanded to include Badabazar, the commercial warren in the near north of the Fort, and the areas that are now called Alipur, which were directly south. Of its three arms, one short stubby one ran up north, one dirty tentacle ran south-east, and the third snaked directly south, leaving a huge gap in between. This three-pronged, underground monument of British engineering was then thought to be 'more than adequate for the foreseeable future' – Victorianese for 'future-proofed'.

The tunnels were built with a new construction technique that took the normal, rectangular, brick and made it curve to make perfect tubes, huge, thirty feet in diameter in fact, a scale unheard of till then in any metropolis including the great cities of the West.

What the early city planners paid no attention to – to the peril of their posthumous reputations – was the night-soil the native population living in connected areas might produce, and how this would affect the Raj administrators and the Box-wallas they were trying to protect from the dreaded tropical diseases. And as to the sanitation needs of the natives not living near the European enclaves, the planners thought absolutely nothing at all.

The engineers who had constructed the thirty-foot wide tunnels to carry the shit of the Raj were then called away on another job – the construction of train lines in London. There, they used the technique perfected in Calcutta to take the Great Commute underground, a phenomenon that would last well into the twenty-first century.

By that time another, very different, overground exodus had begun on the Gangetic plain, one that would have echoes for an even longer period of time. The drought and famine of 1874 turned great tracts of Uttar Pradesh, Bihar and Orissa into uninhabitable wastelands, and Calcutta became the only hope of survival for hundreds of thousands of peasants. Within ten years of the completion of the Calcutta sewage system, the population of the city trebled, pushing the sewers towards early obsolescence. Additions were built, new outlets added, but there was a limit to how much could be done without ripping up the whole city once again. Despite the fact that the actual size of the system was almost doubled, the pressure remained on the big tunnels that had formed the original network.

By the time a young Subhash Bose became the Chief Executive Officer of the Calcutta Corporation in 1927, it was clear that a major overhaul was needed. Despite Bose's best efforts as Chief Executive, and then as

Mayor, this never happened. Within two years Bose moved on from Calcutta's municipal concerns and climbed onto the grander stage of national politics. He left this small defeat behind in the hope of greater victories, but what actually awaited him were much, much grander defeats.

The people of Calcutta continued to live with Bose's small defeat till the end of the century, till the year 2007 in fact, when raids by Pakistani warplanes flying in from airstrips in southern China ripped open the old sewers and forced the State Government to build a completely new sewage system.

To be fair to the British engineers, their great tunnels coped very well for the first forty years or so, managing, somehow, to shift volumes of waste no one had dreamed of: what was designed to carry small amounts of transformed porridge, cabbage soup, beef stew, roast chicken and mild kedgeree, what was made to receive the liquid exchanged from pots of weak tea and whisky and sherry wine, ended up carrying a far more thickly cosmopolitan mixture than that.

From many roundabout routes, the system received the waste of the great kitchens of Bengal, the remains of meals from the great babu-badis of north Calcutta, intestinal translations of the ordinary daal and rice and fish of the majority of Calcutta's citizens, it took the broken-down sattu and gur that the thela-wallas and riksha-wallas ate on the sidewalks before working it out in back-breaking labour, it took the ghee-rich rejections from the Marwari havelis in Badabazar, it took the authentically pungent defecations of one of the biggest Chinatowns in the world, transmogrified noodles, prawns, chicken in the finest honey and chilli sauce, it took the destructions of the complex Lucknawi and Hyderabadi menus from the kotha-badis and whorehouses of Sonagachhi, as, in 1911, it took the Viceroy's final efforts on the throne at Viceroy House, on the day he caught the train to build his new palace in New Delhi. It took the embowelled offerings of poets and writers and theatre people – of which the city had many – and the massive droppings, meagre in real content, of the poor in the rapidly burgeoning bastis. As revolutions grew, it took the thin strainings of the tortured from the modern dungeons of Lalbazar Police Headquarters, and sometimes the last morning rites of the condemned. And then, through the early decades of the twentieth century, alongside the minuscule flushings of French haute cuisine, foie gras and filet mignon and riz de veau and champagne and Pomerol squeezed through the collapsing livers of the expatriates at the exclusive Diaghilev Club, the system began to receive increasing traces of the best cuisine in the world. From Badabazar, Bowbazar and Bhawanipur, came more and more the deconstructions of delicate patra, of dhokla and undhyu, of the simple rotli, daal, bhaat aney bataka nu shaak, of bhakhri, of puri and kadhi, of thepla and proper, thick, masala-wali-chaa, and on the days after big occasions, remains of laadu, magas and shrikhand. In 1940, by the time Mahadev Bhatt reached the final destination of his exile, Calcutta had a population of around sixty thousand Gujaratis.

• • •

Mahadev had been leaning out of a train window, watching out for nearly an hour, when he finally caught a glimpse of the new Howrah Bridge. Something tall and grey, something criss-cross and steel stalking the train between two ramshackle railway colony houses. There it towered on the other side of a wall of rain, and there it stayed, playing hide and seek, coming closer and closer, revealing more of itself from different angles as the Mail from Ahmedabad wound its slow and bumpy path through the outer yards of Howrah Station.

Mahadev wanted to feel elation, but something in him sank when he saw the bridge. The bridge of legend actually existed and, if it was real, then so was the fact that he would never have Suman as his wife. Just before he closed the suitcase for his trip to Calcutta, Mahadev had covered all the things he had packed with a towel – the towel of unreality – and tucked in the sides. He had taken the train as if stepping onto a running dream, a film that he could walk out of, a masked performance by life that would end suddenly, life ripping its mask off and grinning at him, freeing him from these fake and poisonously mesmeric rhythms. For three days and the two nights in between, Mahadev had stared out of the window of his third-class bogey, looking for a sign of real life, of the truth that he wanted to be true, of the reality he wanted to be real. One by one the stations had passed, Nadiad, Bhusawal, Nagpur, Mogulsarai, Patna, Burdwan.

One was a noon-time circus, another an empty, eerie stage in the middle of the night. At another, Mogulsarai?, at dawn, a chai-walla had looked at his face bereft of any sign of sleep, and silently handed him a shakoru of tea and refused to accept any money. Each station was in itself the tip of a whole new universe, and each station was a mark that he had lost the battle of his life at the age of twenty-one. Each new smell, each new guard-house with its sign, big block letters in black against a rectangle of yellow, each saying the same thing in different ways. Wardha saying Suman is gone, Benaras saying now begin your empty life, Patna saying now begin your barren life and water it with duty.

By nature, Mahadev was not a dramatic man. He was a product of the modern age, in that he was rational, systematically curious, untrusting of most things that had gone before and at the same time cautiously optimistic – the optimism based on a faith in himself rather than any outside power. There was a part of him that registered the landscape changing around the train, a part of him that enjoyed pushing his eyes through the fluttering curtain of smoke into the fields of what he imagined was his country. As he looked at the figures punctuating the fields, people that he thought were his people, there was a strong part of him that kept saying what had happened was right, that what had been done was not only normal, common, but correct and useful in a way that those that had done it would not even be able to begin to imagine. He may have lost the battle of his life as a person, but that had actually freed him up to fight, with proper muscle and free breath, the battle for the freedom of his country.

The noise of the wheels changed as the train got closer to the station. Mahadev was already standing up, trying to pull down his bistra from the top berth, when the train reached platform number 8. Suddenly, the tracery of tracks and signal gears was erased by a wedge of concrete that climbed up from the mud and flattened sharply into a flat grey that curtained the windows. A flash of dirty white dhoti against the grey, then a blur of a red tunic, then more dhotis, more red, brass badges on red arms shining dully in the monsoon light. Bare feet running, first on concrete, then on wet concrete and then splashing across a thin film of water that covered the platform.

As the train moved in, the coolies slowed down, their hiked dhotis now showing signs of wet.

Mahadev had heard about the great platforms at Howrah, just as he had heard about the great platforms of Bombay Central and VT before he saw them. That day, Mahadev suddenly realised that he would not see the platforms of Howrah Station. As the train screeched to a stop, Mahadev felt something take a grip around his ankles, just below his dhoti something slightly cold, something being very familiar with his feet, something with no sense of shame, something that could reach up to his knees and carry on climbing.

By the time he looked down Mahadev knew what it was. And years later, when he saw Neil Armstrong stepping off the ladder onto the moon, he would have a vivid memory of the first time he arrived at Howrah. From then on he would always feel that he had known since the year 1940 what it felt like to walk on another planet. He knew what it was because, when he bent down a bit, he could see it from the window. He could see it stretching from his train to the next. And, though it wasn't like any water Mahadev had ever seen, he knew he couldn't call it anything else.

'O bechara ki korey bujhbey? Jiboney jol dekheyni t̂o. JOL! Eta Real WHATER! Not that watery water that passes for water in Gujarat! Not like that watery thing that passes for daal in Gujarat! Poresh! This was not water it was JOL! Madhuda had never seen it, this thing!' Kalikaku's pleasure would crackle like electricity gone wrong. He would slurp his tea – 'the watery tea that passes for tea in Bengal,' Paresh would think, when the urge to retaliate got the better of him – and giggle his deep giggle.

'Mr Bhatt was stepping into the primordial swamp of Indian Urban Life! Of course the platform was submerged! Of course his pocket was pickpocketed! How else could it *be*?'

Kalikaku had many names for Paresh's father, Madhuda, Modhuda, Modhusudon Bhotto, Mahadebshaheb, all of them affectionate, each an attempt to disguise his deep respect for the older man. There were stories he told Paresh about his father's life that Paresh would never have got from Mahadev Bhatt himself.

'Poresh! You have to remember this was 1940! This young man was coming from a backwater, and what was Ahmedabad then but a complete puro backwater – backwater without water – to CALCUTTA. And what was Calcutta? This city that all of you now sneer at, it was then the Paris of the East. There was nothing more cosmopolitan between Cairo in the west and Shanghai in the east. Madras? Full of Madrasis and that awful, ki boley? Carnatic music. Bombay? Parsees, Gujaratis, shopkeepers, money, the sea, nothing else. Karachi? Also sea, but full of Sindhis. Nice kababs I'm told, but what else? Lahore? Drunken Punjabis whether Hindu or Muslim, lying around in kothas trying to speak Urdu like Lucknawis. Some few very beautiful women, some poetry, bas. Delhi? A debased tradition in the rotting old town and a barren wasteland of government bungalows in the new part – nothing, no culture, but that too not even today they have any. The Ingrej may have taken their capital there but they could not take the Second City of the Empire with them. That stayed here. And into it, this then Cosmopolis, came your baba, Shri Mohadeb-bhai Bhawtt.'

The coolies splashed into the carriage as Mahadev began to wade out towards the second city of the empire. 'Samaan sahab?' 'Samaan, samaan samaan.' Four or five of them brushed past Mahadev looking for families because they usually had the most luggage. One old man reached for Mahadev's bedding. 'Samaan lelu sahaab?' Mahadev pulled the bistra back and reached for his meagre Hindi, saying, 'Nahi chahiye.' Then he looked through the window and thought again, by which time the old coolie had already picked up both the bistra and the little suitcase.

It was only when the man stepped down, out of the carriage and into the bellydancing carpet of green, that Mahadev realised how deep the water was. As he watched from the door, the man deftly balanced the suitcase on top of his head, slung an arm through the strap of the bistra and waded forward. A few feet away he stopped and turned around slowly, like a dancer with a pot on her head, and then looked at the young man as if to say, 'Are you coming?'

That image would always stay with Mahadev. Whenever someone mentioned 'Calcutta' in an abstract way, whenever Mahadev thought of Calcutta as a thing, he thought of the old coolie, his red tunic cut off at the waist by a sea of grey-green, hands in a delicate mudra holding the suitcase, looking at him in a question – 'This is the place. Are you coming, or are you going back to where you came from?'

Mahadev took in his breath, pulled up his dhotyu and tucked it into his waist under his kurta. Then he stepped down into the enveloping welcome of real jol and began to push his way along behind the coolie.

Around them Howrah Station was in chaos. Coolies' shouts bounced off the high roofs and collided with panicky calls from passengers before tripping over the metronomic chanting of the chai-wallas. Train whistles cut the crackling announcements in half before chasing off after engine smoke, up into the pelting rain. In the drive-way between platforms 8 and 9, an army truck, loaded with Englishwomen in drenched skirts and drooping summer hats, honked repeatedly as it bullied its way past porters' carts and stranded motorcars. And everywhere, over and under everything in this half-cut world, the mad orchestra of the monsoon. Rain drumming on the platform roofs, rain stitching into the flood water around the trains, rain sizzling on the hot skin of exhausted engines. Rain slapping on people's heads, making nonsense of umbrellas, turning tarpaulins porous, turning fingers into prunes, turning clothes into rags, walls into vertical fields of slithering moss, daylight into a dark grey there-was-never-a-morning-there-will-never-be-a-night smudge.

It took Mahadev and his coolie twenty minutes to reach the big hall at the end of the platform. For the last five of those minutes Mahadev had the feeling that he was wading in the same place. Then, suddenly, through the crush of people Mahadev could see the arches leading to the city outside. As the crowd pushed them to the right, the arches revealed the bridge, much closer now, its size and grace much clearer.

As they came out of the station, Mahadev felt something smooth slide across the outside of his right thigh, and then again something which touched both legs as it bobbed through between them. Mahadev took his eyes off the bridge and looked down to see himself surrounded by a small school of dead fish.

Before he left Ahmedabad, Mahadev's younger aunt Vinodamashi had given him several instructions. The last one had been 'As soon as you see the Ganga bow your head and do pranaam'. Mahadev had imagined himself doing pranaam standing grandly on top of the bridge, a great calm of river stretching before him. Now, looking down at the fish bobbing around him, the young man realised that the Ganga had come out to welcome him and he brought his hands together. Then he bowed his head as he had been told to and whispered out a small prayer.

'This is where the pickpocket must have struck. I mean, bhebe dakho, what could be a better target than this nice young Brahmon doing pronaam to a few kilos of rotting ilish? And mark two things – first, the water is from the river but it is not as if it has come over the bank, it has come up from some overflowing sewers, and two, the fish are probably from a bori that has burst while being loaded onto a truck, otherwise why dead?'

• • •

Kalidas placed the oddly familiar smell in the hut when Bose finished talking about the dolphins.

Through the day the old man had swayed in and out of consciousness, talking sometimes and at times just gesturing. Once he had focused on Kalidas and pointed to one of the desks. Kalidas obeyed instantly, went over to the jungle of papers and waited for further instruction. But Bose then just said one word: 'Podo!' Kalidas didn't know what he was supposed to read but when he looked down he saw the two clippings from *Izsvestia* and glanced over them very quickly. When he looked back up he saw that Bose had gone back into his dreams.

Once Bose had done a pranaam to one of his guards before muttering, 'Jo aap theek samjhe, Bapu.' Which Kalidas had deliberately mistranslated as, 'Whatever you think is correct, Father,' missing out that the only person Bose would have called Bapu would have been Gandhi, the Bengali word for father being 'baba' and not 'bapu'. Then, later, once again in his Bengali-accented Hindi he had snarled at Alexandrovich, 'Ponditji tum hamaara baat nehi samaajhta hai!' which Kalidas passed on as, 'Priest, you do not understand what I am saying,' again leaving out that the 'Pandit' in question would have been Nehru. And then again, after a lot of effort, a whisper that Kalidas had to lean forward to catch: 'O'r meyta ke watch koro. Dainjheraas.' 'Watch his daughter. Dangerous.'

By the time Bose began talking about the dolphins, Kalidas was exhausted. He had been ordered not to sleep and the only food they had eaten was a bowl of thick soup made with some foul-tasting meat. It was the middle of the night when Bose began to shake his head and moan. Mr Alexandrovich was sitting in a chair, looking fast asleep, but at the first sound his eyes sliced open.

The moaning became recognisable sound. Bengali this time.

'Prothomey, teente dekhlam, shudhu teente.'

At first I saw three of them, just three.

• • •

Three of them, then down, out, then three of them again, up out of the water in a cappella, a tripled curve, then down. Then more following, twinned, single, once five young ones bridging across the waves together, the sunlight a single wet rippling on their grey bodies.

They had left Kiel harbour twenty days ago, set sail at night and dived deep as soon as they passed the continental shelf. The Captain had ordered a steady slow speed, keeping the engines at a low hum to minimise the chances of detection on enemy sonar. The U-boat was not on attack patrol and the cargo it was carrying was precious – it didn't matter if the rendezvous was reached a couple of days late, but it was crucial that it was reached safely.

A line where the two oceans meet. The Atlantic a blue-grey, the Indian a dull green, Indian Ocean, his ocean, the dolphins crossing over the water border heading past both the boats. Heading east. His escort back east. His pilot cars.

The cargo had kept to himself after an initial tour of the submarine, reading his books and making notes in his tiny handwriting. Once, as they headed south past Portugal and the mouth of the Mediterranean, they passed under an enemy convoy and the Captain went himself and escorted Bose to the control room. He called him Herr Kommandant-Marschall, which was technically correct, because Bose was the Commander of the Azad Hind Fauj in Europe and about to become Commander-in-Chief of the Indian National Army on the other side of the world.

Sunlight slits his eyes after several days. The submarine a sadhu's gufa. Will they have a desk for him in the other one? The next leg of the trip would be longer. Singapore waits for you, SIR!

The Captain had no English but a translator had accompanied Bose as a bolster to his limited German and the Captain spoke through him.

'Does the Herr Kommandant-Marschall notice the mountains on the graph of the sonar?'

'Yes, what are those?'

'That, sir, is an enemy convoy protected by only two destroyers, which are the two little peaks on either side of the row. For me to pass them by without attacking is exactly like a tiger passing by a herd of plump cows. But I obey my orders with pleasure, Herr Kommandant-Marschall, and I know my counterpart on the Japanese submarine is at the moment doing exactly the same.'

'My apologies, Herr Kapitan, but you will one day have the gratitude of an entire nation for your self-restraint. After the war I shall arrange for you to go tiger-hunting *im Frei Indien!*' In his excitement Bose had tripped into German for the last three words – In Free India. 'You shall have a Bengal tiger as your medal.'

The Captain clicked his heels and smiled a wide smile through his beard.

'May I thank the Kommandant-Marschall for his generous offer.'

Standard procedure, first thing upon surfacing, sailors on both submarines take off the waterproof covers from the heavy machine-guns fixed aft of the conning towers. The Germans idly tracking the dolphins with the Spandau as they whip away across the water, surely the gunners just whiling time as dinghies ferry luggage and documents from one boat to the other. Surely that was all?

Except for once, when they had surfaced off the coast of Guinea-Bissau to let Bose have a look at the African coastline, the U-boat stayed under water till it reached the Cape of Good Hope. Once well south of the Cape shipping lanes, they made contact with the Japanese submarine on a pre-arranged frequency and fixed the exact point of meeting.

Another school appears far to the left, solid dots glistening in and out of the waves. The German machine-gunners see them too. The two captains standing next to him on the conning tower of the German boat, laughing. A German-speaking Japanese seaman translating. The rope of alternately soft and sharp Japanese colliding happily, twining around the guttural buoy of Herr Kapitan's Hamburgian German. The Japani notices the Spandau following the dolphins. Surely they would not?

That morning Bose awoke early and packed his suitcase himself. While packing he felt a strange joy, the joy of a man about to be released from jail. It was the same joy he had felt when he had packed his suitcase the day before his famous escape from house arrest in the house on Elgin Road.

From Elgin Road Bose had made his way to Kabul and from there, via Samarkand and Tbilisi, to Berlin. In wartime Germany he had been feted, wined and dined and given time by high officials of the Third Reich. He had met Mussolini and he had even met Hitler thrice – once at a formal dinner in Berlin and twice at his retreat, Berchtesgaden. He had been promised help to raise an army to fight the British, and indeed one had been raised for him from the Indian prisoners of war captured in Europe and Africa. Bose had stipulated that his soldiers would fight only against the Allied armies, not on the Russian front, not against the Soviets. This demand had been met and, for a while, Bose was satisfied. But something in him began to balk when reports of the first casualties of the Azad Hind Fauj began to come in from North Africa. He was at ease with the idea of losing one's life in order to free one's motherland. What he could not reconcile himself to was his soldiers dying, fighting somebody else's war on the other side of the world.

The Japani Captain takes the loudhailer from his German counterpart.

When the possibility came up of raising another army in the Pacific – from Indian troops captured by the Japanese – Bose became incredibly excited. It was what he really wanted. An army that would fight, directly, the Battle for India. An army that would cut across Burma and reach India through its north-eastern back door. Assam first, then East Bengal, then Calcutta and then the Gangetic plain and then Delhi. Dilli Chalo! Bose could think of nothing else.

'I WANT FRESH FISH FOR DINNER!' the Japani captain calls out to the sailors manning his machine-gun. The sailors look at their captain, take a couple of seconds to

comprehend, then do a quick double bow, 'Hai!', and train their gun on the dolphins. They find their aim and open fire. The Japanese gun has a high staccato like a sentence with underlined blanks.

Herr Kapitan laughs and calls out a command to his men. Something with the words 'Feuer' and 'Fisch' and the Spandau opens up a few moments after the Japanese gun. The German gun has a smooth rattle, deeper than the Japani gun, and the two chorus across the water. The Japanese aim at the nearer school while the Germans courteously try and catch the first school, which is now much further away, a much harder target.

Three of them, then down, out and then up and one is hit, the curve broken, cleaved in half, then another twisting in the air, then two at once, the blood making its own bridges over the sea, the ones coming behind, at first not understanding what was happening, then an adult knocking two babies down out of sight before catching bullets, flipping half-alive, churning up the sea surface, its tail slapping the water, thrashing left and right, left and right, till the gunner fires another burst to silence the sound. Sunlight rippling wet on still grey bodies. Sunlight on the blood as it spreads on the still sea.

'Shto? Wyot woz dat?' Alexandrovich chewed out the question.

'He is saying, "Blood on my water. Innocent blood on my sea." Something about fish.'

'He wants fish? To eat?'

'No, he can't eat this fish.' Kalidas leaves out the words 'Japani sabmereen'.

Bose was asleep in his armchair, the dream twisting his body under the blankets. Suddenly a guttural 'Hai!'. Then 'Ey ma!' then 'Ilish. Shorsher tel e ilish!'.

'Oh Mother. I want ilish in oil. Ilish is special Bengali fish.'

Alexandrovich shakes his head in exasperation but makes a note of this in the little book he has been writing in.

'Kono desh nei, shudhu ilish. Ilish abar pelaam na.'

'There is no country. Only ilish. I could not get ilish again.'

'Desh nei, shudhu maachh, shudhu maachh.'

'No country, only fish, only fish.'

Suddenly Kalidas places the smell.

'Paresh, it was mustard oil. Fish fried in mustard oil, but their fish, herring or something, strange ekta combination, sea fish and shorsher tel. They must have got special oil for him all the way from Bengal, but where to get ilish from?'

• • •

Nothing in the world smelled as wonderful as ghee on a hot bhakhri, thought Vaju as his mother put the thali in front of him. Vaju's cousin Mahadev had shown him drawings in some Inglish boys' magazine, things called flying saucers that were supposed to come from outer space.

'Look Vaju! Don't they look more like flying bhakhris?'

Mahadev was always a bit odd, but sometimes he said things that stuck in Vaju's mind and he could not shake them off. Ever since Mahadev had shown him the magazine Vaju had always thought of bhakhris as flying saucers. And since Vaju's mother made the best bhakhris and was the fastest in the whole family at making them, it did feel like they were flying in from her tawa, ekdum garam garam, puffed up, black at the edges, the ghee melting on the spotted surface like some strange, rich, atmospheric condensation. How plain flour could become this magic Vaju never could understand, but he was grateful for it, as he was for the daal and the finely diced dry potato shaak that competed with the daal for the attention of the bhakhris.

Sometimes Vaju would start with just a bhakhri, tearing it open to let the steam escape before putting a bit of it, unaccompanied by anything else, straight into his mouth. On other occasions he had a trick of dipping it whole into the daal before biting into it to get the taste of the daal, the bhakhri and the ghee, but with the lovely sting of the steam pushing the whole thing onto his tongue. Today he began straight, because he was hungry and he wanted it all. He broke open a bhakhri and took a piece of it to wrap around a bit of the shaak before dipping it into the scalding hot daal and bringing it up to his eager mouth. The symphony of taste exploded, sending Vaju into ecstasy. The sensation led to a feeling of deep love for his mother and from that love came, again, a feeling of the deepest gratitude for what she had just given him. He chewed on his food for a while before letting his gratitude speak.

'Sumu was there today, when Mahubhai woke up. They looked at each other,' he said.

When Vaju spoke, his mother was squatting next to the chulha with her back to him. Even before she turned her head, Vaju could tell he had made a very bad mistake. Tell just from the way her back went hard, just from the way her neck stiffened upwards. Then she turned and looked at him. Such was the effect of his mother's stare that Vaju, the next bit of bhakhri still in his hand, bit down on his tongue. Bit down so hard that he could taste blood.

An hour before Vaju told his mother, my father's sister Mrudula went to the mandir for the evening bhajans and, during a boring sermon on 'purity of the nation', informed her best friend, my mother's cousin Shantilekha, that Suman and Mahubhai were planning to run away and get married. This was a few months before my parents got the idea themselves.

My father's aunt was his aunt by marriage to his mother's brother. Bhupatmama ran the matrimonial affairs of my father's family because my grandmother was dead and my grandfather was too busy with his work to pay attention to these side matters.

In bed that winter night, my father's aunt gave her husband Bhupat Kumar a lecture on incest.

'Nanabhai is Mahu's father. Mohanbhai is Suman's father. They are second cousins. This marriage can't take place, it's mixing one's own blood with one's own blood. It will lead to deaf and dumb children. We are not some Muslims that we can encourage this.'

• • •

'All Muslims,' says the man, as they cross the Pakistani coast near Karachi. 'From now on, next four hours, all Muslims below us. Let's hope the guy doesn't have to crash-land.' The man snorts briefly at his own joke and then puts a finger up his right nostril and gouges around as if trying to get rid of some Muslim hiding in his nasal passages.

Viral looks around again for an empty seat elsewhere. Nothing. The jumbo is jampacked.

'Funny,' the man starts up again, still sniffing, 'you are Gujarati, I am Gujarati, can you smell athaanu? Are you carrying some your mom's pickle or something?'

Viral can't stand the accent. Part Charotar, part New Jersey is what it is, but Viral doesn't know that yet, all he can tell is that he is stuck till Frankfurt next to this nasal cocktail of Gujju English and some rancid American twang.

'Chhundo. But it's in the luggage,' says Viral defensively.

'Must be strong chhundo for me to be able to smell it up here,' chuckles the man, now wiping the nosed finger on the paper napkin the hostess has given him with his Scotch.

'Naah, it's not chhundo. Chhundo is sweet neh, this is more athaanu, kaink like, marchu ne limbu, you know, lime-chilli pickle?'

Viral knows. He gets up and goes to the toilet again. Inside, he takes his penis out and puts it over the edge of the sink. Then he uses both his hands to try and operate the hot and cold water switches together, trying to make sure this time that he doesn't scald himself or freeze himself. They have been airborne for an hour and this is the third time Viral has tried to wash the athaanu off. All through check-in, immigration and customs he has been in pain. There has been a circle burning around his cock and he has had difficulty walking, a difficulty compounded by carrying heavy hand-baggage.

There has been difficulty urinating, his cock burning from base to tip as the piss swells up against the veins. There has been difficulty looking at the Government Duty-Free shops – 'Make sure you buy some Black Label for Arvindkaka! We don't go empty-handed as guests,' his father has said to him, and with difficulty – the itching and the burning criss-crossing his crotch at the exact moment he shows his boarding card and pays out the precious dollars – Viral has bought a bottle of Johnnie Walker Black Label, the last thing his uncle in New York needs. Then there has been the difficulty looking at the TWA air hostesses.

He has tried to avoid thinking of Sandhya, but every now and then she has pushed past his guard, pushy ghaatan that she is, and stood before him, mother's green-gold sari, gold-coloured blouse, lipsticked mouth, hard, appraising, eyes. Once or twice he has felt her mouth on his cock and it has hurt, the erection carrying up the pain, the burning, the hard eyes.

Viral comes out of the cubicle thinking of Sandy and the aircraft shudders as if it's sharing his memories.

'Kaink bladder problem chhe?' asks the man solicitously. 'I get that sometime, you know, loose bladder when flying? I fly a lot in my work, domestic, within the US mostly, but a lot. Scary sometimes.'

'Achha?'

'Yeah. But *never* tell the guys you work with. These goras use it against you, you know, like, bhosadina, over a drink, boss ne keh, "You know, this Eendyun guy Parekh is chickunn, Parekh shits bricks when he flies, I'll take that job." Stupid, bhenchod, gora byaastards, you know? Supp-posed to be yor colleegs, you know. Never trust these goras.'

The gori air hostess comes along the aisle, sweeping up empty glasses as she passes.

'Rr you finshed with that, sirr?' and before the man can answer his little plastic glass is gone.

The man leans into Viral's ear, his whisky whispering loudly.

'Bhosadi bitch. But they all give, hawn? You have to know how to play it but aa baddhij aapey hawn, sooner or later. Dying for it, you know? And actually from us. Indian men somethin' special . . . one or two told me, maney actually kidhu, actually told me, ke we last longer . . .'

Viral looks out across the man, trying to look out of the window.

'Nothing down there buddy. Just desert and a whole lotta Muslims. Next three hours, forty-five minutes or so, you just furrgetbout it. I'll show you when there's somthin' to look at. Kaik jova-jevu bataadis, trust me.'

After a while, Parekh pulls down the window shade, pushes his paunch forward, undoes the top two buttons of his pants and then turns his head away from Viral and shuts his eyes. After a few minutes he begins to snore softly and it is as if he carries the whole plane to sleep with him. Suddenly, there is silence. Viral can hear the quiet throb of the engines over Parekh's snoring, over the rustling sleep of other passengers. People have pulled down shades on the windows. Here and there overhead spots light up the darkened cabin. Viral gets up and goes to the rear exit and looks out of the window. The plastic inner peel of the window shivers as if it's about to sheer off, but it doesn't.

Red mountains spread below the jumbo. It is the end of August and Viral can see that the snow has retreated up the slopes, just covering the peaks in little white caps. Sharp spines of rock work their way out from under the caps, hard, red-brown, dropping down to flatten out into barren valleys. A road in the lap of two mountains, a dark brown nail scratch across some face of flat land, straight, thin and insolent between two peaks. At one point a small cluster of brown industrial freckles on both sides of the road, buildings, a factory of lonely rectangles, then more mountains, the valleys gone, the lines of rock now talking to each other more directly, the dialogue between the flat and the steep ended, the jumbo shaking, sending a current up Viral's legs as it rises in response to the changes below it.

Strange mountains. Parekh's Muslims still camping in his mind, Viral suddenly connects the mountains with Id in Haji Ali and thousands of little white caps going down in namaaz. The sound of the sea at Haji Ali smudges into the hum of the jumbo's engines.

His mother's face at the airport waving goodbye turns into Sandhya's face as she gets into the lift to go back to her floor.

'Bye Viri. Bet delivered, okay?'

'Yeah. Will you write?'

'Viri, don't get senti now. I'll write if you write. Now GO now.'

'Sandy . . . that was . . .' The lift doors slide shut by the time he says 'great' and he is glad because that is a wrong and limited word.

At Santa Cruz Airport, his mother, Chandra Patel, regarded by many as the most sophisticated of hostesses, suddenly looking old, a fragility quite foreign to her pushing through the crowd of expressions on her face as he lifts his bag to go.

'Johnnie Walker Black Label for Arvindkaka! Samjhyo beta, remember!' says his father, cheerful, forceful, a Personnel Manager giving nothing away. His mom not crying but somehow . . . shaking.

'Have you got the money reachable, Viri-beta? Keep the money reachable,' is all she says, but it's not like her, people around her have never had to be told to keep the money reachable, it has always been reachable. The lime-chilli pickle suddenly burning, Viral realising that the boarding card was not just for him. It was also for the pickle of departure that was cutting him into two.

• • •

Later, Kalidas would keep feeling the hand on his left shoulder, as if it was still there, like they say about people who lose limbs. A cold hand, quite meek in its touch, but enough to tear him awake from his paper-thin sleep.

'Eijey chhele. Otho. Amaake jetey hobey.'

Kalidas almost started translating before he opened his eyes – Here, you, boy. Wake up. I have to go.

The old man stood above Kalidas.

Kalidas struggled out of his chair as fast as he could.

'Ser!' he said.

It was all he could get out. He almost saluted, but stopped himself in the nick of time. He could smell tea being brewed in the kitchen.

'Cholo. Bairey!' The old man's eyes were on fire behind the thick spectacles.

From the corner of his eye, Kalidas could see Alexandrovich standing in the kitchen doorway. For a moment, Kalidas was caught between the need to translate and the need to act. He gambled and went for the act.

'Ser,' he said calmly, and took the old man's hand. What would happen later would happen, for now he had to do what he had to do, which was to take Bose outside.

'Tomar coat ta porey nao. Naholey morey jabey.'

Bose took his hand away while Kalidas followed the great man's instructions and found his greatcoat and put it on. Coat and hat on, Kalidas received Bose's hand back on his forearm.

For months afterwards, Kalidas would feel Bose's left hand as if it was still there on two different parts of his body – his left shoulder would remember the light, asking touch that woke him up, and his right forearm would remember that last grip.

'Paresh! Ekdom vice-like. The moment outside door opens, I felt actual pain in my arm where he was holding me. It was his only reaction to the cold. At that time, I thought how is it possible for the same hand that was so timid just two minutes before to become so strong? He had a walking stick in right hand, left hand was on my arm, squeezing all blood from it, so tight, such strength, such . . . life!'

Outside, morning had broken. There is something that happens to light when it has to come fighting through extreme cold and Kalidas, later on in life, would go searching, go to the mountains, cross glaciers, looking for the light that he saw on the morning of 11 January, 1963. One day, while looking for that light, he would realise that he was also looking for the deep silence that went with it.

The old man's footsteps stuttered around the steady sound that Kalidas found himself making with his own boots. The snow had several layers. The first was almost fluff, light, the latest fall, the last trace of the blizzard just before it cleared up. It is what the ankles brushed aside when moving forward. Beneath the top layer was something more crunchy, the stuff they actually walked on. And under that was a hardness, ice almost, and Kalidas stepped lightly in some way, because he didn't want his boots to have anything to do with that slippery finality.

The old man was actually better than Kalidas at walking in the snow, it was just that he was so weak that it was difficult for him to balance. Every now and then Bose would slip a little bit and grab Kalidas's arm tighter. Then the grip would loosen, not a lot, and they would progress, a jointed contraption, precarious yet firm, two Bengalis catching the sub-arctic sun.

They walked around the compound twice, doing a pradakshina of the little hut, the only thing coming from Bose being his breathing and the Morse code of his grip tightening and lessening on Kalidas's arm. A little distance behind them, Alexandrovich followed with one of the guards, something stopping them from coming too close. On the third round, the old man looked up into Kalidas's face and asked, his thin voice loud in the silence, the Bengali making it seem even louder, 'How long have you worked for them?'

'I don't work for them, ser.'

'Then why are you here?'

Kalidas began to explain. The only thing that allowed him to speak to Greatness was the situation, the life and death of it, otherwise, whenever he thought of it later, Kalidas would shiver at the thought of addressing a legend with such ease. But his memory remained that of a young man trying to explain something gently to an elderly man on the verge of death. As Kalidas began to explain, Bose lost interest. Kalidas could not tell whether this was because the famously sharp mind had captured the facts very quickly and jettisoned the young man as being of no importance, or whether the last slide had begun and the old man was no longer capable of grasping anything outside himself and what concerned him directly.

'Tumi cigarette smuggle koreychho?'

'Yes ser.'

Bose broke off the circling around the hut. He suddenly found a self-sufficiency without Kalidas's arm and moved to the barbed-wire fence, looking at the sun. Kalidas stayed a little behind him. The Russians stopped where they were, about twenty feet away.

'*Die ich rief, die Geister* –' Bose looked over his shoulder at Kalidas, the wind making the glasses vibrate on his nose. 'Goethe podechho?'

'Aggey na ser, I am knowing a bit of Russian but I have never read German.'

'Faust. *Die ich rief, die Geister, werd ich nun nicht los.*'

'Ser?'

'Read Goethe's *Faust*,' commanded Bose and his head dropped like a bird's as he reached to unbutton his greatcoat. 'Ektu help koro,' was the second command.

A fumbling of four gloves, Kalidas behind Bose, no time to be embarrassed, his arms around the old man, holding him up with the side of his elbows while the gloves did what they needed to do. Kalidas felt the thin shoulder jamming into his chest, realised that the old man needed to urinate immediately and that he couldn't, not without help. His arms around Bose, Kalidas realised that he was holding the old man's shrivelled little penis on the tips of his gloved fingers. Bose's hands clutched Kalidas's arms for support.

'These –' Kalidas could feel the old man's body struggling to eject the urine.

'Those I called, these . . .' The voice subsided into a sigh.

As the urine finally began to spurt out Bose leaned back into Kalidas, his voice now orating.

'Those that I called, these ghosts,
I cannot now get rid of . . .'

Bose's penis jetted out the urine and it froze before it reached the ground, falling on the snow in small curved icicles, making a sound like branches cracking. The final curve was a long one and it froze in an arc which began between Kalidas's fingers and ended in the snow about three feet away.

Kalidas stared in amazement at the fragile bridge of frozen urine. It sparkled in the sunlight like a glassblower's mistake, a shard from a rainbow, stopping Kalidas from realising for a few moments that he was propping up a dead man.

• • •

Many years later, while lecturing his freshman class at Wharton, Viral would describe his first international flight as the 'Big Bridge'.

'. . . Now – ladies and gentlemen – you have to understand that this *thing*, this innocuous elephant, nothing more sinister than a wide-body civilian, passenger, jet aircraft, able to carry about three hundred people, *is* the one thing, the one man-made object, that is the principal instrument of change in our times – in the last third of the twentieth century. It is the one thing that has turned your world and mine topsy-turvy, upside *down*, more than television, more than the telephone, more than Bill Gates, and I know there are some of you who will howl in protest, but certainly, *certainly* more than rock and roll or the cinema.'

It was a well-practised lecture, but gripping nonetheless. It was called 'All That Is Solid Melts Into Air – a turbulence of technologies'.

The main title had two antecedents: first the original phrase, which was from Karl Marx, writing in the nineteenth century about modernity, and second the book by Marshall Berman of the same name, the title quoting Marx, in which Berman, an American literary theorist, examined the modern condition in the late twentieth-century West. Like a chopper using a heli-pad in enemy territory, Viral would take off from the heart of Marxian and Marxist critical theory and embark upon his journey into the future well-being of the multinational corporation.

Somewhere towards the middle of the lecture Viral would bring in the story of the first time he disembarked at a US airport. He would speak of what a moment that was for young men like him, young men and women from all over the world. He would vividly recall the sense of fear, of awe, of being torn from his moorings.

'While one was nervous, and possibly quite exhausted by the flight, there was a difference in reaching the US in this way – you were not a poor Mexican trying to crawl in under a border fence, neither were you part of a herd, just off the ship after seven or eight days, thrown into the terrifying mêlée at Ellis Island – you'd travelled in rather comfortable circumstances, air-conditioning, food, drinks, from the early '80s onwards you'd maybe even seen a movie on the flight or looked out of the window and seen half the planet pass under you in the space of hours. You had just crossed the Big Bridge, possibly the biggest bridge you would ever cross in your life – and the first time is the hardest, but also the most exciting – but you didn't have to do very much in order to cross it. You were better prepared to face what awaited you.'

Viral would talk eloquently about what awaited him at John F. Kennedy International Airport on that August day in 1979, but what he would not mention was the smell from the middle of his pants. He would make no reference to Parekh – whom he'd managed to lose during the changeover at Frankfurt, and who found him just where the signs began to bifurcate the arriving passenger flow.

Two blue signs with white lettering. One that said 'US Citizens Only'. And the other that said 'Non-US Citizens'.

Parekh breathed out a mixture of stale whisky and paan, temporarily wiping out the smell of the pickle which still rose up from below.

'Okay, boss. Awhey good luck, hawn? Remember –' Parekh leaned even closer, making Viral lean back slightly, 'remember, aapdey loko t̂o aalokona *modha* ma mutariye,' then his voice dropped into a whisper as he did a rough translation, just in case Viral hadn't understood, 'Us Indians, specially Gujaratis, you know, we can piss in these people's mouths, okay? Okay, I gotta go, or I'll miss the shuttle to Newark, so good luck.'

Parekh then gave Viral a friendly jab in the stomach and turned away towards the corridor marked 'US Citizens Only'. After a few steps he turned and called out, 'I'd give you my phone number but, you know, I'm a busy guy and I wouldn't really be able to help you out or anything if you needed help, okay?'

Viral nodded, his ability to speak slaughtered by the vision of Parekh, his dick smelling of Gujarati pickle, pissing into an American's open mouth.

In the lecture, Viral Patel would talk about the excitement of approaching the immigration officer with his passport.

'It was . . . like bungee-jumping. You had a cord, yes, but you didn't know if it would hold. You had to take the dive. And when you came through there was an exhilaration that is hard to describe.'

What Viral would not talk about in the classroom is the look the man gave him, his face mostly obscured by the reflection of the parked aircraft on the plate glass of his booth. In a shadowy part of the reflection he could see the man's eyes, flicking down to the passport and then back up at him, then down and then back up. What Viral would tell a girlfriend, many years later, was, 'There was a kind of, I don't know, a kind of "Shit, this sonofabitch is gonna get past me, I ain't got nothin' on him" kind of look, you know, kind of like a deer-hunter missing at point-blank range with his last bullet on the last day of the season?'

Through all his teaching, Viral would never mention moving from the hard stare of the immigration officer to the sneer of the customs officer though it was Viral's first genuine, twenty-four-carat, Brooklyn, New York, Italian sneer.

'Whawchyugawt in there buddy? C'mawn, tell me! I ain't got all day.'

'Er . . . nothing, sir, just some clothes and some books. One or two presents.'

'One or two *prresents*? Nuttin' else, huh? What? None of your mother's pickle stuff?' and then, without waiting for an answer, turning to the man next to him, 'Am I smellin' somethin' weird here or am I smellin' somethin'?'

The second customs man was middle-aged, black, large. He nodded slowly, as if receiving difficult instructions on an invisible telephone.

'You smellin' somethin', I'd say.' A growl that came out of a nod.

'Uh, yes, I am carrying two jars of pickle, it's only like a jam kind of thing –'

'*Jam* kind of thing!' said the black guy and laughed a laugh like a steamroller reversing fast. The word 'jam' seemed to send him into another world and Viral could not understand why.

The Brooklyn Italian was unmoved.

'No dwugs or anythin' hunh, my friend?'

'Oh no sir!' Viral now in terror.

'Whywoudjya need 'em? Mamma's pickle smells like it'll do it for ya.'

'Whooo! Yeh!' nodded the black man, all trace of humour suddenly gone.

The two customs men looked at each other significantly while Viral waited to be told what to do next. Then the Brooklyn guy's eyes caught a young woman standing behind Viral in the queue.

'Anything to declare, miss?' he called out to her. Viral wondered if he was being asked to wait.

Brooklyn suddenly noticed him again and Viral realised he had been dismissed even before the man snarled at him.

'Woouldjya please move on, sir? You're blawcking the queue.'

Outside, the adrenalin that had welled up inside him slammed into a wall of clammy heat and made him reel. For a moment he panicked. Had he gone up, circled around for twenty hours and landed right back in Bombay?

A voice brought him back to his senses.

'Nickelbag, dimebag. Nickel bag, dime bag. Ta-ake your pick!'

Viral looked at the man and the man gestured downwards with his eyes. Viral looked down and saw the man holding two little packets of something wrapped in cellophane. They reminded him of the quack medicine-sellers who prowled Chowpatty beach in the evenings. The last thing he needed just now was some home-made aphrodisiac.

'Uh, no thank you. Could you direct me to the taxi stand?'

The man looked at an imaginary companion.

'Polite boy! *No Thank You* he sez! Could you di-*rect* me, he sez! Hey man? Don't you know what this is? This is Sens man! Real genuine Sens! You missin' out!'

Viral began to move away from the man. Later, he would wonder why a man with dirty blond hair and spotted pink skin had a black-sounding accent. At that point he just said, 'No thanks, I don't need incense. There's plenty where I come from.'

The man doubled up with laughter as Viral moved towards the row of yellow cabs that he'd spotted. Then the man straightened up and limped his way over to another man standing a little distance away, gesturing to him to come closer so's he could tell him the joke and pointing to Viral and doubling up again.

The cab driver rolled down his window.

'Where to?'

'It's 347 East 64th Street. Please, how much will that be approximately?'

'You talking East 64th, Manhattan, right?'

'Uh, yes, New York.'

'Manhattan, Upper East Side, you talkin' sixteen to eighteen dollars depending on the rush. And about five more for the luggage. You got the money?'

Viral calculated 18 + 5 = 23 plus 10 more in case the guy created some trouble. He had it, plus another 2, 35 dollars, kept aside exactly for this. He'd get more from Arvindkaka once he reached their apartment.

'Yes, yes, I have the money.' Keep it reachable, his mother saying.

The taxi driver drove silently and fast, the radio on low. It was evening when they left the airport and by the time they got out of Long Island it was dusk.

The lamp-posts on the parkway were a strange yellow colour, quite different from the dim green tubes on Marine Drive and much brighter.

The lights whipped by rhythmically, flashing the inside of the taxi as it passed under them. A slight breeze squeezed in past the air-conditioning, coming in from where the driver had kept the window open a crack to let his cigarette smoke escape. Through the half-open glass partition Viral could hear the murmur of the radio and the meter on the right of the dashboard clicking on, big black numbers set against curving strips of white, with a little lamp over them so's the passenger could see. After a while, the driver suddenly switched off the radio and pushed open the glass partition fully.

'Where you from?' he asked.

Viral was startled by the question, wary of all the traps he had been told New York was capable of springing on you. Was this one of them?

'I'm from India,' he replied cautiously.

'Thought so,' said the man, 'figured you were either Indian or Pakistani.'

'Not Pakistani,' said Viral, too firmly, a slight trace of offence creeping into his voice despite himself, 'I'm from Bombay.'

'Bombay?' the taxi driver laughed, 'but that's not India, my friend, I'm told that's a whole another country. Just like this town ain't America.'

'That's true, you're right.'

'So what do you reckon? Think she'll make it back?'

'Uh, what?'

'Indeeracandy, think she'll get back into power? I mean this old guy, this guy who, like, drinks his own piss, is that right? Think he can hold her off?'

Viral was startled. He had to make an effort to get back into that world. The cab driver didn't wait for an answer.

'I mean, y'know? Talking about piss, did you ever hear that joke about Harry Truman? About him having guys who hated him on his cabinet, and when someone asked him why, he said, "Because I'd rather have the bastards inside the tent pissing out, than outside the tent pissing in." Now, it sounds to me like your man, what's his name,

DeSize, Day-sigh?, sounds to me like he's got a problem – he's got guys *inside* the tent, but they're *still* pissing *in*!'

Viral burst out laughing, as much in surprise at the taxi driver's knowledge as at what the man was saying.

'You know a lot about India,' he finally managed.

'Ye-aah. We got radio, see? Driving all day, ain't much you can do 'cept listen to the radio. Now you have a choice. You can listen to shit, you know, wall-to-wall Barry Manilow, or you can tune in to one of the better news stations.'

'Good news stations here in America?'

'No, no, not in *America*, in New York. Out there . . . out there –' the man poked a finger at his windshield but he was obviously pointing over New York to the darkening continent that lay beyond the city, 'out there they know *nothing*. And they're workin' hard on knowing even less.'

The parkway rose under the car. Suddenly there was a crowd of highway signs passing over the taxi like guillotine blades waiting to fall – Manhattan, the Bronx, Queens, Brooklyn Bridge, Newark, Rochester.

'This your first time here?'

'Yes, this is my first time.'

'You seem like a nice guy, so I'm gonna give you a chance, I'm gonna warn you.'

The driver looked over his shoulder and smiled wickedly at Viral.

Viral's knees suddenly felt heavy.

'Warn about wh-what?' he stuttered out.

'About what you are about to see. What you are about to see is very, uh, very *seductive* at first sight, but beware.'

'I don't understand.' Viral was now really scared. He looked at the door handles to see if they'd mysteriously fallen off. No, they were still there. The driver continued, obviously enjoying himself.

'I only warn people I like, and I like you. You seem like an intelligent young man. Do you know what a gulag is?'

'It's like a concentration camp? A Russian concentration camp?'

'Eight out of ten, buddy. It is a *Soviet* concentration camp – the czars had the idea first, but they never managed those economies of scale – my family lost a couple of people there . . .' the man paused to light another cigarette, 'look, if you like, I'll turn around and take you right back to JFK, no charge, but if we proceed I must warn you, you will be entering a zone that is very difficult to get out of. It is . . . a concentration camp of the mind.'

'I thought we were going to Manhattan?'

The cab crested the slope and before them, on the other side of the river, danced the most famous skyline in the world.

'Indeed we are. Look at that stuff. You still want to go there?'

'Yes, er, yes please,' said Viral leaning forward, pushing his paunch back and staring through the windshield at the photograph he had seen so many times before – Manhattan at night.

'Okay my friend, you've been warned. Let's go.' The driver took the exit for the Williamsburg Bridge.

As they crossed the river, he glanced back at Viral again before looking away. 'Welcome to the gulag,' he said cheerfully.

December 3, 1985

Bhopal meeting today.

This one woman – what she said.

And then this Andolan guy saying it was like a Nazi gas-camp – literally like Auschwitz or Dachau except the gas-chamber was bigger, like a whole city turns into a gas-chamber. This woman talking first – telling us about that night and I couldn't stop crying. Aarti helped me control.

Now I just feel anger, like cold, cold, cold anger. (Ya, so what you gonna do babe? Walk out on Ai and Dad?!!!!!)

One year today, one whole year gone and this bastard Government's done sweet FA.

Okay, it happened right after IG's assassination and some of these Rajiv supporter types went around saying – Oh bichara, poor guy, his mother's just been killed so give him some time – but now it's a whole year and it looks like him and all his management pals in the Cabinet are going to do bloody Zilch.

This woman (name I think Jahanara Begum?) she said it without showing much on her face, just very calmly, I don't know where she got her calm from (Learn! Learn how!) – ki Rajiv, ki he may be the pilot of the plane of the country but he should not forget that he is also sitting in a larger plane, that of the world and that has a different Captain. "Yeh duniya ka pilot Khuda hai aur unko ek din wahaa jaake report karnaa padega ki unhone kya kiya, kya nahi kiya." Doesn't sound the same in english, but still I kept trying it out – "Allah is the pilot of the world and he will one day have to go and report to Him, what he did do and did not do."

Also, besides what RG did/did not do, she said he should remember what happened to his brother and his mother . . . they had all the power in the world but still they were taken. Just like That. Just like us.

Came back home – don't know how – could barely drive. Don't know how I saw the bloody traffic through the tears. Aarti saying Sandy slow down, slow down, getting us killed won't help anyone. "Total Irrational!" – as Dad would say – but feeling that getting killed is better than this feeling that you can't do anything.

Sitting here in my nice room. I can see the sea. Put on Joni Mitchell tape that Viri sent. Was hoping it would calm, but nothing works, nothing. Just switched it off.

Aarti says it's a common phenomenon, when rich-shits get a bamboo of conscience up theirs, she calls it "de-rooting".

I feel de-rooted, oh yes, tonight feel de-rooted alright.

Dec 5, 1985

Went down to call Mom from the Patels' coz upholstery-walla came. Some material for sofas. Something – when I walked into that house. Suddenly remembered again ki Patel Uncle was in Union Carbide. Saw this f-ing plaque, or whatever you call it his staff had given him when he retired. Nearly threw up on P aunty's nice new Ahuja carpet. Should have. Should have. But didn't. Used my rich-shit control and controlled myself.

Remember the night after it happened last year and everybody had only vague information, Patel uncle knew more than others. Remember P uncle very drunk – coming up to talk to Dad – late night in his pajama-kurta – Dad and Ai almost in bed. Sat down in drawing room like he was going to be there for a long time. When Dad came out P uncle sez, "Sunil, Sunil, there should be somewhere a memo I wrote. Believe me. When they started the plant, I told them workers' safety should be, had to be, taken into account Sunil!" And Dad saying in his Firm and Final voice "Narendra it is not your problem. You were Personnel, this is the Engineers. Their problem!" and P uncle saying "Sunil, am I first and last an Engineer or not? What am I? What is my degree from MIT? It is not Personnel Management. First and last I am a Chemical Engineer, you know! When I first started in Carbide in '53 for five hundred rupees a month it was a good salary and an honourable job. We built it in India as engineers. Chemical Engineers!" and then starting to shake like he was freezing or something and Dad pouring him another Scotch. And Ai saying "Narendrabhai it is not good for Chandra for you to be like this. You stop it now. It has nothing to do with you, you retired five years ago." And Dad with his logic coming out with a top card. That when P uncle had retired, the Bhopal factory was not under him. "You may be an Engineer but you did not design that plant." Guess that's what P uncle wanted to hear coz he went home happy and he's never mentioned the Bhopal word again.

So, nobody's problem. Just like Germany. Not the train driver's. Not the architect who made plans for the death camps. Not the soldiers who rounded them up from the ghettos. Not Marketing's problem. Not Personnel's problem. Not Finance's problem. Not P uncle's problem. Nothing that kept Dad awake at night. Or Ai. Nobody. Some Carbide CEO, Warren Anderson, some shit who could run back to his Country Club. His problem but also actually, really, not.

My problem? Is it?

Dec 24, 1985

All day out at Senapati Chaal talking to the women. Amazing understanding. We didn't even need to finish our talk before they were talking, asking questions. Talk about seeing the ball early, these women . . .

Thought it was stupid to try and go into too much detail about WHY Bhopal affected everyone but didn't say anything. Aarti would have bulldozed so kept shut. But these women – they knew from their own factory, just knew it. Like what it would have been like. When Aarti was talking about the smaller children in the affected areas one woman didn't say anything – just held up her baby. Just held it up – two month old baby coughed. She just let us hear the coughing and then she put baby back on her breast like putting a knife away without using it and just looked at Aarti. There was in her eyes a "what are you telling me? I know!"

That shut me up, inside and outside both.

It's impossible to talk to A about these things. Coz A doesn't see.

Ai's shouting outside the door about some new sari she's got me.

Party tonight at Abhay's. Don't want to go. Don't want his creepy hands on me. Don't want his creepy corporate anything anywhere near me anymore.

No. Think will go. And say bye around midnight and leave. Time to get this finished. Tear up the contract, so to speak, do a demerger between Mathur and Agarkar – he should understand that, if I put it that way.

Think I'll wear that little shirt, silk black one. And the tight Levis. No need to make it easy for anyone.

Dec 25, 1985, 5 a.m.

Diary, diary,

Wake up! Listen to me! I'm back.

Demerger completed. Almost didn't, almost hesitated – but in the end did it, just fut-ttack!

Ain't you proud of me baby? I finally dumped the son-of-a-bitch.

Wanna know how it happened? I'll tell ya anyway.

Once I got there I thought ki I'll leave early and write AM a note like today–tomorrow–day after. Then I met this guy who I really used to like a while back, friend of Viri's called Paresh from Calcutta. Paresh Dave or Paresh something Gujju or the other – on a trip here and knew someone who knew Abhay so he'd come to the party. He's still kind of quiet, doesn't say much, nice guy, not too cute or anything but tallish and okay-looking. I used to like him before Viri left for the States but then never had any contact after V took off. Anyway, so he said hello and at first I couldn't recognise him in the dark and then I recognised him. He's a photographer now. He's sort of grown up a bit from eighteen. (Guess we have too, DD. Quarter century already approaching, no?)

Anyway, we were on the lawn sort of chatting and looking at the sea and AM kept coming up and asking me to dance and I kept saying no. He doesn't see how much like a boss he sounds, trying to manage something, nothing in what he actually says – "Sandy! This one?" you know, but it's like an order. So I kept saying no, no, no. Then one bad Madonna number came on and he came up again and this time he went for Paresh. "Hey listen man, do you mind leaving my girl alone?" and I thought this poor guy, but he didn't take it like a "poor guy" at all. Ya, no, at first he didn't know what to say, then he just said, "No, I don't mind at all." But, you know, he didn't move. I'm here, she can go if she wants, like.

I went with AM, just to avoid a scene – idiotic Agarkar! – but Abhay didn't know what to say after that. It was just a very clear "I am not holding her here by force and you're a fool for doing what you're doing", all said without saying. But like no-nonsense tone also, like – "Why blame me if the girl doesn't want to dance with you?" And if that was bad what happened on the floor was like the worst.

First there was this lousy Madonna tune and AM kept trying to close-dance when it was a fast number. Then some Wham number that was slower and I kept moving his stupid hands away from me but he didn't get it – thought I was playing hard to get or something – kept grabbing with this stupid smile on his face. Then the song finished and the DJ got brave and put on the Stones – Jumpin' Jack Flash. And I was almost starting to have fun, coz it's a good track and even AM couldn't try close-dancing to that one. Then they switched on the smoke-machine and the song was going, you know, gasgasgas. And one bastard, one of AM's pals from Siemens or somewhere, shouts "Hey, Abhay! Where's that Bhopal Victim Sandy?" and then he comes and falls down near me and starts to pretend-choke – croaking "Bhopaal! Bhopaal!' and everybody took this up and started to choke and fall down and bloody f-ing AM found this very funny and began to act out this choking too. And that was it. DD, that was IT.

DD, he was on his knees in front of me, looking at me and laughing with his hands on his throat going "GasGasGas" and I gave him one jhaapad, tight one straight one, straight on the face – yeah in front of everyone – and my hand still hurts but I like it, this hurting. And I walked off. No words. No words. One Slap. He fell over not believing it. And before I knew it I was outside opening the car door.

Suddenly I hear this guy's voice. Er Sandy, which way are you going? Maybe, can I get a lift? And I turned and saw this Paresh character. I'd almost forgotten about him. So I said Nepean Sea Road and he said he needed to get to Altamount, so I told him to get in. He too looked glad to get out. Said so actually, after we were out of the gates.

Talked on the way back and it was nice. He's studied Photography in America and was getting work there but decided to come back. Now he's Cal-based but travels a lot to shoot. Didn't seem that interested in money – which makes for a nice change in this town I tell you. Also earlier he'd sounded kind of surprised when I told him about me working with the women. So in the car I asked him about that. Maybe I was a bit aggressive – don't know – you know me – sed to him something like "So you imagined I'd grow up to be just another rich bimbo, huh?" And he smiled and didn't say anything. Then I poked him again and he says "well . . . you always were good-looking and I guess your family's not exactly poor . . . so it might have been possible for you to go the rich bimbo route, no?"

"Possible for you to go . . ."!!!??? This was not like he'd been talking before so what was all this cautiousness, like suddenly? Pompous ass. Or actually nervous-pompous. I looked at him and I was almost sure he blushed. Then it was I realised he was getting a bit tongue-tied – which was cute. Could have pushed it more but I let it be coz it was nice the way it was. Coz he doesn't have these eyes that you expect. I mean earlier I could see that he noticed the black shirt and jeans and all, but it was okay. There were other things he noticed too, like when I told him what I was doing. I wasn't just a chick in tight pants. He listened.

Maybe that's just his trick but still – like him.

Also I still like him like him.

Though you know, after tonight, anyone could have looked subtle compared to Abhay f-ing Mathur. Maybe that's all. But all the way back from Bandra we talked about Bhopal and he saw the scene on the dance floor and it got him angry too. I asked him were you dancing? And he said I don't dance.

Feel like I want to make him.

Dec 28, 1985

DD! DD! He *does* dance! Only he doesn't know it.

He came with me to the Century Mills chaals today. I was talking to the Purshottam Gali women and later there was a meeting and like he'd said he took some photts. At first tˆo he just disappeared. Don't know how to explain it but I was talking to Saraswati Tai and he was there, taking photographs, and then he like just blended into the scenery and I basically forgot he was there. Then he came up behind me and asked something and I gave a jump. Nothing creepy but – don't know how to put it – like he had some quiet blanket wrapped around him so you didn't really notice him.

Later in the evening he gave me some high funda theory about how many people have a problem with that kind of photography. Something about "the photographer should be seen" and you should know who is photographing and why and where they stand . . . too much. Some shit about this new jargon – all this Post-Modernism. Sounds like management-speak, like everything can be explained in every way, just depends on what mood you are in at that moment. Me, I had no problems with someone not being loud and pushy and shoving everyone around to get some "great" picture. Other men photo-wallas I know are generally like that.

Anyway, DD, I saw him dance.

What happened was a fight broke out between two chaal women and this Textile Union guy. And they were shouting and the Unionwalla was shouting – like happens – and P began to move around them clicking and it was amazing. Diary, he moved exactly like a dancer – very still one time – and then like a cat he's slinking up to perching somewhere, then he's down on the ground squatting down, then just like standing just behind the Union guy like he's his sidekick and getting a shot of the women waving their fingers at him. His moving – you could put music to it.

Of course, I haven't seen the photographs yet!

Maybe all this is just show-sha and he is a shit photographer. That's what I told him later, when we went to Naaz for a beer – didn't want him to think I was giving him too much bhaav, like.

And Diary? Are you listening? Listen, this guy's a bastard, okay? You know what he says? He thinks like deep thought and nods and says "yeah, like I have no idea if you're any good at singing." Bastard, no? Doesn't go for my work, I mean he can't, he's seen me do it and he's said that the women really seem to trust me so he can't. Wish I hadn't told him about the singing. Then he really does it, he says "anyone learning from a direct shishyaa of Hansabai Joglekar, I suppose one would expect a lot from . . ." This, you see, is in reply to me being nasty about his States' training when I said "I don't know about all this America-Shamerica, Paresh, I want to see it in the photographs, all your training." Maybe I shouldn't have said that. Last thing he says as I drop him off at his aunt's is "I'll show you the photographs if you let me hear you sing." Like hell, you Gujju bastard, no deal. I'd rather die first.

Diary, I haven't told you till now, but I asked him. He has a girlfriend in Cal, some bengali Brain-type, some Sociologist egg-head who understands all this Post-Modern bullshit theory-sheory . . . Diary, what do I do?

Gulag Ranchhodlal

As I grew older I stopped believing many things my parents told me. At some point I started doubting many of their stories, stories that I used to love as a child. Some of the stories remained, useless but treasured, like heirlooms you hang on to for sentimental reasons. Some disappeared, forgotten or barely remembered, their clarity scraped off by the sandpaper of passing years. Others I made up, for Para, for my own sanity, for the sake of having a complete picture, a virtual pillow I could sometimes rest my head on. A few things my parents told me survived, built houses in my head, became more real as time passed, became the bannister to support me whenever I took the fragile staircase to the past.

For instance, I still believe my parents loved each other with all the passion in the world, at least until the time I was born. I believe their love for each other was strong, very strong, for instance at the time in 1952 when my mother caught her flight to Calcutta to secretly marry my father.

Every time I think of that flight, I imagine two predators stalking my mother's Vickers Viscount, two Second World War fighter-planes with shark's teeth painted on their engines, their airscrews whirring, pointy noses blood-red, one piloted by Fear and the other by Worry, both from the Future Squadron. And I imagine my mother oblivious to them, her love keeping her airborne, the discovery of flight, the thrill of it, banking into the greater adventure she had embarked upon. Sometimes I feel sure

I'm wrong in this. There must have been doubts, the gravitational pull of hesitation. Despite the little picture of Krishna she was carrying in her purse, she must have heard the different pitch of single engines, their contrary sound gnawing into the throb of the Viscount's four turbo-props. I know there was a lightning storm somewhere above Bihar because she told me, and she must have been scared, even though she always denied it. She must have slept, fitfully, and she must have had dreams.

'Pappa?'

'Hm.'

'Mon père? M'sieur Père-eche?'

'Para, *what?*'

'Did Dadaji ask Ba to marry her?'

'Yes. Twice.'

Yes, at one point, Mahadev Bhatt asked Suman Pathak to marry him. It was a hot day in late August 1939 and time was running out, not just for the world but also for a nineteen-year-old boy and a sixteen-year-old girl. Time would run out for both them and the world. And time would then reinvent itself, reappear like some clown Dracula, rise out of its coffin with bits of dhokla, shrikhand and human flesh hanging from its fangs. The blood of vampired empires smearing its cheeks, burping nations and lovers, it would come out again, time, with the hunger for more polishing its eyes into a deadly shine.

Between her saying no to my father and finally agreeing to marry him, thirteen years would go by, the longest thirteen years my mother could have imagined, thirteen years that my mother would spend in her first prison – the concentration camp that was Ahmedabad.

By that year of 1939, Ahmedabad had spilled well over the walls of the original fort that gave the town its name. It had grown so much, in fact, that the fort walls had already become no more than a mere tracery of the old defensive conceit, submerged now in the static deluge of houses and mills and market areas.

Across the Sabarmati River, new colonies had already begun to appear, low bungalows with gardens, straight roads, the occasional lamp-post, all surrounded by barren land dotted with dry brush. These new Societies were the seeds from which, in time, would grow the gargantuan business cosmopolis of the twenty-first century, the glutton city that would swallow the fall-out from both Bombay and Karachi. That would come. But old Ahmedabad was, at that time, still a small town hiding from the desert that had threatened it many years ago. It was also, in a sense, a town hiding from itself.

Both my parents lived in Hajira ni Poel. Like other poels, Hajira ni Poel was also a jigsaw-puzzle of interlocking houses. A maze, where a public route from one point to another could, for example, start from the lane, go up a short flight of steps, bisect the dark womb of someone's house, past the half-light of somebody's else's ohtlo, through the beam of sunlight coming through yet somebody else's courtyard, through the ink-black shadow of another lane and out into the hard bright light of an open chowk, after crossing which you walked into yet another dark knot of galis and khanchas. It is, to my mind, the worst place in the world for two people to fall in love. But my parents, having had no alternative model, did not know that.

On that hot day in August, Mahadev made his way from Hajira ni Poel to his cousin Nalin's house in Vaanka Kaka ni Poel. Nalin let him in without a word. Mahadev went up the narrow wooden stairs to the second floor. He went into the dark anteroom and climbed up the ladder to the wooden trapdoor that opened onto the roof. He unlocked the heavy padlock that secured the trapdoor, pushed the slab aside and climbed up into the naked glare of the afternoon sun.

Just as there was an intricate web of lanes in the poels below, the tops of the houses in old Ahmedabad made up another world, a roof-world, quite different in sound and smell from the streets. Slopes of corrugated tin butted up against old cement. Narrow pathways went around the square gorges which opened the centre of each house to the sky. The only protection against the forty-foot drop into someone's kitchen were the rickety low railings, the wood chewed into by the combination of sun and rain, the brass joints shaken loose by the wind, the rusty nails barely managing to keep the rotting wood in some mimicry of what it was supposed to be.

The year before, during Uttarayan, a young nephew of Mahadev had crashed through a railing while chasing a kite. The year before that a policeman had gone over during a raid in Raja Mehta ni Poel. That time the police were chasing Batukbhai, the man in charge of Mahadev's cell. Batukbhai had managed to escape but the policeman had slipped on chillies drying on a sheet of cloth. Suman and Mahadev had themselves escaped over the roofs three times, carrying diaries, illegal newspapers, and once a small sack with something in it that could have been a gun.

That day, though, in August '39, Mahadev wasn't worried about the police of the British Empire, he was worried about a different system of surveillance. As he stepped carefully over the hot tin, Mahadev kept an eye out for the foi-mashi vigilantes, the eagle-eyed network of aunts that could be far more dangerous than any policeman or informer. He needn't have worried. The hot sun had driven even the most ardent pickle-maker to her siesta and the roofs around Nalin's house were deserted.

Mahadev worked his way around the railings, careful not to lean on them for support. He climbed up a steep slope of tin and crossed over a low cement barrier at the very top. From there, he slid down into another terrace and reached a small turret of a room. This was where the cell kept some of the printed material and it was a safe room, in that its door was hidden from other roofs and windows by a wall on one side and some piled-up old furniture on the other. Mahadev unlocked the room and squatted down in the shade of the doorway to wait.

After about ten minutes he heard the tapping noise he had been waiting for. He got up and went around the room to the narrow ledge that stuck out behind. This was the most dangerous part of the operation. The ledge looked over a very narrow lane, the gap only about four feet wide but the fall still many feet below. Across the ledge was a roof that was lower by a few feet, and Suman had to take a little run up to gain the momentum she needed to cross the chasm of the lane. Going back was easier, because of the height, but Mahadev had to be there on the ledge to catch her whenever she came to the room. It was a moment he looked forward to because it was the only time she ever came into his arms.

Suman looked across at Mahadev and smiled. She always did that before starting her little run down the slope of the roof. Once he had asked her why and she had replied, 'In case I fall. I want you to remember me smiling.'

Today Mahadev did not return her smile, he just nodded that he was ready. Suman came down the slope in a patter of small steps and pushed herself off the roof.

On the first airplane flight she ever took, Suman Pathak would dream of the moment when she hung for a second over the narrow lane, the moment when the world would go silent, the moment before her body came slamming up against Mahadev's, the eternal moment before his arms locked around her, holding her tight, kick-starting her heart back to life.

'Why did Ba say no the first time?' Para asks, chewing her question out through a bite of croissant and blackberry confiture. Magali looks up from her newspaper and backs the question by lighting a cigarette.

'Yes. Why did your mozzer say no?'

In five minutes Para will leave for her summer painting class. I will lean out of the window and watch her saying hello to her friends as she gets into Alain's car in the narrow street below. I will keep watching till the car joins the flow of traffic on Rue St Antoine. Then I will go into the kitchen, walk though the smell of coffee and Magali's cigarettes and open a cupboard. I will reach up to the top shelf and bring down the packet of condoms. Magali will keep reading her newspaper, keep sipping her coffee, as if all this has nothing to do with her. I will get down on my knees in front of her and push up the long t-shirt she is wearing and part her legs. The smell of coffee will make way for another, darker, aroma. The first time the tip of my tongue rakes across her, Magali will arch her back slightly, but carry on reading. After a while her hand will fall on mine, which will probably be on the outside of her thigh. Then, just as I begin to get through to the taste of her, she will put her coffee cup down on the floor, get rid of her cigarette and grab my hair with her other hand and push hard against my mouth.

I've got my timing down pretty well and I will probably manage to enter Magali while she's still coming. That's what we've been doing for the last few days, but, suddenly, I'm not sure that that's what we will do today. Though I've told her the story twice, I have still not managed to explain to Magali the centre of my mother's 'no'. It is as difficult to explain to her as it is to Para even though, at twenty-eight, she is sixteen years older than my daughter. I love many things about Magali – though I'm not in love with her – but I hate the way her mouth touches Suman Pathak when she says 'your mozzer'.

My mother said no because she was the only one earning money in her family. She was the only support for her widowed mother, her useless brother, his wife and their children. She said no because their elopement would cause a scandal, not just in the two immediate families Bhatt and Pathak but in the entire Bhatt-Mewada naat. My mother said no because she didn't want to ruin another woman's life. My mother said no because – no, it's no use.

Years later, late one night when I came home after seeing Ila, my mother heard me trying to shut the door quietly. I thought she was asleep on the sofa so her words caught me in the knees. '*I wish I had said no the second time.*' At first I thought she was talking in her sleep but she hauled herself up and shook her head as if trying to clear some fog, still trying to retrieve a 'no' from the wrong 'yes', and stared at me and hissed, there is no other word, hissed.

'I wish I had held on to my no. If I had known what was to come, that you were the son I was to be blessed with, I would have never have said yes. I would never have said yes to this prison.'

However, the first time she said no, the only time in fact, Suman Pathak had no idea of the prisons lying in wait for her later in life. The only prison she knew then was the prison of duty, of dharma, and that prison made her shake her head. A young woman shaking her head, clear-eyed, firm chin, the mouth set as if it had never smiled.

My father had this way of feeling his left arm with his right hand whenever he had something difficult to say, as if he was massaging it, and I imagine he did this as he told my mother. I imagine they were standing in front of the open door of the safe room on the roof, the afternoon sun beating down on them. Mahadev in a crumpled kurta payjama, the sleeves of the kurta rolled up. Suman in a printed salwar kameez, the sweat making a dark valley between her shoulder blades, squeezing out the colour from the cloth, what he was about to say squeezing the colour out of Mahadev's face.

'They want me to marry Sharda,' said Mahadev. 'They are trying to fix the date.'

My mother had a way of turning her head away when she heard something she didn't want to, as if she had been slapped hard, and, again, that's what I imagine the sixteen-year-old Suman Pathak doing when she hears that the man she loves is to be married off to another girl.

Suman looked away, first to her left and then to her right, trying to hide the kick she had just felt in the centre of her being. Then she let out her breath, took it in again and with the next exhalation rushed out the words,'So. Marry her. Congratulations.' The last word in English.

'Suman . . .'

I saw this scene many times when I was a kid. In some darkened movie theatre, my hand smelling of stale potato chips, Paradise or Roxy in Calcutta or Regal in Ahmedabad, Dharmendra reaching out to Asha Parekh, Rajendra Kumar in *Palkhi* reaching out to Saira Banu, tears glycerining from eyes.

Mahadev reached out. Touched Suman on her arm.

'Suman . . .'

In the cinema, the girl would snatch away her arm, turn and sprint, shaking with her grief. Or the wronged man would turn away and, voice traffic-jamming with emotion, bravely grit out, 'Aapki . . . aapki suhaag ki zindagi . . . *aapko* . . . *aapkomubarakhobegum*,' before walking away, never running, always walking away quickly. As the music rose I would feel Minakshibehn begin convulsing next to me, the glycerine transmitting off the screen and coming out as real tears from the receiver of her eyes, the smell of her Pond's talcum powder suddenly stronger, her handkerchief running all over her face trying to catch the sobs escaping from various parts.

Suman didn't run, she had nowhere to run to. She took Mahadev's hand in hers, firm, gentle, eyes dry. She shook her head.

'Na,' she said, answering the question just before it came out of Mahadev:

'. . . Will you marry me?'

Mahadev registered the shock of the answer at the same time Suman caught the fact of Mahadev having said it out loud. They both looked at each other, caught in the headlights of time.

After a long while Mahadev spoke again: 'Suman. She won't have a husband, she will have a living corpse.'

Knowing my father, there would have been no melodrama in this. It would have been the cold statement of a judge ordering an execution, no matter that the execution included the death sentence on his own married life.

'That's your problem,' I hear Suman say, and I know it rings wrong, she would never have said that, not then, or even later, even when she meant exactly that, not in those words. Those words belonged to my women, to Ila, to Anna, to Sandhya. To Magali saying it in French, 'Ça c'est *ton* problème.' Not to Suman.

Suman wiped the sweat from the side of her face while clutching Mahadev's hand tighter.

'Try and make her happy,' she said. 'You know if there was a man I would marry it would be you. You know I have my Ranchhodlal. I am as married as I will ever be.'

Ranchhodlal. Ran = Hrin = debt. Chhod = release. Lal = son/youth. The-young-man-who-releases-you-from-debt = Krishna, another name for Krishna Kanhaiya, the debt being spiritual rather than monetary, though with Gujaratis you never can tell. When I was a child, for the longest time I thought Ranchhodlal meant something different: Ran =

field = the battle-field. Chhod = leave. The one who escapes, or helps you escape, from the battle-field. And yes, in a sense, I was right, he is the one who helps you leave behind the debts of the battle-field of life, the cosmic banker who releases you from the tithe of war, from the maya of wanting to pay back blood with blood. Like all bankers, though, there is a chargeable interest, and the interest here was devotion. Suman Pathak had the walls of her devotion to protect her from the battle-field of marriage, and she quickly took up a position behind the ramparts.

In the labyrinth of her soul Suman found an escape route away from trouble, away from pain, both hers and that of others, but what she didn't know was that the maze would ultimately bring her back to the same point. That day, Mahadev helped Suman leap back across the gali for the last time. As she jumped away from him she felt, for a moment, like a kite that had been cut loose.

A few months later, my mother attended my father's marriage to his first wife. A loose kite of despair floating within the walls of her heart, its sharp corners poking, Suman watched as Mahadev and Sharda went around the fire. The women around her were from the groom's side and their voices shrilled out songs, extolling the virtues of the boy, pointing out the shortcomings in the girl. *O the bride she is dark, and O doesn't she have a slight squint? Isn't she lucky, O isn't she lucky, to be marrying our Mahadevbhai, he who is so fair and tall?* A corner of the kite poked into one part of her and then floated to scrape against another. Across the hall sat the bride's people, their women answering in song, carving into the boy and praising their girl sky high. *O the groom may be tall, but he isn't so fair, he looks a bit dumb. What will our graceful Shardabehn do, with this clumsy boy?* and then, given that everyone knew of Mahadev's political activities, *O will he just be a martyr for the country? Will he not do his duty as a martyr to marriage?* Suman had an answer, but she didn't respond. My mother was one of the best singers at these marriages, her witty improvisations feared by the other side, but on that day no sound of praise for her distant cousin left her throat, nor a single word of mock-viciousness for the woman who was now, technically, her sister-in-law. The kite had taken her voice with it and dropped it onto some distant terrace of longing. *O isn't she lucky? O will he just be a martyr?* Mahadev's face was a flat mask and he kept his eyes trained on his feet as he slowly led his bride seven times around the fire. Suman's face was equally empty of expression as she avoided meeting anybody's eyes. Sharda's face no one could see, for the sari covered it like a monk's cowl.

On the flight to become Mahadev's second wife, perhaps these songs of marriage played in Suman's head. She knew that in the small temple in Calcutta there would be no chorus of praise for her, no lilting sarcasm for her husband. There would just be the two of them, the pandit to conduct the ceremony, and Nalin as witness and photographer. Nobody else.

After a while, the gentle bouncing of the Viscount lulled Suman into a sleep where she had a dream of kites. A red kite fighting a green and yellow one. The strings taut, sawing against each other, some unseen hand tugging rhythmically, another invisible hand also pulling, trying to trick the air into helping. *O our Sumanbehn is fair, while Mahadevbhai is black, isn't he lucky, to wed a beauty like her?* A gust of wind sending the green and yellow kite exclaiming upwards, straight up and hard, the red kite shaking in one last frapping sound and then its string cut, from tight, to flaccid, the string falling away, the kite spinning, catching the evening sun one last time, then flattening, jinking from side to side, like a drunken dancer, the life gone out of it, floating away, slave to the whims of the breeze, carving a soft, invisible calligraphy as it meandered down toward the roofs.

Magali's fingers loosen from my hair as her tide recedes. Her legs go slack around me till I only feel the weight of her left heel against the bottom of my spine, like a big round full stop. And the back of her right ankle cupped into the back of my knee, also heavy, like a plane that's landed. The sound she makes when she comes still in my ears, a long low-stringed groan washing inside the left side of my head, sometimes with a word wrapped in it, either a 'merde' stretched out or else a 'oui' falling off a cliff – 'woe-eiiii'. A seed, from which will come some temporary calm, a solace that will network with other small sanctuaries from other mornings and other nights.

She lies there, her eyes closed, breathing more gently now, but I can still feel her pull tight around me every time she breathes in. My face is quite close to hers and gradually the smell of her mouth changes and I can smell the whiff of her cigarettes again.

Magali opens her eyes and looks at me. She smiles a question. She puts a finger on the centre of my forehead, right on my third eye. 'You were somewhere else, no? All 'ere but somewhere else, also. No?' I look back at her, trapped, too fresh and weak to put a lie on my face. I start to answer, and the sentence is halfway down from my head to my tongue before I register a sound that has peeled up from the traffic in the streets below. Two connected sounds. Alain's car honking a signal that he's dropped Para off, Para's heavy trainers clumping up the stairs. Someone has let her into the building and she is almost at our floor, almost at the door. Oh shit, which today is not locked because I forgot to do it.

Magali's eyes widen, following mine and then she gives a little gasp as I yank myself off her. She gets up quickly, just as Para pushes the door open, 'Hey you guys! Are you deaf or something? I've been ringing that bell – ' I grab the condom wrapper from the floor, narrowly avoiding the ashtray, but my foot hits the coffee cup as I tear on my pants, 'What's happening?' Para appears around the door. 'You in the middle of a fight?'

Magali is fine. Her long t-shirt never came off and she has it down and all in place. She has even managed to light a cigarette in this time – 'Only a Frenchwoman could do that,' I find myself thinking, resentful, angry. My jogging pants are up under my kurta but I haven't had time to tie them. If I move they will fall down.

Para looks down at the overturned coffee cup, then looks up and stares at me. Fast brain on the girl.

'Oh. Having fun, were we?'

• • •

I never asked my parents how they actually began their courtship. I never asked them how their third contact happened, so when, many years later, Para asks me, I don't have an answer. Like I don't for many other things. Like, what did they say to each other at first? Was anything said at all? Was it all eyes? What was their love about, what did they love in each other?

Para began asking me these questions when she was about twelve, in 2006, which was, let's see, from 1934, about seventy-odd years after my parents conducted the first phase of their romance. There was no way I could answer these questions. Sometimes, when I got irritated with Para's questions, I would come up with absurd answers.

'How did they communicate?'

'Smoke signals.'

'Did they touch? Did they make out?'

'Yeah, they met on the street corner every two weeks and looked at each other. That was sex in those days.'

'PUPS! I'm serious. The game needs some answers.'

The game indeed needed some answers.

The game was called Megalopolis 3000 and even though it was an expensive adult game it had been bought for Para in the hope that it would get her off her addiction for shoot-'em-up games like Half-Zone. In the hope that it would give her something else to think about besides the three advanced flight simulator fighter modules on the Web that she had gained free access to as her prize for defeating someone with the game-name of Aaron.

After she beat him in the Air Duel World Final, Aaron had tried to get in touch with the man who had defeated him three times out of three in brief but intense jousts played over the course of a week.

The closest Aaron had come to getting his opponent had been in the first round – his Spitfire MK IV versus the Messerschmidt ME109 flown by game-name Sudarshan. For the first round the planes and specifications were set by the Game Committee and round one was a close-fought dog-fight somewhere over Holland in late 1944, with a storm brewing. Aaron had badly damaged the Messerschmidt before going down himself because of a lucky shot causing a leak in his fuel pipe.

Partly correctly, Aaron had concluded that his man was young, hot-blooded, completely dependent on hand–eye reaction and with not a lot of understanding of strategy or older engines.

In the second round, Aaron had the choice of battle-area and aircraft and he had chosen a plane he knew well – the F4 Phantom from the Israeli Air Force – with the joust taking place at high noon in the clear blue skies over the Sinai peninsula during the Yom Kippur War of 1973. Sudarshan, from all the contemporary aircraft available, including the Dassault Mirage III and the British Hawkers, had made the lunatic choice of the MiG-21 as modified by the Indian Air Force.

The battle lasted exactly seven minutes, after which Aaron had to pay a visit to the cardiologist and I had to massage Para's shaking calf muscles before taking her out for a hamburger. Despite the Phantom's greater fire-power and superior overall technology, Sudarshan had managed to wrong-foot the overconfident Aaron, dragging him into a chasing dive that he couldn't pull out of. The beauty of it, as Aaron told the doctor, was that the bastard in the MiG had won the battle without firing a single shot.

What scared me after the first two rounds was the complete absence of any sense of triumph in my twelve-year-old. It's true that the final was far from over, and also true that Para was pitted against a tough opponent, but the normal-wanter in me kept looking for signs that this was just a game where small victories could be celebrated, and I found none. All I saw was a single-minded determination of the kind I'd never had, something of Para's mother, the German Anna, and something again from her paternal grandmother, my mother Suman, a certain war-light that I remembered, lurking anew somewhere inside that thin jeaned and t-shirted body.

For the third joust, it was Para's turn to choose her aircraft and battle area and she showed a typical mixture of intelligence and ruthlessness in her choice.

'Pups, this guy knew that Phantom too well. Like he's actually *flown* it, yeah?'

'Maybe he just practises on that one a lot.'

'No, Pappa, I can tell. I once had a Jaguar-to-Jaguar with a guy I later got to know actually flew Jaguars in the RAF? No way I could get him. This one had that kind of feeling.'

'Okay, so?'

'So . . . he's *old*. Quite old.'

'You think I'm old.'

'You are, but he's even older – he's flown Phantoms.'

'So?'

'So . . . I'm guessing he doesn't like new-tech type stuff. I'm guessing his edge reactions are slow. He's good but he's slower than me. Somewhere.'

'He was faster than you on his Spitfire.'

'Yeah, because I hate the throttles on that 109.'

'Tell me the points again?'

'Okay, the first one we're almost equal even though I won. He got an 8/10 and I got an 8.5/10. Second one I got a 9/10 and he got a 5/10 so that one's a clear lead, but this one I've got to win because I'm not ahead by more than 6 points – so chop chop.'

The choice Sudarshan sent in to the Game Committee was in itself half the battle. The aircraft was the new Anglo-French Elise attack helicopter and the battle-area chosen was south Bombay late on a monsoon night and the strategic situation was FC – Future Conflict – a kind of contextless war that pared down all strategic calculations to just the two combatants.

Sudarshan's specifications created two problems for Aaron: first, the only other helicopter that could come close to the Elise's wide-radar ability was the Sikorsky Cougar, and it was well known by then that the Cougar had recently failed in heavy monsoon conditions in Ecuador as well as in Jaffna. Secondly, if, as Para had guessed, Aaron was actually a fighter pilot, his reactions in a critical situation would be those of a man used to having room in the sky, and this battle was actually a street battle with not much sky involved. The choppers would be stalking each other around buildings, at times pretty much like two soldiers on the ground.

As it happened, Aaron chose the slightly older but more reliable Ilyushin Cetna C-3, exchanging the Cougar's infrared wide-area ability for a radar with a much smaller spread than either the Elise or the Cougar but taking a chopper with proven reliability. Besides being solid in all kinds of weather, what the Cetna had was a big Russian sting in the tail – two backward-pointing heat-seeking missiles, originally designed for hitting tanks on the ground but equally effective against something like another helicopter chasing it.

'That's his main playing card, Pappa. His cannons I can handle, but if he misses with those two heatheads then he's gone,' said Para, practising with the C3 on the computer.

On the day of the match, as I drove her to the Game Room, Para spoke almost to herself. 'It's like Krishna getting his uncle Kauns, yes?' Para was big into Krishna, especially the bloodthirsty part of him. 'Can't kill him in the day and can't kill him at night, can't kill him inside the house and can't kill him outside, so Krishna gets him on the threshold of the house at dusk. Well, Pupso, this guy's day is his experience of historical wars – which I've taken out. And his night is his ability to analyse the terrain, and my radar's better than his. So.'

I was not fully convinced. 'What about his house and outside it?'

'Listen, you have to go beyond the obvious. His house is the sky and lower down is his threshold. It's all about getting the enemy into something that is a grey area for him.'

I looked at my daughter and wondered where she had got that from. I parked the car and walked her to the Game Room, watching her as if she was someone else's child. Not even a child, as if she was some adult stranger in a kid's body.

Every time my mother started something important, like taking me to my school exams, she would do a little Puja, take something sweet, sometimes just a Parle Glucose biscuit, and touch it to her picture of Krishna before giving it to me to eat. As she sat down in front of her computer, Para took out her wallet and flipped it open. In it she had a picture of Suman Bhatt which she tapped three times. Then she whispered something to herself and put the wallet away. It is not something she had done for the first two rounds but this one, as we all knew, was crucial. I don't know where Para got this from, I didn't remember telling her about my mother's Pujas. Maybe Anna had told her about my mother's little rituals, maybe not.

'Good luck, Para,' I said.

'Thanks,' said Para, without turning around.

The Game Controller connected to the site and then spoke into his microphone. He listened for a moment to the reply coming in on his headphone. Then he turned to Para and asked in English, 'We are connected. Are you ready?'

'Yes,' Para replied.

The Game Controller tapped in his final codes. Then he moved away from the console to his own three screens where he could see the game from both the finalists' point of view as well as from outside it. It was more or less the same facility that the thousands who made up the Net audience could see by hitting a button on their keyboards. Since I was Para's drinks man I was not allowed to see anything other than what she could see.

The battle began slowly. Sudarshan entered the zone from the east, scanning his infrared radar for heat from the Cetna's engines. Somewhere over Mohammed Ali Road something flickered at the edge of his radar and disappeared towards Colaba – it could have been a big truck carrying heavy machinery but it had moved too fast for that. The Elise rose into the rain and tilted its snout down to head south-west. Below the chopper the streets were filling up with the heavy downpour. Here and there clusters of cars stuttered in the flood, their headlights reflecting off the shimmering water.

The Elise reached the flooded Maidan and went very low because here, on the flat stretch of open ground, it was at its most exposed. It jumped over the trees at the edge of the Maidan and turned past the

Eros cinema, going low again over the road leading to the Sachivalay, and up again as it approached the Air India Building, curving around to hover over Marine Drive and the rain-lashed seaface. Nothing on the radar. Sudarshan decided to head between the Oberoi Hotel and the Air India Building to get a clearer signal from Colaba and Cuffe Parade. As he passed the hotel, some instinct made him drag the chopper into a steep turn to the left. The missile exploded into the fifth floor of the Oberoi, jolting Sudarshan. Narrow miss. Where was the guy? How come he'd got so close without the Elise's radar picking him up? Sudarshan sent the Elise straight up through the smoke billowing out of the Oberoi. He had to get a visual. Rising above the Air India Building he caught sight of the C3 ducking back down into the middle of a round building. Ah. Gotcha. Stadium. Two stadiums, very close, easy to mistake. Brabourne? No, Wankhede. Wankhede Stadium. Very Good.

The radar on the Elise had a small problem and Mr Aaron had obviously done his homework. The problem with the radar was that it got confused around television installations, often skimming over those areas without registering engine heat. And if there was one place in south Bombay where there was heavy tele-electronic machinery present, it was the broadcast tower at Wankhede Cricket Stadium. Sudarshan put a manual sight-range on one of his six Tomahawks and fired it. The missile jumped over the buildings lining Marine Drive and headed for the centre of Wankhede.

Aaron in the meantime had moved his C3 through a gap between two stands and put himself just above the wires of the Churchgate line. He confirmed that the Elise knew roughly where he was when the Tomahawk hissed over the MCA pavilion and thudded into the pitch in the middle of the ground. Picking up speed, the C3 headed for the open sea, looking for a ship. He had to waste a few more of the Elise's Tomahawks.

Sudarshan saw Aaron on the corner of his radar and watched him carefully. The C3 was at the edge of his Tomahawk's effective range.

Why was he heading out? Ah, looking for a ship. A source of big heat to fool a heat-seeking missile. An old man's trick – he wasn't going to fall for that. He'd wait.

Sitting in the official Game Room in an office building in Haifa, Aaron sipped a cup of coffee with the left hand while the right hand gently held the joystick, ready for action. At the same time, in Paris, Para kept both her hands on the action console while I held the bottle of Orangina under her nose and let her sip from the straw. The rules were strict and I was only allowed to provide her with minimum sustenance and that too only because she was a minor. She could ask for juice and biscuits, but I was not allowed to say a word to her. If I did, she would be disqualified.

Para suddenly jerked her head to indicate that she wanted the Orangina removed. The C3 had obviously decided to stop wasting precious fuel and moved off north, disappearing behind Malabar Hill hoping that the Elise would chase it.

The Elise did not chase it. Instead Sudarshan flew inland, crossed over Opera House and found himself a 'sitting place' from where he could do his sums. Using the Elise's grid-map system, Sudarshan very quickly worked out the two or three routes the C3 could take after coming around Malabar Hill. The next thing he worked out was where he had to place himself in order to cover all the routes on radar. The point was just down the road, forty feet above the steep road that winds up from Peddar Road to the Hanging Gardens. The Elise quickly moved into position and Sudarshan began scanning his radar.

Yup. There he was, C3, on the other side of the hill, coming in fast across Nepean Sea Road after having made sure that the Elise was not chasing after him. Sudarshan would be in his radar range within one minute.

I watched my daughter as she moved the side joystick with her left hand and tapped in commands with her right. My fists were clenched with tension but Para seemed about as perturbed as she would be while doing some particularly engrossing bit of schoolwork.

She moved the helicopter to where the Hanging Gardens road flattens near the Kemps Corner Flyover and my eyes pulled wide as she landed in the thin stream of rain water and switched her engines off. The Game Referee standing next to me went extra still as well. The move had taken thirty seconds, and if the C3 saw her before she saw him she was a sitting duck. But now she was off his radar. She waited in the rain, my daughter, the virtual rain drumming on her plastic-glass outer skull, visibility low. Waited, knowing that her radar could still see him. Knowing that though her rotors were off and her missiles disabled, her movable cannons were still operational.

Aaron scanned his radar as he approached Kemps Corner from Nepean Sea. Nothing, nothing, nothing. Where had the bastard gone? Just out of his radar range, he reckoned, hanging somewhere near Opera House waiting for him to come within range of his Tomahawks. Aaron began calculating how long it would take before Sudarshan released a radar-run Tomahawk and the answer he came up with was two minutes, which made him slow down just before the cannon shells slammed into the right side of his machine.

Sudarshan had calculated the angle of fire beautifully and the C3 caught a full bite of his cannon. But two things happened next, two things that combined to save Aaron from immediate destruction: first, Sudarshan had raked his cannons upwards, assuming that Aaron's first reaction would be to go up. This was sensible, it was a good bet, but it didn't work. It was a measure of Aaron's skill as a pilot, his highly honed sixth sense, the second thing that happened, that he pushed forward on his joystick rather than back, that he, literally, ducked. Dropped from thirty feet to five feet over the road, went *under* the flyover and out of Sudarshan's angle of fire, the cannon shells somehow missing his rotor-blades and shattering the huge Vimal Suitings neon sign on top of the building behind.

It was also a measure of Aaron's reactive abilities that he hit the button for his last missile almost as soon as he came out from under the flyover, just as he went past the 122 bus stand, hoping to catch the Elise, and it was here that he finally lost the game. Because the heat-seeking missile smelled things other than Sudarshan's air-cooled cannon barrels, it sensed the huge wave of heat coming from the two hundred and fifty-eight air-conditioners that were on that night in Akaash Deep Apartments on Altamount Road and, instead of ferreting out the Elise across the Kemps Corner crossing, the missile did a U-turn and headed up the slope of Altamount to the twin towers and exploded, I imagined, in the unpeopled empty triplex apartment of Rusi and Georgina Jeejeebhoy, which had the most air-conditioners running in the whole of Akash Deep, the machines kept on so that Valdemar the greyhound could roam from room to room and floor to floor without the discomfort of a hot and humid monsoon night.

Despite the incredible detail of the game, it did not register the unfortunate incineration of Valdemar and the destruction of the Jeejee-bhoys' collection of paintings, which included priceless works by M.F. Husain, Ganesh Pyne and B. Prabha and two wall constructions by Satish Gujral. What the game did register were the unbelievably quick reactions of both the adversaries.

Aaron, his C3 now limping, his screen informing him that he had been hit in the right arm and with a graze on the right temple, and that his missile had missed badly, decided to turn his helicopter around to get as close as possible to the Elise so that Sudarshan could not fire his Tomahawks without risking his own life. He knew that if he took the Elise down with him the Game rules specified a rematch. Sudarshan, in the meantime, had waited for the C3's anti-tank missile to explode and then immediately hit his engine button. Within thirty seconds he was airborne and away, knowing that he had not managed a clean kill, knowing exactly what Aaron had to do to get a rematch.

The rest was simple, uninteresting. Aaron dragged his C3 back from near Forgett Street to Kemps Corner, by which time Sudarshan was already away, hanging near the BMW show room on the corner of Peddar and Babulnath Road. As Aaron appeared from behind the Chinese Room building Sudarshan released two Tomahawks, both of which hit the sluggish C3, creating a fireball in the pouring rain and sending bits of burning debris as far as Jaslok Hospital.

'Phyooph,' said Para, 'not that slow.' Then she put her head down on the keyboard console. I moved to hold her.

'Felicitations, Sudarshan! Vous êtes la nouvelle championne du monde!' said the Game Referee, forgetting his English as he echoed the screen, which was going crazy with congratulatory messages.

The first message from Aaron came via the Game Committee, congratulating Sudarshan.

'Can we communicate on e-mail? I would like to know how a young man, as I'm guessing you are, developed such patience.' And giving an e-mail address. Para howled in triumph and sent back a message saying, 'What if I'm not a young man? Tell me, sir, have you ever actually flown fighter-planes?'

The reply was quick: 'If you are not a young man then what are you? And as for fighter-planes the answer is yes – I flew for the Israeli Air Force from 1966 to 1975.' And it was signed Ahuva Ron (Lt. Gen., IAF) (Ret'd). With a PS: 'Don't call me "sir" or even "madam", just "Ahuva" will be fine.'

General Ahuva, as Para began calling her, was overjoyed to discover that Para shared her gender and astounded that she was only a child. After the first couple of exchanges Ahuva asked to communicate to Para's parents and, since Para was with me at the time, I was the one who formed a kind of e-mail friendship. It was in one of our exchanges about being parents, in Ahuva's case, grandparent, that I expressed my worry about Para's obsession with warfare. Ahuva understood immediately and her next e-mail to Para was about real war:

> Dear Para,
>
> I want to talk to you about war. Real war is the most horrible thing that man has invented and, having lived through a few, I have not wished any child or grandchild of mine to go through the experience. When you are older I will tell you a few things I

remember, but for now all I will say is that war is (sometimes!) fine as a game on a screen, where there is no blood and no death, but when you see the real thing at close quarters you only wish for one thing – that you were somewhere else.

You are obviously a very talented girl and I want you to use the intelligence god has given you to learn and enjoy things that will be of use to you later in life. I notice that your birthday is coming up and I am sending you a game, a very different game from the ones you have been playing till now. I hope you like it.

With best wishes,
Ahuva

A week later, a parcel arrived marked for Mademoiselle Paramita Bhatt. Para opened it and took out the game called Megalopolis 3000 (Asia).

On the surface it looked harmless, but I only realised what we were getting into when I installed the game and it took up four whole gigabytes on the computer. The basic premise of the game was simple – it took off from the dissatisfaction people had experienced with other games like Sim City where the construction of a city was the main objective. After a while the municipal game became sterile, players wanting human drama, needing to people the streets that they had constructed, needing the meat of character and plot to go with the sauce of urban planning, desiring some history to fill in the blanks between neighbourhoods.

Megalopolis Asia gave you the detailed environment of two hundred and fifty of Asia's major cities along with their basic histories since the year 1900. What you had to do was choose characters – up to seven – and give them roles to play against the architecture of a city. You could select anything from a riot to an intimate dinner for two and the game would put you in that. After you chose your basic situation, the game then plotted back against you, giving you new things, incidents, to deal with, and you could change the balance by adding in additional factors, new elements and the game would then respond.

For the first game that Para played, we had to go out and get an additional programme for Central Europe. The game Para chose was set in Kassel with just four characters – me and Anna and the German artist Jost Wedekind and the Swiss artist Pippilotti Von Traume in the year 1982 – but when she saw the effect it had on me she quickly changed over to another location and another generation.

'Okay Pappa, stop sulking now, we'll leave it, okay?'

'No, no, you have the right to ask.'

'I know, but we'll leave it for now. Can we do Ahmedabad and Ba and Dadaji?'

'If you like.'

By the time she was twelve or so, Para had developed an identification with her grandmother, Suman Bhatt, whom she had never seen. The first point of this connection came from a photograph of my mother taken when she was about fourteen. There were not too many pictures of my mother between the time she was seven and when my father began taking photographs of her, which was when she was about fifteen, so this was quite a rare picture. One day after brushing her teeth in the morning, Para began rummaging in a drawer and came across the photograph in an old album.

'Hey, wait a minute, this looks like me. I've just been looking at myself and now I'm looking at myself again!'

And it did. While Anna and I had done the usual parental thing of finding all sorts of resemblances when Para was a baby we hadn't really noticed how much Para, of late, resembled my mother, or rather, my mother as she had looked when she was young. But once Para had pointed it out there was no escaping it. Without either Anna or me noticing it, despite the obvious differences like the brown hair and lighter skin, the rest of Para's face seemed to have tracked down different components of Suman Bhatt's face in the ether somewhere and one by one inserted them under her skin. Suddenly, from that particular morning, my mother's photograph began to look like a photograph of a slightly older sister that Para might have had. Even more than the individual features – the Studebaker nose, the firm chin, the slightly slanted eyes – what began to fascinate me was that Para had developed some of my mother's expressions, her gestures, her posture.

Even the way she now looked at me, impatiently, waiting to start, was exactly the way my mother would look at me, waiting for an answer to some homework question.

'Shall we start, Pfazzer?'

'Yeah, okay, let's start.'

First we scan the photographs of the two main characters into the computer and name them. Then we give them eyes. Para works very carefully on Suman's eyes. She takes about two hours for what I think is a small thing, scanning one of her own recent photographs, cropping out the eyes and then carefully putting them into her grandmother's face. After this we ask the game to find other local types, giving them names and age as we go along.

'What kind of a horse was Pathankot?'

'I don't know, big is all they told me.'

We find an old picture of Graham Gooch and put him in as Sergeant Green. We take the horse from an old Lone Ranger comic and he becomes Pathankot.

'Okay, Pups, you can go now.'

'Thank you, miss.'

For the next few days Para played out variations of the scene of Suman and Mahadev's first encounter. Finally, satisfied, she summoned me to the computer.

'Popsu, it's taken me three days to make it happen almost like it happened. Just couldn't get Suman's wail right. Horse just wouldn't rear up. But got it, finally.'

'How?'

'You know that James Brown CD you've got? The one that I hate?'

'Yes?'

'Well I took one of the screams, one of the ones from a slow song? And I put it in. Then I changed the pitch, made it even higher. And it worked great.'

'So why "almost"?'

'Watch,' said Para and hit a key to start the scene.

Pandemonium, sand flying, people running away, the whole thing from some strange perspective that I couldn't understand at first. Then I got it.

'It's from the fucking *horse's* point of view.'

'Yup. I can do it from anywhere, but this one's the best. And watch your language please.'

The old lady standing, frozen, her sari pallu dropping, coming closer on the screen, the horse going past her and then the sound of the baton hitting. Thwuck. Then the boy runs across the horse's vision and something makes the horse turn. Then the boy goes past and a harder *thadaak*. The horse turns and you can see the boy lying in the sand. Then the girl on the left, almost on the edge of the screen. Then the sound.

'Jheez-us.' I find I have covered my ears.

Para switches to a different point of view and we are now looking at the horse from a little distance. He goes up, up and Green drops, falls on his head and there is the sound of a neck snapping.

'There's the problem, see? Couldn't save either Dadaji or this guy, Green. Both keep dying.'

'Unh-huh.'

'Green I don't have a problem dying, Pups, but Dadaji dying means Ba doesn't get spermed and therefore neither does Mamma and so I don't get born.'

'That is a problem.' I flinch inside at the word 'spermed' but it is what the kids in Para's school use nowadays.

'Okay, Pappa, let's move on. The girlfriend-boyfriend time.'

'Not so easy. You'll have to get into handwriting.'

'No! Why!?!'

'Because that's how it happened, baby.'

How to explain handwriting? How, especially, to Para, who still hated to write by hand?

'How did it happen?'

I remember my mother telling me about the singer from Nathadwara and I take it from there and make it up. Hell, I even have a CD that's made here in Paris. I put it on for Para.

'Listen to this.'

'Oh god, Dad, is it like that James Brown stuff?'

'Different. Opposite end of the scale.'

'What's it about?'

'Well, mostly Krishna.'

'Krishna huh? Well, okay, I like Krishna.'

The cover says 'Girish Karia – Nathdwara Haveli Drupad' and on the back in English translated from the French: 'For the first time, one of India's most secret music has been recorded – Drupad from the forbidden temple of Shri Nathji in Nathdwara. This Dhrupad in its most unadorned form is the illustration of the origin of this music, before it became a court music.'

The voice climbs out. A slow train, running just this side of melody, winding out of some deep tunnel. The first phrase coming both from below and above, falling around your ears and settling on your shoulders like a thick drape dropped from a great height.

Shri Krshnaay namaha

Then the second one, same but different, thick water, longer.

Shri Gopi Jana Vallabhaya namaha

'What's he talking about?'

'It's a prayer, a chant. He's saying bow your head to Krishna, to the one who pleases the Gopis, to the gurus. It's like a list. Different names of Krishna.'

'Why is he saying Krushna and not Krishna?'

'Because that's how you pronounce it sometimes. If you're a priest and stuff, in Rajasthan and Gujarat 'specially.'

'How would Ba pronounce it?'

'Same – she hated me saying Krishna. It was always Krshnuh.'

'But she wasn't a priest.'

'No, but she was very much a Brahman's daughter.'

'So, how do normal people say it?'

'Oh, a hundred different ways – Krishna, Kishino, Krishno, Kisan, Krishan, Keshto . . .'

'So which one's right?'

'Whichever one you like at that moment – they're all correct.'

'Can't be, Pups. One's got to be right.'

'Why? Shut up and listen.'

Mana Mohana Natawaram!
Mana Mathuradhipati!
Shri GO . . . kula pati!
Shri Bala Krshnammm Bhajaa . . .

The singer from Nathadwara was famous and people had gathered from five surrounding poels to hear him. The concert, though it was not called that, had been announced weeks ago. Everyone knew it was a rare occasion that a pujari from Srinathji actually came down to Ahmedabad to perform. The occasion was the wedding of the daughter of Sheth Popatlal Maneklal, one of the richest traders in the city and a great believer of the Srinathji Krishna. The concert was going to be in his haveli in Vaanka Kaka ni Poel.

'What's a haveli, Poppo?'

'Opposite of a hovel-i. Ha, ha.'

'Hey. Cut out the bad jokes. Answer.'

Easy, thanks to Gen'l Ahuva. I open a dialogue box in the education panel of M-polis 3000 and click on Ahmedabad, then on House Type and key in Sheth's Haveli and it comes up:

Haveli: Mansion, usually built by wealthy traders called seths or sheths, found in various forms across the northern and western

parts of Indian subcontinent, including Pakistan, especially Punjab and Sindh. (*See also:* Rajasthan – Shekhawati – Haveli – Paintings.)
Haveli/Ahmedabad: Many fine examples remain. Tall houses sandwiched between smaller buildings belonging to the less wealthy.

Game situations recommended:
Historically – Business games, trade situations.
Contemporary – Conservation project, games against real-estate developers.
Future – Ideal space for gun game chase, intricate warren, dangerous building factors.

A frame comes up, a tall building with steps going up to the main entrance, which gets filled in – a huge wooden double door with intricate carvings. Studded in the carvings, ornamentations of brass. Inside, a hollow wire tower into which colour gets poured. A large marble-tiled courtyard with rooms leading off on all sides. Three different stairways going up to the floors above. Three floors with balconies looking down into a courtyard. Rooms with windows, occasionally, in the room of a privileged member of the family, a small balcony looking out over the roofs of the poel. Up above everything the dhaabu – the roof from where the sheths can fly kites with the advantage of height.

'Details?' enquires the game. 'No,' I type in. I will provide the details.

So, Sheth Popatlal Maneklal's haveli on the evening of the concert – of the puja – for his daughter's wedding.

For some reason, Mahadev paid particular attention to how he dressed that evening. First, he pushed ahead of his brothers and sisters for the evening bath, having made his mother heat some water specially to pour into his bucket. This was not normal in April but Mahadev had told his mother he had a cold coming on and she had responded immediately with the standard Gujarati prophylactic of ordering him to have a hot water bath.

Bathed and extra clean, Mahadev had gone up to the clothes cupboard he shared with his older brother and quickly pulled out the best dhotyu they had between them – a silk dhotyu with a thin red and gold border. This was normally reserved for marriages and special family pujas and usually worn by his brother, and since Mahadev wasn't usually that particular about his dress he only got to wear it rarely. Today, though, he was planning to brook no argument from his dandy brother or anyone else.

Mahadev shut the cupboard and straightened himself in one of the twin mirrors on the cupboard doors. Then he began the elaborate ritual of putting on the dhotyu. First he wrapped the cloth around his waist and, measuring it exactly, he secured it with a knot on his belly button, leaving two separate drapes falling on the floor. Then he took one side, folded it and wrapped it between his legs, before tucking it in behind him at his spine. The other part he accordioned with his hands and made a kind of graceful soft triangle for the front and tucked it in over the first knot he had made. He looked at it and shook his head, dissatisfied, the balance was wrong. He took out the pleated cloth and folded it all over again. He was just tucking it in when he felt someone yanking hard at the back of his dhotyu. Keshav Kumar Bhatt, my older uncle Keshavkaka, remembered for the rest of his life the slap he got from his younger brother Mahadev.

'Baap re. He was really in love, your father,' he told me, still feeling his cheek in 1972, 'otherwise Mahubhai was the one who would never fight, he was above all that normally, head in his books, but that day he was serious.' Keshavkaka pushed himself back on the swing and slapped the air again. 'Dhadaam! The power of woman, young man, the power of woman!'

Having got rid of Keshav, Mahadev opened the cupboard again and pulled out a clean ganji and a silk kurta. The bruise still hurt slightly as the cloth of the ganji brushed it. He worked some silver buttons into the buttonholes before sliding the kurta over his head.

After tying the buttons, he looked at the finished work in the mirror.

Almost finished. Now for the embarrassing part. The bit he hated. Chotli.

'Pappa, which one's correct? Choti or chotli?'

'Choti is north Indian, also UP and Bihar, chotli is Gujarati. Same way a dhotyu is dhoti in Hindi, dhuti in Bengali and a dhotyu in Gujarati.'

'Okay, stop showing off. We stick to Gujarati. His dhotyu and his chotli.'

Sitting here in Paris, I can't imagine it. Something stops. Even though I see the women on the streets with something like chotlis. Paris has finally caught up with London from where this year's new fashion comes – le 'nouveau-pony' as in ponytail, short hair with a long pigtail sticking out from the back. The tails are frozen by some awful spray into different shapes with things – ribbons, fake beads, buttons, even tiny digital screens with flickering images – all hanging from the tail or woven into it. It's not right, something rings false.

I see the Bastille tower in the evening, glistening in wet November sunlight, and something stops me. It's the wrong revolution, I can't imagine 1789 recognising the handshake signal from 1930. I find the smell of coffee from the cafés assaulting my imagined memory. Something in me wants to retrieve memories of Ahmedabad, this memory of a smell my father must have had in his nose when he left his house and made his way to Sheth Popatlal's haveli. Instead, I smell watered-down Gauloises, petrol, ganja from the vendors standing near the steps down to the métro. I'm looking for the smell of hair oil, or Keshav's precious imported Brylcreem in Mahadev's hair, but what I get is a twin whiff as I pass the Chinese delicatessen on the corner of Rue Beautrellis, something, prawns?, cooked in sesame and soya sauce, being packed for a woman wearing some very French perfume. Something . . . not-Ahmedabad.

Chotli, I explain to Para – a little tail of hair worn till those days and even after by every high-Brahman male. In front, normal hair, short over the ears, proper parting, everything. From behind this little pouch of hair tied into a knot at the end. 'Very useful for non-Brahman boys to pull in a fight. Like those chains you could pull in trains to stop them for an emergency,' I remember my father telling me. Earlier, traditionally, Brahmans used to be completely shaven-headed with only this little island of hair at the back, but that had given way to this compromise.

It was a compromise my father hated but it would be a couple of years before he summoned up the courage to go to the barber and ask him to lop it off.

Anyway, that evening a seventeen-year-old boy, dressed up in a shining dhotyu, shining black hair, lion-waisted but waist well hidden under a flowing kurta, a decision shining in his eyes, made his way to the Haveli of his dreams. In the right pocket of his kurta Mahadev Bhatt was carrying a note he had written earlier that day.

'What did the note say?' Para, almost upset that I'd said the word 'written', an almost 'Why couldn't he type it?' in her voice. I answer without being asked, answer inside my head: 'He couldn't type it because typewriters were few and far between and came only in English and belonged to the police, government officials, lawyers and rich mill-owners' accountants. No one typed love letters in those days, not in Ahmedabad and not in English, love was a human thing and you couldn't express it in English.' What did the note say?

The note said . . . now here is tricky ground, I can only imagine what the note said, I never read it, I only remember my mother saying to me once, 'Your father's handwriting was very difficult to decipher. It was beautiful, green ink, round letters all dancing ras-garba with each other, but very hard to read. But when I looked at the first note he gave me I didn't need to read it, I knew somewhere that Krishna had answered my prayers. The man I had given my heart to felt the same way about me.'

The note, folded, torn from an exercise book, shining in his pocket, Mahadev wound his way through the galis of the poel. There was an electricity in his step that his brothers Keshav and Bhimsen noticed from afar as he raced ahead of them. Mahadev knew his way to Vaanka Kaka ni Poel like the back of his hand and he didn't think about where he was going, he was on fast auto-pilot, drawn by the imagined landing beam of Suman Pathak's eyes, the turbulence of steps, up and down, the circum-navigating of steep houses, the false welcome of flat narrow stone porches, all avoided, as he walked at a running pace towards his –

Para takes the wine glass away from me.

'Pappa! Stop getting carried away. What did the note say?'

Chi' Suman, it has to have started like that, 'Chi'' short for 'Chiranjivi' meaning long-lifed, equal to 'Dear' or 'Dearest' in English. Why? Because every letter I'd ever read from my parents, every letter in Gujarati, started like that, Chi' Paresh, Chi' Minakshi, Chi' Vasu, actually not my mother's letters to my father, which always began with some obfuscated address, because she always called him 'tamey', vous, till the day she died, and you only wrote Chi' for people you addressed as tu/toi. For letters to respectable elders you wrote 'Pu', short for 'Pujya' – worthy of worship.

'What would you call your dad when you wrote to him?'

'Me? Always "Dear Pappa". Why? And always in English 'cause I couldn't write Gujarati.'

'Can I call you Pujya Pupface? How about Pu'Pa?'

'Well, it's better than "bastard", I suppose.'

'Look, Fups, I said sorry about that.'

'Yes, well, anyway.' I pull my wine glass back from Para's side of the dining table.

The haveli was lit up. Para starts to arrange the audience, mixing up the men with the women, and I have to correct her. Men on one side, women on the other, never together, not in those days.

Mahadev entered the haveli and made his way through the men seated on the carpets, weaving his way past the little pillows put there for people to lean on, his radar scanning for Suman, not there, not there, not there, not there, where was she? The singer cleared his throat as a signal for silence and the crowd hushed. A hand reached out and pulled

Mahadev down just as the first phrase rang out over the gathering. *Shri Krishnay Namaha.*

• • •

Before her work changed and she went completely into making installations, Anna Lang made a series of photographs. She did these after returning to Germany from her first visit to India, which was in 1987. The photographs were commissioned for a group show that paid tribute to Frida Kahlo, the Mexican painter, where seven European women artists were invited to make a series of self-portraits. Later, in an interview in *Art Forum*, Anna dismissed the series as 'not serious', the worst thing a German artist can say about their own or anybody else's work, but, even though I personally like her later stuff a lot more, two or three of those photographs still work for me. They affect me on one level, perhaps, in the same way home movies are capable of affecting the people involved, but on another level the images still retain some genuine power beyond the merely personal.

Anna took off not only from Frida Kahlo but also from other well-known self-portraitists closer to her own time, the Americans Chuck Close and Cindy Sherman. My favourite is the one where Anna poses as Durga. Wearing a drab housecoat Anna stares at the camera with her own two arms plus eight mannequins' arms coming out from behind her. In her ten hands she holds the following items:

1. TV remote
2. Scissors
3. Riding whip
4. Small vacuum cleaner
5. Saucepan
6. Breast-pump
7. Bubbling test-tube
8. Biography of Frida Kahlo
9. Chainsaw (small model)
10. Shopping bag from a German supermarket

Anna is standing precariously on a big motorcycle covered with fake tiger skin. And the front wheel of the motorcycle seems to have gone over a man with two buffalo horns coming out of his head. The man is blond, eyes wide open in the rictus of death, and the weapon he clutches is a smashed video-camera out of which tumble the entrails of a tape.

The other one I like is simpler, the background is not a flat red studio backdrop, as in the Durga picture, but a cow-shed in a German farm. The photograph is shot almost naturalistically and there is only a little bit of tampering with the colours. Anna is squatting, wearing a tinny Krishna crown which was one of the things she took back from India. With a plastic peacock feather and all. Around her waist she has a bright orange-yellow dhotyu, Krishna's pitamber. Above the waist Anna wears nothing. But her face, arms and body are painted a shiny black – it looks as if she is covered with engine oil of some sort.

Anna smiles at camera, young Krishna's guilty caught-stealing-butter smile, teeth white, eyes green, tufts of yellow-brown hair poking out from under the crown, and her black arm is buried deep inside a bucket of incandescent cream standing under the oversized udders of a square German cow.

The gallery chose to make this one into a postcard and this was the one Anna sent me, naked, without the benefit of an envelope, just to see what the Indian Postal Service would make of it. 'Of the highlights, quite accidental, around the nipples,' as she put it in another letter.

The Indian Postal Service, which normally had a habit of swallowing picture postcards, for once didn't make anything of this one. It came through, one corner slightly bent as if a calf had nibbled at it but otherwise intact. I was out and my mother received the card along with other letters.

When I got home, I noticed my mother's thali sitting on the dining table, empty steel glass standing sentinel next to it, both shiny clean and untouched. It was a double signal saying, one, that she hadn't eaten her dinner, and two, that she wasn't planning to – she was on one of her fasts-unto-death in protest about something.

With Para gone to spend time with Anna, and Magali in her own apartment tonight, I've set up the game and I have three choices as I walk in and see the thali. The first, as always, is Abort Game (Ctrl AG). The second is Avoid Encounter (Ctrl AE) and the third is Enter Encounter (Ctrl EE). Para has added a new parameter for anything to do with Suman Pathak. She's fixed the short cut K+F2 for the Krishna Factor (KF). If you hold down the two keys and hit plus or minus you can increase or decrease the extent to which Krishna-devotion affects the outcome. I hit Ctrl EE to Enter Encounter, and then very quickly, as my mother comes out of the kitchen after putting away food, K+F2+ the minus key from the numerical keypad. To cut down the KF.

'What, Mummy? Not eating?'

Suman Bhatt looks at me and there is no getting away.

'How can I take food in a house where my son brings prostitutes.'

'Whaat?'

My mother throws the postcard down on the dining table.

'It's bad enough that this whore has to show herself to the world. Art! Why send this filth here? To my house? Where I welcomed her as a decent girl!' My mother's face still belongs to the photograph that Para has scanned in, except she now has white hair and her body is a little plumper. She looks like Para does when she is angry. An angry teenager in a white wig. 'How will I look at the postman again? Today he brings this. Tomorrow he will bring Diwali cards with the same dirty hands, laughing the same dirty laugh.'

In the bedroom my father turns over in his sleep, my mother's voice oversalting his dream. His voice half opens a window – 'Shu thayu?' What's happening? – and then shuts it again. I pick up the postcard and look at it properly. A flash of desire runs through me – the woman I love, the woman I miss. I want to laugh but my mother has put acid on that. I don't want to hit Ctrl AG but I do. Abort Game, Exit Megalopolis. Exit Game Drive. XXXXX . . . Shut down computer. Switch off mains. A lone siren outside. It's late at night. So late I can smell the boulanger's oven downstairs.

Every time I switch out of the game, I face the real thing. The real thing had been much worse, I didn't have a minus button to tap down the Krishna Factor.

My mother had a strange relationship with Krishna and it did not translate well across generations. For example, I found it very difficult to explain to Para how someone could worship Krishna and all the variations of Durga/Amba, the mother goddess, and have almost no time for Shiva and Brahma and Ganesh. All I could come up with was: 'It's like a story you choose over other stories that you like less. It's like this one particular story moves you more than the others and that's why you read it again and again, while the others you read only sometimes or hardly ever at all.'

It's as arbitrary as falling in love with one person and not another – ''aving a story wiz 'eem (or 'er)', as the French like to say – or deciding the borders of a nation, I thought to myself after I finished saying that to Para, but I didn't say that last bit out loud.

'But you said Ba was rich when she was a kid and then she was poor.'

Yes, put baldly that was about right. When Suman Pathak was born, her grandfather was a wealthy man, his wealth built mostly on the bribes he received from various maharajas as the British Agent for the princely states of Rajputana and Baroda. Suman had memories of when her older brother Prabodh had his janoi ceremony, memories of different rooms in their big house in Godhara, one filled with silk saris, another filled with gold bangles, another with sacks of dry-fruit and nuts, all meant for distribution to relatives and connections on the occasion of Prabodh putting on the Brahman's sacred thread and getting his chotli.

What happened was that Suman's grandfather lost his wife and decided to marry again. He married a young woman less than half his age, which was common for rich widowers in those days, and divided his money between his second wife and his only son Vitthal Pathak, my grandfather. Vitthal Pathak received the sum of five lakhs, which in those days was a huge sum of money, and a house in Ahmedabad, in Hajira ni Poel. This would have been enough for any sensible man to build an even bigger fortune, but Vitthal Pathak was not a sensible man. He felt cheated of the rest of the wealth that was his due and he began drinking and gambling and my mother had memories of that too. She had memories of him coming home drunk, well after midnight, and beating my grandmother with the butt of his hunting rifle.

'A bit like you and Mamma fighting,' Para says and I almost slap her.

'Mamma and I don't hit each other.'

'No but you shout, both of you, and it's like hitting.'

'No, hitting is different.' I suddenly remember my parents quarrelling and my answer lacks conviction. In their case, even the silence could be like hitting.

'So?'

So, within a few years, my fool of a grandfather and his wealth parted company with each other. Vitthal Pathak lost his mind and my mother remembered him sitting in the prayer room, in front of a statue of Krishna, asking for the rest of his rightful inheritance.

'Why Krushnuh? I thought Ganesh was the god for money?'

Yes, well, you believe in who you believe in and if you're not too well connected with the others you ask your main man, your main god, for whatever you need.

The night when my mother threw Anna's postcard at me, I remember going into my room and shutting the door. On the other side of the door I could hear my mother in the living room, singing a bhajan through her crying, trying to cleanse the house, me, herself. I could hear the sound of my father getting out of bed and opening his bathroom door, moving slowly, my mother's singing having woken him up. I could tell by the sound of the toilet seat being put up that he was irritated at her bhajan at this time of night.

I looked at Anna's postcard again and then opened a drawer to put it away. Even then I filed things carefully and her postcard went into the large manila envelope which I'd hung on to from my time in New York. It had all of Anna's letters and cards in it, including the first letter she sent me soon after we first met. I found the letter, still in the envelope it had come in.

Two frankings on the stamps, one, very clear, from Duisburg, the date and the letters BUNDESREPUBLIK circling around it, and then the half-legible, faded thappa from the Elgin Road post office. 15 September '82. And then the address – Mr Parresch Bhatt, 6A Lansdowne Road, Calcutta – 20, Indien.

I remembered then how precious that letter was when it arrived, well before I got anything from Lou or Aleyah or anyone else in New York. A sign that I had not dreamed my other life, that I hadn't conjured Anna up from some bad German art movie.

Dear Parresch,

(I am sorry, is it how you spell it? You left your address but never wrote your name!) (Your last name I got from the airplane card you left in the garbage!)

How is it to be back in India? And with your parents? And with your father's tongue and your mothertongue? (yes? is that how you write it? I warned you my English in writing is not so good. Even bad then my spoken English.)

No onion skin; solid, square, good paper. A kind of light purple-blue ink. The letters oddly formed, slanting wrong, like too many elegant Germans sitting on the small uncomfortable sofa of English. But if you pushed aside the letters and looked at the words:

I know this is what I should not say, but it is strange to be without you suddenly. To be without your face in the morning on my pillow. Even though it was only some too short five mornings. My pillow misses the beautiful brown of your face. There is a taste I miss in my life and I think what is it and I think it is your smile.

Jost and Pippi make too many laughters at me, too many jokes, like. This morning I awoke up and decided I would make a laugh at myself bigger then them because otherwise I maybe could cry and that is not good. There is no use for these tears in the work we are doing now, though there should be space (room?) for another kind of tears.

'The phenomenologische-cal self is different from the psychologikal self!' Ja. I mean, yes, I can look at myself now . . . and I must laugh.

It is so strange to be picking up my fountain pen now, after a so long time to write, to actually connect to paper. Some months. I am so used to write on the typewriter and now slowly even computers – which I hate. My pen is not happy with me and I am trying to tell it that I am sorry for forgetting her but she won't hear me. She won't listen. And she doesn't like my English, maybe. Maybe it is like another lover, not her and her dear German. Even a pen can be hurrapatriotisch!

And now I must stop.

I hope you will write.

Your

Anna

PS I will send you a tape of the group you liked, 'Collapsing New Buildings', if you think your post men won't steal it.

I slid back the letter into its own envelope, then into the manila envelope, and then I put away the manila envelope in the middle drawer of my desk. I shut the drawer and opened the one above it. Something set me looking for a photograph of me and my mother taken by my father when we went on the first holiday I remember. I found it and looked at it for a long time before switching off the light and going to sleep.

• • •

One day, in Paris, looking for something else, I find it again under a sheaf of more recent contact sheets. There it is, black and white, matte, printed half-size from Bombay Photo Stores. I remember my mother looking at it when I was much older and calling it her 'prison'. Waving it at me when I got home drunk another night.

'This is a picture of the beginning of my prison! When you were born I thought Bal Krshna had come to fill my lap! If only I had known you would grow up to be . . . this. All my prayers and I get . . . this, this . . .' Words leave her, scurry away from her anger as she flings the photograph down on the drawing-room table and slaps it, slaps it and then slaps herself.

My father must have taken it with the Contax he sometimes borrowed from Narendrakaka. A horizontal frame, shot against light coming in from a window. The light, diffused by chintz curtains, coming into a room that I always thought of as 'not my house', which indeed it wasn't. A room in a guest house in Darjeeling – Kalimpong? – soft, indirect morning light, a pudding of white quilts on a bed with dark grey blankets crumpled on top. On one side, to the left of frame, a woman, Mummy, asleep with a child, me at age five, also asleep. Both of them are turned away towards the window and the woman has her right arm around the little boy. The boy sleeps clutching his mother's elbow, or rather the bottom part of her upper arm where it plumps out from under the blouse. His head right next to hers.

Calcutta used to have photography 'Salons' that ran yearly competitions. Alongside other titles like 'Village Landscape – Dawn', 'Portrait' and 'Still-Life' one of the favourite themes used to be 'Mother and Child'. My father, who rarely entered these competitions, won a prize in the 1966 South Howrah Salon for this photograph, titled, naturally, what else?, 'Sleeping Mother and Child'.

Always some cheap, temporary peace when I look at this photograph. Something about the way the light traces the two faces in a kinship of highlights, something about the absence of worry in the sleepers and the love in the regard of the man looking. Something about having landed. The photograph from the second day of the vacation, the first day spent travelling. Something to do with a memory of the first airplane I sat in and fear and anxiety and elation. A Dakota wobbling low over the fields like a warm, airborne bus. An overexposed memory of the jeep we took from the airport at Bagdogra.

It's getting cold. Mummy's lap, her arms clutching me tighter around the bends. On the right, steep rock, I was told they were mountains, but I couldn't see them. On the left, a twisting sliver of road and then past the edge of road, below it, mist for a footpath. Sometimes, the mist would open up and I could see the drop, the bottom far, deep, strange green falling away, not good, but okay, the driver smoking a bidi, the smell of the bidi enveloped by a larger mountain smell, one that I had never smelled before. An excitement, a back-straightening, in my mummy-pappa that seemed to come from the smell. A fear also, but mostly elation, a together kind of elation where the fear was also welcome, no, not also, just welcome. Because without it there would be no elation. The driver sometimes questioning a bend with his horn. Sometimes, a yellow glow with a sound attached to it, the light coming first, followed by a reply, *bhaawwnk*, and then a truck or another jeep, feral, frightening, leaping at us from behind the rock wall, our jeep sliding left in obeisance, closer to the mist footpath and then somehow through, around, still on the road, back to being a blind and lonely king skidding around its opaque kingdom.

A long time, it seems a long time, I sleep, dreaming mist-footpaths, worrying about Mummy who seems worried, wake up and the jeep is still there, her lap is still there, everything still sliding except her plump elbow, which is around me, still a yellow light pushing at the grey in front of us, still Mummy's shaal behind which I can hide.

I wake up to huts, the mist pushed back behind them, the side of the road now proper grass sloping away but there to see. And the jeep going down. The driver's back now relaxed, the bidi held looser, Mummy also holding me looser, except over the bumps, Pappa now talking to the uniform man sitting next to him. The uniform man offering Pappa a cigarette which Pappa refuses, politely, a hand gently pushing away the air between the open packet and itself. The jeep now not sliding, grabbing the road loudly, the horn honking, looking for goats, for children running across, for mountain dogs.

Then the uniform man gone. The jeep climbing slowly up past fairy-tale houses, me still in Mummy's lap, my feet on the suitcases. It's late and we're looking for hotels, guest-houses, I don't want to sleep in the jeep. Two or three times we stop at one of the houses with turrets and little windows and sloping roofs. Pappa gets off and knocks on the door. Rings a doorbell. Someone opens it and shakes her head. A word, in English, 'Sorry.' And once, a man, 'Sorry, full up sir.' Signboards -- Hill Vista, Greendales, Belmont, I can only read a bit, but Mummy reads them out to me, pointing to the signs. Why do people here name their houses, Mummy? Hotels, baba, they're hotels. Englishword – 'Ho-tull?' I repeat. Pappa has a consultation with the driver. On to the next one. Hotel Como. After a lake in Italy, Pappa tells me later, after we've unpacked and I'm about to go to sleep.

Before that, Mummy ordering hot milk and opening the tin of Bournvita she's brought along all the way from Calcutta. Taking out the theplas, chhundo and alu nu shaak that she's packed for the journey. God knows what all non-vegetarian food these Anglo-Indians might be cooking. Let's not take a chance tonight. No, and anyway I love theplas, much nicer than rotlis, better than puris even. And sweet sticky chhundo.

There's a musty smell in the room and the bed has woollen blankets on top of fat quilts. Pappa lifts the corner of a blanket and checks the little silk brand label sown on the underside. He shakes his head, not one of ours, meaning the textile mill he is an agent for. The windows have funny thin curtains that you can see through. Outside it is now dark. Cold. Mummy takes me to do bathroom, and then washes my feet with hot water. Doing bathroom into a white wash-basin chair. What is this, Mummy? as she lifts up the brown wooden ring. The ring makes a hard sound as it hits the white box at the back. Commode, baba, it's called a commode, remember like on trains? No, trains have steel things to do bathroom in, this is inside a house. Foreigners use these, it's all right. Put on payjamas, take off long-sleeve sweater, put on sleeveless sweater, climb in under the quilt and blankets. Told you not to worry, we were never going to spend the night in the jeep.

Under the quilt is warm, there is a rubber hot water thing near my knee and it feels really hot but I like it. Under the quilt is soft but if I take my arms out and put them on top I can feel the rough blanket through the sleeves of my kurta. I can't decide whether to keep my arms out or put them back under. I try both and settle for the rough of the blanket. It's a nice difference. He's growing, Mummy says, these payjamas are now too short.

Hm, replies Pappa. He has settled himself near a table lamp with an English book. *Dr Zhivago* by Boris Pasternak, I know because I asked. We might as well be home. He turns a page and draws his shaal closer. Mummy sits on one side of the bed and sings a bhajan in a low voice. *Laadakda thai, baalakda thai, balaswarupey jo aáwo, prabhu aawo aawo aawo.* It's the one asking Krshna to become a child and come visit her. I always used to ask why she needed him to come as a child when she had me and she would always explain that he *had* come to her as a child – me. I was her little Runchhamlal, her little Ranchhodlal. Now I didn't ask anymore.

I go to sleep looking at the middle of the ceiling, wondering why it didn't have a fan, listening to Mummy singing softly, waiting for the flick of a page turning from Pappa's book.

December 30, 1985

D Diary,

Oh shit, I did it. Cheap trick, DD, but couldn't help it.

He came to show the photos and we went for a drive after. Asked me to sing again and I thought why not. I mean, thought if I leave it to him he'll go back to Cal without doing anything.

Didn't want to try him with something too difficult so just sang the thumri, the Abeer Gulal one, in Kafi.

We were on, where else D? Marine Drive only – talk about cliché place na! – evening breeze and all . . . and I'm driving quite slowly and singing . . . so he listens. DD, I'm pleased to report to you that his eyes just almost fell out of his idiot head. Actually I went off besur in two places but he didn't notice.

Then I drive up Malabar Hill to the gali off Little Gibbs Road – top Bombay smooching headquarters – "Just behind the Tower of Silence and right on top of the Mountain of Hope" as Aarti says, and what does this idiot guy do? He asks me to explain. Says he likes Indian Classical but doesn't know much about it . . . (Obviously neither does his clever Miss Bengali Theory!) So. So I gave him quick lecture and impressed him with my knowledge – in for a penny, DD, in for a pound no? – so first, basics test: does he know the diff between North Indian Classical yaani ki meaning Hindustani Classical and South Indian Classical as in Carnatic Music? Yes. Tick. Does he know that both

Classicals have things called raags (he laughs at this point but not for much longer) and each raag has a different note progression on which you improvise? Tick. And most raags have a time at which you sing them, like early morning, mid-afternoon, midnight etc. . . . by this time he's getting irritated, Diary, he says "C'mon! What are you, a tourist brochure? I'm not a bloody foreigner okay, I know that much!" (well thank god, otherwise I couldn't have proceeded with anything with Mr America-Returned Calcutta-walla!)

So then I explain that a thumri is diff from a full raag, it's a light classical form, short, and there is less improvisation. And the words matter, I told him – talk about heavy hinting. I was hoping he'd ask about the words but he didn't immediately. What raag was it in? Idiot! What do you care about the raag? Ask about the words no! But no, so okay, it is in Raag Kafi, so can be sung at any time really but most us Marathis would treat it like a late-afternoon raag – 3 to 4 o'clock. Next question, why are Marathis (he said Ghaatis instead of Marathis, getting really cheeky now) different? Because we had Bhatkhande to do the sorting out of all the raags. Who was Bhatkhande, so told him about Bhatkhande and his books. Then back to thumri, told him that it was a form perfected by <u>courtesans</u> in Banaras and Lucknow, a kind of serious ritual of seduction. Still he doesn't take the hint . . . I'm thinking maybe he's not interested and I'm about to say some bye-bye thing like "so get in touch next time you are in town" when he asks – T'NAANG! – Sandy, what were the words about?

So D, I take him by the hand (mentally speaking) and explain. Laali chhaay rahi hai. Red spreads everywhere. Red of what? Udata abeer gulal. Gulal, the red powder you use to colour people on the day of Holi – the Gulal flies through the air. Laali chhaa rahi hai, red spreads – red of what? Red of colour but also red of passion, red of desire, EROTIC desire, you dumb Calcutta dodo (didn't actually say that Cal bit. Just thought). Laal Shyam bhaye laal bhayi Radhika. Laal as in the word for red but "lal" also as is used for "beloved", so Shyam, that is Krishna, is red and beloved and so is Radha and so are all the other "maidens", as they say. Mor chandrika laal bhayi hai, murali laal rasaal. The peacock feather on Krishna's crown has turned red and so has his flute, his murali, and then I just looked at him and something in there must have gone laal-rasaal because, DD, he leaned over and bang! – smooched me! Nope, wrong, NOT a smooch, he kissed me – tender, proper kiss.

And Diary! You didn't ask me about his photographs. They were also good. I know you don't believe me but really – godpromise.

Then dropped him back and he asked if he could see me again tomorrow. I said I would think about it, but I think he knew that I wouldn't take too much time thinking. There goes my New Year's Eve. Bastard.

1 Jan, '96

Godpromise!?! Haven't said that word in years.

Reading old diary – don't quite know why – kind of time-pass – avoiding work, I guess. Anyway, be bindaas Sandy! Why ku work on the 1st of January?

Weird shifts reading stuff from that time. That girl – that language – and this woman . . . me? I suppose there are some things I'd want to hang on to about me from that time but not quite sure what.

And the other thing that strikes – that town and this town. Talking about Bhopal, sudden unavoidable thought re: Bombay – The bastards have gassed us while we were sleeping. Gassed us with godpromise Gas.

Went to Sunday lunch at Nepean Sea last week and bumped into Viral's dad. He'd come up with some Income Tax file to ask Dad for advice. Started going on about how the Sena had been so good for Bombay. Mumbai he called it, Mumbai this and Mumbai that, and I suddenly remembered him snapping at P aunty many years ago, at one of Dad's collaboration parties – some Dutch guy visiting and the party for him – and Chandra Patel made the mistake of referring to Bombay as Mumbai. P uncle just freaked. "Don't call it Mumbai!' his voice frying chillies in Gujju, "Aa Bombay chhe! Bombay! Mumbai nahi!"

Used to be a big Indira fan in the early '80s and then a great Rajiv chamcha. Now it's like Nehru Chacha got everything wrong, we should have had Sardar or Netaji! And the BJP can do no wrong and Bal T. is a great statesman and saviour of the people. He's also re-discovered his "Hindu" roots – he's stopped eating Ai's Hyderabadi style Mutton Korma. Dad is the only one out of the four of them, out of him, Mom, P aunty and P uncle, who at least says that he can't stand all this Hindu Rashtra business.

Three of them were standing there and talking when I suddenly noticed how old they looked. Like not time but this town's managed to shrink them. The flat is still the same but they now seem smaller in it – Ai&Dad – sort of taking up less and less space.

Caught myself thinking again – what if something happens to one of them – don't want to move back to Nepean Sea. Happy here in Versova, happy alone in my little den, so what if the fishing village smell drives me crazy sometimes, at least this place is mine.

As Aarti says, and she has a way of putting these things, as we know, like that one unforgettable dialogue she maaroed two years ago, just back from some conference in Geneva – "Abroad-shabroad is all right yaar, call it chutiatic, but I can't scratch my balls properly anywhere outside Bombay! US-Europe is <u>fine</u>, but you can't really relax in all those please-thankyou countries. Here tô you know, you can stand there and go scritch scritch scritch to your mind's total happiness because you are <u>home</u> no?"

Yes . . . I can imagine Aarti standing in front of Flora Fountain happily and furiously scratching her balls. And yes, Aarti <u>can</u> be damn chutiatic, but she was okay last night – one nice line she came up with – "all these emotions that are dhad-dhadoing through us".

Dhad-dhadoing. Indeed. Actually not too much dhad-dhadoing last night, quiet dinner in fact, like all middle-aged activistas should have, to celebrate New Year's Eve. Prakash talking endlessly about his nuke reactors and how India needed a proper anti-nuke campaign, Smita being supportive wife but changing the subject now and then. And me and Aarti Madam, the two spinsters – the two splinsters more like it. This Prakash&Smita, they still can't handle anything that comes first from a woman's point of view . . .

Not that you always love them, but you have to have some friends I suppose. Anyway, they'd cooked some khau-suway – some Burmese thing which tasted to me like basically bhelpuri soup – and nice pork momos. Aarti'd got some okay French wine through Guillaume, her "friend" at the Alliance (now <u>those</u> please-thankyou balls she is <u>quite</u> happy to scratch!) (Sandhya, now you just STOP this bitchgiri, okay? One day you'll say it to her also and lose a friend!) and I'd taken a choc-cake from Sugar and Spice, so despite political bifurcations, comradely feeding and boozing took place.

Talking about bhelpuri, at one point in the evening found myself looking at the <u>coupleness</u> of Smita and Prakash, like her sev and mamra and lasan chatni etc. caught up with his papdi, onion, meethi chutni, all mixified and inseparable . . . and I tried to put myself in her shoes, like with two children and a proper-pukka husband installed in life. As many times before, in other situations – didn't like the thought – our Sandy the Single! But don't know what set me off thinking about this. The Paresh e-mail from yesterday? Maybe just the sense of another year gone. God knows.

Putting lenses in today, looking at the mirror, when I saw my face. Happy New Year, Sandy Tai. Meaning, everything still functioning, nose, mouth, hair (four white! all on left side of khopdi!) not too many lines, but don't know – something around the eyes. Can't remember who said it, that the eyes are the first thing to age. Putting lenses in suddenly reminded – got to re-frame that photo P gave me of man painting in Durga's eyes. Chokshu-daan he called it. God, ten years ago exactly no? Yeah, New Year's Day '86 he gave it to me. Shit yaar, ten years weren't supposed to pass so quickly . . . And all that excitement at turning 25! Chhah! Admit it, what a tottull Bombay semi-bimb you were, Sandhya. Abhay Mathur of all people – so close to the edge of full bimbodom that was.

Anyway, you're Sandy Tai now and you're okay – and still your own person, single, footloose, fancy-free. Look at Paresh, married, childed, and now splitting also with wife, now that's what we can call *advanced*! And whoever heard of people splitting because of work? No third party, no affair-shaffair, nuthhing, just "the quarrel between our ambitions is now unbearable". Unbearable!?! Why have children then? Words like unbearable are not allowed to people who have kids. Bas khatam.

Well maybe that's not fair, lekin tu tˆo bach gayi Sandy Tai – from becoming a bhelpuri with Bhatt. What a close shave.

Funny, never admitted that about Bhatt before. Must be because it's New Year's Day or something.

Talking about the Durga photo, remember P talking about how he had this synchronicity with the Bong, Ila, that he never found again, this great sharing of seeing things – kya bola tha? – something, "Our frames overlapped well" or some such photographer's bullshit and remember how mega humiliative that felt at the time. What, you and me can't see things together or what? (Thought – didn't say.) And now there's no trace of that. Don't mind that my frames don't overlap with anyone too much. Well, meaning, don't *mind* mind. No frames lapping at each other and no emotions dhad-dhadoing and no ambitions doing jhagda with each other . . .

Anyway, fuckeeeeeeeeeeeeeeeet!

Must find that photo. Like the way the tip of the brush touches the eyeball. Like the tender precision. Chokshu-daan, Giving of Eyes, that's what you have to do, give eyes to your life. The rest is all bakwaas.

Contact Sheet

Clear weather as they had been promised.

There are various sound alarms in the cockpit and this one sounds like the old Hindi movie comedian Johnny Walker laughing, at least that's what Cindy used to say, 'Hic. Hneh, hneh, hneh, arrrey! *Kaun* kehta hai ki mainey jyaada pi li hai? Hain? Nooo whisky, hic. Whichky very risky, make many hichki. *Hic*.' Not the dialogue – that was Cindy mimicking – just the hneh hneh hic hic arrrey. Hneh hneh hic hic *arrey*. There is a readout on the far left of the screen, that's synchronised with the alarm – Six to target, Five Fifty-Nine to target, Five Fifty-Eight to target . . .

Para is calm now, her training sitting up inside her as natural as the sun rising on her horizon. The sound-swat, losing Cindy, now far behind her, no further incident, no further sign of enemy ECM. Formation now intact. Five-Thirty to target. Time to go down.

No signal necessary, the squadron of Ishir fighters put their noses down almost vertically, as if they've just seen a glass wall, like falcons from a wildlife film on TV, comically precise, as co-ordinated as a Broadway musical, from twenty thousand feet to one thousand and then straightening out slightly to go even lower.

Para feels her stomach tighten with the dive, feels her upper-body clamps squeeze, the computer calibrating the g-force and countering the blood as it rushes up, pushing it down, away from her head, just right, only as much as necessary. By three hundred feet she has pulled the plane out of its dive. Her hands are at her side, like sitting in an armchair, working the controls at the end of the hand-rests. There is no stick – in a hard turn there would be so much weight on her that her arms would not be able to move to pull on a stick. Instead, under her right palm, she has a ball which is attached to the arm-rest and this is what she controls, watching her numbers, watching her horizon and watching her floor. She is trained to scan her instruments at the rate of six times a second. She doesn't read them, she senses them. No radar warning yet, they seem to have made it through the hole.

The Ishirs skim over the low mountains like fish jumping over rocks. The planes are painted a dull black, except for the roundels of the Indian Air Force, green dot in the middle, then a white circle, then the orange circle outside. She can tell from her metal-sounder pings that there is a lot of hard stuff on the other side of the mountain range.

Three Forty to target says Johnny Walker and Para switches out the wig. Suddenly the Ishirs sprout hair from their wings and tail, tentacles like a manta ray, fine electrodes that are designed to deceive any anti-aircraft missile, especially the new generation shoulder-held Stingers, which are most dangerous when you come out of the attack dive. The hair gets dragged into brush shapes as the fighters jet forward.

Hneh Hic. Two minutes to target. Hneh Hic. Too late for any air-to-air missile, no enemy aircraft within range, only the SAMs and Stingers left to tackle. The third finger on Para's left hand taps a button at the edge of her arm-rest thrice, hard. Not the thumb or index finger, and not the middle finger, because most people find these the easiest to move and you could make a mistake. And not the little finger, because that is too weak, even in the strongest of men, and if everything else fails this is the finger that has to do its job, so it is the third finger of the left hand that gives Para her eyes.

The instructor saying, 'Girls! You will now have to stop batting your eyes at the boys, understood?' Taking a pause, relishing his moment. 'These eyes can – and will – kill.'

Cindy later saying, 'Zehrili Ankhia. Haay.' And Zoltanpari, the Hindi-less dotard, asking, 'What dat, what dat?' Cindy translating, 'Haay Mizoram ki kali . . . Zehrili – Poison, Ankhia – eyes. What *you* do at *boys*, gettit?'

Para has spent months perfecting the blinks. Three times, twice, once, mentally flicking over the nine specific fire-points on the heads-up display, one directly at the centre, one on the left, one on the right, three across the top and three below, blinking three times, once, twice. Once, three times, twice.

• • •

He knows the focus will be at infinity but he checks anyway. He pulls the focusing ring till the tents become soft blobs and then brings them back into sharpness, making sure that the two halves of the electric pole at the far end align in the centre to form a straight line. Then he presses the shutter. The snap of the mirror going up and down cuts into the conversation between the jeep driver and the journalist. They pause briefly to look at him and then carry on talking. The driver's Bihari Hindi knocks oddly against the journalist's Gujarati-flavoured Mumbai-style patter.

He takes the camera away from his face just enough to allow his thumb to work the winding lever and takes another shot. And then one more, this time including a bit more of the sky and the deep grey clouds.

He lowers the camera and looks at the scene for a moment. Then he takes off the lens hood and reverses it, clicking it into place around the lens before carefully putting the lens cap on again. He finds the cover of the ever-ready case in the jhola on his shoulder and clicks the button into the back of the camera casing. He feels the first raindrops just as he brings the hard leather cover over the camera.

The journalist has walked up to him and they both stand there and survey the camp below.

'Baap re. The last time I saw something like this was in Dilli in '47. When we'd gone from our college to help out in the camps there.'

'Yes. We had them this side as well. I didn't think I would see anything like that ever again in my life. It's almost as if time has – what do they do, those tape-recorders? Rewind – yes, as if time has rewinded twenty-four years.'

They walk back to the jeep and climb in. The driver has already started the engine and he lets out the clutch as they get in. The journalist points down the hill to the camp. 'Chalo bhaiyaji, oodhur camp ko lelo.'

As Mahadev looks down, he sees that a bit of his dhoti is wet with mud that has squelched up and his feet and chappals are completely caked. He leans forward and pulls up the edge of his kurta to wipe the raindrops off his spectacles.

• • •

Poison eyes. When Para taps the button, two beams from inside her visor synchronise with her pupils. These beams will – *pneeep, pneeep, pneeep – pneeep, pneeep, pneeep.*

Radar warning. A ground missile has locked on to her. Her first real one. The Enemy. At last. Hneh Hic. Zero Fifty-Six to target. Just over that hill. Her ECM screen blinks, telling her what's coming at her – TR6, TR6, TR6. Tank-based SAM, just as expected. Good. Hold on to the flares, try the old Cobra first. 'Hold Flares. Charlie Bombay. Charlie Bombay.' She realises she has spoken the last sentence – said it to her whole squadron – well after it is out of her mouth. No radio silence needed now, they are there and everyone has already said good morning. There is an elation in her voice that she will only hear when the mission tapes are played back at base. Her senior officers will mimic her for days, as will her subordinates, out of her earshot. The slightly sing-song, slightly German-tinted 'CHARlie BomBAY!' will go down in squadron history as the first battle call of a victorious war. She will remember later the sudden increase of sweat in her armpits at the exact moment, and the corner of stiff photographic paper poking through her fire-suit into the upper part of her right arm.

Two of the twelve Ishirs go straight up and away in a hard vertical climb, Para being one, Raksha the other. Para can see from the top right of her heads-up screen that she and Raksha are the only ones who've been locked on to, the others are still free, still low over the carpet. *Pneep, pneep, bhneeeh, pneep, pneep, bneh.* The SAM has gone past, missed, the Ishir's steep climb beating the missile's comparatively sluggish guidance system. Raksha is clear as well. Para flattens out of the climb at about six thousand feet and puts her nose straight down again. As she dives, she switches off her eyes because she needs to look. She slows for a beat, two beats, like a sword hanging in mid-air. It is a touch that will win her praise at the debriefing.

'Very good, Bhatt. Most first-timers would have gone tearing in. You stopped to look, you acted exactly like a Squadron Leader should.' Then the sting of sour at the end of the sweet, 'But what happened to Blue Flight Leader? Why did Mahajan, why did she . . . ?' Sentence left unfinished: why did Flight Lieutenant Raksha Mahajan lose it?

• • •

Mahadev thinks the man is saying the soldier did it for fun. The kerosene stove behind the man has levelled into an angry hiss, and Mahadev can't make out the exact words. The children shout as they jump up and down in his viewfinder. Just as he settles on a frame, two more run up and add themselves to the picture. The man's accent is difficult. Mahadev's city Bengali slides off the mud bank of the riverine voice.

The entrance flap whips in the wind, slapping gusts of rain into the tent. Two old women sit huddled near the stove, waiting for the tea to boil. One of them takes a puff of a bidi and passes it to the other, who cups it in her shaking hands, letting the tiny burning tip warm her palms before raising it to her mouth. First we thought it would be like the other villages, only the men. Mahadev understands that quite clearly. Aamra lukailam, aamra lukailam. *We hid, we hid.* And then something, the word 'khelaa' – Bengali for 'play' – and then another impenetrable web of sounds.*

The journalist from Bombay is jotting things down on a little pad, Gujarati mixed with some English words. He turns to Mahadev to ask him what the man is saying. Mahadev shakes his head, turns to the Bengali reporter standing next to him and asks.

The man answers in English.

He is saying that normally Pakistanis were killing the men only and raping the women, at least all young women and girls. When they came to his village everybody was fast hiding. But one family was caught. This time, this one soldier, he made the whole family line up, father, mother, four children. Other soldiers were wanting the young daughter, who was only maybe twelve or thirteen, but this soldier, he said no, he was an officer. He lined them up, this whole family, and, and, and . . .

The reporter's words die in his throat and he starts to swallow. His chest begins to heave.

Mahadev finds himself clutching his left shoulder tight, trying to protect himself from what is coming. The journalist from Bombay is shivering now, his pen shaking uncontrollably in his hand. They have heard other stories too, today, and they have mounted up inside Mahadev. Suddenly, he is struggling to find space to take this one in. The reporter shakes his head, blinking away tears.

The father of the family and the mother of the family were just begging the officer to kill only them and leave the children, but this man, he told the soldiers to hold the father and the mother and then he started from the smallest child first, a boy of two or so, and then, one by one, one by one, one by one.

• • •

Below Para is a vast burlap-coloured plain dotted here and there with white, and the flight tapes have no record of her first thought then, except for a small, barely audible '*Sht!*', which is the clamped-down tip of the iceberg, which is '*Shit! There is no target!*' Had the Armour divided already? No. It takes a further drop of two thousand feet for her metal-sounder to see them clearly. She loses them briefly as she flattens into her attack gradient, and then she's got them again. Satisfied, she taps her eyes on a second time and goes in.

As Para's Ishir comes low over the target area she sees smoke where her pilots have already hit. The sun has now reached down past the surrounding mountains, and the columns of smoke shine, sculpted almost solid by the dawn light. Her pre-programmed target-radar comes alive, joining her metal-sounder in a tightly synchronised dance of flickering digits. Her eyes rake over her numbers, altitude 500, 400, 300, 200, 185, at 185 she blinks, once at the centre, twice-twice on the left, and her Ishir begins its war by decapitating two camels and taking out an Abrams 8 tank belonging to the 2 Armoured Corps of the Saudi Arabian Army.

• • •

They see the burnt-out wreck a little after they pass the milestone that says JESSORE in English and underneath it again in Bengali, black letters against the yellow cap of the slab, and below, also in chipped black lettering against white, 35 MILES, with the Bengali beneath. The milestone looks the same as the ones they have left behind on the other side of the border. Just like the ones in India, one child says, with wonder in her voice. Viral's father, leading the convoy, sticks his arm out of the window signalling a stop, but there is no need. All the four cars slow down and stop as if they are radio-connected. This is the first proper trace of the war and everybody is out, excited, the children running up to the tank first, even before the mummy-pappas are out of the cars.

Paresh asks his father if he can take a few pictures and Mahadev nods. Paresh gets out, taking the camera with him. Mahadev feels the car emptying around him, but he doesn't move. He sits there silent amidst the slamming of Ambassador doors and the excited chatter, his hands still on the steering wheel. He catches the slight alarm in the voices of the women as they call out to the children, telling them not to go too close, but he pays it no attention. The monsoon gone months ago, the war winter nearly over, but the day at the camp sticks inside him like a virus.

'One by one, one by one, one by one,' he can still hear the reporter translating. 'In the end they left only the father alive.' The reporter shaking his head, as if trying to move his mouth away from the words it was bringing out. 'And he ran after the soldiers' truck, screaming like a madman, begging them, just begging them to kill him, but the soldiers, they just laughed and went.'

Narendra Patel walks up to Mahadev's window, shining with pride. He points to the tank, stabbing the air with his finger. 'Juo Mahadevbhai juo, see what our boys can do!'

There is a slash of yellow in the frame, startling against the green of the paddy field, just behind one twisted arc of metal curving out of the wreck. Mustard flowers, some grown-up has pointed out, from where these Bengalis get their funny-smelling oil. Paresh wishes he has colour film, but his father has loaded black and white. I don't think today you will find subjects for colour. Paresh takes the picture anyway, trying to place the sweetish odour. It doesn't smell like a Bengali kitchen smell.

It's a ghost of a machine, and it looks as though someone has carved out the insides, scooped all the substance out, like a knife scooping out the insides of a coconut, leaving just the shell. Paresh looks closely at the strange slashes of Urdu script, white on the dark green side of the tank. There are also some crudely painted normal numbers and Roman letters and, as he looks closely, he can see another row of stencilled numbers, faint under the new paint. The stencilling much sharper, foreign numbering, not from here.

His mother's voice suddenly, just behind him, dripping with disgust, talking to Viral's mother.

'What is this awful stink, Chandrabehn? They must have been cooking something non-vegetarian.'

Viral's father replying, 'Sumubehn! These Pakistanis weren't cooking, they were cooked! They are the meat! Our General Manekshaw is a real non-vegetarian! Now to even you – especially a patriot like you – have to become non-vegetarian.'

Paresh looks around to see Viral's father chuckling at his own joke.

His mother's face knotted with revulsion and anger. Her voice sharp, cutting through the laughter, 'Kai nahi Narendrabhai, kai nahi, I don't mind, sometimes you have to fight the Asurs. This is Durgamata's land and she has awoken to answer these demons!'

Viral's mother nods in agreement as his father walks off to share the joke with others.

Paresh turns back to the tank and focuses on the numbers. He shoots a couple of pictures, pretending he is a Time-Life photographer under fire in Vietnam. He is about to take another one when he feels a prod in his back.

Viral prompting him, 'Ei, Paresh, why are you so close? Shoot the whole thing, no!'

Paresh keeps looking into the viewfinder as he replies, 'No need. Somebody's already shot the whole thing.'

He takes his eye away from the camera and looks at Viral. Then they both straighten their backs, throw their jaws up and chorus it over the fields together.

'WAR! Means making the OTHER poor dumb –' and their hands come up to slap over their mouths at the same time, cutting out the next word. They stand like that for a moment, staring at each other, the laughter igniting slowly from behind their clamped fingers, pushed back till they can hold it no longer.

• • •

Para comes out of her first pass and climbs again, automatically checking the status of her fighters as she does. Something is not right and it takes her a few seconds to place it. Blue Flight Leader is not following the planned attack pattern. Her plane should be ahead of her, above her by now, ready to go in again. But it's not, it's still engaged, still firing – what the hell is Raksha doing?

She puts her plane into a turn just as Red Flight Leader's voice cuts into her ear. '*Skip – Red One to SQ1, Red One to SQ1. Blue One's gone mad, repeat Blue One's gone mad.*'

She starts to respond but her voice-file refuses to open. She can now see Raksha.

'Look at her, what she's doing. This is from Blue 2's camera, which has the best angle,' the CO's finger jabbing down on the buttons to bring up the exact segment once again.

The camera is above Raksha's Ishir, which is forty-five degrees nose down, engines on hover, spinning over the sea of tents at about four hundred feet. The screen is scratched by a steady line of white from the Ishir's wings connecting to the camp below. Occasionally there is an explosion at the end of the line denoting a hit, but otherwise the stream of missile bullets keeps disappearing into the soft carpet of brown and white. There is a constant movement of dark dots between the tents, like black static on the screen, people trying to run away. There is the flicker of fires suddenly dotting the camp, smaller, different from the huge plumes of smoke where the tanks have been hit.

The CO freezes the image and goes back. 'Let's see it with the colour-segmenter. You will see she is using her entire bloody spectrum.' The image starts up again, this time in black and white with just Raksha's plane and a rectangle around it in colour. 'There, look there's the armour shells . . . now . . .' The colour of the lines changes in contrast to the surrounding black and white, taking on an edge of yellow, 'That's her 60 mm cannon . . .' – there are flashes of orange flame from under the wings – 'and now she's chucked her missiles into the khichdi, complete, total, random! I'm amazed ki she didn't jump out and start shooting with her machine-pistol!' The CO's voice is now angry, the voice of a woman who feels personally betrayed. At slow speed, Raksha's plane spins like a phuljhadi, spraying different colours into the ground. Para watches, saying nothing as the CO and the senior Squadron Leader both shake their heads.

'And this is where you stop her, Bhatt,' says the CO unnecessarily as Para's voice comes on the sound.

'SQ1 to Blue One, Blue One break now, break now, break now Blue One, that's an order. Blue One, I'm locked on you and I *will* release, last time Raksha, *break NOW*.'

'Ma'am, I should have thought of the D-code earlier.'

The CO pauses the disk and shakes her head. 'Nahi, theek hai, it's good that you thought of it at all. I would have deleted her there and then.'

Sitting two thousand feet above Raksha Mahajan, Para almost opens fire but something stops her at the last moment, and she looks away to her side. She switches off her eye-trigger and punches in the code to disable Raksha's weapons. The function is there to wipe out a fighter's weapons computers in case it goes down, to stop them from falling into enemy hands. It has not been intended for this, but the CO and the other two senior officers commend Para on her quick thinking.

'Blue One, I've disabled you. I've taken out your teeth, Blue One, I've disabled you. Order – head home. Course Delta Zebra Fox Two Five, repeat Delta Zebra Fox Two Five. Stay away from our return highway. Try and head home. Good luck and get out.'

On the screen, the white lines disappear and the sun flashes on the Ishir's wings as it continues to spin for a few moments before putting its nose up and moving out of frame.

'So, three whole minutes wasted over target, though she did get two tanks. And a pilot stripped of active duty, but at least you saved us a plane, Bhatt, so theek hai, you made the best of a bad scenario.'

'Yes, Ma'am.' Para keeps looking at the screen, trying to stop her eyes from blinking so much.

• • •

Mahadev says nothing as people climb back into the car. He waits for the doors to shut and starts the engine. The convoy waits for Viral's father, who comes out from behind the tank, adjusting his trousers. He gets into his car and hits a celebratory note on the horn before pulling out onto the highway. The other two cars reply but Mahadev keeps his hands away from the silver horn ring on the steering wheel.

Paresh opens his mouth to say something about the tank, but the different kinds of silences criss-crossing the car stop him. He is sitting in front next to his father and he can sense something tight and dark coming from him. Behind them, on the back seat, are his mother and his father's sister Vasufoi – Photofoi, as he always thinks of her – who's visiting from Ahmedabad. There is another colour photograph there, Vasufoi in her widow's white sari and, in contrast, his mother in a bright cotton Dhakai print, the red dot on her forehead large today. What is not in contrast is the way the two women rustle with a barely repressed triumph. Paresh can tell, just from the way her elbows are on the top of the front seat, that his mother is sitting very erect, that she is suddenly very alert and happy. Vasufoi's eyes are large as she looks out of the window, searching the landscape for more signs of victory.

After a while Vasufoi breaks the silence. 'Kharu kehvaay hawn – ' she starts, but Suman interrupts her by starting a bhajan in a clear voice. 'Devi Bhrahmaani Rudraani Mammaaya, Devi Brahmaani Rudraani Mammaya!' and Vasufoi stops herself and begins to hum along. After a moment she brings her throat out of the side road and joins the highway. She is a much better singer than Suman, but today she keeps her voice low, sticking to the tune and letting Suman's strident voice lead the way. Paresh doesn't understand all the words but he knows it is a song to Durgamata, something about her being fearsome yet merciful. And he knows that while his father would have sliced into anything either of the women might have said, he will have to keep quiet while they are singing.

Sure enough, Mahadev says nothing. He just keeps driving, concentrating on maintaining his distance from the car in front. After a while, Paresh opens up the camera case and starts to focus idly on the passing fields. 'Narada nritya karey torey aagey, Kaanada bain bajaaya.' He sees something that catches his eye and leans forward to get the camera out of the window. 'Devi Brahmaani Rudraani Mamm – don't do that! It will fall out!' says his mother sharply. 'Shut it and give it back to Pappa now!'

Paresh asks his father if he wants the camera back, which is a deliberately silly question given that Mahadev is driving. What Paresh does not expect is his father's answer. Mahadev shakes his head. 'No, you keep it. You keep it from now on. I'll take it if I need it.' Suman pauses to argue, but Vasufoi's singing drives her on and she keeps to the bhajan, her voice climbing back up.

Mahadev remembers the pleasure he used to feel at hearing the noise of the Nikon's shutter. Another linked sound, the film being pulled forward as he worked the winding lever. He remembers the satisfaction he used to feel in his hand when he did that. The smell of a new roll of film as he opened the little can. Suddenly, these things are gone from him. The sound of the camera clicking just brings back the story, the father running after the army truck, then flipping over and over on the ground like a fish snatched from water, trying to scream but no sound coming out from his mouth.

Suman and Vasufoi finish their bhajan and start a new one. Mhaarey maathey hajaar haath vaalo, akhanda mhaari raksha karey. Paresh knows this one – protecting me from above is Him of a Thousand Hands, but he tests me cruelly with difficulties. He can hum along to this one, and he does as they pass a village on the left. A clump of huts, the thatching slightly different from the ones they've left behind in India, a little pond with steep banks, palm trees bending over the water as if they are dipping to have a drink. The water an uneven circle of opaque bright green, shimmering in the winter noon – 'maney karvaa na deto kadi chinta, kasoti mhaari kapari karey' – but no people that they can see. Four dead goats on one side of the pond, their swollen bodies covered with a sprinkling of crows, but Paresh can't see any people.

• • •

Para looks at the photograph again and she feels as though she is now seeing it from the other side, as if she has climbed through its cloud cover and is now looking at it from above. It is an old picture and it hangs, as it has always done, on the wall to the left of the bar in the officers' mess. A gilt frame surrounds the big black and white print of a handsome young Sardar, his beard and mustache black, still fresh and thin on his face, his gaze directed slightly upwards to the sky, aviation goggles perched absurdly on his turban. Taken slightly from below, most of the area behind the young pilot is a deep grey sky with luminous white clouds. Just to the bottom of the picture is a bit of the cockpit and fuselage of his fighter-plane, the legendary old British Gnat trainer that the IAF used so effectively against the far superior Pakistani Sabre jets in 1965. Below the photograph is a yellowed cardboard strip with neatly hand-painted black lettering:

'The People of our Motherland are the wings we fly on.'
– Sqdn. Ldr K.S. Ahluwalia, Param Vir Chakra (Posth.) 1965.
Tally: 11 PAF Sabres.

Para's CO sees her looking at the photograph and laughs.

'Bhatt! Not already thinking of a posthumous medal after just your first mission, I hope.' She jabs Para on the shoulder as if to wake her up. Para opens her mouth to reply but just at that moment she notices the station commander standing next to their table and she leaps up to salute him.

'Sit down beta, sit down.' Group Captain Raza turns to Para's CO, 'No Kamala, this girl may be thinking of a decoration but I don't think she is thinking posthumous.' He pulls up a chair. 'You don't mind if I join you two ladies.'

'Sir, I was just telling Bhatt –'

Raza holds up his hand to interrupt. 'Drink. What will you two have?'

'Thank you sir, a Cokecardi please,' says Para's CO promptly.

'Nothing for me sir, thank you,' mutters Para, almost under her breath.

'NOTHING!?!' the Group Captain and Wing Commander turn on her together.

Kamala Bhowmik puts her hand on Para's arm. 'You know Bhatt it's traditionally considered major bad luck in this Air Group if you refuse a post-op drink from a superior officer?'

'Sorry ma'am, I didn't know that. I'll have a Cokecardi too, sir.'

Raza raises his hand and the waiter comes up at a jog.

'Dˆo Rumcoke aur ek badaa JB Scotch,' he tells the waiter. Then he turns to the women. 'Rum!' he snorts. 'Talking about tradition, I don't think you girls realise what your tradition is. You know that in the old days,' he points to the photograph on the wall, 'you know that you didn't get rum in air force messes? It was regarded as lower class! Good enough for the ground boys, and of course the navy-wallas, but *not allowed* in our IAF messes – we were the elite and the elite did *not* let rum pass their lips! Low-grade fuel, as my old CO used to call it, and he would hesitate to consider someone for promotion if he caught him drinking rum, even though by then it was available at the Officers' Bar. One of the first things our junior officers told us when we arrived at base.'

'Anyway,' he looks at Bhowmik meaningfully, 'last Ops Update says you and your girls are not on again till day after.'

'What's the latest, sir?' Bhowmik asks, all business now, but Raza ignores her question. He takes a pista from the bowl on the table, snaps it open and crunches on it.

'So you can relax, dammit! Have three-four drinks!' he says, dropping two more nuts into his mouth. 'Some of us, on the other hand, some of us have to work tomorrow!' He pauses to swallow before turning to Para.

He is about to say something when the waiter brings the drinks and puts them in the middle of the table. Raza distributes the glasses and the cartons. Para ducks her head in a thank you and watches him pour the mixed whisky-soda into his glass. Bhowmik waits for him to finish before opening her own carton of Rumcoke. She fills her glass and then nods to Para, giving her permission. Para picks up the carton and checks the date window. The words 'Consume by:' are printed next to a liquid display that has the numbers 7/2018 blinking in it. The Coke and Bacardi logos float in and out of each other on the side of the carton. Para takes the red tab and snaps it back to open it. As she pours, the carton softens in her hand, making the sound-chip play the Cokecardi jingle and she remembers the time when Cindy had booby-trapped the Sukhoi simulator with thirty of these set to go off when –

Raza stands up, motioning to the women to remain seated. He raises his glass. 'If there's one thing a genuine airman hates, it is flying a desk.' His voice is loud now, and he pauses to make sure the other officers in the bar are listening. 'And it was my job this morning to sit and watch on my command screens as a squadron of the bravest pilots I have ever seen did what I always liked to do – take the attack to the enemy and put the fear of God into him.' Raza moves his glass towards Bhowmik first and then towards Para. 'Wing Commander Bhowmik.

Squadron Leader Bhatt. On behalf of this airbase and Air Group 6, may I congratulate you and your girls on a sterling display of skill and courage.' The other officers in the bar stand up and applaud, and shouts of 'Go, Bhowmik!' 'Go, Bhatt!' drown out Raza's last words. 'Jai Hind. Victory to the IAF!'

Before the applause has died down Bhowmik is on her feet. Para sends her chair back with her legs as she jumps up, knowing what's coming. Even before Bhowmik begins to speak Para screws up her eyes, trying to order them into staying dry. Somewhere, outside her, she can hear Bhowmik saying 'Flight Lieutenant Sindhu Mundkur' and something else and then something more. She has her glass in her hand and she lifts it along with Bhowmik and Raza, meeting their eyes briefly before taking a sip, no tears, all under control. Other people shouting 'Cindy!', 'To Mundkur!', her own voice saying Cindy's name quietly but clearly, her eyes locked on two pistas spilled out of the bowl, looking at the tiny barcodes on the shells, as other officers turn back to their own groups, air force etiquette – musn't make too much of it, could be any one of them tomorrow, acknowledge and move back to normal mode, everybody now sitting down, someone turning on the big TV that hangs above the bar.

Raza grips Para's shoulder firmly. 'Para, beta, are you all right?'

Para nods back crisply. 'Sir! Yes sir. She was a damn good pilot sir, and we'll all miss her . . .' but Raza cuts through her standard reply. 'Don't be afraid to grieve for her beta, and allow your girls to also – you know – it is important. But don't dwell on it. We have a war to fight here.' Para nods again, saying nothing. 'I will of course do the needful in terms of letter to family and all that, but if either of you want to write also . . .'

'I would also like to write a letter, sir, if I may. I know her people,' Para says.

Raza nods a yes and changes the subject. 'You know, Kamala, damn good pictures, I have to say. This Bhatt and her girls – damn good – among the best we've seen today. I've sent a download of the whole mission to the Air Strat chaps at Secundrabad and I'm sure I'll be hearing good things from them.' He pauses to drink. 'And I don't think this Mahajan business will matter too much. The kill ratio is too beautiful.'

'I hope so, sir,' says Bhowmik. 'First time everybody was seeing action, I hope so ki they will factor that in . . .'

'Yes, of course they will. And anyway, you asked about the latest, well, they should be happy about the whole scenario at Strat HQ. Their plans have worked out well it seems – 7 Corps's airborne light armour was about twenty kilometres from Pindi GHQ at eighteen thirty IST and their rear is already linking with elements of Pillai's thrust from Amritsar.'

Kamala Bhowmik's eyes light up. 'Pindi! Already? Sir! Sir, so you were right. When you said a little more than twelve hours, I didn't think it was possible –'

'Once there was the will that was never going to be a problem, Kamala – they've stuffed Pindi–Islamabad sector with too many brass and too few soldiers. Counting totally on their air chaps, and their missile command! Chaah! The problem was going to be what we have sorted out for them this morning. And the north. That will be not so easy but . . . dekhi jaayegi . . . so far so good.' Raza knocks his drink back and gets up to go. 'Well girls, well done again.' Para and Bhowmik are standing up as well. Para takes the plunge.

'Sir . . . ma'am . . . can I see her once?' Raza gives Bhowmik a look, as if to ask, What's this? Para speaks again, getting the words out quickly. 'Sir . . . Mahajan, can I see her at least once before she goes?'

Raza doesn't meet Para's eyes. He gives Bhowmik a quick glance, a slight flick of his eyes to say no, to say you handle it, and walks away. Bhowmik turns back to Para. 'Sit down Bhatt. Have some water.' Bhowmik's voice is warm but it is still an order.

Para sits down, her back erect, at attention. Bhowmik finds a waiter. 'Paani. Ek poora jug,' she orders, before turning back to the table and sitting down herself. She waits for the waiter to bring the water. Para pours herself a glass, drinks it, and pours another. Bhowmik waits until she has finished half of the second glass before saying anything.

'It's not a good idea, Bhatt. You have to move on.'

Para says nothing. She finishes the second glass of water and pours a third. Bhowmik treats that as a reply and answers.

'That's the way it is, Bhatt, in war. Someone dies without managing to fire a single shot and we salute her. And someone who loses discipline and fires too much gets taken off. Anyway, she's lucky to be alive.'

'Because Red Flight were good today, ma'am, they thokoed the SAM chip-boards pretty fast. And the Saudis didn't get their Stingers together in time. As you saw, ma'am, there was nothing after those first two that locked on to me and Mahajan.'

Para gulps down the water.

'What you girls did wasn't easy, Bhatt. Get that idea out of your head.'

'No ma'am. I'm not saying that . . . but we were lucky. And the civilian casualties.'

'Forget it, Bhatt. Sometimes, at the beginning of a new war, you have to fight in an old way. Sometimes you have to fight an old war first, before you can get to the new one.'

Hands trying to grab her as she slides. The roar of the sea far below, and the grass suddenly very smooth under her. She blinks her eyes, trying to shoot away the memory. Some of the pilots have gathered to look up at the TV but she can't hear the sound. The sea has turned into a buzzing in her head. Soft punches around her ears that get harder and become painful. She swallows some water and shakes her head. She stretches her neck and shakes her head one more time. Suddenly, after a few seconds, it goes, and she's clear again.

Bhowmik is watching her.

'Stop it Bhatt. You couldn't have known. And you had your orders.'

'The camels, ma'am, the camels were a sign, I should have pulled the girls out after that first run and checked.'

'Checked how exactly please? By landing and opening each tent? Squadron to hover at five hundred feet and get fired at by Stingers while Squadron Leader goes social-servicing? Excuse me, maaf karey, so sorry to disturb you, but are you Irani refugees in here or are you a Saudi tank? Oh sorry!'

'The children, ma'am.' Para picks up her glass to move it away.

Bhowmik leans forward and grips Para's hand, forcing her to put the glass down. Her voice is angry now. 'Don't get sentimental, Bhatt. Any war will have civilian casualties, okay? Don't tell me there were no children in Mumbai.'

'Ma'am.'

'Bhatt. Your planes took out thirty-eight tanks in one sortie. Thirty Bloody Eight. Do you understand what that means? Even the Russians in the Second World War didn't have that sort of kill ratio against German Panzers caught in the mud without ammo. And why do you think we sent you girls in? Why do you think we didn't send in the Remotes? Can you imagine the civilian casualties in an RPV attack? Whole place wiped out, everyone dead? Think of it like this – those coward bastards were holding those refugees hostage. Now they'll think twice before parking their weaponry in the middle of civilians.'

'Yes ma'am.'

'Don't you bloody yes ma'am me. That was part of their spearhead. Was. You girls was-ed it and I'm fucking proud of you. We didn't want to overload you girls in the pre-ops but those tanks were headed for the oil fields in Kutch. Eight hundred more kilometres, basically two more days, and they'd have split up into three tank squadrons leading Pak ground units straight into Bhuj and then Rajkot. You think there are no children in Kutch? Are Kutchhi children less important than Irani children?'

'Ma'am . . . are Irani children less important than –'

'Shut up, Bhatt. Have another drink or I'll put you away for insubordination.'

Someone turns up the sound on the TV. A woman reporting to camera, people carrying bodies on makeshift stretchers behind her.

'Good evening. This is the news on ABCNN. The main headlines. It's war between India and the Pakistan–Saudi Arabia alliance. Early this morning fighter-bombers of the Indian Air Force attacked a refugee camp in the Kharan area on the border between Pakistan and Iran. The target, apparently, was a small squadron of Saudi Arabian tanks parked among the Iranian refugee tents . . .'

• • •

Viral looks absently at the dolphin knocking on the glass. 'Trained,' he thinks, pulling on his whisky, 'like everybody else here.' Behind the dolphin there is a couple getting married. The groom swims up to the bride, who's doing a stationary paddle next to someone who might be the priest. Viral is guessing that the bride is the bride because the goggle rims, diving vest and tanks are all a fluorescent white. The groom wears black but his legs are a very cold pale in the greenish water. He takes something out of a pouch on his side – the ring – and puts it on the bride's fingers. The bride does the same thing back. Viral notices that she has nice legs. A bit Chinesey but nice, the calves not too fat as they come out of the white flippers.

A school of bright orange fish curtains past as man and wife turn, holding hands, and bow towards the bar. There is clapping from the families grouped together this side of the glass. People pour champagne and clink glasses at each other and at the newlyweds. The couple bows again and twin streams of bubbles rise from their masks, catching the lights as they flurry up. Viral sees another diver taping the whole thing, swimming around the couple and the priest, the little light on his camera reflecting off the shiny surfaces on their suits.

The dolphin knocks on the glass again. It seems to be smiling at him directly, but Viral doesn't respond. Something has caught his hearing. He turns away from the glass wall and finds the source of the sound – a TV monitor at the next table. It's a small flat screen and Viral knows it slides up when you press a button.

The BBC anchor twists in his chair and looks at a man. He makes a little gesture with his fingers as if wiping away the air in front of his nose. 'Jack Macpherson, you are the leading air strategy analyst for *Jane's Defence Weekly*. Can you explain to us how the Indian planes got through what was supposed to be a formidable air-defence system – indeed a system set up by the Americans and, according to some reports, actually manned by US personnel?'

It takes Viral a while to latch on to the man's Scottish burr, but once he gets it, it's not too difficult. 'From what we can tell, it seems there was a "hole" in the Pak–Arab electronic wall, and by the looks of it the Indians found it.'

The anchor is quick to interrupt. 'What does that mean exactly, a hole?'

The screen suddenly comes at Viral, sharp, taking him over, his drink, his air ticket, his travel plans.

The man at the next table looks at Viral and nods towards the monitor lying dormant on Viral's own table. Watch your own TV, don't look at mine. Viral reaches for the buttons to switch on his TV, but he doesn't take his eyes off his neighbour's screen. The expert is well into the reply by the time Viral finds BBC World.

'. . . so, it is still a matter of the resources you have available, even with the best of new technology. Our conjecture is that the Pakistanis gambled on the attack coming either very low over the ground or very high – the Indian Air Force sending in their Sukhoi bombers well above the Pak–Saudi fighters' top altitude. They gambled on covering the high and the low, if you see what I mean, and it's a gamble they lost – the Indians obviously had a good idea of where the danger lay, and they managed to find what we call the "bandwidth", which was, by and large, unguarded. They came in through the middle, so to speak, and that is unusual, to say the least. Also, curiously, there seemed to be no sign of the HAARP weather interference that the US Air Force usually deploys in situations like this.'

A weather develops out of the screen to envelope Viral. A dark bank of question-bearing clouds pulling a storm front of unwanted answers. Was this the one that was always coming? Would they fuck it up? Had the Japs put all the money in place? Or had the Government morons gone out on a limb of promises? He had seen no telltale footprints on the markets, so how had they done it?

The anchor turns back to camera. 'As we reported earlier, the attack began with a raid by a crack women's squadron flying Indian-made Ishir 650A fighters. The tanks the Indian Air Force attacked, were, by all projections, headed for recently discovered oilfields in the Kutch area on India's western border.' A map comes up on screen as the man continues. 'The strike on Kharan seems to have been the first component of several pre-emptive attacks across Pakistan and Pakistani-occupied Punjab by the Indian Air Force, and was followed by armour-led columns of the Indian Army breaking across the line of control at several points.'

The map develops three arrows striped orange, white and green, the northernmost curving from Amritsar towards Peshawar, the one in the middle coming out of the Delhi border area and pointing straight towards Rawalpindi/Islamabad and the southern one curving out of Rajasthan to stop almost over Karachi, which is shown in black, as they tend to do cities decimated by nuclear bombs.

As the map begins to track southwards, Viral shuts his eyes. He knows what will come next, the other blackened bit, his bit, south Bombay. He has seen it many times now, but it still knifes into him. The peninsula, the southern half blackened out, as if by a censor's random black marker. The caption 'Mumbai' on one side. He opens his eyes and sure enough, there it is, their-Mumbai-his-Bombay, at the bottom of the screen, at the very edge of the theatre of war.

• • •

As the lift doors open he raises his fingers slowly to his face, not aware of what he is doing, wanting to smell her smell again. She notices, gives a start of laughter and slaps his hand away from his nose – Ei, you just stop it now – she grabs his hand with both her hands and tries to push it into his jeans pocket, glancing up again and again to make sure none of the drivers and darwans are watching – Just . . . keep it in your POCKET, you asshole, IN your pocket! I want everything back in your pants, okay? This is, we are in, PUBLIC now, and you may not believe it but, like, I have a decent rep here, okay?

– Okay, okay, sorry, sorry, okay.

– *What am I doing with a total footpath-chhap like you anyway?*

Her car's with the mechanic so they get into a taxi and she sits as far away from him as the Fiat's back seat will allow, her fingers hooked on the window glass – which doesn't go all the way down like it does in Ambassadors – her jaw on her knuckles, looking away from him, pushing her face into the afternoon sea breeze.

At the Udipi near Churchgate she makes him first go and wash his hands. As he comes back to the table he is suddenly very aware of the mess of sound around them. The traffic on the road outside, the metallic announcements filtering through from the station across the gali, the waiters calling out their orders as if reporting crimes to a lower court magistrate, the clink and clank of steel on steel as people factory through their food, the rrrrrrrp of thick liquid, a toasted smell on the back of it, as a waiter pulls ropes of coffee between two small glasses at impossible angles. As impossible and beautiful as making love to her, as risky and fragile and rock-sure as her sitting across the table from him.

Slowly the sharp smell of the sambar and the thick coconut tang of the chutney take over his soap-smelling fingers. She watches him eat, a half-smile playing on her face, her green eyes wide, as if watching a strange animal in a zoo. – Hungry, huh? she says after he's demolished two idlis and one of her vadas. – *Aren't you?* he asks and she smiles a full smile and bites into a vada.

The waiter comes past, slinging two dosas on their table as he goes. The steel plates slide a bit and one comes to a stop a little to his left. Hers spins to a stop just in front of her.

She looks down at the dosa and she loses her smile, like a plane going into a cloud. She keeps her eyes away from him and moves two fingers lightly over the slope of freckled brown, tracing something private. When her hand comes away he sees that her fingertips are shiny with oil. He keeps watching her as she goes completely still. He hesitates to touch his own dosa, needing to wait, needing to see what she does. She absently pushes a strand of hair back from her face and then, suddenly, she tears into the dosa, ripping away a bit, revealing the yellow innards of the alu masala. She takes the bit of the dosa, captures some of the potato and dips it into the sambar. He waits for the rest of the movement, for the hand to take the dosa out of the sambar and up into her mouth, but it doesn't come. She pauses, letting the sambar lap around her fingers. She looks up at him – It's not . . . it's not like it's . . . love-shove or something, is it?

Her voice is thicker than normal, as if she's put a filter on it. He hesitates, finds something in him like a stranger who's suddenly walked in through the door, something violent, not wanting to give away the possibility so easily. A whole train goes before he can make himself say anything. In the end he plays it safe because he doesn't want to lose her. The words coming out of the wrong scabbard – No, no, ya, not love. No.

She grins, but the relief doesn't quite climb up to her eyes. – Guess, just this damn town Bombay, no? – then, almost to herself – That's good. That's good that it's not any of that love-shove ghichpich, then she leans forward quickly and puts the dripping bit of dosa and alu in his mouth.

On their way out they stop to watch the man making the dosas. He takes the cream-coloured liquid from a bowl, the ladle dripping slightly, and pours it in the centre of the smoking tawa. The liquid hesitates for a moment and then begins to spread in a circle. The man waits for its natural movement to begin before gently coaxing the mixture out into thinner and thinner circles with the back of his ladle.

They watch as the liquid sizzles into a skin, the rings alternately translucent and slightly fat, the pores opening as the heat works into it. He suddenly remembers an archive film he once saw, a hydrogen bomb spreading into clouds, filmed from a high aircraft, rings pulsing out of the midriff of the mushroom column. He turns to her to tell her this and sees that she is stifling some great laughter. Before he can ask she has grabbed his hand and pulled him out of the Udipi. The sun hits him straight in the face, making him screw up his eyes as she leads him towards the sea. – What? What? he keeps asking but she doesn't answer, she just keeps ducking her head and gulping back the laugh till they've crossed over Marine Drive.

Once across, she opens her mouth and gasps for breath before finally finding the words.

– See, you footpath-chhap photo-walla from Calbloodycutta, see what kind of thinking you've reduced me to!

– Achha, enough. Will you tell me now?

She clutches his hand tighter, as if needing help to control herself.

– No, it's too stupid . . . it's just too damn . . . okay, okay, I'll tell you. You see, once I'd gone with my gang, gang means me, Aarti and Nilofer, once in college third year we decided to go see . . . you know – one of these morning shows, you know? Like Sunday-morning shows? You must be having them too, in Cal, you know like –

– Yeah, yeah, I get it. So?

– *Well*, we decided to see what they would say if suddenly these three chicks landed up, like in the middle of this sea of dirty-minded men with their dicks hanging out of their eyes, like. And this movie was called something like Her Secret Knowledge or something, Hindi mei translated something like Gupt Stri Gyaan. And in the middle of all this bharchak meat on the screen, suddenly, there was this . . . this like diagram of a woman's body. Like a Films Division educational film? And there was this commentary about 'when a woman reaches her climax' and then! From between the legs, okay? From between the legs comes this – dhan tan tadaank! – come these CIRCLES and with music going up and this woman's voice on the sound going aaah, aaah, aaah!

– You girls were mad, you could have got –

– Nutthing ya, nutthing, so when this, uh, this ORGASM happened all the audience started clapping and when we saw them doing this we just screamed because it was so funny.

– And?

– And so they kicked us out! Guy comes with his torch, you know, '*Aap bai log disturb kar rahaa hai! Bahir niklo!*' So we left, meaning we'd had enough by then anyway, but afterwards, always we had this gang joke, you know, like if we saw some guy one of us liked then we wouldn't say anything, we'd just take a pen and draw like these circles for each other. And go aah aah aah under our breath also.

– So, like why remember this just now?

She looks at him, not believing he hasn't got it. He gets it just before she tells him. – The guy making the dosa, you dodo, didn't you see the circles?

She is still grinning as she waves down a taxi. They get in and she doesn't sit so far from him this time. As the taxi pulls out she looks at her watch – still about four hours before Ai and Dad come home. – Hm, good, he answers. She brings her fingers up to her nose and takes a deep melodramatic sniff and then doubles up again, biting her lip and looking up at him. He blushes and looks away out of the window. He can smell petrol and he can smell the sea.

• • •

Viral can smell the sea, but he knows it's not the glassed-off water next to him. It's a Bombay memory-sea he is smelling.

The anchor turns to another man sitting on his left, who is a political commentator on South Asian affairs. Viral strains to hear his name, but the blood pounding in his head makes it difficult. He shakes his head to clear it, takes another pull on his whisky and tries to concentrate. The man is giving a quick rundown of the last twenty years of conflict in the subcontinent, things that everybody knows – Kashmir, the Kargil mini-war in '99, the 2007 attack by China and Pakistan that left parts of the Indian north-east under Chinese control and half of Kashmir and Punjab under Pakistani occupation . . . the terrorist loose-nuke that devastated south Bombay in '12, the maverick return strike on Karachi by one Indian missile commander even though there was no direct proof of Pakistani involvement . . . the list chants through Viral's head like an old, old litany. There is applause when the analyst finishes. The newlyweds have come into the bar now, changed into suit and gown, and the families cheer and throw little bouquets at them. A cake is wheeled in. It has bright blue wavy water lines all around the sides and two sugared divers embracing on top.

'What's the difference this time?' asks the anchor.

Viral knows what the difference is this time, but he still forces himself back into the rectangle of the screen. The political analyst pauses to clear his throat before replying.

'Well, I would say the difference centres around three things: first and foremost, the India–China balance has changed. After the newly elected government in Beijing reached an agreement with the Indians on Tibet and Arunachal there has been a massive de-escalation of armed forces on both sides. So, China being firmly neutral, it could even be said pro-India, in the sense that that is where the real Chinese/Japanese economic interests lie, so, that being the case – unlike last time – the Indians are not fighting a war on two fronts. And, with the US unable to intervene directly at the moment, I would say that the Indians have found the gap in the middle, not only militarily, but in the political sense as well.'

Behind the analyst, the new Chinese flag gets a white cross across it.

'Secondly, unlike last time, neither side now possesses nuclear weapons. The enforced disarmament after Mumbai and Karachi has changed the equation back to the old counting, of what used to be called "conventional" weapons, and in these India has always had the advantage – in short, it has more planes, more tanks, more ships and more soldiers. And they've had the time and the money to build these up over the last ten years, whereas Pakistan's internal troubles and, I would stress, its various Central Asian misadventures, have led to a situation where the military is overstretched and yet again totally dependent on the US and, of late, Saudi Arabian backing.'

A missile icon appears under the Chinese flag and gets a white cross.

'Thirdly –' Viral wonders for a moment what the familiar buzzing sound is, till he realises it's his comm-pad. He reaches inside his jacket and pulls it out to see who it is. The message is from Andy Wong of the Biznasia Network in Hong Kong. Can he change his ticket and appear on their morning show tomorrow to discuss the economic fallout of the new war? Viral doesn't reply. He had predicted this war five years ago and talked at length about the economic fallout. He has nothing new to say and he doesn't feel like repeating himself. He doesn't feel like changing his travel plans.

His eyes wandering, Viral sees the man on the next table tap something on the side of his screen to change his picture. He looks at the borders of his own screen and locates the button for Multiple Picture. He picks up the swizzle stick with the Singapore Airport lion and uses the sharp end to tap the button. The analyst's voice continues, but the pictures change. The scrolling type across the bottom of the screen informs him that he is looking at the American airbase on Diego Garcia Island on full alert. A line of fat military transports slowly rolls down the tarmac, reminding him of waitresses pushing dim-sum trolleys.

Viral watches this procession for a while, listening to the BBC analyst talking, and then, keeping the BBC sound on, he starts going through the other channels, one by one, pausing, checking to see what each is carrying about the war.

The bar is dark, each table lit from above with an individual spot, except for the area where the marriage party is gathered, where there is a bright pool of light and noise. Around Viral there are several other First Class transit passengers, many alone, the glow from the table TVs lighting their faces. Some twosomes, one or two groups, their hand baggage in little piles next to them, the sea-world constantly unfolding in the background. There is a buzz of excited conversation from three or four of the tables where Indian passengers are sitting, the news now having spread.

Viral tilts the glass against his mouth without looking at it and finds the whisky finished. He turns and waves to a waiter. The man sees the fat guy signalling. He checks the passenger's name against his palmtop as he goes over. 'Sir, what can I get for you?'

'Another Macallan, a triple please this time, and no ice, yeah? Just like last time, some water on the side.'

The waiter bows. 'Right away, Mr Patel.'

'Thanks buddy.' Viral turns back to surfing his channels.

NippOnLine has a karate tournament on its home-screen with two little inset boxes, one with a news commentator and the other with an animated map of the war zone. The moving arrows on the map develop a strange contrapuntal rhythm to the feints and kicks of the two men fighting.

'Your whisky, sir.'

'Thanks,' says Viral, without looking up. He absently puts his left palm on the I-d sensor the waiter holds out, takes it off, and then picks up his glass. He takes a sip and realises he has forgotten to add water. He pours a tiny amount into the whisky and takes a large gulp. The fire weaves down his throat as he taps his TV again. The screen trips on to Doordarshan World. Fighter aircraft landing in pairs. A sheet of heat pulsing off the desert behind them. The lurid orange, white and green circle of the DD channel symbol spinning in the top left corner of the screen. The scroll at the bottom informing him that these pictures – from an unspecified fighter base in central India – are exclusive to

Doordarshan. A tele-shot of a fighter nose filling up the frame. Then another shot, the cockpit hood sliding back and a pilot climbing out. Another angle, the pilot, now on the ground, taking the helmet off and looking at camera.

The yell catches the waiter just as he reaches the bar, right in the middle of his back like a blast from a sawn-off shotgun. He whirls around in panic, thinking there must be something wrong with the whisky. The fat guy is up, his chair knocked back, the water jug smashing on the floor, people at nearby tables pushing back their chairs in fright, the dolphin flipping away on the other side of the glass.

The fat guy is bent forward, screaming at the TV.

'Go baby GOOO! Go baby go! Fukkkin A!' His fists hammer the air around his ears, another yell rollercoastering out of him, almost before the first one has finished, *'Fuck 'em up! Fukkin FUCK 'EM UP GOOD!'*

The waiter is a brave man, and though he doesn't understand what's going on, he is the first one to react. He runs to the table. By the time he reaches it, the fat man has collapsed onto his knees. The spotlight shines down on his bald head, and catches the tears as they stumble out from the shadowed sockets of his eyes.

The waiter is thinking emergency and ambulance, but as he gets closer he sees the man is actually not physically ill. He is now holding the edge of the table, still staring at the TV. His voice is now almost down to a whisper.

'Yes, Para beta, yes . . . do it for Virikaka. And remember . . . the other poor dumb bastard . . . remember, not you, the OTHER poor dumb bastard.'

• • •

A Stars and Stripes filling the whole screen. They must have used a lot of Signal toothpaste for the stripes, Paresh thinks. War drums going Thak-Thak-Thak, Thak-Thak-Thak. They're seeing it for a third time in less than a week, but the cheese roll is still suspended in front of Viral's open mouth as they wait for the first scene.

A dot at the bottom of the screen, growing into a helmet and head, tiny against the flag, then the rest of the body as he comes striding up to stop with a red stripe behind him as broad as his head. Cavalryman's riding boots, riding crop, short green tunic crowded with decorations on the left, the green helmet with a general's three stars and below it an A *in a circle. The camera goes in as he begins to speak, left hand on waist, the crop held in his fist. The voice rasps into their ears like a broken gear-box trying to push a truck uphill.*

'War!' he says, and they mouth the words along with him, 'is not about dyin' for your Cuntreh!' He pauses and looks around. 'War is about making the OTHER poor dumb byastard die for HIS Cuntreh!' The last bit they both chorus aloud, and shh-ing noises wasp out from the people around them. Viral bites into his cheese roll. Paresh draws on his straw to pull up some Coca-Cola.

After the movie, standing outside on the wide steps of the new cinema hall, one of the older Patel cousins says, 'Hmmh, achha. I always thought Patton was a Pakistani tank.'

'It is an American tank that they gave to Pakistan. It's named after this guy,' says Paresh, who is feeling informative. 'In the Second World War the Americans had Sherman tanks, which is what they showed in the movie, they were named after Tecumseh Sherman, who was an earlier general of theirs.'

'For a Cal kid you know a lot,' says Viral's cousin.

'Better than being a Bombay know-nothing.' The words are out of Paresh's mouth before he can stop them. The older boy stares at Paresh, wondering whether he can get away with slapping him. Paresh stares back, Rommel with his supply lines cut off staring at Patton. The cousin decides against taking it up and moves away to talk to someone else.

Viral pushes Paresh in the other direction and changes the subject. 'If Dad gets transferred to Bombay we might get a flat in Sherman Apartments,' he says, looking at the evening crowd buzzing around the new cinema. 'When are your momdad moving here?' asks Paresh. 'Oh, not soon. Maybe in five years' time, if Dad gets to be Senior Personnel Manager.' He pauses, thinking about it for a moment. 'I like Bombay,' he adds.

'I like Bombay for holidays,' says Paresh, 'but for living I like Calcutta.'

• • •

Viral looks out of his window and sees the engines swivel. Even though he knows what will happen now, he pauses the TV and waits for the announcement. Sure enough, after a minute or so, the voice comes up in his headphones.

'This is the Captain speaking. We have been asked by Calcutta Air Traffic Control to stationarise our position because they are having a stack problem. We shall be in this position for not longer than fifteen minutes, I hope. Please continue to enjoy your flight.' He pronounces it 'Kalkoota'.

These guys are good, Viral thinks, a lot of the new cowboy carriers wouldn't even bother telling you. They would just start the spin and let the passengers figure it out for themselves.

Through the window he can now see two aircraft below them, one a little bigger than the other, because it's closer, and they look like two paper cut-outs pinned to a wallpaper of clouds. They look as if they are not moving, but Viral knows they are doing exactly the same thing as his own plane, spinning in place, while the traffic controllers sort out their mess. Viral watches till the window loses them, moving on to a different patch of sky as the plane continues its rotation.

The air hostess comes up to his seat and smiles down. 'Your coffee, sir.' She places the tray with the fresh cup and the little cafetière in front of him and pushes the plunger. Then she picks up his old cup and saucer and begins to move away. His thank you is too loud because he's forgotten about his headphones and she smiles over her shoulder to acknowledge it. It's his sixth pot of coffee since take-off three hours ago. He knows there is another hour and a half to go before they land at Ahmedabad and he needs to sober up before then.

As the plane moves around, three other aircraft come into view, still as insects suspended in lab jars. Except he can see a beam of sunlight change off the green tail of a Cathay Singapore A360, which is the one closest to them. Viral has been in these traffic jams many times before. There is invariably one when approaching the Heathrow–Gatwick–Stansted cluster, and quite often one over Tegel Two, when flying in and out of Berlin, but he has never seen one over India. Trust them to stack up over Cal, Viral thinks, where else?

He knows that even in the old days, even when not many carriers landed there, Calcutta was a major touch-point for international flights. Despite an airport boasting regular landing by only three international airlines – Air India, Aeroflot and Lot – thirty-five thousand feet above Calcutta was a crowded place. Airliners flying from Australia and the Far East reported to the Dum Dum control tower before turning their noses towards Europe. Coming the other way, planes flying west to east also radioed Dum Dum before finally leaving the land mass of Eurasia to head south-east. Now Calcutta has two airports – the big sprawl of Netaji Subhash Bose International, sitting on the ghost of Dum Dum, and the newer and slightly smaller Rabindranath Tagore, where the old airstrip at Barrackpore used to be. Two airports handling the traffic of three, given that Mujib International was now shut down, covered by a high speed rail-link that got you from Rabindranath to Dhaka in two hours.

Viral gulps down the cup of coffee and pours some more from the cafetière. No sugar, no milk, no messing around with decaf, just good, strong, black, kadvi coffee.

He decides he needs a cigarette with the second cup and pulls his headphones down around his neck. He switches off the infrared connection to the TV and tries to haul himself out of his seat. The seat-belt cuts into his stomach, holding him back. Viral looks down and sees the little white button on the buckle turn orange. Viral taps it and the light turns green. After a moment, the buckle opens and the belt straps get sucked down into the sides of his seat. He is free to go.

Had the light turned red instead of orange, he would not have been able to get up from his seat. Viral knows that this new feature has little to do with passenger safety and everything to do with insurance companies now refusing to cover airlines for minor injuries sustained during turbulence. He knows this in some detail, because he has been instrumental in finding money for research into different hygiene systems to enable passengers to evacuate their bladders and bowels without moving from their seats in emergencies.

Holding his cup, Viral walks past the seat clusters and reaches the corridor where the privacy booths are located. At the other end of the parallel rows of doors he can see the instructor putting two women through their paces in the gym cabin, none of the three under six feet four. 'The Flying Dutch,' he thinks, and then, 'This is not a good time in history to be short.'

He sees a green light on one of the doors and walks up to it, hoping it is a smoking booth. He checks the door for the cigarette sign, taps in his credit code and puts his left palm on the I-d scanner. The door slides open, sending a whiff of some air-freshener straight up his nose. He goes in and presses the button to shut the door.

As the door begins to slide shut, a woman knocks on it and the door stops sliding. 'Asseblif? Meneer?' She smiles at him enquiringly. 'I'm here to offer you our Emmanuelle Service.' All but the last two words in Dutch.

Dark skin. Indian, or possibly Sri Lankan, with a perfect Dutch accent. Short little tunic and pants, very different from the air hostesses' uniforms. There is a slight murmur of blood between his legs, but not enough. He may have considered doing something with her, but he knows she's not available. She's just there to show him the menu. He isn't really in the mood, but he asks anyway. 'Can I see who is free?'

'You certainly can, sir,' she says, switching to English as she comes into the cabin. She flicks her remote at the screen next to the couch.

'Would you like to meet one of our young ladies, sir, or one of our young men?'

'Oh, women only, please,' says Viral.

The woman nods as if she's guessed right. She waits for the first face to come up on the screen.

'Let's see . . . at the moment we have . . . Rita . . .' her sentence slopes up into a question.

Rita's face comes up on the screen, bright smile – Punj, Viral guesses. 'Rita is from Delhi,' the woman confirms brightly, 'and she tells me she is feeling full of energy today.'

As the picture changes to a full-length shot of her walking down the

First Class aisle, Viral wonders how Rita feels on other days. Sari and choli, nice body, not too tall but not short either, long black hair. There are two icons on the left side of the screen – a mouth, and what looks vaguely like a woman's derrière. Both are crossed out.

'And then we have . . . Anke here, from Utrecht, in Holland. I'm sure Anke would love to meet you.' Anke is blonde, no smile, but with a classic, fake, I-want-you-now pout. The next image is of her long body draped across a First Class sleeper-seat, skirt and blouse in disarray, pretending to wake up, ruffling her hair before looking into the lens, and then her eyes going down to the camera's crotch and widening in awe. The mouth icon is uncrossed but the derrière is blocked. The woman senses Viral's disinterest and quickly plays her next card. Viral doesn't hear the name '. . . which means little flower in Cantonese'. There is a close-up of the Little Flower's eyes and then her whole face. A cross on the mouth icon, but the derrière icon clear . . . no, nothing downloading for him today. Viral raises his hand to stop the woman.

'Thank you.' He smiles at her, 'They are all very lovely and so are you, but not this time. Thank you.'

The woman smiles back, semi-genuine, and points her remote at the screen to wrap up her goods. 'No problem, sir.' She seems not at all put out. 'All of us at Emmanuelle look forward to serve you next time.'

Viral lights his cigarette as the door wipes shut. He looks around him, noting with satisfaction that the booth is spotless. These things are charged per every half an hour and they cost a packet, but what the hell. A sleeperette with a pillow and blankets, another seat for those who don't want to stretch out, a TV screen and a window. A fridge and a drinks cabinet on one side with a scanner that will automatically record whatever he takes out. But he won't be needing that today, just as he didn't need the sex service. He remembers other flights and imagines the mess being with one of the women would have made. He is glad he said no – right now he needs neat and tidy.

He pulls the window screen down, blocking out the bright cloud-light outside. He switches the wallpaper imaging from floating tulips to rainforest, dims the reading light and switches on the TV. All around him, the walls grow a thick vegetation. Rain drips down from leaf to leaf and the light follows it, hardly there, trickling down like the water through the sieve of dense green.

Viral settles himself down in the chair and watches the two arms of the seat-belt come up around his waist. He takes a drag from his cigarette and puts his headphones back on. He works the channel button on the right headphone to find BBC World again. Aerial shots of the dry mountains around Kharan make a rectangular oasis of dusty brown against the lush jungle on the wall. He recognises the Scottish burr of the *Jane's* man well before they cut back to the news desk. The anchor and the analyst are still there, obviously pulling an all-nighter, proper old-fashioned wars like this being hard to come by.

The anchor asks another question: 'Jack, now what about this ammunition that the Indian fighters are supposed to have used?'

'Well, basically what we are talking about are munitions made using depleted uranium or DU. It was discovered that the material was much more effective for penetrating armour than normal tungsten-based munitions. It is what the US Air Force and the RAF first used in the Gulf War against Iran in 1991 and then again in the NATO strikes in the Balkans in the late '90s and early this century. There was a hue and cry at the time, because DU-based bullets and shells supposedly leave radiation and many attributed the "Gulf War Syndrome" and, later, what was called the "Kosovo Strain" to their deployment, but there has never been any conclusive proof connecting DU-based munitions to radiation-related diseases.'

'I seem to remember – didn't the Russians object at the time?'

'Yes they did. And after all the fuss they made, it was found that they'd also armed their tanks and planes with similar ammunition against Chechnya. In any case, the use of DU was discontinued in 2005 in Europe, but by then Britain had sold the technology and a fair amount of actual ammunition to some countries, and India was one of them.'

Suddenly, Viral feels anger coursing through him like electricity. Fuck you, you holier-than-thou hypocrite scumfucks, he thinks, first you make it, then you sell it, then you point fingers when people use it, fuck you. He realises he has said the last words out loud. And, before he knows it, he has clicked out of his belt, got up and reached the drinks cabinet. He takes out a tumbler and smacks it down on the little shelf. Then he finds the little bottles of single malt, grabs two of them and pulls off the air-tight seals. The pilot's voice interrupts the TV sound just as he empties the second bottle into the glass.

'This is the Captain. We have just received information that there is heavy, unseasonal rain over Karnavati. The rainstorm is likely to continue for an indefinite period so we are obliged to divert to the nearest Heavy International Airport, which is Bangalore. I regret this diversion, and we will be doing our best to put passengers on the first available domestic flight to Karnavati. All Karnavati-destination passengers please contact your cabin steward for our free-call service. Calcutta Air Control has cleared us for Bangalore and we will now be coming out of our stationary position.'

Viral feels the plane make a small movement as the pilots pull it out of the spin, vaguely like a train carriage bumping as new bogeys are added. He takes his whisky and goes over to the window. He slides it open and looks out. He can tell they are now moving straight, the other spinning aircraft flicking past the window as the plane gradually crosses over from stationary power to cruising airspeed. The anchor stops in mid-sentence. His voice goes up slightly.

'We have just had unconfirmed reports that the US may be using HAARP weather interference across the front to try and slow down the Indian Army columns. Jack, if this is indeed a manufactured storm, how long can the Americans make it rain?'

BOOK THREE

The Passenger

. . . Where the clear stream of reason has not lost its way
Into the dreary desert sand of dead habit;
Where the mind is led forward by thee
Into ever-widening thought and action –
Into that heaven of freedom, my father,
Let my country awake

RABINDRANATH TAGORE

Oh the passenger, he rides and he rides
He sees things from under a glass
He looks through his windows high
He sees the things he knows are his
He sees the bright and hollow sky . . .

'The Passenger'
IGGY POP

16 November, 2030

To hell with connecting all the dots. Sawnrry lady, never been in that business, as Sam Spade might have said. Me, I'm . . . like, just talking okay? It's not as if I'm Chandler writing a thriller or anything, novel-types you know, all the body-bags of narrative tied up neatly by the end, all the stiffs delivered intact to the precinct morgue of your mind. Not that there isn't a pleasure in that – being the receiving officer at the morgue – 'At least wid a fuckin' DOA you kinda know what ya got! But you get some half-finished dame, or some friggin' low-life in a coma in de middleawda night, and it's pissin' down wid rain outside, what happens? *You* get to hold your bladder, get me? You can't read it, 'cause the ball's still curvin'. You're the case officer and you end up not knowin' if you can go to the john or not.'

Not that someone like you has ever opened and read one, you know, a *whole-complete* bodybag of a book. What you would call in Gujarati a 'navalkatha'. No, cut cheap jokes now, not novel-katha and not navel-katha either, navalkatha, what my father used to write. 'Upanyaas' in Hindi, Bengali – 'boi', though Bongs used to call a film a boi as well, so bright nomenculturally, Bongs, same word for book and film, or another word for film same as picture as in painting or photograph, chhobi. Boi, indeed. I could, you know – write a nov – anyway, fuck explaining.

The books just sit there on my bookshelves, all old finished explanations, bound and gagged, surrounded by the profound unfinishedness of photographs, different invisible stories coming out of the four sides of each picture, besieging those books, done for those books, matter of time before the fort walls are breached, but it won't matter to you and you will never read one because you can't imagine it, opening one and holding it actually in your hand, this boi jinish thing, and reading from start to finish like we used to do. Now you fuckers have it all on your screen.

Download pages at random, just like you do porn clips, I like this pussy, add it to this piece of ass, add it to Dietrich's fingers holding wine glass, take glass out, flip the hand and fingers around and you have this ersatz collage. 'Woman'. 'Fingering herself'. Same thing with 'books', this chapter from here, this character from here, make up your own story, your own bloody random soap all doing nothing but framing and fingering the 'I'. At least it's more difficult with photographs. Why?

Because people have been cutting up pictures from way before they did with text. So now people are tired of that, now tˆo of course everyone craves the whole image, Archaeology Zindabad! 'Can we have the original frame please?' 'Can we have the photographer's own original unfinishedness back?' Yeah, *nishhchoi* bokachoda, *sure*, why not? Some of us spent a lot of time making those frames, risked blood sometimes and more. But it's true also, somewhere – why shouldn't you? What are books? Books? What books, bloody? Something even more basic, okay? Thik achhey, okay, fine, how do you explain water?

Remember the @ years?

Aqua_paani_jal_tanni_eau_wasser_agua_voda_jol@H2O.wat?

I explain, cannot explain, hell with you, Sonali, water, like this: first of all, moving thing; next, if real water then no colour, not really, after air and even in the air, main moving thing that you can see that has no colour. Third, effect on tongue and top of mouth and inside of cheeks as if something coming home, nothing else like it. But Sonali's seen it, I mean, not like she hasn't seen it. Tasted it, not that she hasn't. It's just that – it's just that.

Okay, not water, but . . . *A glass of water*, this is the difficult.

One day, when the supply was behaving itself, I tried to give her, Sonali, a whole, full glass, clear, plain glass of water. See what it feels like, see what it tastes like, I said to her, and she shook her head and backed away as if I was suggesting some unnatural dirty act. Some perversion remembered from the past. No, no, no, you are crazy, you can't waste so much, fill a whole glass, crazy. I can't bear it, take it away. Crazy.

When I was about four years old or so, my mother used to show me a picture of a whale. Not even a shark, a blue whale in a picture book, coming at you, mouth open, and I would be terrified. If I was naughty, all she had to do was say, 'Parubaba! Whale-machhli dekhhadish!' just threaten to show me and I would comply with orders. Actually, she only took the book off the shelf in very serious situations. Otherwise it was always 'dekhadish!', a 'will-show'. Next gear up was 'dekhadu-*chhu*', an 'am-about-to-show'. The nuclear option was the book open – 'Aa jo! Aa rahi!' 'Look! Here she is!'. . . I feel like doing that with Sonali. Just fill a glass with good water and chase her around the room. And her screaming in terror, Yes!, and finally willing to do whatever I want. Anything. Only put that thing away. Not that, you understand, I need to do any of this to get her to do what I want – it's just a thought.

I mean, in Europe you still get water. And in America there are states where it's not banned, even after New York. They have what they call a CPDP, 'Citizen's-personal-decision-policy', and you can drink if you want, same as smoking a cigarette – part of 'constitutional freedom' – but you have to sign a statement indemnifying the State Government. Here, in Grater-Bengal, they say there are a couple of ponds in Bankura and one in Nadia and one in Murshidabad where you can drink without fear. Also, apparently near Sylhet there is a spring that is constant and fresh and supplies whole villages, and yes, up in the mountains it's clean, but there you have to be careful, because the Jap water companies own a lot of it, or their sub-patentees, whole stretches of rivers, specially, exclusively, licensed streams, and if they find you poaching they get the cops to put you in jail.

That's where they cull the water for the tablets – you know the ones for Bengal/East? Which is the market that stretches from somewhere in Bankura, Darbhanga, Purulia to the Burma border 'including former Bangladesh' as the market analysts put it. They have these cheeky fish floating in serene Japanese ponds taken from old paintings. Not Hokusai – him they've done to death – more like a carp or something by Zeshin in the nineteenth century. The tablets come in little ammunition belts, a bit like those round, soft, plastic bags with sealed little boils of ice that you used to have in the late '90s, except you don't need to put them in the fridge, though you can if you want to. And there is a grinning blue fish on each boil of tablet. You take the transparent tablet out and put it in a glass. After a few moments of contact with air, the tablet turns into about an inch and a half of clear liquid that looks like water. You drink this and it tastes nothing like water. What it does is hydrate your body and get rid of thirst for some time. One tablet is supposed to be like drinking four glasses of water.

The first time I heard of the tablets was from Para. They were developed for the army in '15, after Pakistani infiltrators sprayed the snow around Siachen with poisonous chemicals and Indian troops lost their main source of water. After the army carried out its own tests, the tablets made their way to the air force, where pilots were given a belt each to carry, in case they had to bail out over enemy territory. *Very funny stuff, Ffubz. Some of the girls threw up at first, but I didn't have any problems. Must be the Cal water you guys gave me to drink when I was a baby.* Which was complete nonsense of course, and written precisely to irritate me. There was nothing wrong with the Cal water Para got as a baby and I remember all the boiling and all the sterilising tablets that went into it, what we gave her when she was small, and it didn't, I'm sure, taste anything like this.

Sonali says I'm imagining it, that I'm completely paranoid, and there is no taste of fish in this. But I am convinced I can taste it. Sonali says get the West/India ones. The ones with the palm tree and oasis on them – also Jap naturally – but balls to her, it's not her money that goes, does it?

They cost thrice as much as the local ones, which are quite expensive anyway. Kumarbabu the stationery-walla stocks them, keeps the Oasis brand, I suspect, for just one customer, just for me, me being the old sucker. In his old-smelling shop. Like a pusher-man with an addict – 'Aashun ser, good morning Bhawtt-shaheb!' Asshole. Old sleaze-spine. Blue-lined, onion-skinned, lizard. Extortionist. Stationortionist. Knows I will buy colour cartridges. Knows I will buy fountain-pen ink. Knows, just *knows*, the paper-pimp, that I will buy writing pads made of real paper, and knows, of course, yeah, yeah, you can laugh at me if you like, I give a – that on occasion, I will buy the water tablets. For my birthday I buy them. One belt only, containing twenty-four tablets, and I drink them for the next few days and I imagine I can actually taste the water from Amdavad, savour it you know?, one of the extinct tastes of my childhood. Not that I grew up drinking Ahmedabad water, mind you, my water home-page is Lake Gardens, just south of here, where we lived till I was eighteen, and I've never tasted water like that again.

Sonali, thankfully, doesn't like these Oasis ones, just like idiot north Indians who never managed to appreciate the taste of Hapoos, 'Oye! What is this Alphonso nonsenso yaar? Call it a mango? Give me a Chausa anytime', just like those moron Punjabis, choosso-ing *Chausas*, poor sucker-fuckers! I'm sure it was a crate of Chausas they hid the bomb in, the one that exploded Mein Herr Generalchodissimo Zia's plane in the late '80s, and yeah, I guess they are useful for that sort of thing. Can't imagine anyone wasting a crate of Hapoos on Zia-ul-Faq.

Anyway, Sonali, she sticks to her fishy liquid. Ki aar bolbo? That's what she's grown up on, like mother's milk I suppose, and that's what she wants when she's thirsty. Drinks it in relief, can you believe it?

Sonali is . . . how do I say this? . . . Well, fuck it, she's twenty-two or so, and so yes, younger than Para, yes, by about sixteen years, Para being thirty-eight now. The irony is that Para, sitting in her little war-shop up in space, is now one of the few Indian citizens who get to drink proper water. It's not like being in a fighter-plane, being in that bhakhri. Now they have more *space*, heh, heh, very funny, I know, and it's typical of the military everywhere. You invent something and it trickles down to the civilian world. You, in the meantime, claim back the luxuries of the past. *Nothing but the best for our Jawaans. For our Sailors. For our Airmen and Airwomen.* Sitting in Varun Machaan, Para and her colleagues get deliveries from this unmanned craft that goes up every two weeks. They call it the Ice-Cream Cart and it drops up goodies, including a fortnight's water supply of ordinary, floating, water. I suppose I shouldn't be resentful, given that they are on a 'frontier posting' and, what is it?, oh yes, forgive me, 'risking their lives for the nation'. But I can't help it, I miss my water and there is no way Sonali will understand what this means.

Sonali was born in 2008, which was around the time normal water really began to seep out of our lives. I still remember the day I really began to worry about water. It was either in 2009 or 2010, can't remember exactly, I'll pull out the catalogue just now and look up the year if you want, though I'm sure it was '10 and not '09. It was the time when Anusha Nayar, then the curator at Tropical Light in Delhi, put together a retrospective of my photographs. Now this, you have to understand quite clearly, was a combination of two things I hated and still hate: New Delhi and the idea of a retrospective. First, I've always thought retrospectives are like glorified obituaries, like those Greatest Hits albums by rock groups who've run out of energy. And second, Delhi was, as Shibu-BMW put it, the Imperial Graveyard. Or, to put it ektu more accurately, the Imperial Cesspit into which drained all the cultural and political gutters of the country.

The show was called 'Shadowing the Nation – Thirty Years of a Life in Photojournalism', with a second, inelegant, subtitle: 'Paresh Bhatt – A Retrospective'. At the time I went along with it, tried to think of it as a punctuation mark in the ongoing sentence of my career, as a kind of stocktaking pause before continuing.

Susan Sontag, an American critic, said once, long ago, that people take photographs in order to forget the thing they are photographing. In the same way, maybe we used to exhibit photographs in galleries in order to then forget about them. In order to forget about those trace-frames of earlier forgettings . . . these ghosts that you can't put back . . . unhh, I know, I know all that's a bit too convoluted, but anyway, what people, friends, told me was that it was an honour at the relatively early age of fifty, that I shouldn't complain, that it was a mark of my 'importance', or, as old man Rajadhyaksha wrote in his slightly long-winded catalogue essay, that, god help me, I was – 'one of the few contemporary Indian photographers who have achieved genuine international markage'. Not that I wanted to be in same category as those other Indian 'international status' bastards with their coffee-table defecations, all the sub-Raghu-Raghubirs, but some egotist in me went along with all that crap.

All the press previews, lazy bastards, quoted from the essay without doing much research of their own. Mentioned all the signposts from the catalogue like a litany. The Calcutta photographs from the '80s and early '90s, *om swaha*, the signing by Magnum in '98, *om swaha*, the European pictures, *om swaha*, the '02 solo show at the Photographer's Gallery in London, *om swaha*, the prints from the Vahlabhai collection bought up by MoMA in New York when the textile empire collapsed, *om swaha*, the Ten-Year project, which I was still doing then, funded by the Rijksmuseum in Amsterdam, *om shantih shantih shantih* . . .

The exhibition was in the winter of '10, and in those days Delhi didn't normally have any water shortage in winter.

• • •

While other people are clinking glasses Talukdar is now wanting to clink cameras. He totters towards Bhatt. Anusha Nayar looks at Bhatt to warn him but he is caught up in some deep talk with Ramu, this Achinto fellow and Saha. They are saying the name of Calcutta a lot. They are all from Calcutta, though Saha lives in Delhi and Bhatt is now tˆo almost a foreigner. Foreign ex-wife, half-foreign daughter, now people say some foreign, French, fashion designer girlfriend who is half his age. A flat in Paris. I have even seen his name written 'Parech Bhatt' in one French exhibition catalogue.

Talukdar is still as he was twenty years ago. A staff photographer. Except now he is senior staff photographer. Not much difference, really, every day he goes to the HT office and they still send him out to photograph politicians. As over the last twenty years. His, this Talukdar's big jump, he is also from Calcutta, was when he moved to Delhi in 1991. And his big moment in life came in '92 when he got the best photo of the Babri demolition. These two RSS fellows shaking their fists as if they had taken a wicket or something. That was his high moment in life, after which he never did anything much.

Just now Talukdar has drunk many pegs and he is now doing as always he does at these parties. He is going to pick a fight with someone more successful than him. I am not a photographer and I don't know why at these exhibitions all these photographers come wearing their cameras. Like one of these . . . how do they call it . . . a fashion accessory. No, actually it is more like a guild badge or something. Every member has to show. Bhatt is wearing kurta-payjama but even he has a small camera like a garland around his neck. Talukdar has a bigger camera, I think it is a Nikon something. He gave it to me to hold when he went to the bathroom and it was quite heavy.

For some time Talukdar has been looking at those four standing there on the terrace and muttering things in Bengali which I hardly understand. Then, just now in English, he told me – I will show him, this bastard, who does he think he is? Let's see if his Leica can take my F4! I will give him cheers! – and he has gone towards them. I know I should stop him, but let us watch the fun for a bit. Let us go closer. Ohho, look, Anusha Nayar also has the same idea but I don't think so ki she wants to watch the fun, she just wants to stop it. These gallery curators are like that only, at heart they are sort of party policemen, but she is too late! Talukdar has made it.

He is short and Bhatt is tall.

'Abey! Saala Poresh!'

'Eijey Borun!'

'Oy. Baanchod!'

'Oy.'

'Poresh . . . congratu-gratu-*lations!*'

'Borun, gaandu, stop it.'

'No, no, congratulations! . . . Ekta kotha chhilo, just I wanted to know one thing. I just wanted to know how with that ancient little instrument of yours you have managed to get so much mileage?'

Bhatt looks up at the sky above him and raises his shoulders exactly like a Frenchman, but before he can give his reply Saha speaks up.

'Han, Borun, I was just wondering the same thing. Also, *how*, despite that huge old hydrocil F4 of yours, you are still where you were twenty years ago.'

Talukdar draws himself up to his full complete height, which must be being about five feet four inches.

'Shibu Saha, I am warning you! I am talking to Poresh and not you!'

Anusha Nayar has reached the action and I am just a little behind her. She holds on to Talukdar's arm.

'Borun-da, Borun-da, please come this side, someone wants to meet you.'

But Talukdar is now not going to go anywhere. He is supporting on Bhatt as if Bhatt is the terrace wall. His arm is in the air and he is trying to find his finger, which is what he is actually wanting to raise.

'Do you know?' he says quietly. And when nobody says anything he continues. 'Do you *know*? Do *you know*! How long have I known my friend Poresh?'

Still nobody is saying anything.

'Do you know that Poresh and I began to take photographs together in . . .1978? That is a full thirty-two years ago! Who are you people? Who are you *people?*'

Now tears are coming out of his eyes like an overflowing water tank. Bhatt is putting his arm around Talukdar's shoulder and talking downwards to him in a kindly voice, like a father with a child.

'Borun, Borun, it's okay guru, you relax now, just relax.' But Talukdar pushes away.

'NO relax Poresh, NO relax! Tui bhaalo bhaabe jaanish jey I have never been anything but happy when I hear of your rise! But eraa, baanchoder dol,' he points to the whole party, covering all the men and women on the terrace and finally stopping at Saha, 'all these fucking bastards who all praise you today! They are ALL jealous! Behind your back they are all bastards jealous! When you are in Paris or whatever you don't know what they say!'

I am now standing next to Achinto Sarkar and I ask him one question quietly because he is a Bengali also.

'Achha, Achinto, what is this baanchoder dol?'

'Dol is, you know? Dal? Like a political Dal or some other Dal. Baanchoder Dol it is a gang or group. Of sister-fuckers. According to Barun we all are, and Barun is of course the only one who is not a baanchod.' Then he is looking at me again, particularly at me, this bald snake. I smile at him for the time being. But his time will come.

Talukdar is now doing what he does every other night at the Press Club. He is holding on to Bhatt and crying full loudly and also he is using Bhatt's nice kurta for wiping his nose. Bhatt does not seem to mind this. He is looking at Saha as if they have some understanding.

Saha says, 'Chalo, I have my car. Let's get him home.'

Bhatt says, 'Where does he live? Still trans-Jamuna?'

Saha says, 'No, no, he moved out of Atal Vihar three years ago. He is this side now, quite close by. Amar Colony.'

Talukdar suddenly realises they are talking about him.

'Shibu, you bloody racketeer! Just because you can offer me a lift in your new bloody BMW does not mean I don't know you. I *know* you!'

Bhatt takes his little camera off, puts it in a bag and hands it to Anusha Nayar.

'Anusha, can you please keep this? I'll go with Shibu and just drop Barun home. We will be right back.' She takes it with a smile. I think maybe Bhatt is having something with her.

Then Bhatt takes Talukdar's heavy Nikon camera and puts it around his neck.

• • •

As Paresh puts Borun Talukdar's camera around his neck, a truck goes by on the road below the terrace. Something about it makes Shibu Saha look down and he nudges Paresh. The truck is a water tanker and the white sign painted on the side says *Mehrotras Water Supply*. It rumbles away from them and disappears around the circle, leaving a dark gash of leaked water in the middle of the dry road. Strings of water slide out in one direction from the central trail, marking the slope. It is a full moon night and the streetlamps and moonlight catch the water at different points, giving it different colours. Suddenly there is a scuffle of paws and four dogs run out of a lane on the side and head straight for the spilled water. They are followed by two more. But before they can get to the water, there is the sound of another large engine and another tanker comes into sight from the left.

The dogs start out of the way, to the side of the road, but their hind legs are coiled, waiting to jump. As soon as the tanker passes, the dogs leap at it, smashing into each other, clawing and biting each other in mid-air, all trying to get to the big tap that sticks out at the back. One of the larger dogs, a big whitish one, manages to hang on to the tanker and for a few moments Paresh and Shibu can see its jaws pumping violently on the tap. Then one of the chasing dogs manages to knock the big dog off and the two roll on the road, going for each other. A third dog takes advantage of this, a fawn streak and it's on to the tanker with its mouth locked around the tap.

'What the fuck?'

'Let's go,' says Shibu looking at his watch, an urgency in his voice.

'Haaaa-aann! Bokachoda! Paris-returned-Poresh!' Talukdar is now next to them, leaning on the concrete parapet and looking down. 'Welcome to real life! Here there is no retrospective, baanchod, here is only futurospective! You have to watch your paarspective! What . . . the . . . pfack, indeed!' Borun rolls away on the parapet like a fish going belly-up and his elbows slam against it trying to keep his balance. His knees bend, trying to take his weight.

'Borun-da . . . I think these people will now take you home,' says Anusha Nayar firmly.

'Certainly,' says Talukdar, '. . . ssss . . . ssartainly,' and his head lolls and then comes back onto his neck again. He focuses on Anusha Nayar and his look seems to send her Kanjivaram sari sliding off her shoulder. Anusha pushes it back in a reflex gesture. She is about to turn away, scanning the rest of the party, but Talukdar is not done with her yet. 'But tell me, Anusha . . . when . . . when . . . can I have a retrospective? Or do I have to be tall, dark and semi-handsome like my friend here.' Anusha smiles an empty smile that doesn't go higher than her gold nose-stud. She looks away again, searching for a way out. Talukdar puts his hand on Paresh's arm as if to support what he is saying. 'And, oh. Do I have to be living in Paris? I mean, you know, I have seen the *Shadows* of this Nation in a much bigger way than this – this *art* photographer!' and then turning to breathe up at Paresh almost in the same sentence, 'Ei, Poresh! Don't mind! Kichhu mone koro na, okay?'

'Borun-da, I'm away in Buenos Aires from the end of the week, for the Salgado show, but why don't you give me a call next month? Let's talk then? Hm?'

'Arrey! Kabhi Buenos Aires, kabhi Los Angeles, kabhi Sydney, Australia, Anusha! Sometimes you should put your feet on the ground of this country you know. Let your beautiful body cast a shadow, cast a *shadow*, on the streets of this poor nation, han? What do you say Poresh? And Shibu? You bloody ex-photographer, tumi ki bolo?'

Paresh says nothing and neither does Shibu Saha. They each put one arm under Talukdar's armpits and help him towards the door. Anusha deletes Talukdar from her presence and along with him her fixed smile.

Her face is ferocious as she moves swiftly towards a bearer holding a drinks tray.

Paresh and Shibu guide Talukdar to the door of the terrace. As they go, they pass a man in thick glasses wearing a denim jacket with several layers of sweaters underneath. Talukdar salutes at the man as they go. 'Okay Ramesh boss! Jai Shri! Okay boss? . . . Aah . . . jai shri . . . ah, Jai Ṣhri Whatever! And Vandey also! Vandey, okay? Milengey! See you!' and then he takes his salute back.

As they reach the road, they see the troop of dogs coming back from the chase. One sees them and lets out a howl. The others pick up the chorus and two of the braver ones break into a run, barking and coming straight at them. Before Shibu or Paresh can say anything, Talukdar tightens his armpits around their arms, lifts himself up and lets out a loud roar. The dogs scrabble to a stop and then they turn and run, barking over their shoulders as they go.

'Jai Shri New Dilli baanchod! See Poresh, dekhechhish baanda? At least someone is scared of me in this town! The one in the back? That last one, dog? I know his name . . . his name is Ramesh.'

Shibu reaches into his pocket and comes out with his engine lock-release. Chyuooonk Chyaa, the BMW flashes its tail-lights in response and the engine begins to turn over to start the heating.

They put Talukdar in the back and put the seat-belt around him. He protests but Shibu insists on strapping him in, the new traffic laws being very strict. Then Paresh and Shibu get in the front and they pull out onto the road. They follow the trail the water tanker has left.

Shibu reaches for his music board. 'What do you want to listen to? Association or Nusrat?' He puts on the Nusrat without waiting for an answer.

As they reach Bhogal Market, Talukdar starts feeling the upholstery and making a noise like a truck having problems with its gearbox. As if he's trying to ruin the rich, low, purr of the BMW engine.

'Hmmhrr, hrrhmm, hnraah . . . Bee, em, daablyuu . . . hnahrm . . . very nice, very nice, Mr Shibu Racketeer . . . who paid for this? Which funding agency, hanh? Danaid na Norad na Oxfam? Or na ki ektu from here and ektu from there?'

Neither Shibu nor Paresh reply, but this doesn't stop Talukdar, who continues, 'Saala, BMW – ei Shibu, put down the window yaar.' Shibu presses the button quickly, thinking Talukdar is about to throw up, but the guy just leans out, evacuates something from his throat into his mouth and spits it out before sinking back into his upholstery.

'Okay, shut it . . .' Shibu looks back to make sure Talukdar is done before buttoning up the window again, '. . . you know, I still remember the time when I used to think white Ambassadors were fancy. You, Paresh, do you remember the ruling days of the white Ambassador?'

Paresh grunts something, his mind on other things. Talukdar carries on.

'In my early days, remember our early days, Poresh? In the early days all I had to see was one coming around the corner, around the Writers' Building or the Parliament drive-way or something and I would feel a, a kirom ekta sharp pain in my stomach, you know? An automatic, "photograph coming!" kind of feeling . . . I can still remember the power of the white Ambassador with Government plates!'

A wave of drink washes over him again.

'But now? Now it's the reign of the Mercedes, guwu! They are all these politicians all bloody Benz-chods!' Talukdar doubles up at his own joke and Shibu looks back again, worried about vomit on his upholstery. But Talukdar doesn't throw up. After a while he drags himself up again.

'You know that bastard I was standing with? That Ramesh Kumar Upadhyay? Supposed to be an art critic, but you know who he is really? He is the advance spy-dog of the Trishul Commando! A real Vandey Hitleram, bujhechho tˆo?'

Paresh becomes interested. He turns and looks back.

'But I thought Junior Madam had defeated them. What can their spies do now? They are not in power.'

'Oh Paresh . . . still so naïve . . . they are not in power in name only.' Talukdar slumps lower in his seat.

Shibu takes it up.

'Junior Madam? Junior Madam can do what? She can only follow their Hindu agenda and put her own branding on it. Just like Grandmother tried to do with Khalistanis . . .'

'But . . .'

Shibu changes the gear and his anger goes up with it.

'But what Paresh? *Ki?* Could she stop the temple being built? With a paatla majority of twenty here, with UP firmly in Parivar hands, did Junior Madam have the guts to send in the army or paramilitary? What those people could not do when they were in power they could do now, now that they are not in power! And she is shitting bricks, consecrated bricks, this so-called Iron Lady! It took the Parivar seventeen years since they demolished Babri, but they did it. That is called Focus and Stamina. And she couldn't say chyoo, she would have lost her support from the outside parties.'

Talukdar leans as far forward as far as the seat-belt allows and pokes his head between them. Alcohol fumes swim into their ears.

'Ei. Ekta! Have you marked one thing? Masjid was broken when PV Narsimha Rao was in power and now, temple is inaugurated when Madam PV is in power!'

Paresh leans away from Talukdar as he laughs. Talukdar turns to Shibu, wanting to collect his laugh-payment from there as well. He pokes him.

'Ei, Racket-Master! PV to PV, han? Recent history of modern India, han?'

But Shibu is not listening, he is staring at the traffic radar on the left of his dashboard.

'Shit, I knew it. Problem.'

Paresh and Talukdar speak in unison.

'What problem?'

They are going up the flyover on Mathura Road, heading towards the Ashram crossing. Outside, below them, the fog has already spread its dirty grey quilt over the rail tracks. Wisps reach up, climb over the edge and through the wire netting on either side of the flyover.

The halogen lamp-posts have already developed halos. In about an hour and a half the fog will have occupied the whole flyover. In a couple of hours the lights will be completely invisible, just bright incandescences alternating with the dim. As if anticipating this, Shibu drops down two gears into first. He looks down at his radar again before replying.

'Behind us, in Nizamuddin there is something, around the petrol pumps. Ashram crossing is clear so maybe we can get to New Friends. But Ring Road, both sides of Moolchand looks serious. It's growing, this thing.'

'What kind of problem?' Paresh doesn't like the underscrape of fear in Shibu's voice. An unease starts climbing into him like the fog.

'Water problem,' answers Talukdar, who has understood. His voice has lost its slurry edge and, for a moment, he sounds a lot more sober.

Shibu turns to Talukdar and quickly speaks to him in Bengali. Motherfucker, I can't get you home now, understand? Let's get back to my place and you call Susmita from there. Tell her you're okay, okay? Talukdar offers no resistance to this. Yes, okay, I hope she will be okay. She should be, they won't come inside the colony. Do you think they will come inside the colony? No, I don't think so, say both Shibu and Talukdar. Shibu reassuring Talukdar, Talukdar reassuring himself.

Paresh asks about going back to the party and Shibu says forget about the party. If it's reached Nizamuddin it's bound to reach Jangpura and Bhogal soon. We can't go back. They were asking for trouble, running those tankers through Jangpura, trying to avoid the main road, and now they will catch it. The security guards who let them in will catch it first, and then anyone who tries to interfere. Paresh says, shit, I knew there was a crisis but I didn't know it was this bad.

Shibu puts speed under the BMW as it comes down from the flyover. The mist is thicker at ground level. The BMW's headlights are powerful but even they can't cut through the fog beyond twenty feet. Paresh wants to tell Shibu to slow down but now he can sense the tension that stretches between Shibu and Talukdar and he keeps quiet. Despite the cold outside and the heating on low, Paresh can see that Shibu is sweating. Shibu slows down as they approach the Ashram crossing and hits his horn once. He takes the crossing quite carefully, checking both left and right on the Ring Road for the tell-tale glow of headlights. At first they see nothing but the huge electronic hoarding on the left, the red words CASIO floating in the yellow-grey fog. Then three massive, articulated trucks parked one behind the other, dormant under huge rounds of straw wrapped in thick plastic.

As soon as they are past the crossing, Shibu speeds up again heading in the direction of Nehru Place.

Look, Shibu says hitting a button under his traffic radar. See that there? Near the entrance to Nizamuddin East? The small oblongs are a lot of cars and they are around the big oblongs, which are the tankers. He hits the button again. And there? Moolchand flyover? Only big oblongs, tankers, but they are not moving. Which means they have blocked the roads with something and probably surrounded the tankers on foot. That must be the people from Def Col naala. There is a moaning from behind. The booze has risen in Talukdar yet again. Ei Shibu, if there is trouble I don't want to be tied down. How do you take this belt off? There will be no trouble, Shibu says, there will be no trouble, we are almost home, keep quiet.

Talukdar doesn't keep quiet. He begins chanting in a low moan. Water, water everywhere, not a drop to drink. Waterwater everywhere, notadrop to drink. Waterwaterwater everywhere. Not-a, not-a, not-a, drop. To drink. Ei Poresh! Did I tell you that white hair suits you? PV Madam would give her right hand, she would give, fucking, her Home Minister! For one streak of silver like you have your whole head! Koto *distinguished* you look! Even if sitting in gay Paree you know nothing of what is going on here. *Extinguish* the fire in the belly of my country! O Ma! Waterwaterwaterevery where? Not a drop, not a drop, not a drop . . . Talukdar nods off as Shibu turns left into New Friends Colony and by the time they come up against the tail-lights he is fast asleep.

• • •

My water ration goes like this, see you've got me explaining again, Ramonchandlering again, but you have to understand this, my water priorities do go like this:

1. Clean running water received through laser filter per week (average): two litres, or roughly fills four of the large glasses that I still have from the hey-days, tumblers, 'hand-blown, green-tinted' as the catalogue described them, £120 for a dozen, not cheap for those days, maybe Made in India but I suspect they are hand-blown Czech, but this thing called Conran's was then a posh shop in London, so four of those glasses per week or, rather, one of those glasses, four times a week, the other three surviving ones stay on the shelf and once every six months I find the water to clean them because I like to see them shining for a few days before the grime dulls them again. So, the clean running water goes for the coffee and to add to the whisky. Two litres.

2. For drinking/hydration: I go through about forty of the fish tablets a week. I drink more than most people but then Sanyal-doctor says I need it, so, like medicine, I take my tablets.

3. Ablutions: the situation is such that there is a complete divorce of the act of defecating from the touch of water. I mean it. Nothing to laugh about, I really mean it. It is as if I was a European or an American or a Japanese or something. Sometimes, I find myself hoping that once, just once before I die, I can wash myself with water. Maybe I'll have to fly to Paris for that. Because otherwise why call yourself Indian? Not that I do call myself Indian but my passport does, this crippled passport in its wheelchair, and I feel like throttling Prabodhmama as he wheens out one of his patriotic songs, except I can't because Prabodhmama is long dead. *O Bharat ma, we spread our blood before you, come bathe in the Sea of Sacrifice your sons have filled for you!* Except he didn't say 'bathe'. In the original Gujarati, he actually used the onomatopoeic word 'chhabchhabiya', which is closer to the sense of a child bongoing the surface of the water with its hands.

To which I say – Blood maybe. If you must. But shit, no. What good is a nation if it doesn't allow you to shit like a human being? A traitor horse inside my head prances sideways away from the crumpled pile of its rider, away from the orange, white and green uniform, goes and positions itself next to the pillar of an old bridge and lifts its tail over sand. As Kalikaku once told me, which fell on deaf ears when I tried telling Para when she joined, 'If you don't get rid of this Nation idea, it will get rid of You!'

Yes, no, okay, there are improvements, especially for the young who are still learning and the old, like me, whose knees can't take it anymore, and also it's apparently supposed to be helpful to women in advanced stages of pregnancy. You sit down and put your feet on the pedals on both sides and then you press the switch and the pedals hydraulically take you up into the squatting position. You don't have to be stuck doing the Rodin Thinker, this much is still Indian and it's a good local innovation. I even have little pads that support the inside of the knee, making sure you don't stretch the tendons too much, and these are useful too. After you are positioned, you do what you need to do. It plops on the aluminium cup, and when you are finished you press the evacuate switch. And that's where the trouble starts.

What happens is – and look at my stupid computer console, waking up now, out of turn, it's not supposed to do that except for emergency messages, but it does it every few days or so – and this is another example of the way my problem starts, and Japanese or no Japanese, somewhere Cal will be Cal, because even though the commode and the hydraulic system are made somewhere near Igatpuri, in the new Bharat Vitreous factory, the chip, the bloody chip and the bloody circuitry that control those hydraulics are local.

What *should* happen is the following: first, the two flaps of the aluminium cup should shut into a ball, capturing the stool and turning over, dropping the stuff into the pipes. And then, out of sight, well sealed off from the body, jets of water should then blast it clean and you should only hear the sound. In the meantime, the tube with the moulded plastic cup attached should snake up to the anus and fix itself around it. The cup is called a 'sanitation module', the company's euphemism for 'ass-wipe'. It felt weird at first and several older people complained of feeling unclean for a long time afterwards, but everyone has got used to this by now and most are convinced by the manufacturers' claim that this is actually cleaner and more hygienic than water. But as we know, the point is there is no other option – you can't let the water close to any opening in your body, not if you want to live for any length of time – and so, these many hundred micro-jets of hot air blast up your bum, literally blowing away the – Fuck, I can't believe this computer, it's clicked on again, both the screens this time and it's flashing its emergency sign. Switch it off. There. Some pada computer whizz-kid getting smart. This happened last week as well and when I clicked on to see what the fuss was about, I found a porn cartoon going on – nothing wrong with *those* hydraulics, though it puts me off from touching Sonali for weeks, something like that.

What does happen, not always but every now and then, is that the suction cup comes and stops just short of the body. Just two inches away, but it's two inches too far away for something like this to work. Then the jets of air have a committee meeting among themselves and some hot air spills out, but nowhere near enough to clean. This is when there is a choice. Either I physically pull the pipe up, which is dangerous because it is quite hot on the outside and I have to gauge exactly how long I can hang on to it without burning my hand. Or, I have to reach for one of my precious newspapers, which I hate to do, because I haven't hung on to them for wiping my ass, I have kept them because they are precious, a reminder of a time when there was a new one every day and you could sit on a proper loo with water and everything and read. But, in times of desperation, the yellowing newsprint has to be sacrificed in the interest of a clean backside and I grit my teeth, curse the circuits and tear off a bit, but only as much as I need, mind you, only as much as I need.

The problem, yes, yes, you may as well ask all the obvious questions, the problem is when you have a loose stomach. What happens then? Well, if you have diarrhoea or dysentery then you go down to the local centre and plug yourself in – their pipes are better, 'professional quality' as they say and the design is different. For twelve hundred rupees an hour you can actually sit down and let the stuff get carried away constantly. They put a monitor in front of you and you can watch TV or link up to your computer and work if you want. Every now and then someone will come around with water tablets and rehydration pills and if it's really bad then they have doctors who can inject you with whatever you need.

Sometimes, some centres have a problem with their pipes, but the one I use is a good one. It's on the corner of Lansdowne and Raja Basanta Ray Road in an old bungalow and it's not like one of the cheaper ones that have come up of late, spread like those telephone STD/ISD booths in the early '90s. They all have big signs, red letters on white saying HC for Hygiene Centre and you get all kinds of cowboy operators running them. Some of the stories I've heard . . . *what?* What do you mean what do the poor do?

Listen. Listen, just fuck off. Don't you dare start that bullshit with me.

• • •

Good brakes, says Paresh, but Shibu can tell he hasn't understood. Then Paresh sees Shibu's face and his own expression changes. Ki? he asks. Shibu nods towards the thing in front. Tanker.

So? . . . Oh. Paresh is now beginning to get it. Can we turn around? he asks. Shibu tells him no, because this damn thing is between us and the only gate to D Block that is open at this time of night.

Shibu reaches over and shuts off the music. The noise of the tanker engine comes through, muted by the BMW's sound insulation. The mist is thick around them and it seems to have a rasping breath. Actually it's Talukdar slumped on the back seat, his seat-belt barely holding him upright. His hands are folded together and squeezed between his thighs as if he is very cold.

You think trouble? Paresh asks. No slums around here, says Shibu slowly, talking to himself as if he's doing arithmetic aloud. But there will be the colony gangs. He strokes his steering wheel, his hands worried. Paresh can tell Shibu is wondering if something will happen to his car.

Colony gangs? repeats Paresh and, as if in response, a pair of headlights glare up from behind them. Shibu looks at his rear-view mirror, shit, man, shit! He tries to inch the car to the right, trying to go around the tanker, but it's too late. The tanker has crawled to a stop and the BMW's nose is almost under its bumper. The car behind has jammed up against them.

Suddenly there are cars on both sides of them, very close, so close that there is no way of opening the doors. Shibu sees that Paresh has put both his hands on the dashboard in front of him, where anyone can see them. As if he is playing a piano. A sound makes Shibu turn away and peer through his windshield. He sees the tap on the back of the truck dripping onto his bonnet, thick drops plopping just to the left of the round BMW badge on the nose.

The window of the car on the left comes down first. Someone shines a big torch into the BMW, moving back and forth from Shibu to Talukdar to Paresh. Then a hand reaches out and slaps on Shibu's window. The gold bangles make a sharp clinking sound in contrast to the flat thud of the slapping. Shibu pushes the button and brings his window down halfway. The woman is in her early forties, with short hair. Her eyes have gone small trying to peer into the car and her lips are stretched tight across her face.

Which colony? The question comes across her from the driver's seat. A man turned towards them, wearing a shiny black ski jacket with the word *RUTGERS* in white on the front, *RUT* on one side of the zipper and *GERS* on the other. New Friends, says Shibu, but we have nothing to do –

New Friends which block? snarls the woman. Shibu tries to answer, D Block, but we were just driving and – The woman is now speaking into a phone, holding the torch so that it points straight into Shibu's eyes.

Han. We have one here. Says New Friends, D Block but we don't know . . . What number D Block? The man spits out the question at the same time someone bangs on Paresh's window. Paresh looks to see a man shining a torch at him from the other car. The man signals to Paresh, telling him to lower his window. Paresh stares back, not moving. D 1103, second floor, says Shibu, tenant of Shravan Kumar Jaiswal. The woman repeats this into her phone – He is saying Jaiswal ka tenant hai, D 1103. Han? What? Han, yes, red BMW, yeah, okay?

She turns to the driver and says okay. The man nods and begins growling into his collar. Yeah, no, wrong number, this guy is New Friends D Block. I thought it was Taneja's BMW. I was going to just fuck him. The woman switches off her torch and says, You can go. The man leans over her and says, You are damn lucky buddy. If you were from Maharani Bagh your ass would be grass by now. If you are New Friends you should be with us on patrol. Either you are with your Colony or you should get the fuck out.

As the car pulls away Paresh sees a huge sticker across the back window that says *Northwestern* and another, smaller one that says *Jai Shri Krishna Bhagwan Ji Ki*. The car behind them reverses and the tanker moves forward again. Shibu lets out the clutch and they move forward slowly, still caught behind the tanker.

• • •

4. Bathing: For bathing I first put on the special mask. The eyeband fits tight over the eyes but you can sort of see through the lenses. There is a special breathing net for the nostrils which allows air to go in and out but blocks off the water. The mask seals the ears completely and it is strange because you can feel the water but you can't hear it. And, as far as I'm concerned, water that you can't hear properly is not water.

Along with the mask you also have to put on the crotch-patch which seals off your downstairs, talk about bodybags, and if you have any cuts or open wounds then each has to be sealed by the special bath band-aids. I really try hard now, not to cut myself shaving, because funny-sounding or not I like to feel the water on as much of my face and body as possible. If I have to put a seal under my chin, which is where I usually cut myself, then it puts me in a bad mood for days.

Sonali, god bless her, uses the big soap and water wipes that you get for children. They come in two sizes, 'big towel' and 'small towel', and they look pretty much like those packets you used to get on aeroplanes to wipe your face, those ones that said 'Freshener', except, of course, they are bigger and have two layers that peel off from each other. First you use the soapy layer to lather yourself and then you throw that away and then you use the 'water' layer to wash away the soap and then you dry yourself with a normal towel. I hate this stuff and I would rather stay dirty than use it, but then that's me, the Dirty Old Man as Sonali calls me when she's feeling flirtatious.

She'll sit there on the bath stool sensuously wiping herself with the soap towel, trying to entice me. Nothing I say can make her understand that this is, like, the biggest turn-off. All it reminds me of is wiping baby Para's bottom with soapy-wipes, and call me kinky, but that never got me going.

One day, I happened across a letter Bethan wrote to me in the late '90s, when Para was about five and her two children were, I think, seven and four. I took the letter to where Sonali was sitting drying herself and read it out, trying to explain to her the central happiness of water.

Bathe with your children, Bethan wrote, *bathe in their presence, let their voices too loud in the morning, their whining and their wailing, be the scrub that cleans out the armpits of your soul, the toenails of your heart. It is one of the true sunlights. There are few others.*

'So what is the sunlight of your soul doing in the air force anyway?' Sonali asked yet again and I had no reply.

I folded the letter back into its envelope, put it away in its file and went out onto the terrace. It was a couple of months ago, a night just after the monsoon and the breeze still had a slight whip of wet. There is a chai-walla's booth in the lane below, on the footpath, just inside from where the lane meets Lansdowne Road, sort of half under the big neem tree and half on the road. I leaned on the railing and looked down into it. Ronaldo-da, the old guy who owns the booth, was having a busy night. He'd obviously got a tank of supply from somewhere on the black market and the local pada guys had gathered to have a proper cup of tea. Someone was gesturing to one of the mini-TVs Ronaldo-da runs on the power he steals from my mains board on the ground floor. I don't mind him taking the power, I can afford it, especially with my solar panels, and his shop provides me with something to look at when I get tired of my flying prison.

Most of the pada boys like wearing these shirts that are fashionable nowadays, they have a small replaceable chip with a different set of images in each chip and the fibre optics in the shirts splay out the images. The quality of the pictures themselves is not very good, quite crude they are in fact, but the novelty's the thing I guess. One boy down there has snakes running down his sleeves. The guy who's talking to Ronaldo-da has a loop of a ski-jumper and from where I am it looks as if the jumper is coming down straight out of his neck, growing larger as he comes down to the guy's waist and then disappearing to start his run again.

Some of the more expensive shirts even have chips that are controllable. I've seen two youths have a fight without using any spoken words, one turning his shirt red, the other a bright purple with the words 'Your Mother' flashing across his front before they took to blows. Sonali thinks these are very cool. She has a couple of saris she wears and one I particularly hate has a, how do I say this, has a group of synchronised swimmers, big blonde Australian women doing their stuff in an Olympic swimming-pool, and Sonali has a terrible habit of getting them to do things to underline some point she is making in conversation. She will say, 'Well, you are wrong!' and her sari pallu will drop. As she pushes it back, the swimmers will perform some number, like suddenly their legs coming out of the water, impossibly straight, you know, wagging their legs like fingers. I just hate it. I can't have a conversation with her when she does that. I end up shouting at her and if she sees I'm really upset then she puts her swimmers away, returning the sari to its base pattern of loud batik.

It sounds bizarre but actually it's not. Everything is, somewhere, still ordinary, still recognisable. Everything has a parent of memory and there is not too much mental orphaning . . . but, then, if you let yourself look at it the other way, it can get quite scary.

As I looked down, I could see the ski-jump boy tugging at Ronaldo's shirt. I could hear his voice coming up, saying something about what he was watching. 'Naldo-da! Naldo-da! Dekho! A beauty from your time. It's Madhuri, look!' I couldn't quite see the screens but I could hear the tinny soundtrack from an old film – *Ek Do Teen! Char Paanch Chhe Saat Aath Nau! Das Gyaara! Bara Tera! Tera karu, tera karu, din din gin ke . . . intezar, aaja sanam . . .*

A whale of memory rose to the surface and spewed it up.

• • •

A year after Bombay, Delhi in '13. Nothing to do with the film, because the film was already very old by then. Maybe because Sonali asked. Or maybe it was the Bombay chip in my mind getting activated. Maybe it had to do with tea. I'd ordered tea that day because, by then, the coffee they served in the coffee-shop was so bad. There was a part of me that really couldn't blame them. I mean, when you lose the mainsail of a ship it's bound to be difficult to steer. And you had to take into account that now their sir-Taj was gone, the real ur-hotel of the whole chain, the whole tradition, the back-to-front pride, the sea-face, the Sea Lounge, everything. And Mansingh was never designed to be the headquarters of the chain, it had always been the Northern High Command and now it was having to cope with both being a border-town hotel as well as the hub of the entire chain, from Kuala Lumpur to Cairo. And it showed up in the way the coffee tasted.

All Para had said to me when I said, 'Meet me in the Machaan,' was, 'Okay, I think I can get away for a couple of hours around four.' Get away from where? But I didn't wonder too much, and I didn't ask, because you don't ask twenty-one-year-olds too many questions, not if you want to stay recognised as a parent.

I reached a bit early, I think, and got myself a two-seater next to the big windows that look out over the swimming-pool. There was a comfort I always found in five-star hotels, a kind of soiled sanctuary, in the nice-smelling air-conditioning, in the little bread rolls, in the combed pats of butter they used to have before they replaced them with little foil-covered ingots that you unwrapped and invariably wasted half of, especially if you were trying to feed children. Then there was the clean cutlery and the sparkling glasses. I remember Sandy always liked checking the glasses at Samarkand at the Oberoi in Bombay.

She'd always find a speck or a smudge or something and summon the waiter. The man would shift from foot to foot while Sandy twisted the offending glass in her fingers, peering at it closely like she was Sherlock Holmes. 'Hmm,' she'd say, taking her time and then looking at me, 'Kya re, Watson?' I'd sink deeper into my chair while she put on her version of the local Ghat accent and let the waiter have it. 'Hello? Kai ku? For vot we are paying five-star prices, haaan? Glasses tˆo at least clean mangtai na?' The waiter would try and take the glass away before the neighbouring tables noticed anything but Sandy was a real haraami. At the last moment she'd pull the glass away and put it on her other side. The man could have it only after she was finished with him.

'You know where I am just coming from?' she would ask him.

'Ma'am? No, ma'am.'

In a ringing voice Sandy would cut across his mumbling and tell him. 'I am just coming from Dharavi, haan. You know of Dharavi, na? It is famous. It is the biggest slum in the world, or now maybe number two, second after only Mexico City. And the women there give me tea in a cleaner glass.' The waiter would reach across, trying to snaffle the glass, and Sandhya would finally take pity on him and let him take it. 'Remember my friend! No five-star prices in Dharavi, okay?'

And now no five-star prices at Nariman Point either.

I looked at the waiters moving about and thought, 'Sandy-fodder,' and then I stopped myself thinking along those lines. No point thinking about Sandy – it must have been pretty instantaneous where she probably had been at that moment. And that was that, so – no point.

I looked at the waiters moving about. I glanced down at the menu and noted that they were still sticking to the old theme. On the cover was a tiger's body, sunk low in the grass, as if seen from a tree, from a hunter's machaan. Inside, the titles were still twee:

The Shikari's Breakfast – to sharpen the eyes.

From the Continental Jungle – our European Specialties.

Reeled in from the Sea – fish and seafood.

The Last Bullet – desserts.

A Change of Calibre – light snacks for those who want to keep alert.

Which included the Egg-Chicken Paratha Roll. Many years ago they'd had the nerve to call it a Nizam Roll, after the famous Calcutta Nizam's, till someone objected and they took it off.

Double Barrel – drinks.

I looked up towards the entrance and caught a glimpse of a waiter's uniform, some short guy wearing a strange uniform. 'An Exotic Animal,' I thought, my head still in the menu . . . and then.

Leave aside the face, I would have known the walk anywhere.

Not a waiter. My daughter. Wearing some strange new fashion. Not like her at all, odd light blue, which was not her colour at all. Grinning at me as she came up, taking off some strange cap.

'Hello Liver – Pater. What are you drinking?' She sniffed down into my cup disbelievingly. 'Tea? What, *you*? How come you're not having a drink?'

• • •

There is no surprise about it, just the sick fist of the inevitable punching out from inside his stomach. It happens just as Shibu manages to get away from behind the tanker. The fog has thinned for a stretch and as they move to their right they see that their tanker is actually the last in a convoy of three. It's almost as if they've been waiting for the BMW to move. It all happens at once. First, a tangle of headlights criss-crossing the fog somewhere near the first tanker. Then, suddenly, the sound of several horns being pumped, as if a pre-arranged signal. One set of rear emergency lights blinking. Two cars screeching in from a side lane, cutting off the second tanker from the first, blocking the road. Figures jumping out.

Shibu is clicking his radar buttons, trying to see what's behind them, to see if there's a way out. No. There are several cars behind them, moving towards them. Moving slowly because of the visibility but spread out across the road. No, no way out. The driver of the second tanker is being dragged out of his cabin. The door of their tanker opens and a big man jumps out. At first it looks as though he is going to help the other driver but no, he disappears around the front of his tanker.

Shibu scans his radar again, decides something. He reverses the BMW a bit, it's our only chance, and then swings the car forward and right giving himself space to take a sharp left turn and spins them through between their tanker and the second one, taking them to the other side of the line.

How far is the gate? Hundred yards, I think. The lead car blocking the second truck. Its nose sticking out in their way, but Shibu knows the roads around here and he bumps his left wheels up onto the sidewalk and manoeuvres past. The people from the cars are all out and on the other side, dealing with the driver, and no one notices them. They come off the sidewalk with a hard bump and Shibu grimaces. Bloody fancy low suspension, wish I had an Amby now. Next up ahead is the riot in front of the first tanker. Paresh is now sitting erect, his window down, watching the edge of the wheels brush the sidewalk as Shibu inches forward. The headlights catch a movement ahead and to the left of them. The driver of the third truck flat against the wall, looking for the same gate as them. He probably has a security card he can show the guards.

As they come alongside the first truck, Shibu brakes and switches off his headlights. There is enough light from the other cars to see. In front of them is an overturned three-wheeler with its tyres sticking out sideways, poor bastard must have left it for the night, and a heavy Kawasaki bike that's leaning on its stand, tail-light on. The bike guy's in there, fighting, Paresh finds himself saying, and he knows Shibu is thinking what he is thinking.

On their right something happens on the other side of the truck. More cars arrive, more people, doors opening and slamming, someone saying, A Block is here! The sound of screaming as someone is hit. Someone shouting get out, get out, too many of them, get out. Metal smashing into metal and then the wail of an engine in pain, trying to pull back out of some other metal. Shibu sees a way past the overturned three-wheeler and the motorbike. Shibu is now sweating a lot, Paresh I'm going to have to go for it. Paresh nodding, then saying it, Go for it Shibu, go for it.

Shibu calculates it nicely and, in his head, Paresh drives with him. The BMW jumps forward. The right headlights will hit the bike's handlebars, hopefully knocking it out of the way. The left side will hit the three-wheeler's tyres and they should act like a buffer. The idea is good but neither calculates for the bike guy running back to his Kawasaki.

His leg and arm act as unexpected padding from the bike but otherwise it is what they wanted. The bike goes over. One of the three-wheeler's back wheels catches in Paresh's open window and then rolls over the closed back window. Brake korbi na, Paresh finds himself shouting, just brake korbi na.

As they slam past, they see the Rutgers man standing on the road with a rod in his hand. He raises his thumb at them, well done, score one, and then he leaps back as the BMW nearly knocks him over. Beyond Shibu, Paresh can see more iron rods silhouetted in the high beams, a cricket bat, a woman crouching behind a van, pulling something out of her purse that looks like a phone and then looks like a small gun. Two men are smashing the windows of a jam-packed Lexus, smashing the glass onto the people sitting inside. An old Cielo has its nose puckered into the side of a big Japanese four-wheel drive and there are two people slumped out of the right back door, one piled on top of the other, not moving, blood trickling out of the bottom of the door as if someone's left a tap running. Don't brake, just brake korbi na Shibu, just put your foot down. Shibu brings the car to a stop.

The guards shine their torches into the car. Then they step back and raise their sub-machine-guns away from them. The gates slide open. One of the guards salutes as they drive past and Shibu nods back without meeting his eyes.

• • •

Inside New Friends Colony the silence folds in around them. There is a nick of sound, small, regular, from somewhere in front of the BMW, but otherwise the car seems to have come through intact. One by one, they pass the high fortress walls of the houses. Electric wire, spotlights, surveillance cameras positioned well away from the road, beady infrared eyes following the car as it passes, little pillboxes in front of some of the wealthier houses, the twinned cameras of one house leaving them as those from the next one pick them up.

Paresh stares at the houses. 'Shit, this is worse than Johannesburg,' he says.

'Yeah, you haven't been this side, have you? Here, GK, Anand Lok-Gulmohar Park side, Sundernagar . . .'

'Jangpura wasn't like this.'

'Jangpura is always a little behind. Soon it will become like – '

'Anusha living somewhere that is a little behind?'

'Arrey, you don't know Anusha,' Talukdar says. He sounds as if he's been awake for a while, 'Anusha just keeps that little pad for entertaining because Jangpura is avant-garde. Her family owns houses in all the grand old – everywhere – Golf Links, Mehrauli, you name it!'

Shibu looks over his shoulder. 'Oy baanchod! Woken up after all the trouble's over, han?'

'What trouble, bhai? I thought I heard some noise . . .'

'*Some noise*, bokachoda,' mutters Paresh, shaking his head.

Talukdar is now sober enough to fiddle with his seat-belt and he manages to get it open. He wriggles around and is free of it as they take a left. They turn into a lane lined with the side walls of houses. Not too many gates here. And, in the middle of the road, with no barrier, just coming straight out of the asphalt, three trees in a row. Paresh is about to say something about the trees when he sees the feet sticking out from behind a tree trunk. Shibu sees them too, but Talukdar is still chatting away.

'Well, you know me. I am calm, always. If there was any genuine trouble you could have depended on me. What do you bastards think? I have seen more trouble than the two of you and your, both of your fourteen generations of forefa – ki? What?' he stops as if they've hit a wall.

The feet belong to a big man who is on his knees, looking up at two men standing over him. One of the men is holding an iron rod.

'It's the driver,' Shibu says.

'Stop,' Paresh says, just as Shibu presses down on the brake.

'What, what?' Talukdar is still asking, but Shibu and Paresh are already out of the car.

The men look up briefly but pay no more attention to them as they walk up. It's as if they are part of the team. The man with the rod is now poking the driver in the throat with it. The other man is speaking. 'And who was going to drive the truck? Your daughter-fucking father?'

'No, sir-ji, no. I would have gone back but –'

'And if they had taken the truck? What then?'

The man with the rod moves it to his left hand and pistons his right to slap the driver twice in the face, hard. He is less in control. 'Then what? What will my children drink tomorrow, you fucking pimp? What do we pay your owner so much for?' He lands another slap. Flecks of blood from the driver's bleeding mouth fall on his overalls. A line of red trickles down, impossibly straight, through the middle of the 'M' of the *Mehrotras Water Supply* printed across his chest.

The driver is covering his head with his arms now, sobbing through his elbows. 'Sir-ji, mistake, I made a mistake, but please think of my children also.' The other man looks around. Then looks at his watch and then at his partner. His voice is completely flat, as if negotiating a business deal. He says it in English.

'Listen, just kill him now. We have to make an example. Otherwise this will go on and on. These bhenchods have to understand we are not joking.'

The driver seems to understand what they are saying. 'Sir-ji, Bhagwan ke khatir, I beg you, no kill, sir-ji, please, no kill, I will bring in three trucks tomorrow, come what –'

The man lifts the rod high above his head, ready to bring it down. His fluorescent green ski-jacket stretches tight over his thick stomach, the zipper opening a bit with the strain. Before Paresh or Shibu can say anything Talukdar stumbles between them and the men. He has his hand raised in front of him, the fingers splayed out in a stopping gesture.

'Arrey bhai, just a minute, just a minute! What is the problem?'

The quiet-voiced man looks at Shibu and Paresh. 'Who is this?' he asks them.

Talukdar answers before they can. 'My name is Borun Talukdar. I am from Press. Please stop gentleman! Please relax! Let us just talk through it!' He starts to move towards the man with the rod, unsteady on his feet, weaving a bit, both hands out now, as if he's going to push a stalled car.

Green Jacket brings his rod down, just missing Talukdar's head, smashing into his shoulder. A shrill sound saws out of Talukdar's throat as he goes down.

Paresh has no memory of taking the camera off his neck and no memory of wrapping the strap tight around his wrist. There is just a bit of slack so that the camera can swing. The rod is heavy and the man is just beginning to lift it up off Talukdar when the camera catches him with force on the side of the head, just behind the eyes. There is a noise of small glass breaking as he stumbles sideways, shaking his head as if vehemently saying no to something, now using his rod to keep himself on his feet, but Paresh is already on the back swing, the camera smashing into the top of the man's skull this time, bouncing up, almost coming free of Paresh's grip, a sharp pain shooting up from his wrist through the middle of his forearm all the way up under his ear. The man goes down on his hands and knees. The viewfinder assembly shatters as it hits the road.

Paresh pauses for a moment, lost. He doesn't know what to do next. Out of the corner of his eye he can see Shibu grappling with the other man. He decides to hit Green Jacket again but before he can swing back the camera he finds himself rolling on the ground. He puts up his left hand to ward off a blow but finds no one attacking him.

The driver has the rod now and he is a strong man. He swings the rod into Green Jacket's neck, just once, but it is enough. Then he turns to Shibu and hisses, 'Hat jaao!' Shibu tries to fling himself back but he is still close enough when the rod smashes into the back of the second man's skull and the man's forehead catches him on the nose. He reels back, holding his nose, blood pouring out from under his hand.

Then the driver is gone, gone before the rod stops clattering on the road, the sound loud as it echoes off the walls. A dog begins to bark somewhere. Not a stray. A trained guard dog, single alarm barks, each like a gunshot. A voice shouting from somewhere, but muffled and tinny, 'Jimmy, where are you? *Kya ho rahaa hai? Give me your location!* Tell me kahaan ho! Repeat, give location!' Paresh sees the phone on the ground, alive and talking, and he steps away from it.

Nobody speaks. Shibu and Paresh move with speed, with a co-ordination and an attention to detail that would surprise them later. First, they lift Talukdar, careful to avoid yanking his left shoulder, and put him in the car. Then, as Shibu gets in and lets out the clutch, Paresh bends low over the road and picks up as much of the viewfinder as he can find. There is one small bit of optical glass, which he crushes under his shoe and brushes to the side of the road. Then he is in the car and Shibu pulls away quietly. Within two minutes they reach Shibu's house and the guard lets them in. As Shibu drives past the guard he has his handkerchief clutched over the bottom half of his face, as if he has just smelled something bad. It is dark and the guard doesn't seem to notice anything.

Paresh twists around and watches as the guard's uniform gets narrowed by the closing gates. He waits for the sound of the gates shutting and then the electronic bleep of the security alarm coming on again. Then he gets out and opens the back door to look in at Talukdar.

• • •

I quickly tried to hit the arrow key, trying to make her rewind up off the chair and walk backwards, back out of the coffee-shop and in through the doors again. I could hear the two disks running against each other, whining in frustration and the screen coming up – *Selected Move Not Possible. Try Another.* This is not a waiter. This is my daughter. Green eyes but different shade, this is not Sandhya who is dead, this is Paramita, my daughter, who is still alive. Like a kid with a Barbie doll, I tried to take off the stupid air cadet's uniform, tried to put another dress on her, mini-skirt and tight top from the '80s, retro hippy kurta, long skirt, sandals, all from the late '90s, one of Magali's outfits, and then even a sari – *Move Not Possible.*

Why the fuck not?

Ser, you are yasking, 'Vaaynot'?

Yes, why not?

Ser? Vaay did the chicken cross the road, ser?

What?

Ser, the chicken woss crossing the road becoss . . . Zimpdly. Zimpdly, becoss.

I remember the teatime sunlight jumping up at us from the stone slabs around the pool. Reflecting from below, coming up like it does in May in Delhi, hard even in bounce, crude, catching a loose thread in the stitching between her shoulder and sleeve and making it radiate. I remember thinking maybe this was the magic clue. Maybe if I tugged hard at the thread the whole thing would become something else, light blue to bright yellow, a loose Brasil t-shirt, Ronaldo, and baggy jeans and sneakers, like I knew she liked. 'What's the problem with violence, Father? Hunh? *Hunh*, Pupfart? Since when?' Laughing at me, being affectionate – *humouring* me. Maybe I was not hitting the right keys, maybe find the game manual, the game's four whole GB after all. 'Real life won't fit into four gigabytes,' I could hear Mahadev Bhatt snorting. 'Though, yes, your brain might fit into something much smaller. Try something else.' The waiter arrived with the Australian sirloin steak and caramelised onion on baguette. 'Your sandwich si –, madam.'

Uniform to uniform. He smiled a hesitant smile as he put it in front of her, bowed and nodded from the waist like he had certainly not done with me. 'Do you have any mustard?' 'Yes, ma'am. I'll immediately get it.' Catering doing pranaam to Slaughtering. Then retreating as if before royalty. *Go, no!?! You go and do what she's about to do, you son-of-a-bitch. Swap jobs! Let her serve South African orange juice to fat ladies from Agra-Mayfair! You go, YOU, go get your ass shot off!*

'She may be even stupider than you, but at least she isn't going to spend her life hiding behind a camera.' My father could be mean as well as nasty sometimes.

Erect, just like Mahadev Bhatt, erect, unlike me with my overlong spine, the posture made for a uniform. My father's was a khadi dhoti-kurta, hers was this. A fly buzzing around the metal badge with the roundels. Just above her breast pocket. Orange outside, then white and then the green bullseye in the middle, little brass edging between the colours and below it in white against black – Air Cadet Bhatt. The fly simpered around the badge, checking the colours for food, found nothing and flew off.

Other people see a woman in her but I couldn't then and still can't – even now. I saw my little girl and somewhere that girl stopped in my head at twelve or thirteen. *Il est strong, eh? Mon vieux!* Suman's face, but different body, lithe, Anna-like, but shorter, 'a conqueror' I think, not a watcher like me, not a bystander. I watched her bite into the sandwich and there was a way she tilted her head, ducking into her food, that came straight from my mother. 'I wouldn't let your mother see that meat if I were you,' Mahadev Bhatt tapping me on the shoulder, 'What is it? Beef? Well, in that case even I don't need to see that.' He was right, he didn't need to see it and I tried to stuff him back into the other game where he belonged, but my software was faulty and he kept tripping into this, which was none of his business. No longer his business.

I had asked, though I didn't need to. She was going to tell me anyway.

'Pap, you remember that time you told me what Ba said about Gandhi and Godse?'

No, she was not starting on that, was she? I put us in the Sea Lounge, looking at the little boats bobbing outside, India Gate glowing in the evening sun. Now there was a proper, classy coffee-shop, and there was Para in normal clothes telling me she wanted to go to Burma to help with the epidemic. *Fine. I am proud. Go. Don't forget your immunisation patches.* Good coffee arrives in a nice silver service. Para gets her steak sandwich. The light winds its way through the tables, polite as a waiter, weaving through the rich-shits taking their evening tea. A spot of sunlight reflected off a porthole out on the water carves a yellow half-circle on the shoulder of a muted red armchair. A seagull squawking outside one of the big windows, a middleman sent up by the beggars waiting on the quay below.

But we were in Delhi, no seagulls, and the only thing knocking against the windows was the hard May light. 'Why did you and Mamma have me, Pups? I wish you'd thought about it a bit. I wish I didn't have to do the thinking for you people now.'

The thinking for you people now. Call this thinking? She removes a bit of onion from the corner of her mouth and looks at me. The expression on her face is almost warm, not like Anna's when she was about to tell me a home truth, nor like Suman Bhatt's when she was about to pull out the whale, and her voice is soft, soft as a boxing glove. 'I mean, I could argue that it's an act of violence, no? I could argue it is violence, having a baby in a world you don't like or trust. Having a baby with someone you're not sure you like-trust. And you two did that, didn't you?'

Such absolutes. *Ab-Salutes*, as Para would have punned when she was younger.

Or, have a baby with someone you love-trust and then fall out of love, like Mummy and Pappa. That can happen too. Or: Pfupps, I'm going to have a baby with someone I love and trust and because you and Mamma fucked up on me you will never see me again or the baby ever. *Fine. Can't speak for your mother but as far as I'm concerned – Deal. Go. Go with my love.*

'Sir?' Something breathing on my right ear. 'Sir? Excuse me, sir, can I get you some more tea?'

'I – er . . .' I tried to find something to hide my impulses in, a brown paper bag, but Para was on to it already.

'Yes. My father would like a large Scotch please.'

It was only five o clock and early, even by my standards, but my daughter was concerned for the state of my heart. She was thinking for me. As the waiter nodded and went away the old bhajan started scratching in my head. *Vaishnava jan tȏ tehne re kahiye je piid parayi jaaney re. Par dukhe upakar karey toye mana abhiman na aaney re.* The first four lines skipping again and again, the needle moving back to the beginning and then bobbing on the same groove. *Vaishnava jan tȏ tehne re kahiye –*

Not Subbalakshmi's famous version, wrong-spiced with the Tamil accent, but the straight one in proper Gujarati, like my mother used to sing, like they used to sing in the prayer meetings on the Sabarmati. Friday mornings when I was about five, Subbalakshmi Carnatacking it on the radiogram. What's this bhajan, Mummy? Isn't it the one you sing? It was Bapu's favourite bhajan, baba, he used to love this song.

Him we call a Vaishnav
who knows the pain of others.
He who eases another's sorrow
yet brings no false pride to his mind.

The old Gujju lawyer's favourite bhajan. The one that always brought tears to his eyes.

My father snorting from behind *The Statesman*. 'Whatever his ego, which was big, Gandhiji at least tried to act on those tears. Too many others just had large handkerchiefs.'

'Remember about Gandhi and Godse, Pappa, what you told me Ba said? Remember the G & G game?'

I remembered. But what did it have to do with this lunacy?

'Don't you see it *makes sense*? Someone has to kick back. You have to kick back otherwise we are all sitting ducks. Ba was right, don't you see?'

I didn't see at all. So many ways to kick back. Why join the – I stopped before saying anything. I knew Para and I knew it would have no effect. Try something else, another tack.

'Anyway, you're a woman, they won't let you near a warplane. Helicopters ferrying supplies, maximum.'

Para burst out laughing. A table full of tourists stopped their babble and turned around to look at us. A waiter passing by smiled. So nice to see customers having a nice time.

'Pop . . . oh Pappa . . . you don't think I'd join just to fly supply choppers?'

Didn't work – not working. She knew something I didn't, my daughter the meticulous, methodical, single-minded one, and no, if she wanted to fly fighters she would have checked –

'Do you know what g-force is, Mr Bhatt? Let me tell you. G-force is the pressure gravity exerts on you when you are flying and your plane makes a movement either up or down or in a turn, okay? Like when you are in an airliner and there is turbulence and the plane suddenly goes up and you feel pushed back into your seat? That is mild g-force. And what they've figured out is that women, especially short women like me, are better able to withstand high g-forces than mere men. This, Mr B., is invaluable in a fighter pilot, because a fighter often has to make very sudden and extreme manoeuvres. And it is good if the pilot doesn't black out during these turns and flips.' She paused to take a swig of her juice, her eyes twinkling with pleasure at the look on my face. Hand shaking, I took a retaliatory sip of my whisky.

'So, Ffups, I heard from a pal whose dad was in the air force that they were looking for women, scientifically educated, fit, women who were not taller than five foot three, to form a crack squadron. That, by the way, is classified inf., dear Father, so do not talk about it to your journalist friends or anyone. I, Flying Cadet Para Bhatt, am going to start training to be a head-firster.'

Para Bhatt? Since when did Pararnita Lang become Para Bhatt?

'Remember that old birth certificate you got made in Calcutta? The one just to please Dadaji? It says Paramita Bhatt d/o Paresh Bhatt and Anna Bhatt. Remember you guys telling me how furious Mutti got when you got it back home? About the erasure of her name? Well, wait till I call and tell her how useful that erasure was. 'Cause apparently they get really careful if your parentage is half foreign, unofficially of course, and so best to avoid. So, in the form I filled in her name as Annapurna Bhatt and it worked just smooth. No one even asked me if she was a Christian or even Anglo-Indian! Green eyes, brown hair, my complexion and no questions, can you believe it?'

In a letter she wrote me once, Anna Lang used the word complexion when she meant complexity. As I looked at my daughter's complexions, things clung on to the cliff edge of my tongue. Hanging words, losing their hold, about to slide off into the sea of spoken things.

Two flies buzzed around my head, incorrect, not allowed, yet somehow inside this air-conditioned fortress. A memory of two parallel fighter trails, scratching white across a clear blue summer sky somewhere in Europe. Two other fighter-planes, somewhere else, lower, screaming out of a sunset. At the last moment something pulled my words back up onto the safety of silence. Maybe she didn't need stopping. Maybe there was no saving her involved, she was fine, she would be fine. In the aftermath of Bombay and Karachi there was once again serious talk of an economic federation. People were planning to remove the borders. Para would never see action because the wars were over for the next few decades. Maybe the only war was in my mind, an old war that was still alive, and Para was the main victim of that one. Maybe she should be allowed to get away, to fly, to go where she wanted. Don't try and catch her when she is not falling. Don't say anything. Stop.

A memory of the letter from Anna that came in December '91. The one that gave me the news. *Before we talk and our voices touch each other and make confusions, I want you to be quiet for some moment and think with your heart. Because this is not just my news it is also your news and it will add to the complexion of both our existence.* Purple-blue ink, still, but the handwriting different, surer in forming English words, sentences scratched out where they didn't work, the German hand flowing, flying, confident that I would decipher what was being written, that I was, in some deep sense, hers for the keeping. *Sometimes I am happy but sometimes I don't know what I think. At some days I don't connect with this other life that takes shape now, inside me, like a passenger that will leave me at some time. But then I think maybe this is a passenger not just mine but also yours, ours.*

I folded the letter away. A different handwriting, ugly this one, the handwriting of time, scrawling something across the complexion of my existence, a claw of light scratching an indelible trace of dread on the emulsion of my being.

I looked at my daughter's face and I suddenly found myself missing her mother. After many years, I suddenly found myself wishing that Anna Lang wasn't so far away. I tapped hard at whatever buttons I could reach inside me but I didn't even bother looking at the screen. I knew the move I wanted to make was not possible in this game.

• • •

Paresh stands behind Shibu who is sitting on a stool in front of the phone. As Shibu tries to find a safe doctor Paresh's eyes go up to the noticeboard that hangs on the wall above.

Pinned up among the jumble of photographs, pizza, tandoori and Thai home delivery numbers, nestling among greeting cards and reminder notes, he sees an old snapshot that he knows well. A little baby, about six months old, lying fast asleep on a chatai. On the floor right next to the baby are the remnants of a meal – plates of idlis and vadas, a bowl of sambhar, a green banana leaf wrapped around a torn dosa, an empty bottle of Thums Up. On the left, cut off from above the waist, is a woman sitting cross-legged on the ground, her skirt pulled back a bit to reveal very white knees. The baby looks like it is part of the meal the woman is having. It is naked except for a half-open cloth nappy and its arms are flung back over its head in complete abandon. Paresh remembers the afternoon in Bombay and Sandy pulling out her camera and taking the picture and Anna saying, 'Shall we eat her now or later?' They had just come from the airport, the first time they'd brought Para to India, and everyone had been very concerned about how she would take the heat.

Separated by some other children's pictures was another photograph from the same trip, this one taken by Shibu in Calcutta. Paresh remembers that one well too. Taken on the balcony at home, Anna holding up a grinning baby Para, now dressed in a babygro, and Paresh standing behind Anna with his arms around her and the baby. Everybody looking very happy.

Paresh looks from one picture to the other and back. He pauses on the picture of the three of them and looks at it for as long as he can. Then he turns away abruptly and walks into the living room, where Talukdar is stretched out on the sofa. Behind him he can hear Shibu's voice, low, cajoling the doctor, trying to get him to come for a visit. 'Yes, Doctor, yes, two painkillers we've given him and he is semi-awake but still in bad pain.'

Careful not to make too much noise, Paresh pushes open one of the sliding doors to the terrace. He goes through and draws the door shut behind him.

The cold comes around him and pulls off the heat from the house, stinging his face and hands. He shivers as he lights a cigarette. Something in him welcomes the cold and he moves deeper into it, crossing the broad, open, space towards the line of plants next to the railing.

The fog is now everywhere and Paresh can't even see the house across the road. He can hear a police siren far away, the sound refracted by the fog. It recedes and there is a moment's silence. Then, one by one, as if the siren has tugged them out, he can hear other sounds. A tapping of a night darwaan's stick that seems to come from another time. A street dog barking. A lone scooter scarring through the night. Leaves rustling on a tree he can't see, moved by some thief wind slipping through the still fog. Anna screaming at him, shaking his shoulders, *Do you realise how violent you really are?* A wheel on a gate making a single slow shriek and then the clang of the shutting.

Do you think violence is only in action? A thick riffling of wings as a bird wakes up somewhere. *Only in words? Don't you see there is violence in your silence?* On the other side of the terrace a tap dripping into a metal bucket, long gaps between each drop. An azaan climbing out of one of the gaps, then another, from another mosque further away, the second voice winding itself round the first one.

Paresh turns as he hears the sliding door open. Shibu comes out holding two glasses.

'Whisky.' It is not a question, just information. Through the door Paresh can hear a song playing very softly on the system. He looks at Shibu enquiringly. 'Borun. He said maybe music would help him sleep.'

Even though he can't hear it properly, Paresh knows the song well and it plays clearly in his head. A track called 'Late at Night', Ava Rimbo from her '07 album *Reservoir*. The voice slightly hoarse, French chansonny, the alto sax swimming just under the voice.

Late at night
Late at night
By the water's edge
In the bayou of my heart

In the home for old crocodiles
That is the delta of my heart

In the mangrove swamp

Of my sharp-tooth soul
In the mangrove swamp
Mosquito-bitten by memory

• • •

Late at night
Late at night
Where my muddy heart-water laps

Late at night
The tiger of your love
Creeps up to quench its striped thirst

I don't know if it's just old age or the water tablets, or the air, but the smell of my sweat has changed. I can smell myself now and there is a strange iodinous thing attached to the smell that used to be the smell of my sweat.

Ila's sweat-cocktails. What sweat-cocktail makes me up now? What sweat-cocktail produced Para? Some strange combustion of glands, some strange percolation trickling down through time, making fellow travellers of different memories, of different emotions, things attaching to each other for a while and then peeling off, amounting to nothing. Amounting to the universe, which amounts to nothing. Maybe we mother-fathers are just the wrapping on their real life. The packaging that our children rip open and throw away when the time is right.

So maybe we are, maybe, maybe nothing but passengers in our children's lives. Like, when your stop comes you get off. You maybe climb back on some other time, climb on for a bit again, if their bus stops for you, but if it's full you just wave and stand and watch it go by.

Suman Bhatt's revenge. 'One day your children will do to you what today you are doing to me. Worse than you. They will make you suffer more. Then you will remember me.' I remember you anyway, Mummy. A gesture Para makes, like brushing off a fly from the side of her temple, that comes straight from my mother. 'Well, Fapoopz, the way I hardcalc it is – the universe will end one day, nein?' using German like a smartbomb just to annoy me, 'and before that we will all be long dead. You. Mamma. Me. So, it's not about how people remember me. It's about what I want to do before I go.'

What do I want to do before I go? Already done it, have I done it already? How can I hardcalc it? Both my engines failing, left engine long gone, burnt to a cinder, the Suman engine, a long time ago. No, not when she died but well after – well after – these things have their own run-down time, one day you look, looking for power, and it's a smoking shell and you know why your life's tilting funny. Late, late at night, by the water's edge.

An airplane's own two engines stalking it, sucking out the air from any language you've put together to explain your life to yourself. Fuck language, fuck explanations that depend on language, fuck all explanations, what do you want to do before you go? The Orbituary doesn't matter, where is the real water?

There is a copter jam on Rashbehari tonight. I can tell just from the racket they are making, horns, klaxons, the rotors on low so that they can hover one above the other and stacked in twos and threes, one stack behind the other. I turn away from watching Naldo-da's tea-shop and walk over to the other side of the balcony. It's a real mess out there on the crossing. Some of the copters are dropping rope ladders so that passengers who want to get off can climb down, others are trying to make space so that some of the hanging people can squeeze in. The pilots are shouting into their radios and one conductor leans far out of his chopper, secure in the leather harness that goes between his legs and buckles around his middle. He's got a long stick and he's reaching out and tapping on the cabin window of another chopper in front of him, trying to get the pilot's attention. Some of their radios don't even work, but the route-owners give a fuck. Till an emergency happens and the cops get heavy.

Below the copters the road buses are also lined up all the way past the shell of Priya Cinema, tailbacked as far as I can see up the avenue. One guy coming down a rope ladder sees a bus he needs and steps onto the roof of the double-decker and climbs in through a window. Jesus. This is Cal and I've seen much worse before and it shouldn't surprise me but I guess that is one function of age – you panic about things that never worried you before.

The steady beating of the massed rotors is creating enough of a wind-wall to make the old palm trees lean back. Those trees' days are numbered. One of these days they are going to go, like so much else. In fact, it's a wonder that they are still – 'Ei, PB shaheb! There is some problem message on your machine. You better look.' – there. I mean this town has a habit of raping anything beautiful that it has, anything old and without – 'Ei! PB! Did you hear me? Shono! I'm serious!' – an obvious function. It is bound to go. God, I still remember the purge of the old houses that happened between 1980 and 2000. One by one, all the old bungalows, all the quaint little follies built early in the twentieth –

There is a bug on my left screen, crawling on the Asia weather map that is my live wallpaper. The bug moves over the border from North Punjab Control to Baluchistan Sector in Pakistan, no need for a passport, just traverses from one territory to another. The message is on my left screen and of course it's another prank.

> – accident on indian space station – indian space station varun machaan launched in 2026 suddenly stopped responding to normal communications early yesterday morning the official spokesman at isro confirmed – the nearest space craft, ussv reagan is trying to reach varun machaan –

What I don't understand is – how does the hacker know I have a special news tag for any item to do with Para's bhakhri? It's too clever, it's too much.

I know I shouldn't fall for it but I check other sites for more news.

There is an odd sound in my head, like water being sucked down a drain. Nothing, there is nothing else on my computer but then this is the breaking item so others may not have picked it up yet. Or maybe there's nothing because this isn't really news but just a fucking joke.

Sonali, stupid woman, is holding my shoulders hard, very hard. I break loose and go back outside. The copters have cleared, the air is empty, the road looks like it should at ten o'clock on a November night. I suppose I should wait before having a bath. Let the bodybag come in, wait for the story to finish. Just a thief stealing wires on a rainy night. Wait to see if there's been an electrocution. Or maybe not. I mean there are no surprises here, it was just a question of when. With no ifs attached. So. First put on the Coltrane and then have a bath. No mask, no patches. A real one.

'Bath? Keno?' She's such an idiot, this girl, fucking know-nothing, asking me why I am now going to have a bath.

'Because,' I am patient when I explain things nowadays, 'in Gujaratis, you have a bath after you lose someone you are related to. It's supposed to wash away attachment.'

Love Supreme

Despite my father's pessimism, Ma Thug made a mistake and the impossible happened. In the January of 1977, in the sixteenth month of her Emergency, Indira Gandhi, Empress of All India, decided that she had done enough to regain the people's mandate. She calculated that she had bludgeoned the people of India enough to make sure that a vast majority of them would not hesitate to vote for her and her Congress Party.

When Indira lifted the Emergency and declared elections my father was incredulous. For once, even he was at a loss for words. My uncle Prabodhmama was the opposite. Sitting in one of Havmor's many ice-cream parlours he increased his output of anti-Indira and anti-Sanjay Gandhi songs.

Chi' Suman, he wrote to my mother in one of his Inlands, the letters of the Gujarati script herded together like clusters of virulent germs, deep blue Quink squiggling right up to the edges of the light blue paper, words sometimes getting lost where he had gone over into the gummed edges, *I hope all of you are well.*

I wasn't interested, but my mother made me sit down and forced me to listen as she read it out loud. I let her go through it because it was a rare sight to see her cheerful and the letter had obviously had that effect.

Chi' Suman,

I hope all of you are well. Here, with Sai Baba's blessings we are all fine. (My father snorting at the mention of Sai Baba, my mother defending Prabodhmama and family, saying this was the older, genuine Sai Baba von Shirdi, the one who was dead and not the new fraud I would later call Jimi Hendrix's fat cousin.) *Mahubhai and all of you must be overjoyed to hear the news of the coming elections. Has Kalidasbhai been released from jail yet? If he is not already out, I pray to Krushnah Bhagwan that he will be fine and released soon.* ('Multi-band antibiotic' my father called Prabodhmama and family's proclivity for believing in anything and everything that resembled a god, a holy man or a shrine.) *I am writing songs every day and people here are using them at election rallies. Here is one that is a hit –*

Bhool, bhool, bloody fool (next to which, for my benefit, he'd written in English – 'mistake, mistake, bloody fool' – as if I didn't know what the word 'bhool' meant – bloody fool).

You claimed you were father's daughter,
You claimed you were father's daughter!
But all know that you are only your son's mother!
All know you are only that baldy's mother!
Bhool, bhool, bloody fool!

And son, you planted trees, yes! Oh you planted trees, yes!
You uprooted people from their houses and
Planted trees on their hearts!
But now the nation is back from vanvaas (for me in English – 'forest-exile, like Lord Rama and also the Pandavas'),
Bhool, bhool, bloody fool!

And Mummy you had twenty points didn't you?
And Mummy you tried to teach us to count, no?
But we know that your twenty is equal to zero,
We learned freedom's mathematics long ago,
Bhool, bhool, bloody fool!

And son, you're the prince of operations!
You tried to sterilise the nation's soul,
But we, the real sons of Bapu and Jawaharlal
Are not so easy to turn into eunuchs,
Bhool, bhool, bloody fool!

And now sitting on your truck you say you want our vote,
You want us to renew your licence to rule,
But not for nothing are we the world's biggest democracy,
Every vote will be a nail to puncture your Maruti chariot,
Bhool, bhool, bloody fool!

'Somebody is obviously buying him enough ice-cream,' muttered my father under his breath as my mother paused. My mother ignored this and continued reading the letter.

The mood here in Gujarat is that the Indira Congress will not get even one seat. Astrologer friends looking at her stars say this is the end for Indira and Sanjay. How about Bengal? Is the freedom Jyoti (light) burning bright there? With Durgamata's blessings the CPI(M) is sure to sweep.

Minakshi had gone to Ajmer and there she put flowers at the Dargah of Salim Chishti with a prayer for Paresh to get the best result in his ISC exams. Tell him that he will have to buy his Prabodhmama samosas and ice-cream at Kwality restaurant if he gets first division.

With my regards,
Prabodh

Below which was the usual Om symbol.

The letter put both my father and me in a bad mood but for different reasons. The only thing my father added after my mother finished was a comment about how Prabodh had never bought anyone an ice-cream in his entire life and yet here he was, an uncle, shamelessly demanding a treat from a nephew who wasn't even an adult.

My mother didn't rise to the bait because both she and I knew the real reason behind my father's irritation. The real reason was that there was still no news of his friend Kalidas Dutta, who had been arrested in the early days of the Emergency, a year and a half ago. This was despite the fact that, right after Indira had declared elections, the government had released most of the political prisoners arrested under the Emergency's special laws.

Of late, no one mentioned Kalikaku's name in the house. We hoped he was all right but as prisoners began coming out of jail with their stories of incarceration and torture, more and more evidence began to emerge that the police had used the curtain of the Emergency to 'off' certain prisoners they considered especially dangerous. This was a continuation of the policy of fake encounters and 'shot while escaping' executions that had begun in the peak years of the Naxal movement. And while Kalikaku had parted ways with his Naxalite comrades as early as 1968, he was still very much on the police files as a Naxal when he was arrested in July 1975.

My father only told me all this when I was fifteen, when I asked him why Kalikaku had been arrested. I think it was a kind of passing-on of important information – the kind of thing you do in – well, in an emergency. In case something happened to my father. Which is why he went into it with me, otherwise he might have waited till I was older. Because, for example, a few years earlier, when I was about ten, he had said nothing when the officer from the Border Security Force came for tea. My parents had let me sit and listen. I just thought it was another visitor coming for tea, a policeman this time, and I was quite excited. It was only after he left, and Kalikaku came over and my father and he had a fight, that I realised that there might have been something wrong in the policeman's visit.

'Kalidas, I just wanted to hear what he had to say! What is wrong in that?'

'Nothing, nothing, Modhuda. Listening, after all, is a non-violent act. Even if you listen to a murderer doing justifications of his actions.'

I couldn't remember any justifications for murder and I wondered why Kalikaku was so angry. All Rathodsaheb had talked about was how they had been brought in from Gujarat to fight Naxalites.

My mother had served the tea herself, as she did when important guests came, not trusting the maid. Rathodsaheb took his cup and poured the tea into his saucer and then sloped the saucer into his face. I thought he was going to spill it for a moment, but he had a big mouth and all the tea disappeared into it without a single drop escaping. My mother never liked anyone drinking tea like that, like Prabodhmama always did. 'Mawaali!' she would call people who drank tea from their saucer, but today she didn't seem to mind. Rathodsaheb was obviously a special mawaali. The tea made a slurping sound going into his mouth, like water spinning down a washbasin, and later in life I always remembered that sound at strange moments.

I waited till Rathodsaheb finished his cup before asking, 'So, Kaka, you actually fight Naxalites?'

Rathodsaheb was saying something to my father and he didn't answer me immediately.

'It's a standard procedure,' he said, reaching for the plastic bowl full of chevdo that my mother had put next to the tea. He sifted around in it as if looking through a file and picked out a peanut. 'The administration found that they could not . . . that they could not trust the local police. They were either too scared or the other way . . .' He let his sentence hang as he basketballed the peanut into his big mouth.

My father had his hand in a fist just under his lower lip, with the thumb supporting his jaw and the index finger up along his cheek. That meant he was in his serious listening mood and I knew better than to ask my question again. So I also put my fist under my chin and listened.

Rathodsaheb scuffed some more chevdo into his hand and herded it all into his never-tiring mouth, capturing more than just the peanuts this time. The sound of his chewing changed as he pulverised all the chevda things, the puffed rice and the sev cushioning the harder crack of the peanuts.

'You mean that the police here actually . . .' my father didn't finish his sentence either.

'Well,' said Rathodsaheb, reaching for his tea again, 'not all of them, of course, not all of them, one can't say *that*, but the situation was getting so bad that they had to be sure there were no links.'

'Yes, well, I have heard that too, that they were receiving help from some people actually inside the police forces, but in a situation like this you hear a lot of things and you don't know what to believe, you know?'

'Take it from me, Mahadevsaheb, take it from me. If these people had nipped it in the bud we would not have been called. They have let it get out of hand. Though, saheb, it would be good of you if you didn't write that I said that.'

'No, no, I was just interested in getting some background.' My father reached for his own cup of tea in a reassuring way. 'After all, we are in a semi-war situation here and you, the paramilitary, are being called in chhek all the way from Gujarat to fight our own people. I want to know how things came to this.'

'This is not what we fought for.' My mother had come and sat down.

'No, Bhabhi, you are right. These people are willing to drown all the sacrifices people like you made, real freedom fighters like you . . .' Rathodsaheb poured himself some more tea from the kettle. 'Out there in the camp I miss our tea. Nothing like our Gujarati tea, Bhabhi. Today I am really happy.'

'Please have,' said my mother. 'Please don't be shy. There is more. And I can make more.'

But Rathodsaheb was back to my father.

'Mahadevsaheb, it is not a semi-war, it is a full war. And another full, bigger, one is coming with the Pakistanis. This East Pakistan business – it's only a matter of time, six months, maybe eight.'

My father started to say something but Rathodsaheb had turned to me.

'Yes beta, I fight Naxalites. And you know what I do? I shoot them.'

'Do you use machine-guns?'

'Sometimes,' said Rathodsaheb, 'sometimes. But most times I just use this.' And he reached down to his side and pulled out his pistol from his holster and put it next to the bowl of chevdo.

I stared at the pistol, fascinated.

'Do you know what this is?'

'A revolver,' I said.

'No. It is an automatic.' I kicked myself, I had meant to say automatic, but I had never actually seen a real one and the sudden presence of it had pushed back all my war comics and brought up the first word, the word you use in Gujarati – rivaulver.

'It is actually a Colt .45 semi-automatic and it was given to my father during the Second World War by Colonel Mitchell of the American Army. It is a beautiful gun.'

'A .45 is even bigger than a .38, isn't it? Isn't it the biggest handgun?' I said, recovering.

'Exactly, very good,' said Rathodsaheb. I could sense my father getting tense but I could tell my mother was all right. She was as fascinated as I was.

Rathodsaheb grabbed a quick gulp of tea from his cup before picking up the gun again. He pointed it downward and did something with it and the magazine came away in his hand. He put the magazine down on the table. I could see a bullet perched halfway out of the top of the magazine. A real live bullet.

'A gun is not a toy,' said Rathodsaheb. 'You use it when you have to, but most of the time you have to be very careful with it. Here,' he said, turning the muzzle towards himself and handing it to me, 'here, hold it and see how it feels.'

I reached for the Colt with one hand and almost dropped it, it was so heavy. Then I took it with both hands. It was even heavier than my father's Nikon F.

'Baba! Don't pull the trigger or anything, beta,' said my mother quickly.

Rathodsaheb leaned back into the sofa and laughed, enjoying the tension.

'Don't worry, Bhabhi. I've taken the bullets out. And even if I hadn't, it would take more strength than this young pehelwaan has to pull the trigger. You need a lot of strength to shoot this. It also has a recoil that can take your arm out of your shoulder.'

My right hand had got used to the weight of the gun and I turned away from my parents and pointed it at the window. The gun wobbled slightly as I took aim at a crow sitting on the ledge. It felt strange and beautiful. The metal of the trigger was cool to the touch, and even though I could barely get my fingers around it, the textured grip felt right, as if it belonged in my hand.

I could hear my father controlling his voice when he said, 'Okay, Paresh, enough. Give it back to kaka now.' And then to Rathodsaheb, 'You don't know him. Next thing you know he'll be running to his school and pointing it at his Principal. Empty of course, but they won't consider that when they expel him.' Rathodsaheb gave a little laugh as if he didn't totally disapprove of shooting Principals.

I reluctantly handed the Colt back to him. The magazine made a nice click as it slid back in. The gun was ready again for Naxalites. Rathodsaheb wiped the side of his finger across his mouth and looked at me very seriously.

'Beta. This gun. I don't enjoy using it, you know.' He was finishing all his sentences now and I could tell this was as much for my parents as for me. 'Every time I pull the trigger – I never even put my finger on the trigger unless I am convinced there is no other choice, that I am doing my duty to protect my Mother, which is this great country. Remember that, beta.' With which he put the Colt back in his holster and used the same hand to scoop up some more chevdo.

'Some more tea, Rathodsaheb?' asked my mother.

A few days later a noise woke me up late at night. I listened for a moment, trying to place it, and then I was sure of it. Gunfire. The sound of gunfire coming from the south, from Jadavpur University side. Two kinds of sounds, single reports like random firecrackers, being answered by a rattle, a bit like I'd heard in war movies. There was a third sound, it was raining hard and the noise of the rain blanketed the gunshots and neither of my parents woke up. I got out of bed, slid into my rubber chappals, and crept out to the balcony.

There was a triangular park in front of the flat we lived in then, and just outside the park railings, one on each side of the triangle, were three lamp-posts which rarely worked. Some parts of the city already had the new ones which used tubelights hidden under a long translucent shade, but our colony was always among the last to get new things and these were still the old style poles, with a naked bulb hanging out of a little conical hat which was painted grey on the outside and white on the inside. These were connected to other electric poles by sagging strands of wire. That night the lamp-post on the far side of the park was on and I could see the rain lashing down into its dim yellow light from the darkness above. In the throw of the bulb I could see sheets of water breaking on the mess of wires, making them shake.

Parts of the park had turned into shallow little seas of shining water and the roads around it were beginning to fill up. As I watched the storm I tried to part the sound of the rain and listen for the gunfire beyond. After a while I heard it again, a sharp crack, then a brief stuttering reply, then two sounds that sounded more like explosions and then no more – as if two people had decided to stop a fruitless argument. I waited for a few minutes and then decided to go back to bed. Just as I was about to turn away, a flash of lightning lit up the sky and I saw him.

At first I thought it was my imagination playing a nasty trick on me but then another crack of lightning lit him up like a flashbulb and left no room for doubt. There he was, crouched at the very top of a long bamboo ladder leaning on an electric pole, doing something with the knot of wires that met at the pole. I lost him after the lightning, but once my eyes adjusted back I could see him even in the light of the lamp-post, a shadow in a shadow. The thick rain made everything fuzzy, but I could still see him.

These were the days when the Calcutta middle class had stopped venturing out after dark. Every day we would hear new stories, Naxals killing a policeman, Naxals robbing a woman of all her jewellery as she stepped out of her car on Chowringhee, Naxals killing a jute-mill owner as he slept in his bed in his mansion in Alipur, Naxals – and now, here in my colony, in the deep of the night, right in front of my eyes, a real Naxal perched on top of an electric pole. As I watched, frozen more with fascination than fear, I wondered if Rathodsaheb's Colt .45 could bring the man down.

After a while I saw the man jerk something. One of the wires loosened through the other wires and came crashing down like a whip onto the flooded road below. Then the man pulled at something else and the light went out with a flash and then there was only the black whirr of the rain. Scared now, I used the darkness to feel my way back to my bed, hoping the man hadn't seen me.

The next morning, when my mother was having her bath, I told my father what I had seen.

'Do you think he was a Naxalite, Pappa?'

'No baba, I don't think so. Just a thief stealing wires.'

'Are you sure? How do you know?'

My father snapped his newspaper into good behaviour and smiled down at it.

'Because the Naxalites are busy electrocuting themselves in other ways, political ways. They think they are revolutionaries. They don't waste time trying to commit suicide by stealing live electricity wires on a rainy night.'

I didn't understand what my father meant but I thought about it for many days.

Now, seven years later, that war was long over. As was the war with Pakistan that Rathodsaheb had promised. The end of those two wars brought the Emergency, which was another kind of war, but that was over too. As far as I was concerned, all wars were over for good. There was only the matter of one POW, Kalikaku, who was still missing.

While I was as worried about Kalikaku as my parents, Prabodhmama's letter put me in a bad mood because of the mention of my school finals which I had given at the end of the previous year and which, having given, I wanted to forget all about. The blessings of Salim Chishti or no, I was sure I was in no danger of having to take Prabodhmama to Kwality for a treat. The only thing I was praying for at the time was that I would pass.

My results crawled out of the Board in April, and it was a very good thing that they appeared just a few days after the election results. My parents were both still so elated at the victory of the Janata Party, so triumphant in their different ways about the complete rout of Indira and her Congress, that they didn't seem to notice that their only child had barely managed to scramble over the wall that stood at thirty-eight per cent, separating the failures from the rest.

'An aggregate of forty-five per cent is not bad for someone like you,' said my father. 'Make sure to send a copy of the marksheet to Miss Zeenat Aman's secretary.'

'Hashey awhey, never mind,' said my mother, putting another bhakhri on my thali, 'now you have to concentrate on getting into a good college.' Which for her, the education fanatic who had topped exams all her student life, was generous to the point of lunacy.

A few weeks later, one evening in May, I was sitting on the balcony beating off mosquitoes and trying to read a book by candle-light. The electricity had been gone for over three hours and I was waiting for it to come back, hoping I wouldn't have to try and sleep without the fan in the festering pre-monsoon night. My mother was clattering about in the kitchen, trying to get the maid to clean up properly despite the lights having gone. My father was sitting next to a window in the living room, listening to a raag on his little Hitachi transistor. I heard a riksha stop on the road outside, near the gates of the park and I paid it no attention. After a moment, the riksha pulled away, the riksha-walla hitting his hand bell loudly to ward off the colony dogs and any cars without headlights. I could hear his chappals slapping against his feet as he went off into the unlamp-posted dark. Further away, a couple of dogs took up the chase and I could hear their barks escorting the riksha-walla's bell. I was still listening to this when someone began banging on our door.

My father switched off the transistor. I went in and picked up the torch.

'See who it is, knocking this late,' my mother called from the kitchen.

I went to the door, my father a few steps behind me.

'Ke?' I asked, but since the Emergency was over I didn't wait for an answer before opening the door.

The first thing the beam of the torch caught was the grin wolfing out from the tangle of moustache and beard. Then it caught the eyes, the cheekbones pushing them up into glinting slivers. My mouth must have been open because I remember a mosquito going in just as my father shouted, 'KALIDAS!'

The shout seemed to jolt the electricity, and a tubelight began to flicker on as my father pushed past me and dragged Kalikaku in. The fans clacked awake in welcome. Behind my mother's footsteps rushing out of the kitchen, I could hear the fridge clearing its bronchial passages before beginning its all-night grumble.

My father rarely hugged anyone, but that day he had Kalikaku in a tight hold, as though if he let go the man would disappear back into the night. Kalikaku, on the other hand, was good at hugging people and he had his arms around my father in an equally passionate clinch. The two of them, one tall and one short, rocked back and forth for a while like a badly balanced modern sculpture at the Academy of Fine Arts. It took my mother a moment before she could see Kalikaku's face clearly. When he finally turned to her she recoiled in horror. Her hand went up to her mouth, but the words jumped out before she could trap them.

'Aay haay! What have they done to you?'

'Ehey! Sumandi! You had forgotten how ugly I am!'

Kalikaku put one arm around my mother's shoulders and gave her a sideways squeeze, the kind he always gave her after he had offended her by saying something funny and outrageous about one of her gods. Normally my mother would try and wriggle out, refusing to be mollified, but this time she grinned, put an arm around him and hugged him back. I still had my fingers stuck in my mouth, trying to get the dead mosquito out, when Kalikaku turned to me.

'And – oh my god. Who is this strapping young man? O Maago! It is Pawraish!'

It was only when he put his arms around me that I realised I was now taller than Kalikaku. As he held me I could feel nothing but his bones and somewhere, in some corner of my mind, I realised I was feeling the remains of the jail in him.

• • •

After a few days of going around shocking friends with his new beard and moustache, Kalikaku shaved and returned to being recognisable. Always a thin man, his stay in Presidency Jail had sliced him down even further. But the walk was still the same, jaunty, bouncy, a sailor's lilt to it. His hair was more white and there were new lines around his eyes and mouth that I would always think of as 'Emergency' lines.

'So Paresh! What are your plans now that you have passed your exams?'

'What plans can he have with his marks? I have advised him to go to Bombay and marry some rich actress.'

The relief of seeing Kalikaku alive had rubbed some of the shine off my parents' post-election euphoria. My low marks had begun to appear again and again in conversations.

'Oh, forty-five per cent is okay, Madhuda. Examinations are a bourgeois trick to keep intelligent people away from power. And besides, if you go to Bombay to become an actor your karate will come in use, no, Paresh?'

'Oh, he has given that up. No application at all,' said my mother and my mouth became a mosquito airport. I remembered clearly how much she hated my going to karate class.

'Well, he *is* interested in photography,' conceded my father, before adding, 'so if he does find a rich actress then he needn't necessarily get into acting. She can support this expensive hobby of his.'

'Arrey come on, Madhuda, and where did he get this nesha from?'

'Yes, yes, I know. But I used to shoot maybe one roll of film a month. This boy finishes a roll sometimes in a *day*. Doesn't think, just presses the shutter.'

'Pappa, Time-Life and National Geographic photographers shoot many rolls *in a day*, colour and black and white, and they have motor-drives attached to their cameras.'

'Yes, but they also get a Time-Life salary.'

'Don't worry Madhuda, he will find something. At least he doesn't have his heart set on something like this Computer business. That would have been a disaster, what with George Fernandes having got rid of IBM, there is no future for that sort of thing in this country.'

Fernandes had got rid of not only IBM but also, to my great despair, Coca-Cola. There was still a supply available, but bottles of Coke were becoming rarer and rarer and not every paan-walla stocked them. There was one guy, across the road from Waldorf in Park Street, who seemed to have an inexhaustible supply. While other paan-wallas were trying to foist the new horrors of Double Seven and Campa Cola on us, this guy would open up a bottle of asli Coke for you as if he had been doing it for years, which of course he had.

One day Kalikaku took me out for lunch to Park Street and I expressed a desire for a Coke before eating.

'Yes. Better drink all you can before it disappears from our lives altogether,' Kalikaku said in mock sympathy as I led him to the paan-walla across from Waldorf. The man reached into his rusty red ice-box and took out a cold bottle. He opened it and gave it to me. I greedily took a big pull on the straw and found some impostor of a taste clouding my tongue. 'Chheh!' I said. 'This is not Coca-Cola!'

The paan-walla whirled upon me as if I'd insulted his mother. 'Of course it's Coca-Cola! What do you take me for? I don't do all that chaarsobeesi.'

I offered the bottle back to him. 'You try it,' I said, knowing exactly what I was doing.

The man's eyes flared wide. At the back of his head his choti twitched. In front, his moustache glistened. He put down the paan he was making.

'Are you asking a Brahman from Banaras to taste your jhootha bottle of Coca-Cola?'

Thanks to my father, I had no undue pride in my Brahman ancestry, but at times like these I could pull out a good pretend.

'I am probably a higher caste of Brahman than you,' I said, 'and this is not a jhootha bottle of Coke, this is a jhootha bottle of *fake* Coke.'

The man was large and he was sitting on his perch, cross-legged, his knees jammed up against the marble slab on which he made his paan. Had he not been, he would have gone for my throat immediately. As it was, he had already begun to uncross his legs from under his large belly when a man standing next to us interrupted.

'Mishraji never sells false stuff,' he said authoritatively and underlined his point by putting one of Mishraji's paans into his mouth.

'Paresh, leave it,' said Kalikaku, pulling out money from the top pocket of his shirt. 'Lo bhai, here, take your money,' he said to the paan-walla, but the man was bellowing now, addressing all of Park Street.

'Who does this boy think he is? Here is Jhunjunwalla sahab saying that you can't doubt Mishra and you are showing me your caste?'

Another man, a thin babu in a dhoti-kurta, had stopped to light his cigarette from the rope. He took a tug on his cigarette to make sure it was lit before joining in. His quarrel was with Jhunjunwalla.

'You can't tell who provides real and who provides fake nowadays. All those big businessmen in Badabazar making lakhs and lakhs from adulterating grain and sugar, why can't a paan-walla sell two-numberi Coca-Cola? How can you tell?'

Jhunjunwalla turned his paunch on the man and spoke through his paan.

'Awe you saywing dat I wadultewate food? Hain?'

'I am not saying you, I am saying anybody. Here,' he said, snatching the bottle from my hand and shaking it at Jhunjunwalla, 'why should this paan-walla taste it? *You* taste it. You taste it and tell us!'

I felt Kalikaku pull me away as the paan-walla bent towards the babu. Flecks of spit flew out with his words, some getting caught on his big moustache. 'Do you know who you are talking to? Jhunjunwalla sahab has the biggest jute business in Badabazar!'

The man raised his arm above his head, waved the Coke bottle like a battle standard and summoned up his high voice as if pulling it all the way down from the noon day sun.

'I don't care! These Marwaris have raped Bengal!'

'I'll wape *you*,' said Jhunjunwalla, moving towards the man, the red of the paan now dribbling out of one side of his mouth like a trickle of blood. 'I'll fuck you madarchod!'

A pair of men had come out of the post office next to the paan shop and stopped to watch. They jumped in between Jhunjunwalla and the thin babu, both of them chanting in unison.

'Ki hoyechhe, ki hoyechhe, ki hoyechhe? Kihoyecchekihoyeccheki-hoyechhe?'

A small crowd began to gather. The paan-walla had managed to get his legs out from under him and now he was trying to find a way to climb down into the melee. The babu was screaming at the top of his voice, as was Jhunjunwalla, but neither was managing to reach the other across all the pushing and shoving. I suddenly realised that we were watching the action from afar. We were on the other side of the road, in fact. Without any volition on my part, Kalikaku had managed to extricate me from the tangle. Now he put his hand on my arm and tried to drag me along the street. As we moved away, more and more people joined the jhamela, the crowd attracting them like a magnet attracts iron filings.

As we turned to go, a man in a suit ran up to us.

'Ki hoyechhe, dada?' he asked breathlessly and then repeated the question in English, 'What is happening?' Without waiting for an answer he turned to Kalikaku and thrust his briefcase at him – 'Eita ektu dhorun tˆo!' – before crossing the road and sprinting into the crowd. We could see him wading in, pushing and ducking, till he was roughly at the centre of the dhakka-dhakki. Then I saw his suited elbow go up, hand in a fist, and come down on someone who was obviously lying on the ground, once, twice, thrice, hard. Then, as we watched, the suit worked his way out to the edge of the mess of bodies. He slammed a parting elbow into someone's ribs and peeled himself away.

He crossed the street, weaving through the cars like a footballer and came back to us, brushing himself off and adjusting his tie. He smacked his palms against each other in a job-well-done kind of way before yanking back his briefcase from Kalikaku.

'Sal-laa,' he said, looking back at the scene of his triumph, 'these people have no culture, jaanen tˆo?' He looked at us, adjusted his spectacles for emphasis and repeated, 'NO culture, you know, eder kono culture nei.' And then he walked off.

We mosquito-airported after him for quite a while before Kalikaku spoke, his voice swimming in deep wonder.

'You know . . . the Punjabis have a saying . . . Lahore, Lahore hai . . .we should have one, some such thing about Calcutta . . . something which says Calcutta is Calcutta . . . but we don't.'

'You needn't have pulled me away. I could have handled that fat bhaiyaji.'

Kalikaku looked at me.

'Of course you could have, I have no doubt, but is that what you really wanted to do today? Beat up a paan-walla for selling you a false Coca-Cola?'

'No, but . . .'

'Paresh. Madhuda told me about those two goondas and you saving him. That was different. That was good. This, today, this was with no meaning. You have to save your energy for fighting when it really matters. At your age you may think your energy is limitless but you will find that it is not.'

Even though my hands were itching to hit someone, somewhere I understood what Kalikaku was telling me. Somewhere I was glad that we had come out of the brawl without a scratch. I kept quiet as Kalikaku led me up Park Street to a really rundown-looking restaurant.

As we went in through the swinging doors, two waiters came hurrying towards us. They obviously knew Kalikaku.

'Salaam sahab,' said one, ducking his head in greeting.

'Salaam sahab,' said the other, also ducking his head.

Kalikaku pointed to a table next to the window, which was actually two sofas facing each other with the table in between. We slid in. I stared at the large frosted-glass window behind Kalikaku. The glass had a buxom woman etched onto it. She was kneeling down on one knee and pouring water from a pot. The sunlight came through her and made a rim around the edges of Kalikaku's hair. When he moved to a certain point it looked as if she was pouring the water over his head.

'This,' said Kalikaku grandly, 'is Olympia. Olympia Bar and Restaurant as they call it. It may not look very fancy now but for a long time this was the place you came to if you were a young man with a little bit of money. In the days when Calcutta was an international city, Olympia was famous as the one of the places where there was action, life, intelligent conversation.'

'When was that?' I asked doubtfully as I looked around me. There was a smear of food on the table. As if to welcome me, a small squadron of flies came and settled on it.

'Oh, I believe from the early '40s sometime, through the war, till about the late '60s. I first came here in '61. When we would dock after a long trip we would collect our pay and then we would spruce up.

And this was the first place we would come to. After that it went downhill. But I still like it – it reminds me of my misspent youth.' The waiter brought us the menus. 'And now it's cheap. Probably the cheapest place on Park Street.'

I looked at the grimy plastic-covered menu and I had no problem believing Kalikaku about the cheapness. Right next to the swank Park Hotel Coffee Shop, and Kwality with its crisp tablecloths, and only a few yards away from the pristine pastry counters at Flury's, was this oasis of grime. In my childhood my mother would have slapped me if I had even looked in through the window of a place like this. I was beginning to enjoy my afternoon. The waiter took out a filthy cloth and swiped the table, sending the flies spinning up for a moment. As soon as his hand was away they came back to the spot where the smear had been, nosed around, and then lost interest and refugeed to another table.

'One large Old Monk,' said Kalikaku, 'and one beer, Black Label.'

'Ek bada peg rum, ek beer,' repeated the waiter and went off to get the order.

'Are you going to drink rum *and* beer together?' I asked Kalikaku.

'No, my boy. I will drink the rum and you will drink a glass of beer. And we won't tell your mother.'

'Beer?' I said, really excited now.

'Yes. You need to calm down. Otherwise you will become like that suited-booted idiot. No culture. Coca-Cola. Chhaah! You need some culture and beer is one of the best cultures.'

The waiter came back bristling with things. Under one arm he had a bottle of what looked like beer. Under the other he had a fat dark bottle that I guessed was the rum. In one hand he carried three glasses, his fingers inside the top of each one, pressing them together. They made a sound like gagged castanets. In his other hand he had an ice-bucket and an hourglass-shaped silvery thimble, one side of the hourglass bigger than the other.

The waiter put the glasses and the ice-bucket down. Then, after putting the beer on the table, he reached for the bottle of rum, unscrewed the cap and poured it into the larger cup of the hourglass. He had the measure held over a glass and he waited till it filled to the brim and overflowed slightly, the rum trickling over his fingers and into the glass. He let quite a bit run down before he turned the whole thing over smartly, pouring out the liquid and then shaking every last drop out to show that it was really empty.

'Ek large Old Monk rum, sahab,' he said.

The other waiter had come up and picked up my bottle of beer. He was using a bottle-opener to fight with it. Suddenly a hand reached out from behind him and tugged the bottle away from him.

'Arrey it's Dutta sahab! Leave it, you idiot! I will serve Datta sahab.'

An old bald gnome in a waiter's uniform held up the beer bottle triumphantly. A long white beard cascaded down, almost to the middle of his chest, and his eyes twinkled under a thick pair of white eyebrows. He looked as if he'd just caught a chicken after a long chase. He ducked his head at Kalikaku.

'Salaam sahab. Sorry sahab, the boy is new.'

'Arrey Islam chacha! How are you today?' said Kalikaku, expanding to the old man.

'Sahab, aapki dua se. Fine. Still alive.' The old man smiled back while magically opening the bottle without even looking at it. He moved to pour it and then saw the rum.

'Oh ho? Who's drinking the rum?'

'I am,' said Kalikaku, 'the beer is for my young friend here.'

Islam chacha turned and stretched his deference to cover my side of the table as well.

'Ah, chhotey sahab, sorry . . . here you are.' He tilted the glass and poured in the beer, making sure, as Kalikaku would later explain to me, that there was no more than a minimum of white foam on top of the glass when he finished. 'In Germany they like that sort of thing, it's called a head, the foam on top, it is one sign of the quality of the beer and you can go to jail if your beer doesn't have some specific inches of head as required by law. Here these idiot people don't like it too much, they think the foam is separate, is alien, to the beer. So these waiters have to be very careful how they pour it. I've seen drunk customers send back bottles because there isn't enough "beer" and too much head!'

The old man placed the full glass in front of me like a courtier putting a chalice before a king. I looked at it and then at Kalikaku, who was now putting ice and water into his rum. After making sure that we had everything we needed the first waiter put a pink slip into the third glass that he'd brought along. Then he reached across and put the glass out of the way, near the wall at one side of the table. Then all three waiters left.

'Cheers,' said Kalikaku and lifted his rum.

'Cheers,' I replied and lifted the beer.

'Cheers, Kali-da, cheers, cheers,' said a voice behind me. Kalikaku's head jerked up and when he saw who it was, he laughed with pleasure.

'Eijey! Anir-baanchod! Come, come, sit. Just when I was wondering who was going to pay the bill. Come and sit.'

I moved up against the wall and a young guy with a ponytail plonked himself down next to me, taking up more than his share of the sofa.

Kalikaku made a mock court-gesture with his hand, 'This is Mr Anirban Dey, the Bob Dylan of Ballygunje Circular Road,' and then to me, 'and this is young Mr Paresh Bhatt, the Lartigue of Lake Gardens, soon to become the Evans of Elgin Road.'

The guy gave me the once-over in what I imagined was a Bob Dylan-like way.

'Lartigue-ta ke? Evans? Evans-ta abar ke?' He was staring at me sourly, but the question was for Kalikaku.

Kalikaku took a pull of his Old Monk.

'Jacques Henri Lartigue, great French photographer. And Walker Evans. Great American photographer. Don't worry, you wouldn't know. They were both before rock and roll.'

• • •

Earlier that day he had known something from Calcutta was going to come and get him.

It happened at Nation, where he was changing lines, walking with his daughter Para, bringing her back from her Hindi class. He heard the guitar well before they reached the corner. The high notes hitting the ceiling of the underground corridor, coming around past the posters in sharp shoals, the low notes slapping off the tiles and the floor, carpeting the station with a menace, with an otherness that tugged at the blurry mask of métro sound. Para jerked her head and lifted one side of her Walkman headphones because she had heard it too. Then she shook her head, not interested, put the headphone back in place and carried on mouthing her Hindi pronunciations. Paresh slowed in his walk and almost stopped, for some reason not wanting to turn the corner. But then he kept walking, following Para as she bounced ahead. The man looked up as if he had been waiting for him but he didn't pause.

Paresh tried to walk past but it was as if the man had put up an invisible wall across the corridor and he had to stop. He looked at Para walking away, oblivious, and almost called out after her. Something made her turn around and catch his eyes before he could say anything and then she too stopped, slightly exasperated, and turned and came back. The man waited for her to reach Paresh before he opened his mouth to let his voice out. The high black throat stretched up from the loose kaftan, and a long note entered the air, pure as a line of spilt milk travelling fast across a dark red floor. Para took her headphones off and put her hand in her father's. They looked at the man and the man looked back at them both, but mostly straight into Paresh's eyes.

Later, back in their apartment, Para asked Paresh what the man was singing about and Paresh had no answer for his seven-year-old except that it was some African language and that it sounded like an old song.

Later, after Para went to sleep, Paresh poured himself a drink and turned on his computer. The man had finished his song and smiled. A wide white grin, almost a laugh but not quite. Paresh had reached into his pocket for change to add to the small pile in the open guitar case, but the man had raised a hand, indicating that it wasn't necessary and Paresh had stepped back. Para had tugged at his hand, impatient to go now that the rope of the song had loosened, and they had walked away. The man's eyes followed them for a while but, by the time Paresh looked back, the cap and the head were down in his guitar again. Something about the song had filled Paresh with a longing and with a foreboding. As he clicked on the Net connection his sense of unease raced ahead of him, downloading the pages of his past inside his head, searching them for a sign of what he did not yet know.

Paresh went into the Web and started going through Indian newspapers. *Times of India*, *The Hindu*, *Indian Expre* – no, no, he needed a Calcutta newspaper, news from Calcutta, *Statesman* . . . *Ananda Baz* – *The Telegraph*. Once there he found it quickly and then there was no getting away from it. There it was, under the Metropolis button, well away from the front page and the headlines about the military coup in Pakistan.

> **NOTED MUSICIAN DEAD**
> Anirban Dey, well-known singer and song-writer, died yesterday afternoon following a massive heart attack. Dey was 47 and is survived by his wife and a son and a daughter. Dey was best known for his synthesis of Western rock and blues with traditional Bengali folk and popular music. He began his career in the late seventies when he formed his band The Calcutta Blues Association, better known as 'Association' . . .

There was no picture button with the news item, the *Telegraph* Website being primitive, but Paresh knew exactly which photograph they would have given to the newspapers and also the other one that they would use for the Shraadhh and the singing. He had taken them both – one in 1979 and one after he had come back from America, in the mid-'80s sometime.

'Use this one after I'm gone,' Anirban had said to his wife Kuku in front of Paresh. Kuku had disagreed. 'No, I like the one he took last year, oita, where you're playing guitar for Darya, you look less rock-star-like and more human, a proper father – which of course you will never be.' Finally they decided to use the earlier one for the public image and the later one for the personal. 'If this is how you want to remember me, then okay,' Anirban had said, and everyone had laughed and everyone had had some more rum.

• • •

'My life is ruled by two monks,' says Anirban. 'Ekta is Guru Thelonius Monk and the other is Shri Shri Old Monk.'

'Hm,' grunts Paresh. 'Don't see much Thelonius in your music, boss, but I see lots of Old Monk.'

Kalikaku snorts a laugh into his drink. Anirban turns on Paresh.

'You. Now you understand everything do you? Photography, music, sex, politics, *shob* kichhu bujhish tui, just because you once spent three years in America? Bokachoda, if the piano solo and in fact the whole tonal arrangement in "Baby Gone Bombay" is not from Thelonius then where is it from? Elton John?'

'Engelbert Humperdinck,' says Paresh, 'Elton John would have been tolerable.'

Anirban clutches his glass of Old Monk as if he's going to throw it at Paresh, but Kalikaku butts in.

'Not just America,' Kalikaku says, 'we have also trained him before and after America, for how many years now? Let's see '77 thekey '79 and then '82 to . . . now is '86, so that's nearly six years under our influence. You have to admit, Baan, that he has been growing up.'

'Little bit. Not enough.'

Paresh starts to tap his glass on the table and hum a pastiche of 'Baby Gone Bombay'.

'Ooo, oohoo, baby gone, baby gone, baby gone Boooombeh.'

They are sitting upstairs in Olympia, behind the wooden partitions of the Family Section because they've got Kuku and Joyeeta with them. A large fat man in a sweat-stained safari suit sits at another table with a heavily made-up woman. Every now and then the woman takes the man's hand off her thigh and puts it back on the table. The hand stays there for a bit, a cheap gold-coloured watch glinting against the marble-patterned sunmica, lifts a glass, grabs some of the stale mixture from a plate, transports one or the other up to the mouth and then drops down again. The man doesn't look at the woman. He is unhappy and he stares into the mirror above the opposite sofa as he kneads her sari. The woman is talking to him in a low voice, complaining about how he treats her. The man scowls into his moustache and says nothing. Every now and then he looks over at their table and stares balefully at Kuku and Joyeeta.

'. . . only because he's upset about Ila,' says Kuku, 'I should leave you Baan, then you would know. I'd like to see you sing BGB then.'

'Yeah, he might even get some feeling into his voice then. And it's not because I'm upset or anything, it is a stupid song, oooo, ooo, baby gone, baby gone . . .' Paresh's voice trails off. Kuku reaches over and squeezes his hand. Paresh pulls his hand away. 'Ei Kuku. Stop it. I'm fine.'

'It's not about the words, it's about the tune and in that sense it is a good blues,' Kalikaku pronounces, ignoring the low-level melodrama going on. 'The essential sense of loss is there. And Bombay does become a metaphor for an unreachable space where the loved one has gone. It could be another lover, it could be death, it could be some other sort of immigration away from the love that the singer offers –'

A rat runs across the carpet between two tables. Joyeeta gives a small shriek and lifts her legs up onto the sofa, pulling up her sari and tucking in under her knees. Anirban smiles. 'Was that M. Karamchand na S. Chandra B.? Those two are okay, but Priyadarshini is bad. Bites also.'

'*Anirban!* It's not funny! I don't know why you guys like coming here.' Joyeeta tucks in her sari some more. Kuku shudders.

'Because,' says Anirban in a patiently explaining voice, 'this is our Office. Our Place of Work. Where else would we go?'

Paresh looks around at the bar. Two huge pedestal fans churn up the humid April air, their rusty heads moving slowly from side to side like two old rogue elephants looking for a place to lie down and die. The tubelights throw a tired green wash onto the cream walls, bringing out the grime of many years. A lizard hangs close to one tubelight, stalking something in a corner of the ceiling. The rat-boulevard of the filthy red carpet is empty at the moment, but it holds the promise of more scurry. The faded polish on the dark wooden partition screens catches smudged reflections from the tubes. It is hot here, and dirty too, but it is still a kind of sanctuary from the many different cities colliding outside.

The fat man has now turned to the woman and put his face very close to hers. He is spitting something into her ear in a very low voice, something that's making tears river into the thick layer of talcum powder that plasters her cheeks. It is as if he has an invisible instrument stuck into her. Every time he speaks, she twists and turns and shakes her head as if trying to get away from what he is saying. A fly crawls around, exploring the foam inside the top of her glass, but she doesn't seem to notice.

'It is like two ideas of Nation dancing a tango with each other.' Kalikaku is unfolding himself onto his favourite subject. 'A game of seduction, as if two bodies are playing a musical chess with each other. And the fact is, they are both in bad faith, both cheating-experts. Because –'

'Ei gelo,' says Kuku as the electricity goes.

'Because the idea of Nation, like the idea of Love, needs to be questioned,' Paresh finishes in his mind, as the darkness changes the sound around them. The tubelight hum and the rattle of the fans suddenly gone, the traffic outside seems much louder. They can now hear a waiter and a cook having a fight in the kitchen below them. As the huge fan blades slow down, they make a rhythmic clanking, and the heat seems to rise with each rusty clank. Unlike the downstairs with its huge windows, the only bit of daylight comes through a small, yellow, frosted glass window behind one of the fans. Paresh watches the silhouette of the wire cage and the blades guillotining down, getting slower and slower, the gap between each chop of black increasing as the momentum dies away.

The table falls briefly silent, as if to pay respect to the darkness. There is the slash of a match being struck and Anirban's face flares up for a couple of seconds before disappearing back into the gloom, leaving only a glowing cigarette tip to mark it. The flies, no longer kept at bay by the fans, now get bolder and start buzzing around people's ears. 'Shobbai, keep your feet up!' says Kuku, a slight panic in her voice as she remembers the rats.

This breaks the silence and Kalikaku starts asking Joyeeta about her mother, who is not well. Anirban and Kuku begin discussing a problem they are having with Darya's Montessori school. Paresh is not required for either of these conversations and he is happy for the cocoon of darkness. Despite the sweat mashi-pishi-ing all over him he is happy to be on an island of quiet where he can worry his memories in peace.

He pulls out a happy one – dancing with Sandy at a New Year's party. Two bodies playing musical chess with each other. John Lee Hooker singing 'Boom Boom Boom'. *When you walk that walk, and talk that talk, when you whisper in my ear, tell ME that you LOVE me, I loove that talk!*

You wouldn't have guessed it if you watched her singing a Thumri, but she could really dance. Some song would come on and she would start moving and then movement would feed upon movement and she'd be going, bringing out parts of her body that she normally kept hidden. *Don't move your lips, don't move your legs! Just shake your hips baby! Just shaiyk your hip-pa . . .* Jagger now pretend-cockneying it in the early days, Sandy doing what he asked, and then another Stones song, one he'd danced to alone, *I've been sleeping on the lawn, I've been hustling through the dawn, 'cause I miss you!*, the accent now gone American, *ooooo bai-bee where you been so long? Oooo baby, where you been so long . . .*

• • •

People think she's crazy. Sitting there next to the door with stones clutched in her two hands. She doesn't look like she wants money. Her eyes are closed and there is none of that asking eye-contact that you get from some of them. There is no baby with a tin, no open cap, nowhere to drop coins, even if you wanted to, and no palm-scan like some of the more advanced ones carry around with them. She just sits there, hands resting on knees, a round stone in each fist, swaying back and forth with the carriage. When the keening comes it's as if the train is pulling it out of her.

People in the carriage stare at her, their voices snatched by shock. Madwoman singing too loud, intruding, interfering. Don't move your lips, don't move your legs. Just shake.

She shakes out her words in something Slavic, he can't tell, but the song reminds him of another one, a ghost of a tune he can't push away. Anirban. Gone Bom Bombay . . . baby gone Bombay . . . baby gone Moombye . . . baby gone Goombye . . . baby gone to Bombay . . . baby gone Bombay . . . Her hands move over the rocks like pale-skinned water, tight sometimes, as her breath empties from her, then loose, then tight again with the song, gripping the stones hard, then caressing them lightly as she breathes in. The knotted fingers moving constantly, and yet, somehow, always still.

He can't bear to look at her anymore. Instead he stares at his own reflection in the window behind her as it goes dark between stops. His hair catches the hard light, a white smudge against the black of the glass, and, under it, his face, almost as if it's looking in from outside.

Sixteen years since he noticed the first ones, the night he got the news about Anirban. Now it's no longer a question of a few of them, it's all emergency, the whole railyard of lines around his eyes. His nose is pushed out, and the mouth and chin now collapsed slightly inwards, though sometimes he tells himself only he can see this. He remembers going to wash his eyes in the bathroom. He remembers splashing water on his face and arms for a long time. And then going to Para's room, standing in the doorway, like in some film, and watching her sleep. Remembers thinking, 'No matter who is born now, or who dies, no matter who comes and goes, I have this. This, at least, I have.' A clear memory of standing there, borrowing breath from the little girl sleeping, before going to the phone and trying to get through to Kuku in Calcutta.

• • •

'So what does your lady love say about this Wall business?' Kuku shouts over the noise of the fans and the generator. 'Is she happy?'

'What can she say?' Kalikaku demands, a piece of Chateaubriand suspended on his fork. 'The whole mess of German psyche, all the mud and blood and bread that forms the Teutonics' collective memory, has been pushing at that thing since it was put up. How long can this jinish, you know, made of brick, mortar and barbed wire withstand on top of this quicksand mental ground?' He puts the steak into his mouth like an answer to his own question.

Anirban throws a crumpled packet of Wills at Paresh. 'At least our loverboy here is happy. Just look at him.'

Kuku, Anirban and Shibu look at Paresh and burst into laughter. 'Oh fuck you guys.' Paresh sighs and looks away, shaking his head, but smiling despite himself. Kalikaku ignores all this and concentrates on his meat. After he finishes chewing he continues his lecture. 'It is not a question of happy or not happy. The wall is always there, inside,' he taps his chest with the end of his knife, 'and all that matters is how you shift it around. It is a question of how one moves one's walls.'

'Lady love phone korechhey?' Kuku asks, sticking to what interests her.

'Na, phone's been dead last one week.'

'You just mark my words, today this is looking like it is torn down, but tomorrow it will reappear somewhere. From inside their Berlin they will put it outside . . . all around Europe . . . you just watch.' Kalikaku segregates his peas from his carrots and takes a gulp of his beer. 'They are all – all these Europeans, they will not lose their concentration camp habit so quickly.'

'And neither will you, Kali-da, you old bokachoda!' Anirban slaps his kurta pockets, looking for cigarettes and matches. 'Ekhono, still, everything for you is oijey ekta Gulag, and ekta, one, imaginary Subhash! Still living in that fantasy!' Shibu proffers his Charminars but Anirban shakes his head, looking up for a waiter. 'Ei Chhutku! Ei Salamat! Idhar aao.'

Salamat comes to the table, smiling. Anirban hands him some money. 'Dˆo packet Wills Filter, aur ek maatchis ka baxaa. Theek hai?' Salamat brings his hand up in a 'han sahab' and goes off. Anirban turns back to Kalikaku, who has his mouth full again.

'Still holding the dick of that story! Still expecting us to believe that this old bugger was Subhash and you held him as he died!'

Kalikaku looks up as he chews, his forehead puckered in a pained expression. It is not the first time he's hearing this from Anirban. Kuku slaps Anirban's hand, telling him to shut up, but he is firmly on the warpath. He looks around the table. 'Who here believes that the Russians would let Kali-da go if he had actually seen Subhash Bose in their Gulag? Tell me. Raise your hand, anyone.'

Shibu raises his hand. 'Why not?' he says. 'Kali-da says they took him for a simpleton. They even told him the name – Bidyut Kumar Banerjee, arms dealer. The Russians didn't need to kill some little sailor . . . even if he had cottoned on, who would believe him?'

Kalikaku shakes his head in disagreement while trying to get rid of his piece of steak. He swallows mightily and gulps down more beer to stop himself from choking. 'Mm, mm, mmm, *na*! Bhool! You are making a wrong mistake! If they had thought I had even a faintest inkling then that would have been Kalidas Datta Hari Bol Hari Bol. I managed to convince this Alexander that I had *no* idea who the old man was. After he collapsed in the compound I even asked Alexander who the old man was and what he had done . . . Tomake ki korey bojhaabo . . .' Kalikaku shakes his head at the futility of trying to explain.

'I don't know, I like the idea,' Paresh says, 'and it rings true, somehow.'

'Chhaah – idiots!' Anirban looks up impatiently to see if Salamat has returned with his cigarettes.

Paresh suddenly remembers his old Principal Dwivedi's face 'Well, when I was a kid I used to imagine these Japani fighters coming up from behind and shooting down Netaji's plane . . . so why not this?'

Kalikaku laughs as he wipes up the last bit of gravy with a piece of bread. 'That, Poresh, was your quite understandable resentment of the Bengali Will to Order the Knowledge-World! It had nothing to do with Bose, it had to do with your Maths teacher – ki naam chhilo? Bagchi! Yes, that Bagchi.' Kalikaku puts the bread in his mouth and then forgets to chew it. 'Iph you wasked Lacan, orw swome other less shuttle Phreudian,' he swallows the bread, 'then they would no doubt explain to you that one fighter-plane was Anarchy and the other simply your love for your mother's food and language!'

Shibu ignores this little detour. 'Yes, why should we be so worshipful of the Formosa plane crash? He may have survived in 1945, you know. He may not even have been on that plane.'

Kalikaku pushes away his plate and reaches for Shibu's packet of Charminars. He carefully lights one, takes a deep drag, and then coughs to acknowledge the cigarette. Anirban has started tabla-ing on the table, shaking his head to some tune only he can hear. Kalikaku looks pityingly at him. 'Jaai bolo baba, Baan, a Charminar is a Charminar.' He takes his feet out of his chappals and crosses his legs on the sofa. 'You see, whether you people believe me or not is irrelevant. What you cannot escape, when you look at contemporary India, is the fact that Subhash Bose has survived in many ways for a lot longer than Nehru etcetera,' Kalikaku blows his smoke at Paresh, 'and – as I keep trying to explain to your father – Subhash has not only survived but he has *won*, whereas Jawaharlal, and so also your old Gujju MKG, have lost. It is something your mother, I think, understood in her own way. Though, of course, she would never have admitted it to me!'

Anirban hits the table hard in a sam and stops. 'Holo na Kali-da! All this theorising is avoiding my question – was the man you saw Bose or not Bose?'

'Arre sahab, what are you saying! Of course it was Netaji that Datta sahab saw in Russia!' Salamat puts down Anirban's cigarettes and change on the table. Anirban stops as if shot and glares at Salamat, who stands there smiling. He looks Salamat up and down as if regarding a cockroach. Finally, after he's worked up a sufficiently scathing voice, he asks, 'Achha? And how do *you* know?'

'Islam chacha told me the story many years ago.' Salamat's grin widens as he replies with his ace.

'Oh, I see. And how did old Islam know this? Did he go to Russia with him?' Anirban nods in Kalikaku's direction.

'Nahi sahab! Datta sahab told Islam Chacha. And if Datta sahab told Islam chacha then he must have been telling the truth.'

'QED! Checkmate!' Kalikaku slaps his thigh, leading the hoots of laughter around Anirban, who gapes in astonishment at the ceiling. Paresh throws the empty cigarette packet back at Anirban, aiming for the open mouth but missing narrowly. Salamat's smile gets even wider, revealing the paan lurking behind his teeth.

Shibu is the first one to come out of it. He holds Salamat by the arm as he gasps for breath, trying to find his voice. He waits for a lull in the noise and then asks a question. 'Ei Salamat? Have you ever seen drawings by a man called Escher?' Everybody explodes again as Salamat shakes his head, still smiling, knowing the joke is not meant to include him, but enjoying it anyway. He waits for the table to calm down before gesturing to Anirban's cigarettes. 'Sahab,' he asks Anirban, 'kuchh baksheesh . . . ?'

Anirban does a mock glower at him and raises his hand in a 'I'll land you one'. Salamat doesn't move. Anirban points to Paresh. 'Did you know Netaji Subhash had a German wife? Well, now Paresh sahab here is also going to have a German wife! Take the baksheesh from him, he will – '

'E *Maaaaaaa!*' Kuku has just noticed the rat near a table leg, nibbling at bits of mixture that have fallen on the carpet.

Salamat looks down and makes a clicking noise with his tongue. 'Don't worry, Didi, she won't do anything.' He calmly picks up the one rupee that is his due and walks away, still making the noise and calling over his shoulder to the rat. 'Raani! Chalo, come! Idhar aao, I will feed you, come!' The rat pauses and looks up, jerking her head first to one side then the other, trying to locate the sound. After a moment she turns and scurries away, following Salamat towards the bar.

Kuku is hunched up in the corner berween the sofa and the wall, shuddering, while Shibu has his knees right up against his face.

'There is,' says Kalikaku, capturing a light from Anirban, 'the concept in Vaishnavism of a Nityo Krishno and a Chitto Krishno.' He taps Paresh on the arm. 'Sumudi would have pronounced it as Nitya Krishna and Chitta Krishna. It basically means there is a more easily accessible Krishna – Nityo – that people can understand in everyday terms. This is the one who cavorts with Gopis, the one who lifts mountains on his little finger and kills demons – as a guru once explained it to me, that is the Krishna that lives on the ground floor of your soul.'

As he talks, Kalikaku starts to wipe the tabletop with his paper napkin, trying to clear it of crumbs. Kuku reaches out from behind her knees and grabs his hand. 'Na. You lecture. I will clean this,' she says, and takes the napkin away from him.

'Then there is the higher Krishno – Chitto Krishno – the one who resides on the first floor, who is above Nityo Krishno, and he is much harder to attain. Now, this Chitto Krishno is a good one for even atheists to know.'

'Aha,' sniggers Anirban, 'so in that camp you obviously met the Chitto Subhash, na? The one nobody else could see!'

Kalikaku waves away the interruption. 'Baan, chup koro! Kothaa shono, I am serious. So, in the same way, there is, one can say, a Nityo Calcutta and a Chitto Calcutta – a mundane Calcutta and a subtler . . . a Jazz Calcutta. And this moment we just had with this boy, ki naam?, Salamat, this moment is an example of this Chitto-Jazz Calcutta.'

Kuku carefully puts one cupped palm just below the edge of the table and wipes the crumbs into it. Then she funnels that hand over the ashtray and brushes the crumbs into the hole. 'Aami jaani na baba, all I know is that there is a ground-floor Olympia and a first-floor Olympia, and I'm happy never to attain this first floor again.'

'That is understandable,' says Kalikaku as he pours everyone some more beer, 'the higher, the Chitto plane is never a comfortable place.'

• • •

As the train comes into Concorde the woman suddenly stops singing and pulls back her hands from her knees. She finds a little bag from somewhere and puts the stones away carefully. One she slips into the front part of the bag, the other she quickly wraps in some cloth and pushes into the back, making sure they won't knock against each other.

By the time the train doors open she is up and ready to move out. She waits as the handle on the platform barrier turns from red to green, presses the light, and goes through. Other passengers get off behind her and the barrier gates slide back, bringing the two halves of the mountain together again. The last he sees of her is framed through the triangle of the Alpine peak pulsing on the transparent barrier, the rolling fat red band that says 'Evian' cutting her off at the knees. She wraps a woollen scarf around her head, tugs on a pair of gloves, and then she's gone. As the train doors wait to shut he can see the curve of tiles on the station wall, each tile with a black letter on it.

• • •

'When did you get it?' Kuku puts down the Inland and wipes her eyes with the end of her sari.

'Three days ago,' says Paresh, lighting a cigarette, 'posted from Rishikesh. He obviously read about the Bombay blasts and got worried we were there with Para, otherwise I don't know if he'd have written.'

'Of course he would have. How could he not write after your father's . . .'

'Oh, he would have argued to himself that the loss was as much his as Paresh's,' Anirban runs a hand through his open hair, 'and so there was no need for any exchange of –'

'You two are so cool and macho, na? Here's this guy sitting like a stone, hardly a month after Mahadevmesho . . . and you, his best friend, calmly saying that no words of any condolence are required.'

'I'm not saying condolence is not required. I'm saying Kali-da doesn't believe in such things. Naa holey why did he go off to the mountains, this great atheist, to be like some anonymous fucking sadhu? And he calls *me* a hippie! Hanh!'

'Not only does Kalikaku not believe in all this, he knows my father wouldn't have wanted any great crying or anything. You remember what he said when Kalikaku told us he was going to disappear, don't you?'

'What?' asks Kuku.

'He said, "It's always a good idea to save people the trouble of queuing up at Kalighat!", and he meant it. He would have done it himself, except he didn't like the idea of silence. I think he needed people around to catch the brunt of his tongue.'

Kuku tries to muster up a laugh, but it doesn't quite come. Anirban looks around at the empty tables. 'Ei, Kuku, think I can make one now? There's nobody here.'

'That's all you think about! Joint, booze, joint, booze, joint! Wait till we get outside.'

'It's a pain since they removed the partitions. It was so much easier then.'

Paresh erects himself into a Kalikaku posture, finger pointing upwards. 'But Baan! There is always a partition! It is inside you! It is a matter of how you move your partitions around.'

'Walls, he said walls, not partitions.' Anirban holds a cigarette over a cupped hand and begins to twist it at the cusp of filter and paper.

'Oi aeki jinish, same thing.' Paresh picks up his glass of rum and concentrates on gulping it down.

Kuku absently wipes the table with a paper napkin, clearing up bits of mixture and the few flecks of tobacco that have fallen from Anirban's hand.

'Kuku, you don't need to do that anymore. They've got rid of the rats. It's only a few cockroaches now.' Anirban taps out the last of the tobacco and piles it carefully on a clean napkin. Then he moves his fingers delicately over the paper, making sure there are no kinks in the hollow tube.

Kuku carries on her wiping. 'I still hate the smell of this place. Earlier it was stale fried food, now it's this new paint.'

Anirban pulls out a blade from his Swiss Army knife and sticks a tiny cube of hash onto the point. He brings it up to his nose and takes a deep, pleasured, sniff. 'Once you have this perfume all other smells are secondary,' he says as he flicks on a lighter under the hash and waits for the flame to transfer. After a few moments the fire catches around the cube. He lets it burn for five or six seconds and then firmly blows it out.

Paresh takes another glass of neat rum from the row of eight that stand ready at the side of the table. He pours water into it and takes a gulp. Anirban starts to sing a tune, mimicking a saxophone as he takes some of the tobacco in his hand and begins to mix the powdered hash into it.

'*Pawuppa, pawn-pa pawnpa, pawuppa, pawn-pa pawnpa . . .*'

Kuku joins in, her voice clear and high, '*When the dog bites, when the bee stings, when I'm feeling sad –*'

Anirban stops abruptly and glares at her. 'Kuku! Cut out oi shob Julie Andrews, this is the serious version! There's a Nityo *Favourite Things* and a Chitto one.'

'I don't care, Baan,' Kuku shrugs, 'you do your second-floor Coltrane-sholtrane, I like my ground-floor words.' They both carry on, Kuku's voice leaping from phrase to phrase, Anirban doing a tenor sax in a low growl, the two forming a perfect harmony till Anirban finishes loading the mixture back into the empty cigarette.

Anirban lights the joint and offers it to Paresh, who shakes his head. Anirban passes the joint to Kuku. Paresh leans back and shuts his eyes.

'Ki?' asks Anirban, 'tui thik achhish?'

'Yeah, no, I'm fine. Just tired.' Paresh puts his hands on his eyes and presses down. 'Do you remember Kalikaku saying – ki chhilo ekta? – oh yeah – "It will be impossible to be nostalgic about this city in a few years' time." I think I know what he meant.'

'Anyway,' Anirban takes the joint back from Kuku and takes a deep drag, 'anyway, you can't be nostalgic about a place, you can only be nostalgic about a period of time, na? So good thing Kalida left before all this.'

'I'm sure he can imagine it, wherever he is. He says he gets newspapers regularly, and sometimes he gets to see a TV as well.'

'Radio also. Up there you get great reception – everything – BBC, Nepali Radio, Chinese, shob.'

'I hope he's all right.' Kuku's eyes are wet again.

'Oh, I'm sure he's fine. As long as we keep sending him his money what's his problem? Anyway, he'll probably outlive us all . . . the cold will preserve him for hundreds of years, just like his pal Bose. One day, after we are all gone, Darya and Para will be trekking in Spiti or somewhere and they will come across this ooold budo sitting in a gufa, and he will see them and say – "Listen, you two! This Nation business is an expensive business! And it needs customers!"' Anirban's hand goes up. '"And only those who can afford to buy the products of this business can call themselves citizens!"' Anirban reaches for a glass of rum and the bottle of water.

'Cheers!' says Paresh swaying forward with his glass.

'Cheers! Here's to Mahadevmesho and to Sumanmashi!'

'Here's to them!' replies Paresh and takes a gulp.

'And here's to Kalidas Bokachoda Datta, King Gasbag of Theory!'

'To King Gasbag! May his gas never run out!'

Kuku has her sari pallu pressed against her mouth. A sound breaks out of her and the men realise that she is sobbing, her body moving back and forth, shaking with different griefs.

Anirban puts his arms around her and begins to stroke her hair. 'Ei Kuku!' he says softly. 'Kuku . . . ? Eiii Kuku!'

'Salaam sahab.'

Paresh looks up to see Salamat standing there. For a moment he wonders when they'd ordered more rum. Then he notices that Salamat is not in his waiter's uniform and he remembers. 'Oh. Han. Ek minute.' He reaches into his camera bag, pulls out the envelope, and hands it to Salamat.

Anirban moves away from Kuku and reaches for his own bag. 'How much are you giving him?' he asks.

'A thousand,' says Paresh.

Anirban takes out his wallet and counts out five one-hundred-rupee notes. 'Paresh sahab is giving you a thousand and here is five hundred more from me, okay?' Salamat nods as he takes the money. 'Now, Chhutku, how much more do you need? And has anyone else given you anything?'

'Sahab – Raman sahab gave me two hundred, then Joshi sahab, same as you, five, and then that Didi from the newspaper, she gave me about two hundred and fifty. One or two others, a little bit.'

'So, what will you manage with this?' Paresh asks.

'I should be able to get a new roof, sahab, and then maybe a mattress, for now. The rest I'll send home.'

'What about the other waiters?' Kuku asks, sniffing into her sari.

'Didi, they are all fine. Except Rahman. Someone threw a bottle into his baasa as well, but he managed to put it out quicker than me. The others are okay, they all live around here, all Free School Street–Wellesley side. Rahman and me are the only ones in Tangra.'

'Okay, theek hai,' Anirban says, 'tell me when your roof is done. I will come and see.'

Salamat raises his right hand to his forehead, still holding the envelope and the loose notes. 'Han sahab.' Then he turns to Paresh, moving slowly to protect the thick bandages on his left hand. 'Sahab, thank you, and don't worry, sahab, even if you are in London-Germany, wherever, I will return this in a few months to Baan sahab.'

'No hurry. You can give it to me when I get back,' Paresh says.

Anirban gets up to go to the bathroom. He pats Salamat on the back as he passes him. 'Don't say that,' he says to Paresh, 'you will disappear for years and this guy will coolly forget. Ei Chhutku! You give this back to me when you have it, theek hai?'

Salamat looks up at Anirban. For the first time his face approaches a smile. 'Where will I go, sahab? You know where to find me.'

He puts the money away carefully and does a last salaam before limping away.

Kuku takes a handkerchief out of her purse, dips it into the ice-bucket, and dabs her eyes. 'How's Anna and baby?' she asks.

'Okk . . . kay,' Paresh says, 'she's okay now. I told you, na?, the first week she was back she cried a lot, but now she says she's okay. Para being there helps.' He looks down at the table and shakes his head. Then he looks up again. 'Helps me too, Para being there. Amazing, na?, how much a child helps you put everything in perspective?'

Kuku brightens up suddenly. 'Ei! Shon! I've got Para a small quilt that I saw in Gurjari the other day, you know, your Gujju mirrorwork and bright colours? Nice. And an English translation of *Abol Tabol*.'

'Why English? You think she'll never speak Bangla?'

'Whooo knows! Anyway, I know it's early, but you could start reading it to her from now, na? And I can always get her a Bangla one when it looks like she needs one.'

'Or a Gujarati translation.' Paresh grins.

Kuku refuses to get into the sarcasm. She is happy now and she hangs on to that. 'So, remember, you are taking these two things. When's your flight? You haven't finished packing, na? Keno ki I don't want to hear at the last moment jey you don't have space or something, okay?'

• • •

Even though this is where he's been living for twelve years now, in his mind it's always Magali's stop and not his home station, which is still Bastille. He looks at the information strip with its red letters forming P-I-G-A-L-L-E, and the train status underneath, and thinks once again of how much he misses Bastille and that too with the old station signs with their white letters on blue. No matter what else changed around the stations, the shape of the trains mutating, the smells disappearing, as long as those blue and white signs were there he could imagine himself in some old New Wave movie, or something even older, perhaps during the war, a Maquis operative sliding through the Gestapo Kontrolle points, or a young Cartier-Bresson in the '30s, or, later maybe, more a Robert Frank or William Klein reinventing photography in the '50s. But all that was gone now, *le charme de Paris*, and not everybody missed it. 'Oh . . . je m'en fous!' Magali, bored with his borrowed nostalgia, 'You 'ave tu live and die in *today*! You and me, sometimes I think we are, two of us, on a *completely* different length of wave!' Actually, for quite a long time now, she had stopped bothering about adding the 'sometimes'.

He buttons up his greatcoat and switches on its temperature control as he walks towards the exit. On his way he passes two boys jumping up and down in front of a métro map. They shout as they poke at the touchscreen making the coloured lines glow and dance. He is almost past them when one of them reaches over and slaps his elbow. 'Salut poubelle! Tu a un ciga?'

He stops, turns around, and stares at them. Punks. About fourteen, both of them, big, probably Ukrainian. He'd get hurt, that was sure, but so would –

The other boy grabs the first one by the small circle of hair on top of his scalp and yanks him back, his eyes flicking up to check the angle of the platform cameras. Paresh gives them both a slow up and down before turning away. Any other day he would have upped the ante a little bit, taken a chance, said something in Hindi or Bangla but clear enough for them to know that their mothers were being referred to. He shakes his head to leave the thing behind and moves up the stairs fast, unzipping his right sleeve to expose his wrist stripe for the exit check.

A black guy ahead of him stops a few yards from the sortie point and puts on cream-coloured gloves and a white face mask. The police have always claimed that the métro scanners are colour-blind but everybody knows that's a lie. As the man goes through the gates he makes sure his stripe is on top of his glove, with no skin showing through. There is a moment's tension as the scanner considers its information and then the gates slide open, letting the man through. The man walks out of the scanner's angle and raises his left fist up in the air in a small gesture of triumph. Paresh watches, briefly sharing the man's satisfaction, before going through himself. He knows his skin colour won't be a problem, his stripe being a special Eurartist bande de securité that allows him access to trains and métros all over the Union.

Outside, the cold jumps at his face, making him narrow his eyes and hunch his shoulders. He crosses the Boulevard and heads for the door of his building. In the hallway, he opens the mailbox which says 'M. Martin – P. Bhatt', checking for any last minute papermail. There's nothing except for a card inviting Magali to a private exposition of a new collection of accessories from Vietnam. Not that he'd expected anything, everything having been taken care of weeks ago, but he can't help feeling a small tinge of disappointment. There was something about finding a paper letter that no amount of electronic mail could match. He leaves the card for Magali to find, and swipes the lock-slot on the inner door.

The lift is old, and, as it rattles him upwards, he realises he has always been thankful for its shaking. The doors open on the fifth floor and he gets out and starts to walk up the two flights of stairs to the apartment. Someone on the floor below is cooking fish in butter. It smells like burnt ghee with some herb caught up in it, and the stink tarragons out from under the door and follows him up the stairs like an unwanted cat. As he climbs his legs suddenly go tired and with each step there is a dull pain that revolves up from his ankles. He thinks of the woman on the train pressing the stones down on her knees, and wonders if they had healing properties.

As he enters the apartment he can see his luggage where he has left it, lined up on the floor near the door. Two big suitcases, a soft overnight case, and his camera bag, all ready to go. He shuts the door, takes off his boots and puts them on the shoe-rack next to Magali's army of shoes. He can hear Magali in the kitchen, and the opening and shutting of the vide-ordure as the garbage bags go down the shute.

He wants to sit down but doesn't. Instead he goes to the slanting window that looks out on Place Pigalle and opens it, letting the air knife in. It's a view he has spent hours looking at, but he is greedy for it again, wanting to take it in one last time before he abandons it.

Straight ahead of him the boulevard stretches away west, the row of trees in the middle now bare. Far away, he can see the red lights of the Moulin Rouge windmilling slowly through the grey branches. Nearer, one of the porn houses has hung a video banner across the left traffic lane, strung up between one of the trees and the buildings. '*XXX Bienvenue '17! XXX*' it says, with a girl sucking a lollipop in slow-motion on either side of the words. He follows a couple, a man and a woman, holding hands as they rollerblade towards him. They part to go around two cars that have stopped at the traffic lights, pause a beat to check left and right, and then come through the red light to link up again at the circle just below.

The fake snow on the Christmas trees in the circle is now beginning to pull down real snow and the cold suddenly gets through to him, making him shiver, even though he still has his greatcoat on.

'Finished?' Magali has come out of the kitchen holding a tray.

'Yes. I confirmed all the neg numbers on their archive files and I have a copy on my disk so there should be no confusion.' He shuts the window and comes away.

'What about new photos?'

'If I shoot on film I'll keep the negatives and transfer them via the link. Otherwise it's no problem.'

Magali puts the tray down and looks at her watch. 'You still have forty minutes,' she says. 'Do you want some coffee?'

BOOK FOUR

Knocking on Heaven's Door

You fast fading photograph
in my more slowly fading hands

RAINER MARIA RILKE

'How would you pass through this, Mr Bose?' The examiner is tall, bald. There is an edge of sweat around the tight white collar of his shirt, odd on the pale skin, and Subhash notices it. He also notes the damp feeling around his own collar. He looks down at the tie stretching under his nose. The noise of the insects outside the tall window is loud. English-controlled insects, marshalled to make the noise to distract him. He ignores them.

'Pass myself through this, sir?' His voice is more high-pitched than he wants it to be. What does the man mean? *Eita abaar ki jiggesh korchhe?*

'Mr Bose, you heard me. How would you pass yourself through this ring?'

He can see the green wooden window shutters open against the cream wall behind the panel of examiners, he can see palm trees through the long window. The palms seem to have a hum in the heat. British-controlled heat, designed to make him fail – ignore. Flies. They will bother them more than him. Go for the Ice-Cream Cart, nothing to lose.

He sees the glass paperweights on the large desk in front of him, little flakes of yellow, blue and red caught inside, red pen in holder, black pen in holder, inkwells in the middle, what he wants on his desk when he sits on the other side. Map of India on the wall. The silhouettes of the Ingrej, staring at him, waiting for him to answer, not so easy to cross over to the other side of the desk and have the light behind you. The map behind you. Check engine power, check timing left on module, check seal on door, *think*, GO.

Might as well try.

It must be, it *has* to be to do with writing. He reaches across, always known for daring, and picks up a pen. The black one is the one that comes into his hand. He knows there is a little pile of paper next to the pens. He doesn't ask for permission, he leans forward, takes a slip from the pile and puts it on the desk in front of him. He shifts in his chair, leans forward again, gets his wrist to move. The drop of sweat that escapes from his clenched fingers barely misses the little chit of paper and drops on his knee, but he doesn't think they've noticed. They are too busy watching his face. Too busy looking for signs of their own power on it, but his face is hidden behind thick glasses, the glare from the window straight on the lenses, so he's sure they can't see much. He writes his name in the best handwriting he can muster. One of the examiners swats a fly away from his face. The fan above his head is making a strange noise which he ignores. He rolls the paper into a tiny tube. Take this seriously, whatever you do, don't smile – *face-ta serious koro*, serious face, grave.

He reaches across for the ring, takes it in his left hand and pushes the roll of paper through it. Then he takes both roll and ring and puts it in front of the Ingrej, a challenge, humbly put, but yes, a challenge.

The bald one says nothing. It is the monocle on the left who speaks.

'I say! What was that? What was that, Bose?'

Something pushes down on his shoulders, relaxes them. The moment the man neglects the 'Mr' before Bose, Subhash knows he's through. Fortune favours the brave.

The Ice-Cream Cart. It's her only chance. She has waited for two days and two nights and now her time has nearly run out. Hopefully they think they've killed the whole station. She has been monitoring her radars without touching them to change anything and after about a day she catches it, this thing heading towards *Varun Machaan*, something wading through all the geo-stationary traffic hanging above the earth, making a course that should bring it within range soon. Then she gets an ID on the craft – United States Space Vessel 41/USSV *Reagan*. So that was it – the *Reagan*. She has heard about this one, special US Aerospace Command attack ship posing as a rescue vessel. Less than two hours away now. The grey area in her head has cleared. She has now understood what has happened and what she needs to do.

The water module hanging below the space station, what they call the Ice-Cream Cart. There should still be enough power left in it to make it back through. Time to go. Para Bhatt has already put herself into motion, doing things towards that end about ten minutes before her cognitive brain recognises the decision her body has made. That she is going to try. Time is running out and she has moved quietly, but with speed, almost without realising it.

She has – there is already a 'has' attached to the letter, for example.

First the pen. Old, old green and black German Pelikan 120 belonging to her grandfather Mahadev Bhatt. Found in her little backpack, black cap unscrewed, taken off. Paper found also in backpack, the pad her father had given her a long time ago, with blue lines on it. Pulled out, laid flat on the work-ledge near her bank of monitors. Odd to feel paper on her ledge. For the first and last time. She moves the pad to an angle as she remembers doing from many years ago. Finds a place for her elbow and then a point on the paper to put her nib. The ink a bit reluctant at first, but then, with a bit of pressure, flowing. *Dea* – she scratches the word out and carries on writing:

Pujya Pappa, not in the habit of changing lines after the address, or perhaps because of the hurry, she carries on in the same line. *You were right about one thing*, she looks up at her observation window and stares through it for a moment. There is a massive swirl of fast-moving cloud cottoning out the whole of the Deccan peninsula. It spreads like a mottled white petticoat, in a line from somewhere just south of Surat, curving a bit, stretching all the way over to what she knows is the border between Orissa and Hyderabad Control. Then she looks down at the pad again, *remember when you said the only time you can take pleasure in a nation is when you are away from it? When you can see what you imagine is a whole? Well, now I understand what you meant. Also, I miss the nation of your love, and of Mamma's love, and I imagine I can now see them from here, both entire. Call me sentimental, but sending a scan of Dadi's photo because I know you don't have the negative – don't want your scrapbook to have permanent gaps.*

Systems down, no chance of getting through to Mamma. You will have to go and see her now, perhaps, to give her my love. If there is a body then – please Ffups – no crying. In case I fall I want Mamma and you to remember me smiling. So exactly the same as Suman if possible. If there isn't then that will be clean anyway. And your turn to write a real Orbituary! Otherwise, who knows? Some of your coffee. Here she changes lines and that is her only concession to a final goodbye. *Tired of sitting – gotta fly. Love, Para.*

PS Forgive the handwriting. It goes for six under pressure! Ha, ha, heeeeeeee!

She slaps the note onto the little scanner and sends it through till it shows on her Out screen. Then the photograph. She double-checks them both and switches on her emergency sending channel. It doesn't matter if the Yanks read this. It doesn't matter if they read the next one either. Let them read while she does what she has to. The emergency channel shows an OK and she puts down her access code and then her special code for the computer sitting in the rooftop room on Lansdowne Road. She gets a password on the screen saying that her encrypted link is secure for fifteen seconds. This is an incorrect signal, as she now knows – the link is established but it's also leaking everything to the approaching USSV *Reagan*. She hits the Send key and watches the message transmit.

Only after sending the message does she acknowledge to herself that she is about to go for it. But she has time yet, because she knows how to make time. She waits a few moments for her Received Acknowledgement Code for the first message and then begins to put out gobbledygook through the emergency channel. Hopefully, whatever machine they have monitoring her will take more than five seconds to register the new channel opening up. And anyway, hopefully, their guessing will be that it is an automatic forty-eight-hourly despatch, now that everyone on board was dead. But enough now, no time to hope any more. Next.

Next Para takes the latest readings, concentrating on the borders. She presses the area choice for – PakBor and then ChiBor and then sets three heights, one at five thousand, the other at ten thousand and the third at twenty-five thousand. She sets this going and moves away from her console, first to the toilet cubicle and then to the suit cupboard. The readings are a long shot but even if they work they will take five minutes to collate.

Para takes off her soft boots, strips off her pants and reaches for the stack of diapers. These are still the most effective for preventing leaks during space walks. In the early days people tried catheters, also other kinds of tubes that attached in different ways, but quite often astronauts complained of finding bits of urine floating loose inside their suits. The diaper was then developed, found to be effective and later found use in the civilian world for babies and old incontinents. Para buckles on not one but two diapers, one on top of the other, which makes her quite uncomfortable, but it's going to be a long ride and she doesn't want to take chances.

After that comes the black bodysuit that fits her like a second skin except where it has space around the crotch for the diaper. It's tight because of the extra diaper, but only slightly. It's a good suit, well made, and there is a little stamp on the forearm, where the wearer can see it – *Shambhavi Defence Ltd. Made in Karnataka for IAF* and a batch number, though if anything were to go wrong with the suit it was unlikely that the user would be in any position to write a complaint.

As she puts on the intermediary suit, Para finds her mind wandering into a list. *One, the skin of the self. Two, the skin of the family.* The intermediary suit is a bright fluorescent orange with little computers and sensors at various points to automatically adjust pressure for circulation and respiration. In an extreme emergency, it is designed to knock the wearer out and keep him or her breathing at a very low rate till help arrives. If help arrives. It also has an elementary radar-catcher that activates at a certain altitude above sea level – three thousand feet – and a pouch containing shark repellent for ocean landings. Para has been trained to get out of her spacesuit and swim in this. *No, two is the skin of the fighting unit, three, the skin of the family, four, the skin of the nation, five –*

Para walks over to the console. The light from the observation window has changed. It's now brighter. The petticoat of cloud has spread over the whole subcontinent and become more like a tattered bedsheet. There are now small holes in it and she can see parts of the country through the openings. A knee of coast here, a rash of a mountain range there, all cut up. At points the sunlight has managed to skid under the cloud to light things up. She can see the parts of the Godavari River shining like an irradiated varicose vein. *Five, the skin of the planet . . .*

The Bhakhri gives a lurch as the positioning jets hiccup again. Para leans over the console, working fast, checking all her screens, working slightly fast but no more panic showing than an executive shutting down office computers before rushing off to catch a train. The last batch of readings is in. She scans them quickly, nothing untoward, the troop and armour positions as they were a week ago, more or less, missiles dormant from the looks of it, but she knows she can no longer trust the looks of it. She knows, for example, that she can't really scan the Arabian Sea. The Seventh Fleet is lurking down there somewhere and there is a vast blank created by the new jammers carried by the warships. She pushes the Send button and the main communication channel links up. Para sends the readings down. They will take two minutes to go. As the signal begins to go out she uses her camouflage command and quickly types her own message within it. Again, it should take the *Reagan*'s code-readers some time to disentangle her words from the detailed picture and text that were going out.

> Abandoning ship: Repeat abandoning ship: Will sweep up before exit: Message in the bottle: ETL = + 5: Give it a pillow: Jai Hind: Over and out: GpCptPB.

She hoped Fawzia, her mission controller, would get it. They'd laughed about it many times. Not possible. Possible. Maybe, why not? 'Why don't you try it one day Bhatt? If anyone can do it you can – you are small enough and only you are mad enough. One day we will open the bottle and Inshallah, find you there like a message!' Theoretically, it is as well sealed as a manned craft. And, where there is the little mattress for the technician to get into the circuits, it should be warm enough in a space suit with your oxy-tanks on. The scariest part would be . . . no control and only the little window for sight. 'But you would feel the thing coming down and changing course and coming through the barrier and all that, and if you were conscious that would give you some assurance, you know?, like being in a plane or something a little bit, or in your Mummyjaans's tummy . . .' and then Fawzia Ansari, queen of the ground, would look at the old fighter ace and cackle.

Para takes out the photo of her grandmother and looks at it. For a moment she thinks of stuffing it into her suit somewhere but then she decides against it. Instead she puts it upright, lodged between a screen and one of the keyboards. It should be there to welcome the Aerospace Command bastards when they enter. After all, just like them, there was nothing she was going to do to damage the actual plant of the craft. She looks at Suman Bhatt grinning at her, the flash lighting up the corset-like seat-belt, the three palm trees tilting behind her. That should keep them wondering, no Sergeant, no Green on no horse was going to get her today. She grins back at the photo. This gives her the energy to go ahead with the rest of what she needs to do.

Outer suit on. Check tanks. The suit has soft oxygen tanks that rope around it and they recycle the air through a special chemical that keeps it at breathable levels for ten hours, not great compared to the twenty-four-hour things that the USAC have but it doesn't matter. She won't be needing canned air for that long, either way she'll be out of it in five hours or so. Calibrate air-flow. Check she can move her fingers. Check that the torch, clock and radar signalling device are working . . . Para puts on the headpiece, aligning it with the dots, and turns it till it clicks. The lock light glows green and she is ready.

The last thing Para does is open a drawer and take out the .32 machine pistol. For what it can do, it is tiny, only as big as a mid-twentieth-century .38 automatic. But the gun carries eighteen rounds of ammunition and packs a fair bit of punch. Not that she will need anything more than one bullet for her purposes. If things go very wrong and she is still alive. Anyway, if that happens she is not even sure she will be able to pull the gun out of its sealed holster and lift it to the soft spot in the outer suit which is on the right side of her neck. Neither is she sure the bullet will actually penetrate the toughened suit but it makes her feel better so she slides it in and seals the holster.

And then she punches in the code to open the door of her chamber. Nothing happens for a while and Para feels panic welling up inside her, until she remembers that the door takes half a minute to open from an emergency lock. As she looks at the numbers flickering on her wrist she notes that she has fifteen minutes to get out.

The door begins to slide sideways into the recess in the partition. It goes one fourth of the way and stops. The gap is too narrow for Para to squeeze through. Fucking Indian technology. Para kicks at the door. It stays frozen for a moment before starting to open again. Come on, come on, that's it, that's . . . it. Good old stolid Indian technology. If this was a French or Israeli craft, something made with all those new alloys, the Carve would have turned her into soup by now. Thank god for Indian obsolescence – the door has opened another four inches. It is enough. Roll of paper through first ring, two more to go.

Para comes out into the main control room. The party streamers from Gulati's birthday party are still up on the far bulkhead, catching the sun from the UV-filtered porthole on the left. And the cut-out sign

– *Happy Thirty Goo-Lathi*. She pauses for a moment, looking at the light. She has always thought of it as Kauns-light – neither morning nor evening, neither inside the atmosphere nor out, threshold light.

After about half a minute she forces herself to move forward.

The air she is breathing comes from her tanks and she can smell nothing but pure oxy-mix and she is glad for that. The floor is splattered with blood and shit. Gulati is twisted under his radio telescope, his head caved into the eyepiece, one hand still on the finger pad he was tapping notes into. On her right, Ashok looks like he is asleep on his keyboard except his back looks like someone has smashed a battering ram into it – his ribcage has collapsed inwards and his white t-shirt hangs from his shoulders as if from a clothes-line. His legs in blue jeans look like they are coming out of thin air from under the empty t-shirt. Her external mike picks up the sound before she sees Reba.

It was quite warm in the cabin and they had all been sitting in light clothes when the Carve hit. Reba had come into her chamber just minutes before and showed off her new shorts. 'See, look Para! Aren't these sexy? Do you think it's safe to wear them around the men?' Para had turned and looked at the transparent plastic material, which had some liquid encased in it, opaque colours floating, more concentrated around the private parts and less around the edges. 'No,' she'd replied, 'not safe at all Reba! You'd be safer taking them off completely.' They'd laughed and Reba had gone back into the main cabin. Following procedure, Para had shut her Ops cabin door and sealed it. Some of the things she needed to do the civilians couldn't be allowed to see. Though they always knocked first, her orders were not to take chances. She had followed the stupid orders and, for once, that had saved her life.

She attaches the sound coming through her headphones to Reba's body, which is jammed between a bulkhead and the back of a wire-patch panel. Reba had obviously been crouching behind a panel trying to fix something. Somehow she had been shielded from the first wave, but the second wave had caught her in one part of her head. Para goes over to Reba and tries to pull her out. It is no use. Her suit is too bulky and she can't get herself into the right position. As she bends over her, Para realises that the girl is only technically alive. Her heart is still beating faintly because some part of her brain is still intact enough to give it instructions. The sound she's hearing is Reba's breath getting pressed out of her mouth. Out with great effort and then getting pulled back in. If anything is alive in her, it is in pain.

Para holds Reba's head and tries to feel it through her thick gloves. She comes to a cavity on the right side of the head where the skull has collapsed almost into the centre of the brain. She doesn't understand how Reba is still breathing and she doesn't have time to. She reaches for her holster, takes the gun out and puts it to Reba's head. She adjusts the angle carefully so that the bullet will not go into the bulkhead and pulls the trigger. The report is loud and dry through her external mike. Blood has splattered her white and green spacesuit but the sound has stopped. She puts the gun back, seals the holster again, and moves over to Ashok's keyboard.

She feels Ashok's pulse automatically, for no practical reason, and finds nothing. Slipping on the slush from his burst sphincter, she drags him off the console and drops him as gently as she can to the floor. She looks for the set of switches she needs to find and starts tapping in her access code. The voice, when it comes, sounds very close. She realises the speaker above her head is alive.

'Calling Indian Space Vessel *VM2*. Indian Space Vessel *VM2*. This is United States Space Vessel *Reagan*. Do you read me? Are you guys okay? Is anybody able to respond?' There is a pause, then again. '*VM2*. *VM2*. This is the *Reagan*, we are coming to your aid. Please respond with your situation.' Para looks around and realises that a small microphone tucked away between two of Ashok's keyboards has a light on. Someone on the *Reagan* has obviously heard the sounds. She looks around for the switch, finds it and pushes it to off. This sends the voice on the *Reagan* into another gear – more high-pitched now.

'Indian Space Vessel *VM2*. Do you read me? This is the USSV *Reagan*.' The voice takes on a cajoling tone, 'Hey guy? We know you're hurtin' and we're comin' in to *help*! We are a friendly vessel,' and here the man's voice goes sing-song, trying an Indian accent in case he is not being understood. Para can almost see him shaking his head from side to side, mimicking Peter Sellers, 'Now lissun pleeeze, du nawt du anything, du not du anytheeng, we are cumming to help you, you no? Just wait. We will be there soon.'

Para reckons from her calculations that they are now only about an hour away. Over the last few hours she has figured out that they've been bouncing the Carve signal from a satellite that is much closer to the *Varun Machaan*. But their precision has obviously increased the closer they've come. The screen gives Para the switch code she needs and she punches it in along with two sets of numbers that only she knows. The screen asks her once more whether she wants to destroy all codes and data and she taps in her third authorisation code in affirmation. The next question on the screen is about time. The question has obviously been written by some real gawaar Haryanvi egg-head.

In How Much Time You Want To Activate Full Destroy?

Para looks at her watch. She now has eight minutes left. She taps in the destroy code to activate in eleven minutes. She activates the Ice-Cream Cart to leave at the very edge of its time, in seven and a half minutes. She heads for the hatch. Then she pauses and comes back. She leans over Ashok's main keyboard and brings up his favourite trick, which is to change everyone's screensaver. She knows that ordinary programs like screensavers and personal files will not be touched by the destroy command. Quickly she changes the text that till now has been a joke about Gulati. She types in the new message: *Banzai to you too, good buddy. Best of Luck. You just blew up Pearl Harbor.*

She clicks the screensaver on and notes with satisfaction that all the screens have it scrolling now. She is particularly pleased with the 'good buddy' – it was one of Viralkaka's favourite expressions. The words are in black and the colours in the background are still Gulati's birthday party colours, with the orange, white and green balloons floating by and popping. It looks six-six cool. Would be great to see their faces when they read it. She takes one last look around and heads for the hatch that connects to the water module.

As she opens the hatch she can feel the Carve starting again, trying to find range. Peter Sellers is obviously taking no chances with someone who's hurtin' but has enough ability and presence of mind intact to be switching off microphones. The *Varun Machaan* begins to vibrate gently, different from the position rockets misbehaving, just like the first time. She switches on the light in the Ice-Cream Cart, climbs down and seals the hatch over her head. Then she slides in further, almost lying down, like a racing-car driver and shuts the module hatch. She makes sure her face is as close as she can get it to the tiny porthole and she tries to get herself as comfortable as possible. And then she waits.

The two sealed hatches should protect her unless they've caught on to the module. Chances are they will target the area around the main cabin again. As she looks at her watch she can feel the vibration grow above her head. She hears the sound of soft human things imploding but she knows she is remembering it from last time. What her mike is picking up is the noise of the engines starting on the module. Four minutes, three minutes, two – the light goes off and Para is plunged into darkness. She realises she has stopped breathing and she forces herself to take in air from her tanks. In, out. In . . . and . . . ouuuut. The module gives a heave and she feels it break away from the main ship. Like a kite cut loose.

Para looks again at the numbers dancing on her wrist. She waits for six minutes and pulls up the radio handset attached to her leg. She switches it on and tries to connect to the *Varun Machaan*. After a few seconds, she is through to her own bank of computers. She tries to bring up a file of basic weather information and her screen goes blank. So far so good. Next she tries to get a missile spread from the Lahore Border sector. Again blank. She breathes more easily. Live or die, she has done the best she can. Her body stretches back and she reaches down and puts away the handset.

Underneath her she can feel the hard padding of the mechanic's mattress and the vibration of the module engines coming through it. She has enough room at her sides to move her arms and to turn over. She rolls around to look through the little window. Most of the window is taken up by the opaque curve of atmosphere. At one side she can see the faint intermittent flash of the warning lights on the module. At the other edge is a sliver of dark, which is space. The window is quite scratched and dented and she knows she won't see anything very different for the next two hours till the craft changes course to head down through the atmospheric barrier. She turns over again and shuts her eyes, trying to concentrate on what she has to do, on what is possible for her to do.

The list she comes up with is short. Sleep to keep her breathing as shallow as possible. Wake up in time for the critical moment when the module re-enters the atmosphere. With no force-field or seat-belts to keep her strapped down, the massive buffeting could kill her immediately, crack her open like an egg. Or, it could rip open her suit, which would kill her more slowly. She will have to brace herself and hope for the best.

If she survives the buffeting then her chances of making it will increase slightly, not by much, but slightly. Her next problem will be the sea landing. Newer craft, the ones that ferried people up and down from space stations, landed like aircraft on airstrips, but for their unmanned craft Indian Aerospace still preferred the sea. They still used a combination of the old parachute system and two retro jets that also put a brake on the descent. In normal circumstances only the parachutes were used. It was only when there was something especially fragile on board that ground control spent the money on switching on the jets to 'make a pillow'. Approaching the sea near the base at Car Nicobar Island, Para will have to activate her radar-catcher and hope that her message has got through and that it has been understood. If not, the impact of the sea might be what will get her.

Para calculates the time left before re-entry. One and a half hours.

She can't risk sleep. She will have to keep awake for her possible death. What she needs is to put herself into a semi-trance state as she has been taught. She wishes she had some music, a radio. And then she realises she does have one.

On one of their space walks outside the *Varun Machaan* Ashok had taken her handset and fiddled with the tuning buttons. Floating in sunlight, the stars stretching below her and the earth above, Para had suddenly heard an old Hindi film song come through her headphones. A man's voice, max-lechy but funny too, kind of laughing at himself:

Badan pe sitaare lapete hue!
O jaane tamanna kidhar jaa rahi ho?
Jaraa paas aao
tˆo chaiyn aa jaaye

Para had sort of understood, but once they were back inside Ashok had insisted on translating. 'Very appropriate Group Captain Madam. The great – no the greatest! – Mohammad Rafi singing. *With stars wrapped around your body, O desire of my life, where are you headed? Come a little closer so that I can calm down.*' Not a good idea to get a little closer to a civilian on a combat posting, she'd thought, and left it to Reba to calm him down. Besides he'd suddenly reminded her of Cindy the Filmi-song expert, Cindy whom she'd lost on the first strike on Kharan. Anyway, he was a bit young for her. Pity. Maybe a mistake, but no point regretting it now. Her knees up and down.

Para takes out her handset again. The buttons light up as she pulls it out of its holster. She tries to remember what Ashok had done with the tuning buttons and after some trial and error she gets it – the handset window shows a signal being received. Wheels bouncing on rough roads. After a second, a voice starts to come through her ear-phones. A voice in Chinese reading out what sounds like a series of numbers. The sunlight hot on her throat where the chunni stops. She moves the tuning button. 'Portland-Plymouth. North-West Five, increasing to Six, then Seven. Showers, good.' The Local Shipping Forecast on the BBC. She moves the tuning again. A Japanese voice. Saying something at length but some words springing out, words that she can understand. 'Raag' . . . 'Drupad'. . . 'Pandit' . . . and 'Ustad', then a whole phrase – 'Raag Bhairavi. Ustad Hideo Kono.' Then silence. And then the first sound. The slow, cracked, dance of an old throat. The stomach throbbing up through the lungs to trap a single note in the net of breath.

Her knees up and down, up and down, the pedals talking up to the soles of her chappals, the wheels bouncing on the rough roads, the sunlight hot on her throat where the chunni stops. A taste of dust at the back of her mouth because they've been laughing so much.

Mahadev a little ahead of her, boy, pedalling faster, his payjamas flapping in the wind, making a different rhythm from the up and down, down and up of the pedals. The pedals, all four, together, together, together, together. They've come across Ellis Bridge together, her ahead of him, then him overtaking, her blocked by a car turning left, he waits for her, her out from behind the car and then they've headed out, together, together, together, out to the new societies that are still more or less sand and brush. A lamp-post – surprise! – he goes straight for it – weaves away at the last moment – siiide! Sway and away! Out on the road again, out. She heads for it too, at speed – he looks back – she takes it much later, much more graceful, spins the bike around at the last moment without even seeming to, carving a sound in the dust, his mouth open, calling out, *Arrey vaagshey!* – but no, she's out and coming after him, fast, faster, fastest, faster than a girl has any right to be.

The four o'clock sun high, tadko, some wind, his kurta-payjama flapping hard, and, from around her neck, her hair stretching behind her, shining black streak, a loud advertisement for their love. Who cares, let them look, her knees up and down, talking to the bumps in the path, laughing with them, riding over, over, over them and away. Now ahead of him, him slowing down a bit, slightly out of breath, but not her, him watching as she lifts herself off the seat and pumps the bike up the hill into the sun, spraying dust behind her.

They arrive at the top, rubber scrape of brakes, and get off and look. Around them a spread of yellow-brown thornland. In the distance, two villages. The one on the left closer, the one on the right further away, just a smudge in the haze. They don't say anything, just stand there and look. Now that they're off the bicycles neither looks at the other, they don't laugh, they stand there looking at the land but the other eyes that are inside, inside them both, stay locked into each other.

What breaks it is a sound, a weight of bangles clinking. Just below them, a file of women taking evening water home. Brass ghadaas, big one on the head, medium one in the middle and small one perched on top, hands on the middle one for balance, the sway that comes up the legs from the winding path, the snaking that comes down the spine from the water moving above. Both meeting at the hips. Mahadev, thirsty, wipes his rolled up sleeve across his mouth and calls out to them:

'O Behn! Thodu paani paasho?'

The women come to a stop in unison, like a troop of soldiers. The sunlight moves on the ghadaas as two of them turn slowly to see who is calling. One flicks her eyes at the other and then back at Mahadev.

'Haa. Aapu ne.' She reaches up to the little top ghadaa. The other one says something in village language that Suman and Mahadev don't catch, but it sounds like she's saying, 'Don't give them water. Why are you giving them water?' The first one says something back, disagreeing, and gestures to Mahadev to come and get the water. Mahadev and Suman go down the little slope and Mahadev eagerly takes the ghadaa and turns to Suman, offering it to her. Suman hesitates for a moment and then bends and cups her hands to catch the water.

As Suman drinks, the second woman points to Suman and asks Mahadev something that he doesn't understand. Shu kahyu behn? What did you ask? The woman repeats her question but Mahadev is thirsty, is already tilting his head back, pouring water into his mouth, careful to keep the rim away from his lips. Muhalman chho? Suman gets it before Mahadev does. Mussalman chho? Are you Muslim? The women are looking at Suman's salwaar kameez.

Suman's eyes widen in horror at the thought. 'Ey *na* hawn!' she cries, as Mahadev starts laughing and wiping the water from around his mouth with the back of his hand and nodding his head vigorously. Haa, haa, yes, she is a Mussalman, he says, handing the ghadaa back and poking his finger in Suman's direction.

The women don't know what to make of this, the girl shaking her head, saying no, the boy nodding yes yes in the middle of the girl's no and shaking with laughter. By now the others have turned to look. One or two of them join in the laughter. Then they stand there in a row, all of them laughing, their ghadaas moving slightly, the metal bangles on sun-darkened arms clinking in the evening light. Her face tight, Suman turns away and stomps up the slope, back to the bikes. Mahadev throws a nod at the women and follows her.

Jumps on his bike and races after her as she pedals away furiously. Catches up a little while later, calling out, 'O Begum! O Begum sahiba!' Suman turns her head to look at him once, eyes on fire, then looks away and pedals harder.

The sun hot on their backs, their shadows long on the road, snaking ahead of them, leading them back. The town growing around them, first the odd cement bungalow in the middle of nowhere, then two, then a whole row of them, all different shapes, then a proper street with a few trees, wire fences around the houses to keep out animals, two parked cars, an old Model T and a new American Buick, then a crossing of two roads with a Bedford truck waiting for some cows to pass, then rail tracks, bump, bump, bump, a hard *triiing* from Suman's bell to warn off a little child wandering on to the road – a baby girl, Mahadev notices – in a torn yellow frock, no, red frock, no, actually yellow – yellow frock – matted hair, wiping snot from her nose with the back of her hand as she watches them go. Mahadev now silent, waiting for Suman to say something, to look.

As they come up to Ashram Road the traffic increases. Mahadev pulls up next to Suman at a traffic light. He is close enough, so she leans back and slaps him. Hard. Mahadev's eyes widen and his hand goes up to feel his cheek. As his cheek turns red the light turns green and Suman is off, away, and onto the bridge, Nehru Bridge this time.

'Uh – ooops, error, Ffupzmeister, error. Can't be Nehru Bridge, right?'

'Nope. Nehru's in and out of jail at this time and no one's naming bridges after him yet. Besides, I think Nehru Bridge was built well after Independence.'

'Right.' Para pauses the game and taps in the changes. 'So, back to Ellis Bridge, right?'

Back to Ellis Bridge. The pontoon girders flashing by. Down on the river bed dhobis moving around, pulling up the white sheets stretched out to dry in the morning. A school of goats nibbling at a rivulet of water that runs along the far bank. Two kids playing guli-danda in a patch of sand between two rows of sheets. The boy and the girl weaving their bikes through the traffic, the girl now with tears in her eyes, wiping her eyes with the chunni she's tied on her side so that it doesn't get caught in the bike chain.

'Why can't I put kites on their bikes? It'd be fun on the carriers – them riding and the kites flying behind them. Like satellites.'

Might be fun, but not in traffic. And anyway, the two are like satellites themselves, like kites, flying away from the foi-mashis, away from the poel and the family, tugging free for a while and criss-crossing their private sky before being reeled back.

Well before they reach Hajira ni Poel and Sankdi Sheri their path will bifurcate because they mustn't be seen together. They reach the tea-shop on Relief Road where Mahadev will stop and let Suman go ahead. He will wait for about ten minutes, have a cup of tea and make his own way back home. Two days after they break the thing down.

Suman stops and slides off her seat. She stands there, left hand on handlebar, feet on either side of the curving bar of her ladies' bike, trying to speak clearly through the tears. 'I'll die!' she says. 'You can laugh now, insult me all you want, but one day I'll just disappear into the air!' Suddenly the sky over Moulali is filled with kites. Mahadev feels his cheek and grins at her. 'I'll tear apart the skies and come after you,' he says. 'Where will you run to then?'

She doesn't say anything. Just stands there for two minutes, wiping the tears with her chunni. When she looks at him again her eyes are soft.

'Aavjo,' she says and pedals herself up onto her seat and cycles away.

'Aavjo.' He calls out after her, biting down on the 'Begum' about to roll off his tongue. Watches her as you would a kite moving away to another part of the sky.

Two days after they break the thing down, the old man shuffles out to the balcony to look at the sky over Moulali filling up with kites. Green silhouettes locusting against the winter morning sun. Many with white sickle moons in the middle, though they are too far for him to make that out. Some with the number 786 painted in white against the green. The wind actually weak and the kites finding it difficult to bite, but enough of them up there to tangle up the light. Paresh holds him by the elbow, not as firmly as he should, but as tightly as he dares.

'Hard work,' says Mahadev Bhatt, 'hard work to keep them up there on a day like this.'

Anna wipes a little dribble from the baby's mouth. The baby reacts by turning to her grandfather, her arms reaching for him, the top half of her straining against her mother's forearm. 'Dyaah?' she asks and turns back to look at Anna, her green eyes as wide as they can get – Can I go?

Mahadev looks at the baby and smiles a question to Anna and Paresh – Should I take her? Paresh shakes his head and then speaks to his daughter – 'Nai baba, not just now, Dadaji is tired.' The baby senses some denial, something being protected away from her, and her eyebrows lock up in angry curves. She lets out a howl. Anna tries to quieten her, speaking softly to her in German. The ayah hears the baby crying and quickly comes to the balcony. She firmly takes the baby from Anna and goes away, speaking to her in Bengali, '*Eijey! Maa? Maaa, Kiiiiii holo? Ebaaar kiii hoyessey?*' The high-pitched sing-song immediately shuts the baby up. Mahadev waits for the noise to stop before speaking.

'She has strong legs. Just like her Ba,' he says to Anna. 'Have I told you that Paresh's mother was once women's cycling champion of Ahmedabad? She was very fast.' Anna nods. He has told her this many times now.

Speaking in English. His shredded voice slowing down around the bends of a language that is suddenly foreign again. Changing gears on to another subject.

'It would be good,' he is now looking at Paresh, but addressing both of them, '. . . it . . . it would be good if you did not go out today. Anna may find it . . . find some difficulty . . . to handle things on her own.'

'Don't worry Bhai,' Anna cuts in before Paresh can say anything, 'he is not going anywhere. This is no time for heroic photography. Here now he also has a child to think about.'

Mahadev smiles at her, something closer to a proper smile coming into focus, not as faded as the last one. It is as if looking at Anna has given him some strength. 'Yes, one child is manageable, but you both now must be getting tired of two.' And he points to himself with his free hand. Anna shakes her head and opens her mouth to say no but the old man continues. 'But don't worry, there should be some relief soon. At most . . . one or two days, I think. Initially it will be difficult, but after a few days it will all . . . all will settle.'

'Pappa, awhey please stop it. Evhu kainj nahi thaay.'

Mahadev ignores Paresh. He has seen more grief than Paresh and he knows when it is coming. Talking now almost to himself, his words go soft again, lowered by the calculation.

'Only problem is this curfew. The line at Kalighat . . . may be quite long. Will be long. Only problem . . . otherwise . . .' Otherwise, as the old man has said many times over the last two weeks, there is no problem. Since I have managed to see my grand-daughter.

Anna helps him come in from the balcony, back to his bed.

Later in the day, lying on one side of the big double bed, the old man sends the ayah to call Paresh. Anna is asleep in the other bedroom and Paresh has Para. The baby is half asleep on his shoulder as he enters the bedroom and the ayah offers to take her from him. Paresh shakes his head, comes in and sits down on the edge of the bed, patting Para's back rhythmically.

'Shu, Pappa?'

Mahadev points to his desk on the far side of the bedroom. Then he speaks in English, as if he doesn't quite trust Paresh to understand his Gujarati.

'My Pelikan,' he says, 'get it.' Paresh gets up and goes to the desk. He knows where the pen is always kept. He finds it in the little plastic tray between the old red anglepoise and a neat pile of literary magazines, old *Encounters* from England and copies of *Kumar* from Ahmedabad. He bends both his knees, holding his back straight to keep Para balanced on his shoulder, and reaches to pick up the pen. As he straightens, the baby gives a sudden jerk and he almost drops her. He manages to get his right arm back around her, holding on to her with his wrist, the fingers still holding the precious Pelikan. The baby makes a small noise and flips her head around to press the other ear into the nape of his neck. Then she takes a tight little clutch of his sweater and goes into deep sleep.

Mahadev fights his way out of his quilts and manages to sit up, propped up on one arm. Paresh looks around for a place to put the baby down but Mahadev shakes his head.

'Two minutes, I only need two minutes.' He pushes himself up a little more to sit as erect as he can and takes the pen from Paresh. 'Taney khabar chhe ke –' he grimaces as he turns to pick up the glass of water from his bedside table. He takes a few sips and puts it down again, carefully, exchanging it for his spectacles before turning back and putting them on. Then he looks at Paresh. 'Taney –' he stops and goes back to his English, 'you know fully well that I don't get sentimental about the death of anybody.'

Paresh looks at his father and nods. Mahadev cups his hand around his mouth and clears his throat into it. Then he starts again, his voice slightly easier.

'You know I was upset when Suman passed away, but that was only because of her life of her last years, and that I was powerless about changing it, that only. Not the fact of her actual going, samjhyo ne . . . because we all do have to be going, sooner or later.' Mahadev waves his hand at the little pile of medicines on his bedside table, 'So this also I have no regrets about. Except for the timing of this grand nation-wide farewell party that our Jan Sangh friends have thrown on my behalf.'

Paresh wants to stop Mahadev from talking so surely of death, but it is the only thing the old man is asking for, so he says nothing. He nods his head again and waits for him to continue. Outside, there is no noise of traffic. It is even more silent than a Sunday afternoon – as if a limb of sound has been chopped off. Just under his ear, Paresh can hear Para's soft, even, breathing. More than hearing it he can feel it, her ribcage expanding and contracting against the left side of his chest, all of it contained like a big hollow fist on the area around his heart. Mahadev has paused and turned to sift through his medicines. He shakes his head, dissatisfied with the waste of it all, puts the medicines down and looks up again at Paresh. He gestures to the window and Paresh can tell he has heard the same silence. 'All was expected. Everything. But who would have thought . . . the one thing I didn't imagine was ke Calcutta would also join in this party.' Mahadev's head drops and for a moment it looks as though he has fallen asleep. But he has not – Paresh can see the eyes wide open behind the spectacles, staring down to where the shaal crumples into the lap.

After a minute or two Mahadev suddenly remembers the pen. He picks it up from the bed and gives it back to Paresh.

'Anyway, aa Pelikan pen Parabehn matey chhe. No point giving it to you since you hardly write. But keep it clean, keep it working till she is old enough to use it. Then give it to her. Aney enhe Azaadi aney

Mukti vachhey no pher tyaare samjhaavje. Banney sarkhaa nathi. Aney banney joiye.' And then explain to her the difference between Independence and Freedom. The two are not the same. And one needs both.

Paresh waits to see if his father has finished. Then he says it bluntly in Gujarati.

'Pappa, they have a bed available from tomorrow morning in the ICU at Calcutta General. It was difficult to get but I've booked it. I'll keep the pen, but you can give it to her yourself when she is the right age.'

Mahadev doesn't bother looking at his son as he pushes himself down and pulls the quilts back over himself.

'You were always oversentimental. And wasteful of money,' he says, and turns away and closes his eyes.

At night Paresh settles Para and Anna under the mosquito net. Para is restless as Anna rubs mosquito cream on her hands and neck and face, all the bits of skin that come out of the babygro. After putting on the cream Anna undoes the top of her nightshirt and turns sideways, pulling the baby gently towards her. Paresh watches as the little mouth closes around the nipple. The baby is still for a moment and then her eyes shut and her cheeks begin the beat of a slow steady pumping, one hand coming up to rest possessively on the side of the breast. Anna waits till she is sure that the baby has latched on firmly. Then, without moving her body, she slowly raises her right arm and strokes Paresh's face – go, go and look in on him. Paresh slides himself back out from under the net, gingerly, careful not to create too big a gap as he comes out, and then he quickly tucks the net in between the mattress and the bed, making sure to leave no openings.

For a while he stands there, looking inside the cube of mosquito net, trying to make out by the light of the bedside lamp if a stray mosquito has managed to slip in. Then he tiptoes to the stereo and lowers the volume slightly on the Brian Eno cassette, Para's favourite sleeptime music. He finds his camera on his desk, puts it around his neck and goes out into the living-dining, closing the door softly behind him. There is a thali and a steel glass waiting for him on the dining table, with food next to it. The ayah gets up from where she is squatting on the floor.

'Dada? Kichhu khabey na?' Won't you eat something?

'Na. Tumi ebaar giye ghumou.' No, you go and sleep now.

The old woman hesitates. 'Jaabo?' Should I go?

'Han, tumi jaao. Aami jegey achhi.' Yes, go. I'll stay awake.

'Dada porey kichhu kheye niyo, han. Ei shomoye na khele bhaalo na. Shoril'er dorkaar.' Do eat something later. Not good not to eat at a time like this. The body needs it.

Pulling her shaal tight around her she goes off to her room, which is outside, on the landing between two floors. He shuts the main door behind her, locks it, bolts it and slides in the chain. Then he makes sure the drawing-room windows are bolted before switching off the light and going into his parents' bedroom. As he enters he can see his father sleeping, reflected in the mirror of his mother's dressing table. The little lamp on the floor next to the bed throws up a crazy shadow of the water jug against the wall behind the bed. The little transistor is on, tuned to the BBC World Service, and there is a low scratching of foreign voices involved in a discussion. Paresh goes and leans over his father, watching his face.

Mahadev's mouth is slightly open, and his breath makes little forays in and out of the body, like something tied by elastic trying to develop the momentum to snap free. Suddenly Paresh needs to see if the breath is reaching down far enough. His eyes scan over the still figure, back and forth from the head to the small peak of quilt where the feet are. Finally they come to stop on Mahadev's hands and arms, which are outside the quilt. The hands rest on the stomach, and Paresh has to look for a long time before he can see them rise and fall with the breathing.

After a few minutes he moves over to the balcony door, unbolts it and goes outside. He pushes the door shut gently, making sure that it's closed, and pulls out his cigarettes. He lights up and leans on the railing.

The balcony looks out north, down onto the gap between a tall block of flats and an old bungalow. Through the gap he can see a tiny portion of Lower Circular Road, empty now, the white road divider shining under the yellow halogen lamps. A wall separates the narrow parking lot at the back of the apartment building from the overgrown bungalow garden. The garden is dark, but the parking lot is illuminated by a dim tubelight that sticks out from just below a first-floor balcony. Maybe it's the difference in light, and, looking down, Paresh can't be sure whether he's imagining it, but the winter mist seems much heavier on the garden side, thinning out in a straight line along the wall before tripping over and spreading on the sleeping cars. Somewhere, a tapping of a night darwaan's stick, the noise hesitant, as if the man doesn't really want to be heard. Paresh wonders if he can keep the Nikon still enough for a time exposure. Maybe, just maybe, if he really dug his elbows into the railing. But half a minute? What would he get in half a minute? He decides to try anyway.

He drops the cigarette and stubs it out under his rubber slipper. Then he takes the lens cap off and slips it into his kurta pocket. He looks through the camera once and he sets the aperture to f4 and the shutter speed to T. Then he puts his elbows on the railing and leans slightly forward. The balcony is only about three feet wide and it occurs to him that he can push his feet against the wall next to the door behind him. Pressing down on his elbows to keep his balance, he puts first one foot, and then the other, both flat against the wall, just where it forms a right angle with the balcony floor. The stalk of rubber that goes between his big toe and the second toe bites into the webbing of his left foot, but now he is stable, his body taut between wall and railing, the camera tightly up against his eyebrow and cheekbone. He manages to focus on a banana tree just inside the bungalow garden, the prism sharpening on one frond that catches the light from the road.

The wall divides his frame almost exactly into half, the dark huddle of cars on the left and the thicker mess of mist and foliage on the right, the wall stretching away, from full focus next to the banana tree to a soft line where it meets Lower Circular on top of the frame. He is sure the film will register something but he doesn't quite know what. He exhales, locks his breath out, and presses the shutter. The camera mirror slaps up, blanking out the frame from his eye, letting the light onto the film. The noise is loud in the night and he hopes that it won't wake anyone up. He keeps his left eye open and starts counting in his head – *one thousand, two thousand, three thousand*

Each thousand roughly about one second. He counts to thirty thousand before taking his finger off the shutter and breathing in again. He rests his feet for a few seconds and then does it again. And then a third time, a slightly different frame, the focus still the same but the wall now not quite so central, more to the left of the picture. *Fifteen thousand, sixteen thousand, seventeen thousand*

First he thinks maybe it's blood pressure hissing back and forth between his ears. Like a tide sifting pebbles on a beach. Then it grows deeper, coming from far outside him, and he can't ignore it anymore. He has heard the same sound the night before. The camera starts shaking in his hand and he abandons the picture, taking his finger off the shutter and straightening up. The soft flesh between his toes suddenly beginning to hurt sharply. He fumbles for his cigarettes, quickly wanting them out, wanting one lit before the thing grows as he knows it will. Somewhere he knows he is out on the balcony because he wants to hear it again and it doesn't fail him.

It has started from the left, he reckons about three miles to the west of the house, from Garden Reach and the port area. Many many throats letting go together, changing pitch, getting stronger and stronger till the roar becomes a thick hum across the night. Then other voices igniting somewhere straight ahead of him, due north, beyond Loudon, Rawdon and Park Street – coming from Wellesley Road side – what is now Rafi Ahmed Kidwai Road – and, before that wave climbs to its full peak, Moulali joining in, to his right and slightly to the north, east-north-east, and then the rest of the area around Park Circus and Dhapa, an aural fever coursing through the dark body of the city. The heat of the sound now closer, suddenly very close, too close to the house. The roar developing a shape – *Alllaaaaaaaaaaaaaaaaaaaaaaah Ho Akbar! Allaaaaaaaaaaaah Ho Akbar!*

Paresh looks at the sky, searching for the glow he has seen the night before and, sure enough, he finds it. There, somewhere around the Wellesley area, a lot of light bouncing up. It doesn't look like fire, though it could be. More probably big searchlights mounted on army trucks shining into the eyes of the crowd. He can't really see the sky to the west but after a while he catches it on the right as well, behind the dark tops of some apartment buildings, light coming from around Moulali. The roar waxes and wanes, sometimes stronger to his right, sometimes from straight ahead, sometimes rising out from the left – like someone playing with the speaker balance of a stereo. Every now and then he hears a faint series of cracks which he guesses is the tear gas being fired. After a few minutes the sound subsides, but he knows it's only a pause before it starts again.

Below him, in the parking lot, Paresh notices some movement. Two darwaans squatting in an empty car slot, warming their hands above a small choolha, sticks periscoping straight up out of their tents of shaal, shaking slightly when they shiver.

Normally they would have put the sticks to one side before settling down, but tonight they hang on to them. Out on Lower Circular somewhere, a dog starts to bark, having heard the large noise. Paresh can now see it wandering around in the middle of the road, sending its search-howl into the night, looking for an answer. And nothing coming back. As if all the other street dogs have migrated elsewhere. Behind him he can just about hear his father's radio through the closed doors, someone reading the news on the BBC Hindi service. Through his bedroom windows, to the right of the balcony, he can now also make out the Eno, a low sheet of synthesiser rising. And then it peels out of the silence again. *Alllllllaaaaaaaaaaaaaaaaoakaburrrr.*

AlllaaaaaAllllaaaaaaaaaaaHoallaaaaaaaaaaaaaahoAkbarallaaaaaaAAAA. A raw a cappella of anger, making the darwaans crouch deeper into their shaals, chopping off the dog in mid-bark.

Paresh looks up at the tall apartment building in front of him and he can't see a single light on in any of its fifteen floors. But they can't all be asleep. As the roar reaches another crescendo, he can almost feel them shrink deeper into their bedrooms. He looks down and finds his hands tight, gripping the railing. He forces himself to pull out another cigarette, and his hands shake as he lights it. He takes a deep drag and peers down again. A question sidles through to the front of his mind – will they come through the garden, or will it be through the parking lot, after killing the darwaans and burning the cars?

Suddenly he feels a tight grip around his chest, his heart knocking directly against her arms, as if his ribcage has disappeared. Her face pressing hard into his spine, deep between his shoulder blades. Her muffled voice, as if coming up through his back and into his ears from the inside.

'Paresh? Liebe?'

Stop, she says, stop, and he tries, but the shaking has now taken over, his body like a small aircraft fluttering in turbulence, all of it, ankles, knees, the insides of his thighs, the abdomen spasming to grip his maverick breath, his shoulder joints rattling in some arrhythmic tympani, the smell of the Calcutta winter night pulsing in and out of him, her smell, Anna's smell, sirening in and out of his nose.

She turns him around and grips his upper arms, as if trying to control a skidding motorcycle. Her eyes bore into him. Her voice is harder now, calmer but harder.

'You have to rip yourself together,' she says, 'you have to – ja – rip yourself together Paresh. This is just nothing but the beginning.' He grasps the little girl's hand and strides forward.

He looks at her and looks at her and looks at her. And slowly, his breathing comes back to him. But, just as his bones settle, something begins to shake the floor under their feet. As the vibration grows, she pulls him closer and holds him. After a while the path curves more inland.

'Is she asleep?' he asks into the top of Anna's head and he can feel her nod a yes into his neck.

The rumble of the convoy grows louder. Army trucks from the Ballygunje garrison coming up Lansdowne Road, heading past their building to the Minto Park T-junction where they will turn either right or left on Lower Circular, depending on where the trouble is worse. The wind picks up and joins its voice to the sea. It's not the normal route – they should have gone up Ballygunje Circular Road. Must be some reason. One, two, three, four, five, six, there are a lot of them, and Paresh and Anna hold each other tight as the small balcony throbs with their passing.

A man and a little girl walk out past the empty tables of the Hotel du Falises, climb onto the promenade that runs parallel to the beach and head towards the cliffs on the west. The sun has begun its evening slant and it catches the man's white shirt, making it even brighter against his skin. The man has two cameras hanging from his neck and he keeps looking down and adjusting something on one camera. The little girl skips along behind the man and almost bumps into him as he stops and pulls out a packet of cigarettes. The man lights up, thinking about something, and then, as if he has reached a decision, he grasps the little girl's hand and strides forward.

Pappa's begun smaking. I know it's smoking but I call it smaking when he smokes and shakes at the same time. Now he's smaking. And he's doing a fiddle with his cameras. And he's keeping the cigarette far away from his cameras because he says the smoke is bad for the lenses but he doesn't keep the cigarette far away from his own inside. I ask him what's more important, lenses or his own inside and he says inside, but then he gets grown-up clever like he does sometimes and tells me there are many insides in people. Something inside Pappa is making him smake and something inside is pushing water out of his eyes. He's wiping his eyes because they have water in them, but he's not crying because Pappa never cries. Doesn't know how to cry.

Pappa's holding my hand too tight and walking too fast. I tell him it's a beach, not a road in Paris and he doesn't need to hold my hand and he's walking too fast. Pappa can walk fast sometimes when he's not thinking. And sometimes when he's thinking he forgets to walk and that's irritating. Sometimes he walks too fast and then he starts thinking and then he forgets to walk. I have to push him then. He's stopped now and looking at something. He's looking at the pebbles on the beach.

I ask him but he won't tell me what Mamma said on the phone that's making him smake.

The man has let go of the little girl's hand. He is now looking through a camera, pointing it down at something on the ground. The little girl takes the opportunity and runs up the slope towards the shell of the old concrete pillbox. She climbs in through the slit and looks back out. The man finishes taking his picture and turns to look for her. She calls out to him from the pillbox – Here! Pappa! – and he looks at her, trying to smile.

I can see Pappa from the hole. Pappa said the hole and the whole bunker was made by German soldiers for shooting machine-guns through. A long time ago. I pretend I'm a German soldier and I shoot at Pappa. Pappa drops to the ground like he's been shot and then he crawls towards me, shooting back, pretending his camera is a gun. Then he comes close and really shoots a picture. Then another. I tell Pappa there is not enough light and he says yes there is. I ask him how come he won't let me shoot with my camera in this kind of light and he says there is enough light for his camera but not for mine.

The man and the little girl have an exchange, something that gets lost in the chattering of the sea against the beach. Then the man helps the little girl out of the slit of the pillbox and they carry on walking, heading up to the cliffs.

Pappa's trying to be funny now, like he does when he is upset but doesn't want to talk about it. He's doing funny things with his face and trying to tell me a story, but I'm not listening, I'm looking at the funny candle rocks coming out of the sea. There's one which he says looks like an elephant but I can't see that. I'm also trying to count the birds.

They are up on the cliffs now and the birds circle below them, coming up from the water's edge, scrapping with the air, squawking at the man and the girl before dropping down again, falling away happily into the gaps between the rocks.

Pappa keeps telling me to be careful on the path but he is not paying attention to where he is going. The path is like a bad story. It's bumpy and it disappears and comes back again. Sometimes it's difficult to walk on and sometimes it's easy and if you stay too inside it's boring and if you go too near the sea then it's dangerous. Pappa slips a couple of times and once he holds my hand and helps me when I don't need help. I tell him it's safer without him holding my hand. He says he can't take a chance.

After a while the path curves more inland. The sea continues to negotiate its arrival against the rocks below, like refugee families at a train terminus, but you can no longer see the drop of the cliffs. The man relaxes and lights another cigarette. He finishes the cigarette and then he takes a few more photographs. He is concentrating, trying to catch something in the slope of land, the sinking light. He pays no attention to the little girl as she wanders, orbiting around him in uneven circles. The wind picks up and joins its voice to the sea. Two sounds constant in the background, elsewhere but there, a pair of servants talking in low voices in another room, ready to be summoned, but taking time out.

I can see stars in the sky and there's not enough light even for Pappa's cameras now and he puts on their lids and shuts them off. He takes one of them off his neck and begins to rewind the film. That's his work done for the day. I don't know why he has to work on a holiday and why sometimes he doesn't work at all when there is no holiday, but that's the way he is – a freelancer, I used to call it freedancer when I was four, but Mamma laughed and held me tight and said – I wish he *was* a freedancer. I don't know what she meant but I stopped calling him freedancer after that because I didn't like Mamma laughing at me.

There is a third sound from far away, low at first, then louder, shouldering its way between the throb of the wind and the sharp hiss of the waves. The sunset developing a whine. The little girl sees it first and runs to the edge of the cliff to see it better. The man is lost in his own world, looking down at the camera in his hand and he is slow to react. Then he sees the girl running towards the drop and a shout comes out of him. The girl is very close to where the grass stops and the shout makes her whirl around in panic. Her legs go from under her and she slides away from the man. She slides away from him towards the sea, her hands taloning, trying to grab the slippery grass, but her fingers suddenly too small. The man's body takes two jumps to build up momentum, taking no instruction from the head, and dives forward. The camera he is holding cuts loose from him, goes up into the air and bounces on the grass before disappearing over the edge.

Pappa's got me. He's holding my arms so tight they really hurt, but he's got me. The camera's gone but he's got me. He's staring at me funny and his eyes are very big but he's not moving. He's lying on the grass holding my arms and I can feel his hands breathing hard. After a long time he pulls me to him very slowly. Then he gets his arms around me and pulls me away and then we both lie there and watch as the next fighter-plane goes by almost on top of us and then almost on top of the sea and then gone. Then Pappa's talking, right into my ear, too loud, I can't tell if he's talking to me. I think he's telling himself, You fucking idiot, You fucking idiot, he keeps saying and he's not supposed to use bad words, but I don't mind this time and maybe I won't tell Mamma.

The man crawls backwards, pulling the little girl with him, dragging her with him till they are well away from the edge. Then he gets up very slowly, making sure of his own footing before he pulls up the girl. He lifts the girl up and clutches her to his body. The girl puts her legs around his waist and her arms around his neck. The man shifts his head so that he can see clearly over the girl's shoulder and then he begins to walk back towards the lights of the town.

Which one did you lose? I ask and Pappa says What? I said which camera did you lose? And that makes Pappa look down and feel around his waist. Which one, Pappa? and he says the Leica. Is that the one with my pictures in it? No, baba, it's the other one, never mind, never mind, its fine, I'll get another one. But you lost the pictures in the camera. That's okay, baby, that's okay, Pappa's saying everything twice and he's shaking again in a quiet way but I know he can't smoke because he's not allowed to when he's picking me up. I think he needs to smoke, so I tell him, You can put me down now, Pappa. You can have a cigarette if you want.

They are almost at the end of the path. The man puts the girl down carefully. He reaches into a pocket and fumbles out his packet of cigarettes. Why did you grab me, Pappa? The man doesn't answer. He concentrates on lighting the cigarette, shielding the lighter from the wind. Did you think I was going to fall down? The man looks away and shakes his head, still cursing himself. The girl had turned around when she heard the shout. She had frozen but she hadn't fallen. Not till the man brought her down. I wouldn't have, Pappa. There was plenty of ground. The cliff was quite far away.

I know, baby, I know. I'm sorry.

After a while the two of them walk over a narrow dip onto the cliff nearest to the beach, the one that juts out and makes the famous bridge of rock that painters have painted for centuries. What locals call L'Éléphant. They stand there and look at the stars and the dark wide rustle of sea.

Pappa's told me Ba and Dadaji are in the sky so I ask him to show me. He thinks for a bit and then points to a star and says he thinks that's Ba. I look at it for a bit and it blinks at me, the star, and I ask him to show me where Dadaji is. Pappa points to another bit of sky and shows me another star. But that's light-years away, Pappa, that's very far from Ba. No it's not, Pappa says quickly, 'cause the sky is so big it's just like they are in different rooms, side by side.

The girl thinks for a bit. The wind drops and they can hear the sound of cars on the road that runs next to the sea, the road which goes to Trouville. And where is Mamma? asks the girl. The man gives the girl a startled look. Mamma's not in the sky, Para, Mamma's on the ground. She's catching a train from Duisburg tonight and you'll see her tomorrow, when we get back to Paris. The girl looks at the ground, at her feet, nods and then she has another question. And when will I see you again, Pappa?

Soon, in three or four months.

The girl doesn't reply. She is silent for a moment and then something triggers in her and she spreads her arms. I wish Viralkaka was here, she says, and launches into a sound. The man keeps looking at her. After a moment, he too spreads his arms and joins in the sound, his voice lower than hers, stuttering, coughing the air in while she sends her throat up against the sea in a high whine.

By the time they come back down to the beach they are both laughing real laughter.

Later on that night the man leans out of the window of their hotel room and looks at the tide coming in. The water rides out of the dark, catches the wash of light from the lamp-posts on the promenade, rearranges the thin line of pebbles, and then scurries back into the night. And again.

The little girl is asleep. The man looks at the stars. He remembers his mother telling him about the frock. When his mother was his daughter's age she had a special frock. It was red and it spread out and it had little lights in it. Little bulbs that would light up. There was a little battery at her waist, at the small of her back, and when you switched it on the lights came on, some hiding in the organdy, like stars against a dark red sky. 'Every time I wore that frock, I imagined I was wearing the sky,' she would say. Now she is a light, the man thinks, the sky is wearing her.

Pappa is good at breakfast. And breakfast is good. Hot chocolate for me and awfulcoffee for Pappa. Croissants for me and croissants for Pappa. Confiture. Apricot for Pappa and raspberry for me. I can tell Pappa is happy the way he's eating, when he's not happy he can't eat, he pretend-eats, but I know the food gets lost in his neck. When he is happy I can see, promise, I can actually see the food going down to his stomach. I like it when he burps to annoy Mamma because then I can burp too and then Mamma gets really annoyed. Germans don't like burping like Indians. And I'm Indian when I'm burping.

Pappa's not being an Indian today, he's being . . . European. He's smiling at the waitress. He's not wiping the jam off my mouth like I'm a baby. He's asking for the bill firmly, like he's a lord in olden times. Then he jumps up and says let's go baby and he hasn't finished his coffee.

The man and the girl get into a car. As the man turns the ignition, the back of the car rises slightly, as if an invisible hand is pushing it up. After a few growls, the long porpoise-shaped front noses out into the street. The man drives through the town, following the signs to the autoroute, and within ten minutes they are on the highway, the sun shining in from the left. It is warm and the man has the windows down. The wind ruffles through their hair.

What are you going to do in Paris, Pappa? Are you going to get a new camera? The man thinks for a moment and then smiles. Yes. I'll have to check the insurance on that, but yes, I'll get a new one soon. But first –

The wail of the siren cuts him off, making the man look up at his rear-view mirror. The police car whips around them and almost forces them off the road, a gendarme leaning out, signalling them to pull over. As they come to a stop, a second police car almost bumps into them from behind. What do they want, Pappa? But the man is frozen, his hands still on the steering wheel, staring at the three semi-automatics being pointed at them. After a moment something makes him check his mirror and he sees two more men ready to shoot through the rear windshield. In his peripheral vision two more yet, one on each side of the car, a woman on the right and a man on the left. The girl has also seen the guns by now and her mouth is open in shock. Keep still, Para, just keep still, the man finds himself saying, not looking at her, still unable to move his head. The wind fingers an empty packet of chips on the dashboard, makes it scrape across the surface, and the noise it makes sounds very loud. The sunlight puts a dull glint on the snub, matte black barrels of the guns.

'Yousouf Ali?' rasps a gendarme, the one nearest to the man, the one on his left. The man slowly turns his head to look at the gendarme. 'I'm sorry, this is a mistake.' The policeman asks again, 'Tu n'es pas Yousouf Ali?'

Pappa is scared but he is also very angry and that makes me less scared. I know when he looks like that he is angry and when he is angry like that someone is going to be in trouble.

'Do you speak English?' the man asks quietly, and then continues without waiting for a response, 'My name is Paresh Bhatt. I am a photographer. I am an Indian citizen, and this is my daughter, who is a German citizen.'

I'm as Indian as Pappa but he always says I'm a German citizen if someone asks. The policeman opens Pappa's door and Pappa gets out.

'Vos papiers, s'il vous plaît.' The guns are still up but the policeman has gone official now. The man notices that the 'tu' has changed to 'vous'. He reaches into the car and finds his passport, his identity card from the photo agency, international driving licence, other papers. It's okay baba, he tells the girl, they're just checking something. The gendarme goes through the papers while one of the others gets on the radio in the car in front. He hears him speak rapidly, catches the phrase 'Non, c'est pas lui, c'est pas Yousouf'. And 'Indien, il parle anglais' and the words 'petite fille'.

The police make Pappa open the back and they look into our bags. Then they put their guns away. Then the car at the back goes away. Pappa is standing there doing nothing but he's wrapped his arms around each other and I can tell he is still angry but he's not saying anything.

After a while the gendarme gives the papers back to the man. 'Merci, monsieur.'

The man puts away the papers and goes back to standing next to the car, waiting.

The gendarme points to the girl.

'Ze childe. In ze back seat. In France eet ees not allowed in ze front seat.'

The man turns to the girl and tells her to get in the back seat. The girl doesn't argue, she does what she is told, gets in the back and puts on her seat-belt.

'You can continue, m'sieur,' says the gendarme.

The man can't help himself, the words come out before he can stop them.

'You don't need so many guns to tell me to move my child to the back seat. You scared her.'

The gendarme stops in his tracks as if he's been shot. Then he turns back and comes very close to the man. Close enough for the man to smell the mint on the gendarme's breath.

'Zees is a war. You ahre luucki we don't shoot you. We don't shoot becoz we see ze girl. Vas-y.'

The policeman goes away from Pappa and Pappa gets back into the car. The police car goes away. Pappa opens my door and gives me a hug and then he gets in the front and starts smaking again.

The man sits for a while, smoking his cigarette. The girl watches him, saying nothing. After a while he starts the car and they are back on the road. What did they want, Pappa? They thought I was someone else, baba, they thought I was a bad man. Would they have shot their guns Pappa? No, baba, I don't think so, they were just being careful. I thought they were going to shoot. No, baby, they just act like that because they want bad people to think they'll shoot, just so's people don't do anything silly like try to run away or something. But Pappa? Yes? They didn't shoot because you told them you were Indian and I was German. The man says nothing. Anyway, I knew you wouldn't let them shoot me, Pappa. The man changes the subject. You know what I was saying when they stopped us Para? What I was saying was, before getting another camera, I am going to buy a new coffee machine when I get to Paris. One that looks like a castle. Is it expensive? Yes, for a coffee machine it's quite expensive, it's Italian. Did the police think we were bad Italians when they stopped us. No . . . they probably thought we were Algerian. But Pappa? It's okay, 'cause you've got money now, you can buy an expensive coffee machine. You can . . . aff-lord it. Thank you Para, that's right, I can afford it now. And you can afflord to get me my game joystick. We'll see about that baby, we'll see, we'll talk to Mamma about that.

After a while the two of them fall silent. They have started very early in the morning and the girl hasn't slept enough. After a while her eyes start to shutter. She is asleep by the time the man starts to hum a tune under his breath, something vaguely in Raag Bhairavi. The road picks up an escort of trees. Light and shadow drum across the car.

Acknowledgements

There are so many friends who took turns at pushing this writer through the long, dark and seductive tunnels of uncertainty, indolence and distraction into the hard daylight of print, so many people who now jointly own the thank-sector of my being, that it's probably best to do what the novel doesn't and hang on, as far as possible, to the guide-beam of chronology.

My first thanks, then, go to those long-suffering Calcutta friends who always insisted that I could, and should, write fiction: Ananda Lal, Anjana Basu, Vasudha Joshi, Vivek Benegal, Paromita Ukil, Kavita Panjabi, Nilanjana Chatterjee and Roopa Mehta. This book was first ignited and fuelled by their faith in my literary abilities, and at least some of the blame for whatever flaws or problems it carries can, I'm sure, be laid at their collective door, attributed to their joint and individual lack of judgement during the years 1982–1989.

Next, my deepest gratitude to:

Nayantara Sahgal on whose dining table, late one winter night, this novel was begun. For her graceful and patient support of my work through many testing and almost impossible situations.

Supriya Guha, who sent off the first shard of what would end up as this book to the editors of *Civil Lines* in Delhi. They, in turn, shared her enthusiasm for what was then just a short story, and their refusal to provide me with a rejection slip was enough to send me off on a project of expansion. I'm far from sure that Supriya meant to be responsible for triggering this small avalanche of prose but, once it began, there was no one, critic-wise, who looked less like a St Bernard and yet acted more like one.

Monica Narula, who gave me the courage to change course to a much more difficult trip than one I had originally bought a ticket for. For having the love, faith, curiosity and energy to push me on to the long and turbulent flight that I really needed to catch. And then, for meeting me at various crucial transit points and, through her passionate and perceptive engagement, showing me again and again to the departure gates for the connecting flights.

Sanjeev Saith, for being the first one to put both his money and his soul behind the book as something publishable. For his huge patience, unflagging affection and brusque gentleness. For giving me the approbation without which I may never have gone beyond the initial few thousand words.

Kai Friese for spending a fair part of the last five years pulling me away from more pleasurable activities and pushing me towards my computer. For finally convincing me that being his neighbour, not only in terms of living area but in terms of profession and crafts as well, was something I should reconcile myself to.

Aradhana Seth, for appearing in my life from time to time like an erratic tooth-fairy and, on one crucial occasion, for picking me up and dropping me close to where I needed to be.

Veronique Dupont for the shelter of her house, for re-introducing me to the music that I thought I knew, for showing me that the discipline of sitting at your desk for hours did not mean that you were numbed to life, for being the friend she is.

Harsh Kapoor, for always being there, virtually and as well as in meat-space.

Sara Hossain and David Bergman for the sanctuary they provided at a very difficult time. To David for the use of his study, and to Sara for her many cogent comments on the book.

Sonia Jabbar and Sheba Chhachhi. Sonia for her huge stamina, for her close readings of the book and her precise comments. Sheba for being there before, during and after, providing various oxygens like a (mostly) clement sky, for her ongoing involvement with my work.

Tony Cokes, friend, thinking partner and guide, who kept sharp the perspective on the work we had begun many years ago, of which I hope this is but one pausing point.

All those friends and film-maker colleagues who've cheered gently from the sidelines while waiting for me to finish this aberrant activity and re-join them. Special thanks to Jeebesh Bagchi for keeping the bridge of helpful e-mails open through all the mixed heavy traffic of information and emotion, to Shuddha Sengupta for his unswerving loyalty to the word despite all the many seductions of the image, and to Ranjan Palit for exactly the opposite.

Sanjiv Shah, Archana Shah and Paresh Naik in Ahmedabad for reminding me that, after all was said and done, I should not forget my daal, rotli and shaak, both intellectually and otherwise.

Paromita Vohra for her many readings, hand-holding and timely warning guffaws.

Stephanie Lang for her understanding that spanned the differences in language, and for sending me energies both solar and lunar.

Tilak Sarkar who tried to teach me how to take money and the Net seriously while accepting that this attempt at writing literature meant that I was bound to fail at my lessons.

The learned Doctors of academia Melissa Butcher, Srirupa Roy, Gayatri Chatterjee and, again, Kavita Panjabi, for their readings and generous gift of time and knowledge. For variously mapping the vast lap of ideas on which my words were trying to find a small sitting place.

Sagarika Ghose and Brinda Datta, for reminding me with such regularity that a decent Bloody Mary or three was more important than writing deathless prose.

Peter Hanley for his invaluable advice on matters military and aeronautical.

Mukul Kesavan and Tenzing Sonam, both of whom took time off from their own writing, both putting on hold the fictional worlds they were constructing in order to get into the one I was trying to create – for their detailed readings and energetic disposal of my doubts and fears.

Nilanjana Roy, for the last scan done from the interstices of her busy screen, for the sharing of her great erudition, sharp wit and unshakeable, Brahmo, objectivity.

• • •

In London, I would like to thank (though in this context that is a hugely inadequate word):

Philip Gwyn Jones, for accompanying me on such a long stretch of the trek, for being one of those rare editors who backs his hunches to the end, for having the uncanny ability to click into what I was trying to do and supporting that with enormous patience, intelligence and experience. And, finally, for having the courage to share, without blinking even once, whatever risks I presented him with.

The team at Flamingo, especially Jon Butler, for their undentable good humour and forbearance, and Andrew Wille for a wonderfully sensitive yet tenaciously microscopic line edit.

Heather Godwin, Penny Jones and Kirsty McLachlan at DGA for the calm anchor they provided me through thick, thin, hairy and smooth. It would be impossible for me to chart their huge support through the roller-coaster ride that was the writing of this book.

David Godwin, for making lightning strikes, both good ones and bad, feel like everyday events, for his insight and huge energy-giving laughter, for his verve, panache, faith. For his friendship. And for taking on the lunatic task of representing me.

• • •

One of my biggest and most inarticulable debts is to Gita Sahgal for being more than a reader of the book, more than the co-parent who has taken far, far more than her fair share of parenting of our two children, for being the stern editor of my life, whose decisions I couldn't always agree with, but whose faith in my ability to produce something readable never wavered. I can only hope that when she looks back at this period she will find that at least some of this book was worth all the energy, courage, humour and love she put into it.

• • •

Reaching the end of this long list, I would like to especially acknowledge three people:

Ashish Mahajan, for keeping the machinery of my life and the gears of my spirit in working order.

Meenakshi Ganguly, who time and again generalled the rabble of troops inside me into a cohesive and more or less focused army.

Monica Bhasin, without whom neither this book nor its writer had any hope of reaching a recognisable shore.

• • •

And my final thanks to my sons Kabir and Ayan, for putting everything in its correct place.